,1

THE FOUR OF US

Recent Titles by Margaret Pemberton from Severn House

A DARK ENCHANTMENT

FROM CHINA WITH LOVE

A MANY SPLENDOURED THING

A REBELLIOUS HEART

THE RECKLESS MISS GRAINGER

A YEAR TO ETERNITY

THE FOUR OF US

Margaret Pemberton

This first world edition published in Great Britain 2004 by
SEVERN HOUSE PUBLISHERS LTD of
9–15 High Street, Sutton, Surrey SM1 1DF.
This first world edition published in the USA 2004 by
SEVERN HOUSE PUBLISHERS INC of
595 Madison Avenue, New York, N.Y. 10022.

British Library Cataloguing in Publication Data

Pemberton, Margaret
    The four of us
    1.   Female friendship - Fiction
    I.   Title
    823.9'14 [F]

    ISBN 0-7278-6138-7

Typeset by Palimpsest Book Production Ltd.,
Polmont, Stirlingshire, Scotland.
Printed and bound in Great Britain by
MPG Books Ltd., Bodmin, Cornwall.

The Four of Us is about friendship and is dedicated to:

Linda Britter – a lifetime friend whose help
and advice on all things literary is much valued.

Kathleen Smith – a childhood friend
regained through Friends Reunited.

June Hanchard – a friend who has
taught hundreds to dance – even me.

Christine Morris – a friend who made life
such fun in the '60s and makes it fun still.

And last, but by no means least, for
Mike – who in over thirty years of marriage has
been the best friend any woman could have.

PART ONE

One

April 2003

Seated in the elegant reception area of Marcus Black & Company, Solicitors, Primmie Dove's fingers tightened on the strap of her shabby handbag. She was fifty years old and her only previous experience of solicitors was when her much-loved husband, Ted, had died. That had been three years ago and her sense of loss was still raw.

She took a deep, steadying breath. Now was not the time to be thinking of Ted. All her attention needed to be focused on the letter in her handbag.

Dear Madam, it read. *I would appreciate it if you would contact me with regard to the estate of Mrs Amelia Surtees, the widow of your father's brother, Gordon Surtees. Yours faithfully, Marcus Black.*

Had the childless Amelia, who had exchanged her council house in Redhill for one in Cornwall at about the time of Ted's death, left her a small amount of money? It was the conclusion her twenty-two-year-old daughter, Millie, had come to, but then Millie was ever hopeful where money was concerned. Joanne, thirteen months older than Millie and an office manager at D. P. International, a Mayfair advertising agency, had been more prosaic.

'You're probably going to be asked to deal with some kind of paperwork. Remember when Dad died? Even though the amount of money he left was negligible, there was still paperwork to deal with.'

She hadn't been able to speak about the letter to her youngest daughter, Lucy, who was backpacking somewhere in Australia and her son, Josh, who never travelled out of London if he could help it, had been equally impossible to contact.

3

'Mr Black will see you now,' the woman at the reception desk said, breaking in on her thoughts.

She rose to her feet, fighting down a sudden, irrational feeling of apprehension, and entered the adjoining room.

'Thank you very much for being able to see me so promptly, Mrs Dove,' Marcus Black said, beaming genially. 'And my condolences on your aunt's death.'

'Thank you.' After shaking hands with him and seating herself on the chair at the far side of his desk, she said, not wanting to mislead him in any way, 'We weren't close. I used to visit her once or twice a year when she lived near London, but since her move to Cornwall we've had no contact apart from exchanging cards at Christmas.'

'Really? Now that *does* surprise me.' Once more seated behind his desk, he looked down at the slim file that lay open in front of him. 'I'd assumed you were close, but of course, as she had no other relatives and certainly no *blood* relatives . . .' He leafed through a couple of pages of close print.

'Has she asked that I be her executor?'

'Executor?' He looked up at her, startled. 'No, indeed. We – Marcus Black & Company – are her executors.' He removed a typed sheet from the file. 'This is a copy of Amelia Surtees's estate accounts, for your own records, but if you will bear with me, I would like to go through it with you, item by item.' He cleared his throat and donned a pair of horn-rimmed glasses. 'Assets at date of death, twenty-nine thousand, one hundred and ninety pounds.'

Primmie gasped.

'Balance at National Westminster Bank, eight thousand seven hundred and forty pounds forty-nine pence. Balance in Abbey National Building Society share account, twenty thousand four hundred and seventy-eight pounds. Jewellery sold, four hundred and two pounds. And now for the debit side of the estate, which is payment of funeral expenses, fee for copy of death certificate, the administrator's expenses, my own costs for the winding up of the estate . . .'

Vainly Primmie tried to keep a mental running total of how much was still left, but maths had never been her strong point.

'And now to the residuary estate of twenty-four thousand five hundred and thirty pounds,' Marcus Black said, 'divisible

4

in equal parts between the following six charities: The Sunshine Children's Home, Birmingham; The Children's Country Holidays Fund; Save the Children Fund; The Seal Sanctuary, Gweek; Redwings Horse Sanctuary, Norfolk; Foal Farm Animal Rescue Centre, Kent.'

He clasped his hands on top of the sheet of paper he had been reading from and looked up at her. 'Now, Mrs Dove. Is that all understandable?'

Primmie nodded, understanding all too well that she wasn't one of the beneficiaries. As she had never expected to be coming into money, the disappointment wasn't too great, but just for a few minutes, when Marcus Black had announced the surprising amount of her aunt's assets, that she might have been left something had suddenly seemed a possibility.

'And now,' he said, 'we come to your aunt's largest asset. The property she was living in at the time of her death.'

Primmie blinked. 'I'm sorry. I don't understand. My aunt didn't own property. She had a council house at Redhill, which she exchanged for a council house in Cornwall.'

Marcus Black cocked his head to one side and said, 'Your information is a little at fault, Mrs Dove. True, your aunt-by-marriage had a council home in Redhill. This she vacated in March 1997 when she inherited her father's property – the property she was living in at the time of her death. This property – and its contents – she has bequeathed to you, Mrs Dove, for your lifetime.'

'I'm sorry?' Primmie said again, feeling as if she was being unutterably stupid. 'Are you saying that my aunt *owned* her house? And that she's left it to me?'

'Yes and no. Your aunt most certainly did own her Cornish home, but the property has not been bequeathed to you outright. You are not, for instance, at liberty to sell Ruthven. You are, however, able to live in it, if you so wish, for the rest of your life. At your death, as part of Amelia Surtees's estate, it will be sold, the resultant proceeds being then equally divided between the six charities aforementioned. If you have no desire to live in the property – and if the upkeep of the property proves burdensome – then you can forego it at any time. As part of your aunt's estate it will then be sold and divided between the charities sooner, rather than later.'

Primmie gaped at him. A house in Cornwall. *Cornwall.* A house she could live in, rent free, for the rest of her life if she so wished. It was so out of the blue, so totally unexpected, that she didn't know what to say, or think.

Marcus Black put his glasses back on and removed another sheet of paper from the file lying in front of him. 'It is only fair to tell you that the property is a little isolated and that some of the outbuildings are, I am told, in a state of disrepair.'

'Outbuildings?' Primmie said dazedly. 'It still has an outdoor privy?

Marcus Black chuckled. 'No, Mrs Dove. The outbuildings in question are sheds and barns. If you look at the documentation I have given you, you will see that the property is a smallholding – a type of property very common in Cornwall.'

'And the house?' she asked, too fearful that the house, also, was in a state of disrepair to giggle at her mistake.

'Sound,' he said reassuringly, passing a thin sheaf of paperwork towards her. 'And these, Mrs Dove, are the keys of the property in question.' From a desk drawer he withdrew a large envelope and, opening it, tipped a small bunch of keys on to his desktop.

Primmie stared at them, still struggling for a sense of reality.

'If I could give you some advice, Mrs Dove?'

'Yes. Of course. Please.'

Aware of her situation – that she was widow of modest means – he said, 'Don't make any decision about the property until you have not only inspected it, but have familiarized yourself with it. Your present address is Rotherhithe – and life in south-east London is very different to life on a Cornish smallholding. You may find it impossible to adapt. Also, although Mrs Surtees has left you the property for your lifetime, she has not bequeathed to you money with which to maintain it – and maintenance costs may prove to be a heavy burden.

'But if it's in such a lovely area there'll be visitors – tourists. I could perhaps take in bed and breakfast guests . . . ?'

'You could indeed – particularly as Ruthven is situated only a short distance from the coastal footpath, in an area designated as an Area of Outstanding Natural Beauty.' The

6

horn-rims came off yet again. 'I take it that you are considering accepting the offer your aunt has made you?'

Primmie thought of the beautiful Lizard. She thought of the wonderment of living so close to the sea.

'Oh yes,' she said to Marcus Black as he continued to regard her with interest, toying with his glasses. 'I'm going to move into Ruthven. I'm going to move into it just a soon as I can.'

Two

Primmie eased her Vauxhall Corsa on to the A38, glad to have Exeter behind her. She wasn't in a hurry. The journey she was taking was the most exciting journey of her life – and it was one she wanted to savour. As she thought of how she had always wanted to live in the country, she was seized by a memory from the past, a memory so strong and so totally unexpected that for a second or two she was robbed of breath.

Petts Wood. It hadn't been real country, being a leafy suburb of Bromley in Kent, but to a girl born and brought up in a Docklands council house it had seemed like country. The garden had been vast and beyond the garden had been a golf course, and beyond the golf course trees and yet more trees. She had been eighteen. Eighteen and in love and naively certain that the garden – and the golden-haired man it belonged to – were going to be hers to love and to cherish for as long as she lived.

Regaining composure with difficulty she drove through the village of Dean and then, at the sign indicating Dean Prior, she slowed down. One of her favourite seventeenth-century poets, Robert Herrick, had been the vicar of Dean Prior and she wanted to look at the church.

As she parked in front of St George the Martyr in the spring sunshine, she was overcome by a glorious sense of freedom. With her heart singing like a lark's she stepped from the car, locked the door behind her and walked towards the church gate, well aware that the only one of her children who would understand the impulse that had made her stop was Lucy. Lucy was always doing things on a whim, chasing whatever rainbows came her way. And not only would Lucy have understood why she wanted to make a little pilgrimage to the church Robert Herrick had been vicar of for over forty years, she would also have understood why she hadn't had a second's thought about seizing the opportunity to enjoy a completely different lifestyle in a completely different part of the country to that in which she had always lived.

'Go for it, Mum,' is what Lucy would have said. 'You only live once, so take a few risks. Enjoy yourself. What have you got to lose?'

As she walked through the deserted church she knew she had nothing to lose. Millie, Joanne and Josh would probably not make the trip from London to Cornwall as often as she would like them to do and she would, of course, miss them, just as she would miss her friends and neighbours.

She came to a halt in front of the beautiful stained-glass window that commemorated Robert Herrick's incumbency from 1629 to 1674, her eyes overly bright. No matter how much she would miss her Rotherhithe friends, she wouldn't miss them in the way that, for nearly thirty years, she had missed the friends of her youth.

The garden at Petts Wood was once again so vivid in her mind's eye that she could practically smell the scent of the old-fashioned roses and taste the lemonade that regularly, in summer, stood in a thermos on the low table near to the deckchairs. And she could hear the laughter – her own always a little shy, especially when Kiki's father was present; Kiki's laughter, rip-roaringly unrestrained; Artemis's clear, flute-like laugh, as ladylike as everything else about her; Geraldine's laughter husky and unchained.

Then she thought of Destiny and, even at a distance of thirty years, pain knifed through her, its intensity so deep she could barely breathe. She closed her eyes, wondering if the real reason she had wanted to visit the church was because she had wanted to come and say a prayer for Destiny.

Some minutes later, when her eyes were again open, her hands still tightly clasped, a voice said from a few feet away from her: 'Can I help you? Would you like to sit down?'

She turned to see the vicar. 'No,' she said, feeling apologetic for having aroused his concern. 'I'm not ill. I was engulfed by a memory that is very painful. It took a few minutes to get over it, that's all.'

He nodded sympathetically. 'I'd like to quote some Herrick that would comfort you, but I'm afraid he was a great melancholic. All that springs to mind is the third verse from *The Night-piece*.

> *Let not the dark thee cumber:*
> *What though the moon does slumber?*
> *The stars of the night*
> *Will lend thee their light*
> *Like tapers clear without number.*'

She managed an unsteady smile, knowing he was trying to be kind, knowing that Herrick's *Epitaph Upon a Child That Died* would have been far more truly apt.

In another half an hour, at the wheel of the Corsa, she was crossing the bridge over the Tamar, in Cornwall at last. She had been before, of course, but not for many years. When the children were young, they had visited Land's End and Penzance and had driven across the Lizard to the most southerly tip of the country, Lizard Point. And now incredibly, unbelievably, she was going to live there – if not exactly on Lizard Point, then close to it.

Joy fizzed in her throat as, a little later, she drove into St Austell. It was now nearly three o'clock and she hadn't eaten since leaving home at eight. At the first signpost for a car park she turned in, well aware, as she parked, that with the passenger seats and the roof rack stacked high with luggage and household possessions she looked as if she were doing a moonlight flit.

The nearest pub to the car park was the King's Arms and she strolled inside and ordered herself a tomato juice and a Cornish pasty. Only when she was seated at a window table, the tomato juice and pasty in front of her, did she see the poster on the wall. ST AUSTELL'S GREAT EASTER '60s ROCK REVIVAL WEEKEND – MARTY WILDE – ERIC

BURDEN – KIKI LANE. There were accompanying photos running down the right-hand side of the poster. Marty Wilde still had a rumpled farmboy look about him, even though he was now in his mid-sixties and a Londoner born and bred. Eric Burden, too, still retained the mean and moody look that so suited his gravelly voice.

It was Kiki's photograph, though, that riveted her attention. There were only a few months in age between them, yet though she, Primmie, looked comfortably middle-aged – her grey-flecked hair in no particular style, her sweater and skirt chosen for practicality and comfort – Kiki looked nothing of the sort. Her hair was short, spikily gelled and still the same spicy red it had been when they had been at school together. There was a spotted chiffon scarf tied jauntily round her throat and she was wearing a denim bomber jacket, the collar flicked up. There were still hollows beneath her cheekbones, still a look of knife-edged purity about her jaw line. Only the expression in the green-gilt eyes was ages old and world weary.

Aware that Artemis and Geraldine must also occasionally see photos of Kiki in magazines or on posters she wondered if, when they did, their memories also went spinning back through time to when the four of them had been young and inseparable: always together either at school or in the garden of the house at Petts Wood. Not that their memories of Petts Wood would be the same as hers. Even after all these years, a flush of colour touched her cheeks. Even then – even from the friends who had been as close to her as sisters – she had had secrets.

Well aware that no one seeing her now would ever imagine what those secrets had been, she rose to her feet. Easter was well and truly over and Kiki would no longer be in St Austell or even, perhaps, in England, for she remembered reading in one of Lucy's pop magazines that the majority of Kiki's time was spent in America.

She walked back to the car and in another ten minutes was back on the A390, motoring happily towards Truro, her excitement rising as she headed ever deeper towards the toe of Cornwall.

She continued towards Helston and then, before reaching it, turned off on to a B road. The road was pretty and it grew

10

prettier and prettier, winding through first one small village and then another. A right turn and then a left and she was crossing the thickly wooded shores of the Helford River at Gweek, on the Lizard Peninsula proper. She slowed down, taking from the glove compartment the directions that Marcus Black had given her.

Another village and a little beyond it a left turn. She wound her window down, revelling in the smell of the sea, so near yet still out of sight.

To the right of her now was the signpost for Calleloe. The road towards it dipped down steeply and she caught a glimpse of slate-roofed cottages huddled around a harbour. 'Calleloe is, I believe, where Mrs Surtees did most of her shopping,' Marcus Black had told her. 'There's a general shop there, a post office, a licensed hotel and a restaurant, two cafés, a couple of craft and clothing shops and a prestigious art gallery owned by an American.'

With her heart beginning to hammer somewhere up near her throat, she ignored the road leading down to the harbour and continued on the narrow road that, from a distance of a quarter of a mile or so, continued to follow the line of the coast. Deep in its chine Calleloe slid out of sight and then, as the road again approached high ground, the trees began to thin and suddenly on the left-hand side of the road was a narrow turn-off and the signpost she had been looking for. PRIVATE. NO THROUGH ROAD, it read.

With knots of nervous tension almost crippling her, Primmie turned left. Head-high hawthorn bushes and tall purple-headed thistles scratched at the Corsa's sides and then, after about fifty yards or so, the road made a final twist and there, on the left-hand side, set in the hedgerow, were rusting double gates. There was nothing else. In front of her the single road ran out over a long, low headland to where, almost at its tip, a small church stood in splendid isolation. Beyond the church there was nothing but marram grass, sea and sky.

On unsteady legs she got out of the car and walked towards the gates.

Only by standing close up to them could she see the faded lettering: Ruthven.

Beyond the gates an unmade track meandered up a slope

11

towards a house that looked nothing at all as she had imagined it would. Instead of being long and low, with pretty whitewashed walls, the house, a farmyard and outbuildings to one side of it, was foursquare and built of sombre Cornish stone. There were green-painted shutters at either side of the long-paned windows and the front door was porched, its roof golden-green with lichen.

She opened the gates wide and walked back to the car. It was nearly six o'clock and the sky was taking on the daffodil light of early evening. She had a couple of hours, perhaps less, in which to do all her essential unpacking and sorting out, for once it was dark her only lighting was going to be the oil lamp she had brought with her.

'There will be no electricity until you arrange to have it reconnected,' Marcus Black had said, 'the telephone ditto. You will find the water turned off at the mains when you arrive, unless, of course, you arrange in advance for it to be reconnected.'

Well, that at least she had done. And she would telephone the electricity people in the morning. As the heavily laden Corsa bucketed up the rutted track, she became aware of the two fields, one on either side of her. 'There's some grazing pasture and a donkey paddock,' Marcus Black had told her and, in her ignorance, she had imagined merely small corners of waste land.

Hardly able to believe the riches that had been heaped upon her, she drove into the cobbled farmyard and switched off the engine.

Immediately half a dozen hens erupted from one of the outbuildings in an agitated flurry. She fought the urge to remain firmly out of their way. If there were hens here, then they were *her* hens, and the sooner she got used to them the better. Who, though, had been looking after them and feeding them?

Taking the bunch of keys he had given her out of the glove compartment, she stepped out of the car and picked her way between the hens towards the house.

The front door was painted a green that had seen better days. On the doorstep was an empty bottle with a rolled piece of notepaper wedged into its neck.

She stretched out her hand.

12

Dear Mrs Dove, the note read. *I've looked after the hens and there is a fresh supply of logs and a fire laid. The key left with me, in case of emergency, I have posted through the letterbox. Matt Trevose. PS. The logs are in the woodrick.*

The tension she had felt in the seconds before reading the note ebbed. Somewhere nearby was a conscientious neighbour. Grateful to Matt Trevose for the care he had taken of the hens she took a deep breath, slid the key into the lock and opened the front door.

The stone-floored entrance hall was larger than her Rotherhithe living room. There was a gaily coloured rag rug on the flags, a grandfather clock against one wall, an oak chest with brass corners and side handles against the other. A staircase with wide, shallow treads rose from the centre of the hallway, its faded stair runner held in place by brass rods. On the right of the staircase the hallway was deeper than on the left, running off into a passageway that was blocked at its far end by a door. Other doors, one on the right-hand side and two on the left-hand side, led off the hall.

Leaving the front door open behind her, she crossed the hall and opened the first of the left-hand doors. It was a study with books floor to ceiling on three walls, a small, prettily tiled fireplace and a window that looked out on to a garden. In front of the window and taking up nearly all the available space was an ancient roll-top desk.

The second door on the left led into a sitting room. There was a chintz-covered sofa, a Victorian armchair and a glass-fronted display cabinet filled with china. A glorious Persian rug, its once vibrant reds and blues gently faded, graced the wood floor. There was another rug, white sheepskin, in front of the fireplace, which, much grander than the fireplace in the study, had a bed of knotted newspapers topped by firelighters and logs in its grate. The door on the opposite side of the hall led into a dining room, the door at the end of the passageway into a kitchen.

It was upstairs that the surprise came – though not in the bedroom that had clearly been Amelia's. There, the walnut bedroom suite looked ancient enough to have belonged to Amelia's mother, the overall heaviness redeemed by the golden light flooding in through the south-facing windows.

13

The surprise was in the other three bedrooms. Instead of flower-patterned wallpaper and muddy cream paintwork, one room was painted a pretty lavender-blue, another was painted shell-pink and the third had walls of pale mauve. The furniture in each room – wardrobe, dressing table and beds – was stripped pine, the curtains and bedding beautifully coordinated to the colour of each room's walls.

It was the beds, though, that were the real mystery. Each room held three. A bunk bed and a single bed.

There were no personal items in the rooms, no framed photographs or articles of clothing. Bemusedly she wondered if Amelia had been renting out rooms to bed and breakfast guests. Looking at the bunk beds, it seemed highly unlikely. Tourists would no doubt put up with many minor inconveniences, but hauling themselves up into a child's top bunk bed was surely not one of them.

Wondering if the answer was that Amelia had bought the furniture and furnishings cheaply, as a job lot, she surveyed the bathroom. A chipped white porcelain bath stood in lonely splendour on ornate claws. The lavatory had a mahogany seat and an overhead cistern. The pedestal handbasin looked as if it had come out of the Ark with Noah.

She didn't care. Deeply satisfied with all she had seen she went back downstairs, eager to get on with the task of carrying as much as possible from the car to the house before night fell.

Two hours later, as darkness closed in, she was comfortable for the night. None of the mattresses was damp and she had carried a sleeping bag, pillow and duvet in from the car and laid them on Amelia's bed. Though one of the other bedrooms also looked out towards the headland and the sea, the window in it was smaller than the one in Amelia's room. In Amelia's room the window was wide and deep with a comfortable window-seat, and it meant that when she woke she would be able to see the view out over the headland to the English Channel.

With her most important chore out of the way she carried a cool-box from the car boot into the kitchen and, removing a bottle of milk and a packet of biscuits from it, gave herself a fifteen-minute rest break. Afterwards she lit the fire Matt

Trevose had laid for her and the oil lamp she had had the sense to bring with her.

For the remainder of the time until it grew too dark to continue she ferried her belongings from the car into the house.

With the fire crackling and the lamp glowing, it had been an enjoyable task. Now, having allowed the fire to burn out, she was in pyjamas and dressing-gown and, utterly exhausted, the duvet round her shoulders, was seated in the window embrasure of what had been Amelia's bedroom, a tumbler of whisky in one hand.

The oil lamp she had brought upstairs with her lit the room with a soft glow. Outside, the darkness of the headland was so deep as to be impenetrable. Never before had she slept in a room from which streetlights could not be seen. It was a moment she had braced herself for – a moment when she had expected to feel panic-stricken and nervous. She didn't. The whisky was warming, the light from the oil lamp comforting. She was in her new home and on the verge of a completely new way of life. It was a marvellous feeling – a feeling unlike any other she had ever known.

Still curled in the window-seat, deeply happy and utterly content, she watched as stars began pinpricking the darkness, and then, climbing into bed, she closed her eyes and slept.

Three

When she woke it was to the sound of rain falling against the windows. There were no other sounds. Previously when she woke, there was always noise. The distant roar of traffic from the constantly busy Jamaica and Lower Roads, the sound of people talking as they walked past her front door on their way to the nearby train station and of children chattering and squabbling as they made their way to school.

This morning, there was only the sound of the rain. She

opened her eyes. There *was* another sound. A sound so alien it simply hadn't registered on her consciousness. Excitement coiled deep within her as she realized what it was. For the first time ever, she was lying in bed in her own home, listening to the sound of the sea.

Ten minutes later she was downstairs and in the kitchen, eager to start the day. It was a large room and, even though the sky was overcast and there were still flurries of rain against the windows, it was full of light.

Last night when she had been in the kitchen, she had been too busy finding room for all the boxes she had brought in from the car to take anything more than a cursory glance round. Now she took stock, and liked what she saw.

It was quite obviously the heart of the house. As well as a small deal table beneath one of the windows there was an enormous oak refectory dining table and, adjacent to the Aga, a rocking chair. On the far wall was a tall dresser crammed with crockery and on the quarry-tiled floor were rag rugs, similar to the one in the spacious entrance hall.

She poured herself a glass of milk and drank it, gazing through a window that looked out over a vegetable garden towards an orchard. Hardly daring to hope that the orchard, too, was hers, she began making a mental list of all the things she needed to do, beginning with the need to drive into Calleloe and make arrangements for the telephone and the electricity to be reconnected.

Another thought intruded. Did she need to feed the hens or would Matt Trevose be arriving any minute to do so? And how had Matt Trevose known of her impending arrival? And her name?

Right on cue, there came a short, sharp knock on the front door.

She crossed the stone-flagged hall and opened the door, a smile on her face.

Just as Ruthven had not looked as she had expected it to, neither did Matt Trevose.

For some reason she had expected him to be elderly. Instead, he was, at a rough guess, only a few years older than herself. He wasn't very tall, five foot eight or nine, but beneath his fisherman's jersey he still had a good pair of shoulders and he still had a thick pelt of hair, shot through with silver.

'Mrs Dove?' he said, an attractive Cornish lilt in his voice. 'Yes.' She held out her hand. 'And you must be Mr Trevose. Please come in.'

'D'you mind if I come in via the side door? My boots are a bit dirty for front entrance halls.'

He was wearing mud-splattered Wellingtons, well-worn jeans tucked inside them.

Five minutes later he was standing in the middle of the kitchen, looking indecently at home.

'I can't offer you a cup of tea,' she said apologetically. 'All I can offer is a glass of milk and a couple of biscuits.'

'Thank you.' He stared in disbelief at the number of framed paintings and prints that leaned against every available surface.

'I like pictures,' she said unnecessarily, pouring milk into a glass and emptying a packet of chocolate digestive biscuits on to a plate. 'I didn't really have the wall space for them in my home in London – they always looked a bit cramped. Now, though, in this house, they are going to look splendid.'

'I'll have to introduce you to my friend Hugo. He owns the art gallery in Calleloe.'

Remembering that Mr Black had said that the art gallery was very prestigious, Primmie said, 'I think your friend's artworks may be a little out of my league. Most of my pictures are cheap Athena reproductions. I want to thank you for looking after Amelia's hens for me. I didn't know about them and haven't a clue how to look after them.'

'Then you'll have to learn.' There were webs of laughter lines at the corners of his eyes. They were very nice eyes, amber-brown and full of good humour. He drained his glass of milk. 'Would you like to walk out to the grazing pasture and the hen arks now?' he said, putting the empty glass in the sink.

'I'd love to. Is the grazing pasture one of the fields on either side of the track? And is the orchard beyond the vegetable garden part of Ruthven as well?'

'Yes, to the first question, and if, by the orchard, you mean Amelia's motley collection of old apple trees, yes again.' He hooked his thumbs into the front pockets of his jeans and she noticed there was no wedding ring on his square, work-hardened hands.

17

Cross with herself for having registered the fact, she said, 'If it's so muddy outside, should I be wearing Wellingtons, too?'

'Yes. And if you don't have a pair, don't worry. Amelia kept a pair under the bench, in the porch leading to the side door.

As they walked out of the kitchen towards it, she said, 'How did you know about me? Your note was addressed to me by name. Did Amelia's solicitor contact you?'

'Yes, ' he said, as she dragged a pair of battered Wellingtons into the light of day. 'And Amelia asked me if I'd keep an eye on things until you arrived.'

Making a mental note that her aunt's relationship with him was one of real friendship and not just ordinary good-neighbourliness, Primmie squeezed her feet into Wellingtons that were a size too small.

'And can you tell me about the logs for the fire? Does a supplier deliver them every month?'

'There's a wood supplier in Calleloe,' he said, opening the porch door. 'Though the logs now in the rick are logs I sawed myself at the end of last year.'

Moments later they were squelching across the still wet grass of the field he had referred to as the grazing pasture. In one corner of it were two long, triangular wooden and wired structures.

'This is the best time of day to collect the eggs,' he said as they reached them. 'And you need to do it every morning, because these hens are very good layers.' He squatted down in front of the first of the arks. 'See this sliding door here? It allows you to reach into the nesting boxes. Let me show you.'

For ever afterwards, she was to remember that morning as being one of the most memorable of her life. For one thing, it was her very first morning at Ruthven, for another, it was the day she and Matt made friends and lastly, but by no means least, it was the day she lifted a warm, brown-speckled egg from out of a nest-box for the first time.

That afternoon she drove down into Calleloe. It was an enjoy-able trip. She exchanged pleasantries with the postmistress, who cheerily gave her twenty-pence pieces for pound coins so that she would have enough of them for her telephone calls. Then, with arrangements for electricity and telephone reconnections all in place, she strolled down the main street towards the harbour until she came to the large double windows of the Hugo Arnott Art Gallery.

There was only one picture on display in the first window and it stopped her dead in her tracks. In a heavy ornate gold frame, set on an emerald-green silk-covered stand, was a large oil painting of four young women in a garden. The style was Impressionistic, full of light and pastel colour, the period – if the girls' ankle-length, broderie-anglaise-trimmed white dresses were anything to go by – was Edwardian. Three of the girls were seated on a wide garden swing. Two had their arms round each other's waists, the third, holding on to the rope of the swing, was resting her head against her hand.

The fourth girl was standing looking towards the three of them, a pale blue sash around her narrow waist, a wide-brimmed straw sun hat held low in one hand.

With her throat dry and tight, she saw that the painting was titled *Summer Memory.*

Foolishly, she felt tears prick the back of her eyelids. She, Kiki, Artemis and Geraldine could never have looked so sublimely languorous when enjoying the summer sunshine in the garden at Petts Wood, but it was the four of them nevertheless. The two embracing girls, heads close, one golden-haired, one titian-haired, were, for her, Artemis and Kiki. The girl resting against the rope of the swing, looking coolly and clearly out of the frame with steady dark eyes was, surely, Geraldine. And she, Primmie, was the girl a little apart from them – the girl who looked somehow younger than the other three – the girl with the blue sash and the sun hat.

The tears continued to prick and she blinked them away, suddenly conscious of the people passing to and fro behind her on the narrow pavement. It was a stunning picture and she wanted it more than she could remember wanting anything. It wasn't priced, and she could well imagine why.

Not going into the gallery to ask the price, knowing it would be way beyond her means, she turned away from the window

19

and went, instead, into the general clothing store opposite and bought herself a pair of very sensible and inexpensive green Wellingtons.

All the way home, the picture haunted her. Had the young women, so at peace together in the sunlit garden, been real people, and, if so, what had happened to them? Had they been sundered apart as she, Kiki, Artemis and Geraldine had been sundered apart?

As she stowed away clothes and books – and as she discovered to her delight that the electricity had been reconnected – her thoughts refused to leave the past and when, just after three o'clock, the phone rang and she answered it to a male voice saying, 'Just confirming your reconnection, Mrs Dove' she knew exactly what it was she was going to do next.

She was going to put one of her leaving presents to good use. It was a laptop computer given to her by Josh, who had bought it cheaply from a friend. With excitement coiling deep in her tummy she hoisted it from the bubble-wrapping it had travelled to Cornwall in and, with a mug of freshly made tea beside her, set about registering on the Friends Reunited website.

Everything was straightforward until she came to the point where she was required to enter some details about herself. What on earth could she put that would encourage Geraldine or Kiki or Artemis to get in touch with her? Widowed after being married for twenty years, four children and living in Cornwall? It didn't exactly add up to anything exciting.

She picked up her mug of tea, nursing it in her hands as she thought over the little she knew about her friends' lives since they had last all been together. Kiki, of course, was easy, because she had been able to keep up with Kiki's life through the occasional articles she had read about her in Lucy's pop magazines. Geraldine's photograph, too, in the early years after they had parted, had quite often appeared in the gossip columns, not because she was also in show business, but because she was so regularly on the arm of high-profile businessmen or media-conscious aristocrats. Whether she had married one of her highly eligible men friends, Primmie didn't know. What she did know, though, was that

Geraldine's lifestyle had been worlds removed from her own humdrum but happy one in Rotherhithe. And then there was Artemis.

Her throat constricted. It was impossible to think of Artemis without also thinking of Destiny – and she couldn't do that again, not so soon after the moment in the church at Dean Prior, when thinking about Destiny had so nearly unhinged her.

Artemis had married well. When last she had heard of her, as well as a home in the Cotswolds, she'd had homes in London and Spain, two sons at Eton and a husband who was in the same league as Geraldine's high-flying businessmen boyfriends. Even as a girl at Bickley High, Artemis had been mindful of people's backgrounds and social credentials. Why, then, would Artemis be tempted to get in touch with her after all these years? Considering all that had happened between them, why would any of them be tempted to get in touch with her, or, come to that, with each other?

The tea was cold and she put the mug down, a headache building up behind her eyes. Knowing that the only cure for it was fresh air, she picked up her coat and stepped outside the house, seeing with startled surprise that the light was already smoking to dusk. Undeterred, she wrapped her coat a little closer and set off on foot down the track towards the church and the sea.

The locked church was even smaller than St George's had been. It was also, according to the notice pinned in its porch, nominally in use, with a church service scheduled for the last week in May.

Beyond it, the headland shelved steeply to a small sickle of sand and shingle. There was a narrow pathway leading down to it and she took it, uncaring that it was now dusk and would soon be dark. She was too deep in thoughts of the past to be concerned about the safety of what she was doing. With every step towards the sea, the years were rolling backwards. The '90s. The '80s. The '70s.

At last, on damp shingle, she came to a halt, her hands deep in her coat pockets, the evening breeze tugging at her hair. The '60s.

That was when it had all begun. That was when the four

21

of them had formed a friendship and unity so close it had seemed indissoluble.

She looked out over the silky, heaving darkness of the sea, remembering with absolute clarity the fourteenth of September, 1962.

Remembering the beginning.

Four

September 1962

'Come *on*, Primmie! You can't be late! Not on yer first day.'

Primmie stood in front of her wardrobe mirror, moving the knot of her school tie up a little bit, and then down a little bit. Where should it be? She moved it upwards again. It looked better like that, even though it was half-throttling her.

'Pri*mmie!*'

'Coming, Mum!' She slid her arms into her new maroon blazer and picked up her shiny new satchel from the bed.

'Oh, Primmie,' her mum said to her as she ran down the stairs. 'Primmie darlin', you *do* look smart. I can't tell you 'ow proud I am. No one from round 'ere 'as ever gone to Bickley. *No one.*'

'Well, I'm only going because Mr Moss suggested I sit for a scholarship place.' She tried to keep the nervousness from her voice, wishing her mum wouldn't go on so. She was nervous enough as it was – and one of the reasons was precisely that she didn't know anyone at Bickley High. All her other friends had gone off to local secondary modern or grammar schools last week – and they'd gone off to them in large friendly groups.

Bickley High wasn't a secondary modern or a grammar school. It wasn't a state school at all. It was a fee-paying public school – which was why its start of term date was

22

different to that of her friends' schools – and it was a train journey and a long walk from where she lived.

'Goin' to start talkin' posh now, are yer?' her friends had said tauntingly when news of her having won a scholarship place to a public school had spread round the playground. 'You always did think a lot of yerself, Primmie Surtees. Always top of the class. Always teacher's pet.'

She had hotly denied the jibes, stung by their unfairness. It had made no difference. The nasty, sarcastic remarks had continued, making one thing quite clear: she wasn't going to be able to both go to Bickley High and continue to be accepted as one of the crowd in Rotherhithe. Bickley High's cream and maroon uniform set her apart far too obviously. Through no fault of her own, she was already being regarded as one of 'them' and not one of 'us'.

Her overriding fear, as she saw with a sinking heart that her mother had her hat and coat on, was that her fellow pupils at Bickley High would regard her in exactly the same way. It was why she was now being so careful about the way she talked. Not because she wanted to sound posh – which was what her former friends seemed to think – but simply because she wanted to fit in and not be different.

'You don't have to come with me, Mum,' she said, not wanting to start her first day being laughed at for having her mum with her, as if she were a five-year-old. 'I can remember the way. I ain't . . .' She stopped herself and took a deep breath. 'I'm not going to get lost. The school might be a long walk from the station, but it's a straight walk.'

'Maybe it is, Primmie,' her mother said, removing an imaginary speck of dust from her school blazer, 'but just for the first day, it's best to be on the safe side. Now let's get cracking or we're goin' to miss that bloomin' train.'

The first thing Primmie noticed as she walked with her mother the mile and a quarter from Bickley Station to the school was the amazing number of cars zooming down the tree-lined road, all with passengers wearing Bickley High uniform. There were some other maroon-blazered pupils on foot, but all of them were walking in small friendly groups – and none of them was wearing a blazer as shriekingly stiff and new as hers.

'It's quite a trek, gel, ain't it?' her mother said, puffing for breath as they reached the school gates. 'Still, you've got young legs. As long as you don't miss the train in the morning, you'll be tickety-boo.'

The school was long and low, with lots of large windows. The gravelled area in front of it, too, was large. It had to be, as car after car swept through the gates, crunching to a halt and disgorging two or three or even four girls at a time.

'I think you should go now, Mum,' Primmie said as a white Zodiac pulled on to the gravel within feet of them. 'None of the other mothers are hanging around.'

'W-e-ll, that's p'raps because none of the other girls are new,' her mother said uncertainly, overawed by the sheer number of girls now thronging the area in front of the school.

'Geraldine is new,' a well-spoken voice said suddenly from just behind them. 'And I'm not going to stay with her. I'm driving back into Bickley High Street. Would you like a lift?'

The speaker was the driver of the Zodiac. She was a dark, vital, casually dressed woman who looked years too young to have a daughter of eleven.

'Oh, that's very kind of you, I'm sure, but I couldn't possibly . . .'

Well aware of how deep her mother's discomfiture was and also aware that if her mother didn't accept the offer she would probably still be hovering around her when morning assembly began, Primmie said forcefully, 'Of course you can, Mum. That's very kind of you, Mrs . . . ?'

'Mrs Grant. Jacqueline Grant. And my daughter is Geraldine. She isn't very happy at being here this morning . . . ?'

'Primmie,' Primmie said as Mrs Grant waited enquiringly for her name. 'Primmie Surtees.'

'And so if you would keep an eye on her for me, Primmie, I'd be very grateful.'

Geraldine Grant didn't look as if she would suffer anyone keeping an eye on her. Tall and skinny, her hair was cut in a short bob and was night-black and so shiny it looked like silk. Her eyes were dark, too, wide spaced and thick lashed. As

24

she caught Primmie looking at her, she flashed her a dazzling smile and then, behind her mother's back, rolled her eyes to heaven so expressively that it took all Primmie's self-control to fight down a fit of the giggles.

'Yes, Mrs Grant, I'll do my best,' she said, struggling to keep a straight face.

The minute Primmie's mother began awkwardly to get in the car and her own mother slid again behind the driving wheel, Geraldine said as if they'd been friends for years, 'Well, thank goodness we're on our own. What's Primmie short for?'

'Primrose.' Primmie suddenly felt shy. 'It's a bit old-fashioned and so I prefer to be called Primmie.'

'I'm not surprised,' Geraldine said with wry frankness, 'though the name suits you. You've got fair hair and green eyes and so with a bit of imagination I suppose you could be said to look primrosey.'

Geraldine flashed her another radiant smile and slid her arm companionably through hers. 'Come on, Primmie Surtees, let's find out where we're supposed to be. I didn't want to come here, did you? I wanted to go to Benenden.'

Primmie's eyebrows shot high. 'Benenden, where Princess Anne went?'

'Yes, but not because she went there, but because it's in Sussex and that's where my cousin Francis lives.'

As they were talking, they were making their way through the throng towards the school's main entrance. Suddenly there was the sound of a commotion behind them and they turned round just in time to see a powerfully built man slam the driver's door of a powder-blue Rolls Royce behind him and stride across to a dark-green Volkswagen.

'Are you bloody blind!' he was thundering to the Volkswagen's driver. 'You've smashed my wing mirror and come damn near to scraping the side of my car!'

That he was the owner of the Rolls and not a chauffeur was obvious from his Crombie overcoat and the half-smoked cigar he tossed to the ground as the driver's door of the Volkswagen opened and an attractive blond-haired man in his mid-thirties stepped out on to the gravel.

'*Mea culpa*,' he said a little sheepishly. 'Here's my card.

25

Send me the bill for a new mirror. Best not to lose our tempers in front of so many young people, eh?'

His spare build and the way he was dressed, a much-worn tweed jacket with leather elbow patches, grey flannels and brown suede shoes, was in marked contrast to the other man's flashy ostentation. When the cigar had been tossed aside there had been the glint of gold on his little finger as well as round his wrist. It had looked more like a bracelet that a wristwatch and Primmie felt her interest deepening. In the part of southeast London she came from, Crombie overcoats and gold jewellery were the signature of villains and the man in question was certainly built like a villain – and had a villain's threatening attitude, as well.

'Don't tell me how I should be behaving, pal,' he was saying now, stabbing the driver of the Volkswagen in the chest with a stubby finger. 'Because I don't take kindly to it.'

All round them shocked mothers were hurrying their daughters away from the fracas and towards the shallow steps leading to the school's main entrance. Standing on the top step, and with no parent to chivvy them inside, Primmie and Geraldine continued to watch the scene with fascinated interest.

'And I don't take kindly to being poked in the chest,' they could hear the Volkswagen's driver say steelily. Despite his narrow shoulders, he was beginning to look far less diffident and it occurred to Primmie that her first day at Bickley High might very well be about to kick off with fisticuffs in the school car park. As the thought flashed through her mind, rear doors of the Volkswagen and the Rolls opened simultaneously.

From the Volkswagen a diminutive red-haired girl tumbled into view, yelling, 'Don't you *dare* talk to my father like that, you horrid person!' From the Rolls, a plump, fair-haired girl emerged. With obvious reluctance and deep embarrassment she walked across to her father, taking hold of his arm, saying pleadingly, '*Please*, Daddy. Don't go on about it any more. People are looking.'

Amazingly, the intervention seemed to do the trick. Mr Nasty ceased his finger-jabbing and with a last threatening glare at Mr Nice turned away from him, giving his attention, instead, to his mortified daughter.

26

'Shame,' Geraldine said as she and Primmie also turned round and began walking into the school's spacious entrance hall. 'I thought there was going to be a fight. It would have been the most enormous fun, wouldn't it?'

'You're only saying that because you've never seen one,' Primmie said chidingly. 'Real fights aren't like fights in films, you know. They're ugly and frightening.'

Geraldine's sloe-dark eyes blazed with interest. 'You've seen fights, Primmie Surtees? Where on earth do you come from?'

'Rotherhithe.'

There was no time to say anymore because an official-looking woman was holding up a large placard on which was written ALL NEW GIRLS LINE UP HERE, PLEASE and, underneath in smaller letters, NO TALKING.

The queue was already fairly long and as she and Geraldine attached themselves to the end of it, as did the diminutive girl with the mop of spicy red hair.

'I thought your father was great,' Geraldine said to her, ignoring the instruction not to talk and breaking the ice immediately, just as she had done with Primmie. 'A lot of people wouldn't have kept their temper as he did. Primmie,' she gave a nod of her head in Primmie's direction, 'thinks the driver of the Rolls is a nouveau riche from the East End.'

'I never said any such thing!' Primmie protested, scandalized.

'Silence, please!' the woman holding the placard thundered.

'And what's a noovo reesh?' Primmie persisted, lowering her voice to a whisper. 'A criminal?'

'No, idiot.' Geraldine gave a gurgle of laughter, uncaring of the glare she received from the woman at the head of the column they had formed. 'It's someone who's come into money and has no taste – or, in this case, no manners.'

'We are now going to file *silently* into the Grand Hall for assembly,' the woman said, shooting Geraldine a look to kill. 'After assembly you will then re-form in a line to be taken to your form rooms and given an introductory talk.'

'I don't like the sound of form rooms, plural,' Geraldine said as their column began to move off. 'It means we may be split up if we don't keep together. Let's stick close, shall we? I'm Geraldine Grant and this is Primmie Surtees.'

27

'Kiki Lane,' the red-haired girl said and then, as they entered a huge hall already filled with line after line of dutifully silent pupils, 'And why does Primmie know about the East End? Is that where she's from? Is it why she speaks with a Cockney accent?'

Primmie's reaction was drowned as five hundred voices launched into a spirited rendering of 'Jerusalem'.

No hymnbooks were used and Primmie, who had never sung the song before, was at a loss.

'And did tho-ose feet, in ancie-nt ti-me,' Geraldine was singing in cut-glass tones beside her. 'Walk upon Eng-land's moun-tains green.'

It was Kiki Lane's voice that was the real surprise, though. Strong and rich and with perfect pitch, it sent tingles down Primmie's spine. Deciding that anyone who could sing so stunningly deserved forgiving for the remark about her accent, Primmie hummed along as best she could, looking round the vast hall with interest as she did so.

Enormous polished boards hung on the walls, bearing lists of names of former pupils in gold lettering, along with the dates they had attended Bickley as well as their eventual scholastic achievements on leaving university. On another wall was a reproduction of Jean-François Millet's *The Angelus* and, several yards down from it, a reproduction of Sir John Everett Millais' *Ophelia*.

Turning her head to look behind her to see if there were any more pictures, she saw the plump fair-haired girl whose father had behaved so appallingly to Kiki's father. She wasn't singing the words of the hymn, either, but somehow Primmie didn't think it was because she didn't know them, but because she'd been crying – and looked as if, at any second, she would begin crying again. Her eyes were red rimmed and she was clutching a sodden handkerchief in one hand. Having obviously entered the hall late, she was standing at the far end of the rear row, looking so miserable that Primmie's heart went out to her. It hadn't, after all, been her fault that her father had behaved as he had.

As she turned her head away she saw out of the corner of her eye that the girls further along the rear row were nudging each other and making whispered comments that were quite

28

clearly about the new girl and, equally clearly, were spite-fully unkind.

'Till we have built Jer-u-salem,' Kiki and Geraldine were singing at full belt, 'in England's green and pleasant la-and.'

Fifteen minutes later, when assembly had been dismissed, they and the rest of the new girls had been divided into two groups and led off towards two separate classrooms.

'So far so good,' Geraldine said as they remained stead-fastly together. 'We're the only three in this group who haven't come up from the Lower School, did you know that? It means we'll never fit in with the rest of them and why should we try? I'm only here because I didn't get a place at Benenden. I'm guessing you're here on a non-fee-paying scholarship, right?'

Primmie nodded, happy to have her non-fee-paying status out in the open where her two new friends were concerned.

'And what about you, Kiki?' Geraldine asked as, bringing up the rear of their group of twenty or so, they finally reached the light and airy classroom that was apparently going to be their form room. 'Why did you opt for Bickley High?'

Kiki gave a rude snort. 'I didn't. I wanted to go to stage school but Daddy said no way, not until I'd got what he calls a proper education. He's a doctor,' she added as everyone in front of them began selecting desks and sitting at them. 'He thinks I've got the brains to be a doctor too, and I probably have, but I don't want to be one.'

'Let's take three desks at the back,' Geraldine said, indi-cating the still half-empty back row as it became apparent that if they didn't they weren't going to be able to have desks next to each other. 'So what is it you want to be, Kiki? An actress?'

'A singer. A rock singer.'

'Would you three girls at the back please have the good manners to be silent,' the woman who had formed them into a column before leading them into the school hall now said, glaring freezingly at Geraldine, who seemed incapable of lowering her voice to a discreet whisper. 'My name is Mrs Sweeting and I am your form mistress for the next year. Now, before I give you the introductory talk, can you please tell the rest of the form your names, starting with the girl in the bottom left-hand corner and continuing along each row until we reach the girl seated at the top right-hand corner. I'm well aware that the majority of you have come up from the prep department and already know each other, but I do not know you as yet and neither do any of the girls who have come here from other prep departments.

'Or Rotherhithe Juniors,' Kiki whispered wickedly to Primmie, making her grin.

'Samantha Wade-Benbridge,' an affectedly languid voice said from the front of the class. 'Lauren Colefax,' the girl seated next to her said. Other names came thick and fast. 'Mirabel Des Vaux.' 'Sophie Menzies.' 'Beatrice Strachan.'

The door opened, bringing the litany to a halt. 'I'm sorry to interrupt, Mrs Sweeting,' a lady Primmie recognized as being the school secretary said as she entered the room, 'but the group numbers are uneven and in order to correct them this young lady, Artemis Lowther, has been taken out of Miss Roberts's class and will, instead, be with you.'

The girl in question was the plump, fair-haired girl, who looked even more distressed now than she had when in assembly.

There was an outbreak of giggling from the front of the classroom and Primmie could hear someone say in a loud whisper: 'It's *her*. The girl with the thuggish father.'

Standing a few feet behind the school secretary and in full view of the entire class, Artemis flushed a deep, ugly red.

Primmie wasn't remotely surprised. Her one fear, until an hour or so ago, had been that she wouldn't be able to make friends at Bickley High; that she wouldn't be able to fit in. Thanks to Geraldine and to Kiki, that was a fear she no longer had. Artemis Lowther, though, was suffering exactly the kind of torments she had feared she would suffer, not because she spoke differently or because she was a non-fee-paying scholarship girl, but because her father's behaviour had singled her out as being someone to be ridiculed.

'Thank you, Mrs Bridges,' Mrs Sweeting said as, her errand accomplished, the secretary left the room. 'And now, Artemis, if you would take a desk on the back row please, we will continue with what we were doing.'

The only spare desk on the back row was the desk next to Kiki.

In an agony of embarrassment Artemis Lowther made no attempt to move and the situation wasn't helped by Kiki sucking in her breath and then saying fiercely in a low voice, 'No *way*. Not till hell freezes over.'

It was a remark that Mrs Sweeting, lifting up the lid of her desk, mercifully did not hear. Artemis did, though, and so did everyone else. As the red stain in Artemis's cheeks spread and deepened and as there was a fresh outbreak of barely suppressed giggling, Primmie said urgently to Kiki, 'Give her a break, Kiki. What her dad said to your dad wasn't her fault. And she's like us. She hasn't come up from the prep department. No one knows her.'

'They do now,' Geraldine interjected dryly.

Mrs Sweeting slammed down her desk lid. 'Artemis Lowther, please do as you are asked and take your place at the spare desk in the back row and will the three girls seated at the left-hand side of the back row be *silent*.'

With a deeply disgruntled sigh Kiki raised her hands palms outwards, in a pax sign, to signify to Artemis that she wasn't going to cause a scene if she took her place at the desk next to hers. Primmie shot Artemis the widest, most sympathetic smile possible and Geraldine, ignoring Mrs Sweeting's strictures with careless contempt, said, 'I think our little band has just increased in number, Primmie. For better or for worse, it's not going to be the three of us. It's going to be the four of us.'

Five

July 1966

Kiki opened her eyes, looked at her bedside clock and saw with relief that there was another half an hour to go before she needed to get up. In the bed a few feet away from her, Primmie continued to breathe deeply, still fast asleep.

Kiki put her hands behind her head, thinking about the day

31

ahead. It was Friday, thank God. Tonight there was *Ready, Steady, Go* on the television and it was an event she looked forward to all week. Her singing voice was miles better than most of those who appeared on the programme and she longed for the day when she, too, would make her name as a pop star by appearing on it.

'Are you awake, Primmie?' she asked, wanting to share her good mood with her.

A slight snore was the only response.

She stared at her friend in disbelief. How Primmie could sleep so soundly, never waking until their alarm rang, was beyond her. 'She sleeps the sleep of the righteous,' her father would say about Primmie, always with fond amusement in his voice.

Kiki swung her legs out of bed, marvelling, not the for the first time, at how much nicer things had been at home since Primmie had begun staying at Petts Wood from Monday to Friday.

'Of course she can stay here during the week,' her father had said when she had explained to him Primmie's problem – that not only was the journey from Rotherhithe to Bickley High a long one, but leaving and returning home every day in her distinctive school uniform was causing difficulties for her with her former friends in Rotherhithe.

And so for the past four years she and Primmie had lived almost as sisters.

She padded barefoot across deep carpet to the window, reflecting that her father did do his best to keep her happy. Recently she'd begun calling him by his Christian name, explaining that now she was fifteen she found 'Daddy' too babyish, 'Dad' too common and 'Father' too stuffy. She'd expected there to be a battle about it and, truth to tell, had been looking forward to one, but he'd merely laughed and said that if she wanted to call him Simon it was all right by him.

Pulling back the curtains she pushed the already opened window even further open and leaned as far out as possible.

It was a glorious morning and the scent from the Albertine rose that grew up the wall to the left of her window and the honeysuckle that scrambled up the wall to the right of it was as heady as a drug. Beyond the long rolling vista of the immaculately kept lawn, a heat haze hovered over the woods and the far distant view of the Weald. It was a view she was too familiar with to rhapsodize over, as Primmie always did, but even she, who longed only for central London and Tin Pan Alley and clubs and coffee bars, had to admit that it was pretty breathtaking.

Her father, of course, loved the fact that Primmie thought their garden – and the view from it – so magical. 'Where's Primmie? In the garden? It's nice to have someone so appreciative of it,' he'd say, coming in from evening surgery and dropping his doctor's bag in the hall. Five minutes later, after checking whether her mother was slightly tipsy, very tipsy or just plain sozzled, he would be changing out of his suit and into an old sweater and pair of shabby corduroys, all set for a therapeutic hour of gardening.

'Isn't it a bit embarrassing at times, having Primmie living with you when your mother's on a bender?' Geraldine had once asked her in her forthright fashion.

It hadn't been a question she'd taken offence at. Between Geraldine, Primmie, Artemis and herself there were no secrets where their respective home lives were concerned. All three of her friends knew that her mother drank too much.

'It's OK. It isn't a problem,' she had said to Geraldine. 'Things are much better at home when Primmie is with us. There aren't the arguments there used to be. If Mummy's tipsy when Simon comes home, he doesn't get upset the way he used to. And Primmie is great. Nothing ever embarrasses her. There was a phone call not long since from the local supermarket manager saying Mummy was 'distressed' and in need of being escorted home. What he meant, of course, was that she'd been drinking and was causing a scene. If I'd gone to haul her off home the scene would have become twice as horrendous – we'd have been shrieking at each other like fishwives. Primmie, though, behaves as if Mummy being drunk is nothing to get excited about, and Mummy's never abusive or aggressive towards her – which she might be if it were me or Simon trying to deal with her.'

'Interesting,' Geraldine had said, and had then changed the subject to the one that dominated most of their conversations; boys – and how to attract them.

That their parents would all have pink fits if they knew just how boy-fixated they were was, Kiki reflected, the only thing their parents had in common. Artemis's father would, they had all generally agreed, lay violent hands on any boy he caught taking his precious only daughter out on a date. Geraldine had been of the opinion that it was *her* her father would lay violent hands on if he caught her out with a boy at fifteen and Primmie had said that if she were caught she would never be allowed to sleep away from home again.

She turned away from the window in order to turn off the alarm of her bedside clock before it shrilled into life and then threw one of her pillows on to Primmie's bed.

'Hey, Dormouse,' she said, impatiently. 'Wake up, it's seven thirty, it's Friday and I've got plans for the four of us.'

Primmie groaned and humped herself a little further under the bedcovers. Kiki unceremoniously tugged them off her. 'What say we organize a night of freedom for tomorrow?'

Primmie swung her legs to the floor and pushed a tangle of mousy curls away from her face. 'How? I'll be in Rotherhithe.'

'You don't have to be.'

Kiki padded barefoot into the en-suite bathroom. 'It's the sixth form school play tomorrow night.' She turned on a cold tap and squeezed toothpaste on to a toothbrush. 'If you say you want to go to it, it'll be the perfect excuse for your sleeping here an extra night.'

'But I don't want to go to it.'

Kiki's response, as she spat and gargled into the sink, was, perhaps fortunately, unintelligible.

'And Geraldine and Artemis won't want to go to it either,' Primmie continued, shedding her pyjamas and stepping into the shower. 'It's *A Midsummer Night's Dream* and I saw them at rehearsal the other week when I had to stay behind for tennis practice.' She turned the shower on, revelling in the pleasure of it. Even after living so long at the Lanes', there were still some things she was unable to take for granted. 'They were dreadful,' she said, speaking more loudly so that Kiki would be able to hear her over the sound of the water. 'Truly.'

'Lord, but you're dense!' Kiki wiped her mouth on a towel and paused long enough in front of the mirror to see if her breasts were making much of an impression against the thin cotton of her pyjama top. They weren't. 'The school play would just be the *excuse* for your sleeping over on Saturday night. We wouldn't actually *go* to the silly, sodding thing. Simon's at a conference over the weekend. It's an ideal weekend for arranging for Geraldine and Artemis to sleep over with us because when he's away Mummy always takes advantage and has a binge and she won't have a clue what time we come home. Savvy?'

'Y-e-s.' Doubtfully Primmie stepped out of the shower so that Kiki could step into it. 'But it's a bit deceitful, isn't it? I mean we're all going to have to lie, aren't we?'

Kiki closed her eyes in exasperation and began soaping herself, wondering why it was she was still so flat chested when even Primmie was wearing a bra and Artemis's cup size was an awesome 36C.

'No, we're not, Primmie,' she said, with as much patience as she could summon. 'We all four tell our parents that it's the sixth form play on Saturday – and you three then ask if it's OK for you to sleep at my house. None of us will have said that we're *going* to the play. It will just be *assumed* that we are. So we won't have fibbed at all. Get it?'

'It's a great wheeze,' Geraldine said later that morning as they all four made their way to the science laboratory. 'We'll all have to leave home wearing school uniform, though. It's obligatory for any school event and all our parents know that.'

'Just hide some trendy gear in with your night things.' Kiki flashed a wicked grin. 'We'll stow them in a couple of carrier bags and change in the loos at Bickley Station. Easy peasy.'

'And then where will we go?' Breathlessly Artemis heaved her pile of science textbooks from one arm to the other, struggling not to be left behind as they clattered up the steep flight of stairs leading to the science laboratory.

'We'll cruise the coffee bars in Bromley High Street.' Kiki looked across at Geraldine. 'You OK with that, Geraldine? All the boys from Dulwich College and St Dunstan's hang out there and there's live music in the Two Zeds coffee bar – and that I *really* want to check out.'

That evening Kiki threw the doors of her wardrobe wide and stood in front of its contents in deep thought.

The trouble was that though she had clothes aplenty they were all clothes her mother deemed suitable for her age, which meant they were entirely unsuitable for her purpose. She dragged an Op Art sleeveless shift dress out, wondering if she could get away with slicing three inches off its length. The zigzag patterning was in stark black and white – a sophistication she'd had to fight hard for – and if she wore it with her black knee-high boots and her black leather baker-boy beret she might just look sufficiently groovy to pass as an up-and-coming pop star.

She was still standing in front of her open wardrobe, pondering whether if she sliced three inches off the bottom of her dress she would be able to successfully re-hem it, when her mother walked into the room and sat down heavily on the bed.

'Wha' are you doing, darling?' she asked, her speech already slurred. 'You're not going out tonigh', are you? I thought the school play was tomorrow nigh'?'

'It is.' Kiki closed her wardrobe door, fiercely hoping there'd been no sign of inebriation in her mother's voice when, a little earlier in the evening, she had responded to Artemis's mother's query as to whether it really was all right for Artemis to sleep over on Saturday night.

'Then come and keep me company downstairs,' her mother said, sounding abjectly forlorn.

'OK. But you have to watch *Ready, Steady, Go* with me.'

'I always do watch it,' her mother said, surprising the socks off her. 'Cathy McGowan reminds me of Primmie. She's always so bright and zesty.'

Kiki, usually always moody and sulky in both her parents' presence, erupted into giggles. Long-haired Cathy McGowan was known as Queen of the Mods and that was hardly a title that fitted Primmie.

'Come on, Mummy,' she said, drawing her mother to her feet and sliding her arm companionably through hers, an action so alien she couldn't remember when last she'd done it. 'You know what Cathy McGowan always says when the programme begins. The weekend starts here!'

'Evening, Mrs Lane. Thank you for letting us stay the night,' Artemis and Geraldine chanted in unison as they trooped into the house a little after six o'clock the following day, each carrying an overnight bag.

'That's fine,' Kiki's mother responded, far more animated than usual, 'there's no problem as long as you don't want me to go with you to the play. An amateur production of *A Midsummer Night's Dream* is a joy I can easily forego.'

Laughing and saying nothing, in order not to have to blatantly lie about their plans for the evening, they clattered up the stairs after Kiki.

'Where's Primmie? Isn't she here yet?' Artemis asked as she dumped her overnight bag on one of the twin beds.

'Nope. We're meeting her at Bickley Station at half past six. What have you brought to wear, Artemis? We need to look as if we're seventeen if the evening's to be a success.'

Artemis clicked open her overnight bag, turfed out a pair of pyjamas and, from beneath them, rather hesitantly lifted out a sleeveless, fuchsia-pink mini-dress. 'It's a Mary Quant,' she said before anyone ventured an opinion. 'Daddy bought it for me to wear at my cousin's christening. It isn't *micro*-short, but it is OK, isn't it? I mean, I will look at least seventeen wearing it, won't I?'

'It's ravishing,' Geraldine said, adroitly fudging the issue of exactly how Artemis, whose legs were just as plump as the rest of her body, was going to look wearing it.

Artemis, always anxious for Geraldine's opinion, beamed with relief. Behind Artemis's back, Kiki pulled an agonized face. Artemis was quite obviously going to look a disaster and Primmie almost certainly would look no better, though for different reasons.

'I did offer to lend Primmie something to wear,' she said now to Geraldine, 'but she wouldn't have it. She said she had a new crocheted top with a scalloped neckline.'

'And what is she going to wear it with?' Geraldine asked dryly, well aware, as all three of them were, that money for clothes was in short supply in the Surtees household. 'Her school skirt?'

'Probably.' There was irritation in Kiki's voice. Why Primmie was so adamant about not borrowing any of her clothes she couldn't imagine. It made no sense. And if Primmie turned up at the Two Zeds looking like a fifteen-year-old schoolgirl then the rest of them were going to find it exceedingly difficult to pass as seventeen-year-olds, no matter how stylish their clothes or how much make-up they wore.

'Are we really going to have to put our clothes in carrier bags when we leave the house?' Artemis asked, fretting over yet another aspect of their evening of freedom. 'If my dress is put in a carrier bag it'll get terribly creased.'

Kiki sucked in her breath, about to blow her top at such nit-picking carping.

'It'll be OK if it's folded properly,' Geraldine said swiftly. 'And I'll do the folding, so take that anxious look off your face or you'll get frown lines, Artemis.'

As Artemis rushed to take a look at her forehead in the dressing-table mirror, Kiki gave a hoot of laughter, her irritation vanishing. 'I bet we wouldn't have to go through all this palaver if we lived in Rotherhithe,' she said, flopping down on the bed next to Geraldine. 'Primmie only has to endure it because we do. She says all the friends she went to junior school with go out at night pretty much when they want to – and not only are there more coffee bars in Rotherhithe than there are in Bromley, but there's a working men's club there as well.'

'A working men's club?' Artemis turned away from the mirror. '*A working men's club?* Why on earth would you be interested in a place like that?'

'Because if you're with a member they let you in under the age of eighteen,' Geraldine said, intervening between the two of them yet again. 'And because they have entertainment, singers and comedians . . .'

'And amateur singers and comedians,' Kiki said, bouncing from the bed, impatient for it to be time for them to set off to meet Primmie. 'In the north, amateur singers can become very well known by singing in their local club. Here, the only

38

place there's a remote chance of being able to get up and sing is in a couple of coffee bars in Bromley. Which is why tonight is so important. There'll be live music tonight at the Two Zeds, and whatever the group playing there I'm going to do a number with them.'

'But they'll have a singer, won't they?' Artemis, as usual, sounded bewildered. 'Why would they let you sing with them when they'll have a singer already?'

'Because I'm going to sing with them whether they want me to or not.'

'And what if they throw you – and us – out?' Geraldine asked, an eyebrow quirked.

Kiki's grin almost split her cat-like face in two. 'They won't do that, Geraldine. Not when they hear me. Tonight is going to be a historic occasion. Tonight, Kiki Lane is going to make her public debut, even if she has to chain herself to the mike in order to do so. It's going to be a blast and absolutely, utterly, *searingly* unforgettable!'

Six

The evening at the Two Zeds had certainly been everything Kiki had promised it would be. Even two weeks later the memory of it was, for Artemis, sickeningly vivid.

She yanked off the dress she had put on only five minutes earlier, searching her wardrobe for something that would make her look less fat, wondering why, when she was about to go with her father and Primmie to see a show in the West End, she was again brooding about what she always thought of as 'the Bromley nightmare'. It hadn't started off disastrously, despite her tension and nerves. At first, when they'd changed out of their school uniforms in the loos at Bickley Station, it had been fun. Giggling fit to burst they'd tarted themselves up with all the make-up they'd been able to lay their hands on. Geraldine's contribution had been her mother's lipstick and her mother's perfume. The perfume had been OK, but the lipstick had been bright red and crashingly old-fashioned.

Geraldine hadn't thought it old-fashioned, though. When she and Kiki and Primmie had opted for the Max Factor pearlized pink lipstick that Kiki had bought out of her spending money, with Kiki rudely telling Geraldine that she couldn't wear the red, because only old women wore red, Geraldine had merely quirked her eyebrow and said, 'Really, Kiki? Just watch me.'

Hauling a tapestry skirt out of her wardrobe in the hope that she might look less of a porker in it than she had in the dress, Artemis wondered why it was she could never respond to Kiki's acidly sharp remarks in the languid, indifferent way Geraldine always did. No one, not even Kiki, ever got the better of Geraldine. And when the four of them had finished plastering make-up on, it had been Geraldine – who had been much lighter-handed with it than the rest of them – who had looked head-turningly sensational.

Kiki had looked mesmerizingly hip – which was the effect she had wanted. Wearing knee-length black boots, a black and white zigzag-patterned shift dress given extra shape by the cotton wool stuffed down the bra she'd borrowed from Geraldine, a black leather baker-boy beret on her flame-red hair and with her eyes soot-dark with the help of lashings of black eye liner and mascara, she had looked years older than her actual age.

She, Artemis, had also looked years older than she was and, until they had reached the Two Zeds, she had thought she looked sensational. Her fuchsia-pink mini-dress was an original Mary Quant – and how many people in Bromley coffee bars were wearing one of those? She'd got electric-blue eye shadow on her eyelids and had borrowed a pair of her mother's bat-wing false eyelashes, which Primmie had glued on for her. Her hair had been long enough for her to anchor high on the top of her head and then back-comb into a chignon of large looped curls held in place by hairpins. She'd been wearing fairly high-heeled sandals, and, of all of them, she felt that she definitely looked the most sophisticated and that her fears of being left on the sidelines, if they should achieve their aim of meeting up with some boys from St Dunstan's or Dulwich College, were groundless.

There hadn't been any boys from St Dunstan's or Dulwich College there, though – and with good reason. Packing the Two Zeds to capacity and spilling noisily out on to the pavement had been a whole convoy of bikers. Chrome-encrusted Harley Davidsons had jammed either side of the High Street and the rock music blasting from the inside of the coffee bar had been deafening. To say that it hadn't been what she had been expecting was the understatement of the year. She'd been hoping to meet a boy who went to one of the two public schools in the area. Instead, she'd been faced with a situation so appalling she'd completely panicked, coming to a dead halt, struggling for breath like a beached fish.

'Come *on*, Artemis,' Kiki had said exasperatedly, pulling on her arm so hard a scattering of hairpins had flown loose. 'We're supposed to be making a sensational entrance.'

'I'm not going in there!' she'd gasped in strangulated horror. 'Not when it's full of all those . . . those . . .'

'Bikers?' Geraldine had finished for her, helpfully. 'I can't say I like the look of them myself, Artemis. Why don't we go somewhere else, Kiki? There's another coffee bar further down the High Street. I don't suppose it'll have live music, but there's a jukebox and it'll be groovy in a way Artemis and Primmie can cope with.'

As she buckled the belt of her tapestry skirt, Artemis remembered how grateful she'd been that Geraldine had made it obvious that Primmie, too, was just as horrified as she was by the sight of the dozens of fearsome-looking youths milling about on the pavement.

'Oh, thank you, Geraldine Grant,' Kiki had said with sarcastic venom. 'Thank you very much! Can I remind the three of you why we're here? We're here so that I can get up and sing with a group and strut my stuff. Singing along to a jukebox isn't on the agenda, OK?'

'We're here,' Primmie had said with steel in her voice, 'to have a fun night out and to meet some boys. Those aren't boys in the Two Zeds. They're bikers and we're fifteen years old. I think Geraldine is right. We should go somewhere else.'

'*You* go somewhere else if you like,' Kiki had stormed,

41

looking as if she'd like to throttle her, 'but I'm not! I came here because it's the only place I know where I stand a chance of making an impression with a rock group. Now you can either come in with me and give me some support, which is what friends are supposedly for, or you can jolly well sod off.'

'Hey, girlies. Come and join the party,' a leather-jacketed youth called across to them, drawing the eyes of other youths in their direction.

'Don't worry! I am!' Kiki shot back brazenly and then, facing her and Primmie and Geraldine, she'd said, 'Well, are you coming or aren't you?'

'We don't have much choice, do we?' Geraldine had said dryly. 'We can't leave you to go in there by yourself. We'll go, but we keep together. Right?'

'Right,' Primmie had said grimly.

She'd said nothing. To have refused to enter the coffee bar with them would have meant her having to get the train back to Bickley on her own and would have been an act of cowardice none of her friends would ever forgive or forget. Miserable, trying to keep in the middle of their little group and not look too conspicuous, a difficult task considering her exotic hair-style, she'd gritted her teeth and walked with them into the Two Zeds.

The next two hours had been unremittingly awful. There'd been other girls in the packed coffee bar, of course, but they'd all been dressed in either scruffy jeans and denim jackets or black leather trousers and leather bomber jackets.

A horrible creature with a crucifix hanging from one ear had tried to pick her up and, when Geraldine had come to her aid and told him to 'shove off and leave Artemis alone', he'd begun making fun of her name, calling her Fatimis-Artemis.

Tears of humiliation had burned the backs of her eyes and then Geraldine had inadvertently made everything worse by fishing a packet of cigarettes from the bottom of her bag. 'Let's light up,' she'd said, 'It'll make us look groovier.'

They'd all tried their hand at smoking before, but the experiment hadn't been an unqualified success. Only Primmie – of all people – had successfully inhaled. Now, grateful for any

42

crutch that would make her look as if she couldn't care less about the nickname the biker had given her, she took a deep, experienced-looking breath inwards when she lit up. The result had been catastrophic. She'd coughed and choked and struggled for breath, her eyes streaming, her mascara running in rivers of black down her cheeks. To make it worse Kiki had said wryly, 'A ciggie isn't making Artemis look very groovy, Geraldine. And she's going to look even worse if she's sick.'

She had been very sick. Primmie had taken her into a disgustingly dirty toilet where she'd retched in blessed privacy until she'd got the smoke out of her lungs.

By the time the two of them had reluctantly squeezed their way back to where Geraldine was waiting for them, Kiki was already up on the small podium and was well into a number that had a beat like a sledgehammer.

'How come she's been allowed to sing?' she had asked Geraldine, grudgingly admiring of Kiki's ability to always get her own way.

'God knows – the biker with the crucifix in his ear has taken a shine to her and he's the group's roadie. The only number she knows that they know is 'Dancing in the Street', which didn't best please her. She wanted to do something more R&B. Still, she's got the voice for it and she looks every inch a pop singer, doesn't she?'

'She does if the cotton wool stays in her bra,' Primmie had said with anxiety.

Artemis stared musingly at her reflection in her dressing-table mirror. Ever since the night at the Two Zeds she'd been on a crash diet and had already lost six pounds. As she studied the size of her breasts in relation to her emerging waist, she knew one thing for an absolute fact: Kiki would *kill* to be able to fill a bra the way she did.

Satisfied with the look of the tapestry skirt and the pie-crust collared blouse she was wearing with it, she picked up a purple suede coat and hurried downstairs to where her father was waiting for her.

'You look sensational, Princess,' he said, beaming at her and stubbing out a cigar in a conveniently handy rose bowl.

'Thanks, Daddy,' she said, hoping their daily cleaning lady

43

would attend to the cut-glass bowl before her mother saw its contents.

'Come on, then. Let's be on our way.'

Her mother wasn't coming with them to the matinée. It was going to be just her, her father and Primmie, and the car they would be going in was the Rolls. Being driven in the Rolls through the back streets of Rotherhithe was not an experience she relished and was one she knew that Primmie hated. 'I'll meet you and Artemis at the theatre, Mr Lowther,' Primmie had said, valiantly trying to avoid the crushing embarrassment of having the Lowther Rolls glide to a halt outside her council home.

Her father, however, enjoyed cruising in grandeur the mean narrow streets where, as a child, he'd run wild with his arse hanging out of his trousers, and wouldn't hear of Primmie making the easy journey from Rotherhithe to the West End by public transport.

As Artemis slid into the front passenger seat she reflected that the most astonishing thing she had ever experienced had been her father telling Primmie's parents that he'd been born only a couple of streets away from where they lived. Until then, she hadn't known that her father had been born and bred in south-east London. She had always believed he was born and brought up in Berkshire.

As the powder-blue car slid down the drive she tried to imagine what her life would have been like if her father had never wheeled and dealed his way out of the narrow cobbled streets of his youth, and couldn't. The prospect was just too vile. The only thing she could imagine was that, if they had lived near to each other, she and Primmie would have been friends, just as they were friends now. Primmie, who was always so steadfast and supportive and who never lost her temper or threw emotional scenes.

The Rolls began to gather speed and she remembered the one time Primmie *had* thrown an emotional scene. It had been the night of the Two Zeds nightmare when, on their way home from Bickley Station, an already horrible evening – horrible for her and Primmie, at any rate – had grown far, far worse.

They'd arrived at the station to find the loos locked – which meant they couldn't change back into their school uniforms.

Hoping against hope that they were going to be able to sneak into Kiki's house without being seen, they had begun the walk to Petts Wood from the station.

Kiki had been noisily euphoric, walking along the edge of the curb as if it were a tightrope, over the moon at how successful her evening had been, full of how Ty, the hideous creature with a crucifix dangling from his ear, was going to meet her in Bromley on Saturday afternoon.

Geraldine had been serenely indifferent to the ghastliness of Kiki doing any such thing and had taken her shoes off and was walking along the pavement barefoot. Primmie was rubbing her eyes, complaining that they were still stinging from cigarette smoke. She, Artemis, had just wanted to be in bed. Her high-heeled sandals had been crippling her, she'd lost so many hairpins there were more curls toppling loose than were still secured on the top of her head and one of her false eyelashes was so askew she could barely see where she was going.

When a car approaching from behind them suddenly pinned them in its headlights and screeched to a halt beside them, she was the last of the four of them to recognize it.

'*Hell!*' Kiki had said, freezing into immobility. Geraldine had said merely, 'That's torn it.' It was Primmie's reaction that had really alerted her to the fact that an evening she had thought couldn't possibly get more dreadful was just about to do so. Primmie had given a cry of such distress that for a moment she'd had thought the car was full of youths who had been in the Two Zeds and they were all about to be raped.

The figure that had leaped out of the car, rounding its bonnet with such fury she'd thought he'd been going to hit one of them, hadn't been a youth. It had been Kiki's father.

Geraldine, who never panicked, merely said, 'I thought he was away this weekend at a conference,' as Simon Lane bore down on Kiki, shouting, 'What the *devil* do you think you're playing at?'

As she looked at her friends' faces, captured in the glaring headlights, Artemis was well able to understand his anger. Though stone cold sober, Kiki looked as drunk as her mother often was. Her beret had slipped halfway off her head, her Cleopatra-black eye make-up looked garishly clownish and the cotton wool in her bra had rearranged itself into telltale bumps and lumps.

Geraldine didn't look a mess. Geraldine never looked a mess. She looked years older than fifteen, though. And because Primmie was wearing a school skirt and because her crocheted top was as prim as her name, her heavy make-up looked even more outlandish and tarty than Kiki's did. As for herself . . . She shuddered to think what she'd looked like, with her hair half up and half down and one false eyelash on and the other dangling half off.

'In the car!' Simon Lane had snapped, half throwing Kiki into the front passenger seat. 'You look like trollops, but I suppose you know that, don't you?' Seconds later, taut with fury, he had slammed the driver's door shut behind him and savagely turned the key in the ignition. 'I suppose that was the effect you were striving for, was it, Primmie?' he'd asked, nastily singling her out as she sobbed as if her heart would break. 'So where have you all been and who have you been with? And I don't want any lies – not from any of you.'

That a man usually so mild mannered could be so very angry was, to Artemis, such a frightening shock, she was incapable of saying anything.

'We've been to a coffee bar in Bromley,' Geraldine had said, leaving out the fact that it was a biker's coffee bar. Primmie, still crying, had confirmed it and Kiki had simply remained mutinously silent. Once in the house he'd refused to let any of them change back into their school uniform and had phoned her parents and Geraldine's, asking that they come and collect them. Primmie's parents weren't on the telephone and only Primmie had slept at Kiki's house that night as arranged.

There'd been ructions, of course, but though Geraldine's parents' anger had been directed at Geraldine, her parents' anger had been directed at Simon Lane – or at least her father's had.

'You weren't at fault, Princess,' he'd said. 'It was that puffed-up doctor that was at fault. You were to stay the night at his house, under his care. He should have kept a better eye on that daughter of his. If it wasn't that you're best friends with her I'd have punched his lights out!'

He would have done, as well. Artemis had long ago become aware that people around her father tried very hard not to upset him.

'It's a good thing she couldn't come to the theatre this afternoon,' he said now, breaking in on her thoughts as they flashed past Lewisham clock tower.

Startled that their thoughts had been running on the same lines, Artemis said, 'Who? Kiki?'

He nodded, taking a hand off the wheel to shoot his cuff and look at his Rolex. 'Yep. Didn't this afternoon clash with her singing class?'

Artemis nodded, knowing that even if Kiki hadn't had a singing class to go to, she still wouldn't have accepted the invitation to go to the theatre with her and Primmie. Her reaction, when she had told her they were going to see the Black and White Minstrels – had been to say devoutly, 'Dear God,' and rudely raise her eyes to heaven.

Geraldine hadn't been able to go with them either, because she was down in Sussex, staying the weekend with her cousin Francis.

They were in New Cross now and passing a huge building site fronted by a giant hoarding, which declared that the site was under construction, by J. T. Lowther. Her father slapped the wheel with satisfaction at the sight of it and Artemis shuddered, hating to see her surname so publicly connected with something so manual and dirty.

Francis's family's money came from land. 'Uncle Piers owns half of Sussex,' Geraldine had once said, and she'd found out later, after she'd met Francis, that it was true and that he really did. Meeting Francis had been a dizzyingly important event. He was eighteen and not only was he heart-stoppingly good-looking, but he also had class – real class – and would quite obviously be very, very rich one day.

More than anything else in the world, Artemis wanted Francis as her boyfriend. Geraldine, though, was so possessive of his time she made such a scenario near impossible. 'Why don't you tell Geraldine that you want Francis to ask you out?' Primmie had said to her practically. 'Then maybe she could find out how he feels about you?' It was a thought that had filled her with horror. She wanted Francis to ask her

47

out without any interference from Geraldine – which he might well do if only she could spend time with him without Geraldine being always only inches away.

As her father turned off the main road and into the warren of small streets that ran down to the docks and the river, her stomach muscles tightened. It was snobbish, she knew, but she hated visiting Primmie's home. Mr and Mrs Surtees were always nice to her, but they were also dreadfully common and when her father had once said that Mrs Surtees reminded him of his mother, the grandma who had died before she, Artemis, had been born, the horror of it had made her feel physically ill. If Primmie was aware of how she felt about visiting Rotherhithe, she never let on, but then Primmie never did say anything that made her feel uncomfortable – which couldn't be said for Kiki or even, sometimes, for Geraldine.

Ever since her date with Ty the previous Saturday, Kiki had declared that he was now her boyfriend and she'd also told everyone at school that he wasn't just a biker, but that he was a Hell's Angel. To Artemis's stunned amazement, instead of this exaggeration making Kiki a pariah it had, instead, sent her reputation soaring.

As the Rolls glided to a halt, she dug her nails deep into her palms. *She* wasn't going to settle for a working-class boyfriend covered in tattoos. When she got herself a boyfriend it was going to be someone so genuinely upper class no one would be able to sneer at him – or her. It was going to be someone who had a home that had been in their family for centuries; someone who had been educated at Eton or Rugby; someone who was wealthy. Someone like Francis.

Burning with the determination to be his girlfriend she stepped out of the car in order to knock on the Surteeses' door. She needn't have bothered. Having seen the Rolls enter the street Primmie's mother, in pinny and slippers, was already rushing down the short front path to greet them, calling out in a voice that that could have been heard in Purley, 'Nice to see yer, Artemis darlin'. An' you too, Mr Lowther. The Rolls is lookin' nice today, ain't it? Are yer comin' in for a cuppa?'

Seven

March 1968

Geraldine leaned back against the Drum's shabby red plush seating. On one side of her Primmie was giggling with laughter at a joke someone had just told and on the other side of her Primmie's mum was shouting across to the landlord that they needed another round of drinks, thank you very much.

Her parents didn't know, of course, that when she stayed over on a Saturday night with Primmie, she and Primmie always went to the Drum with Primmie's mum and dad. Their still being a year under age wasn't something the Drum's landlord gave much heed to, unlike the landlord of the Three Foxes at Chislehurst.

He would single Primmie out, saying darkly, 'She's underage, and if she's underage and you're her friends, you three are probably underage as well.'

When there was music playing and lots of talent from St Dunstan's and Dulwich College sixth forms crowding the bar, his turning them out of the pub was infuriating. It was Kiki, as always, who found a way round it. 'She's my little sister,' she would say, 'and there's no one in at home so I can't leave her there, can I? All she wants is a glass of orange and a packet of crisps.'

Because Kiki sang there on the first Friday of every month with the group Ty now managed, the landlord had grudgingly said that, as long as no one slipped Primmie any alcohol, she could stay. Primmie, publicly branded as being little more than a child, fumed over the indignity but never suggested not going with them. Apart from when Kiki was with Ty, or she, Geraldine, was down at her aunt and uncle's in Sussex

49

or staying over at Primmie's, the four of them went everywhere together. Always.

''Ere you are, gels,' the barman said, plonking down the tray of drinks Primmie's mother had asked for down on the table they were all squeezed round and beginning to unload the brimming glasses. 'The guv'nor wants to know when that red-aired friend of yours is coming down again, Primmie. She ain't 'alf got a singing voice on 'er, ain't she?'

'She sings with a professional group,' Primmie said, loading empty glasses on to the tray in order to make way for the full ones. 'If they perform, they expect to be paid.'

'Well, they wouldn't get paid 'ere. They'd be lucky to get a free drink 'ere, but we could 'ave a whip round for 'er and 'er mates. Ask 'er to fink abaht it, Primmie. She's that good she should be on one of them pop programmes.'

When he'd gone, Geraldine said, 'Are you still OK for next Sunday, Prim?'

'The rally?'

'The rally. It's going to be big. Francis and his friends are coming up from Sussex for it. There are going to be anti-war demonstrators from all over the country there. It means there could be some scuffles with the police, so if you're not sure about it . . . ?'

'Of course I'm sure about it!' Primmie's indignation was instant. 'Just because I don't carry an anti-war placard and organize parties in aid of the Viet Cong doesn't mean I don't feel just as passionately as you and Artemis about what's going on in Vietnam! I'll be there next Sunday, Geraldine. Even if you and Kiki and Artemis weren't going, I'd still be there!'

Geraldine grinned. It always amused her when Primmie got het up over anything, because generally she was so unflappable.

Sometimes, over the last few months, the four of them hadn't always seen eye to eye politically. Primmie, for instance, had shocked all three of them by not backing the campaign for legalized abortion and Artemis had nearly forfeited all their friendships by her inability to get passionate about civil rights in America. Where American involvement in Vietnam was concerned, though, they were all in wholehearted agreement. The Americans needed to get out of the country – and

50

that's what next Sunday's demonstration was all about. There was to be a rally in Trafalgar Square and from there, after speeches by leading peace campaigners, they were going to march to Grosvenor Square in order to protest outside the American Embassy.

'Don't wear boots with heels next Sunday,' she said as everyone round the table, apart from themselves, erupted into yet another gale of uproarious laughter. 'If there's a scuffle with the police, we'll need to be able to run.'

'So I've got a problem about Sunday.'

They were sitting on the steps outside the second-floor room used for art classes. The class had just ended and, as there was a ten-minute break before their next class started, everyone else in their form had clattered off to the school shop for a can of Coke or a bar of chocolate.

Geraldine quirked a sleekly shaped eyebrow. It was Kiki, not Artemis speaking, and Kiki never had any problems, now, about doing exactly as she wanted at weekends. For the first time she registered that Kiki not only looked more fed-up than she'd ever seen her, but that she also looked ill.

'Why?' she asked as Artemis fussed with her skirt, unhappy at sitting on a dirty step.

'Because I've got more on my mind than an anti-war rally.'

Artemis stopped fussing with her skirt. 'Then you're being very shallow,' she said reprovingly. '*Nothing* is more important than standing up for what you believe in – I thought we were all agreed on that. If Daddy knew I was going up to the rally on Sunday he'd be *furious*, but I'm still going.'

'Yeah, right on, Artemis. But you're not pregnant, are you? I am.'

The stunned silence went on for so long that Geraldine thought it was never going to end. Artemis's cornflower-blue eyes widened to the size of saucers. Primmie's face drained to the colour of parchment. Even she, who'd long known that Kiki was going all the way with Ty, was rocked by disbelief.

'But you're only seventeen!' It was Primmie, darling Primmie who spoke first.

'I know how old I am, Prim!' Kiki looked as if she was

going to explode at any minute with the force of the feelings she was trying to control. 'The question is, what am I going to do?'

Somewhere in the distance a bell rang, signalling the end of break. None of them took any notice of it.

Making a vain effort to behave as if she'd known all along that Kiki had far outstripped the rest of them in sexual experience, Artemis said, 'Have you told Ty?' And then, as Kiki didn't answer, 'I mean, it is Ty's baby, isn't it?'

'Of course it bloody is! Who else's would it be, Artemis? Mr Hurst's?'

Mr Hurst was their sixty-year-old science master.

'Will Ty marry you, do you think?' There was doubt at the prospect in Primmie's voice.

Kiki gave a howl of anguish, tears spilling down her face, though whether they were tears of rage or distress was hard to tell. 'He might and he might not and it doesn't bloody matter which! *I* don't want to marry *him*. I'm not going to have this baby, Prim! It might have passed you by, but I'm going to be a pop star! And teenage unmarried mothers aren't on *Ready, Steady, Go* – or hadn't you noticed?'

Geraldine fought down her own feeling of panic, aware that if someone didn't somehow reassure her, Kiki was going to freak out completely. 'It could be worse,' she said. 'At least abortion is legal now.'

'Only just and only if my family doctor refers me for one,' Kiki shot back bitterly. 'And who is my family doctor? He's a doctor who works in Simon's practice. Do you *really* think he would refer me for an abortion without telling my dad? I don't think so, Geraldine, do you?'

Well aware that her answer was written on her face, Geraldine kept silent, marshalling her thoughts, trying to work out what the best thing was to do.

Primmie, too, was silent, biting her lip.

Artemis sucked in her breath and said tentatively, 'Perhaps if you told your mother . . .'

'My mother's in a drying-out clinic, as you well know, Artemis. Even I'm not so bloody selfish as to dump this on her when for the first time in years there's a chance of her turning her life around.'

'Then what are you going to do?' Primmie asked inadequately.

'I don't know.' Kiki wiped her nose on the sleeve of her jersey, her shoulders slumped in despair. 'I wish I did know, but I don't. I don't have the faintest bloody clue.'

Geraldine paid very little attention in class for the rest of the day. Kiki's bombshell had unnerved her far more than she was prepared to let on, not just because Kiki's situation was so appalling, but because, if she wasn't careful, she, too, could quite easily find herself in the same position. Not that she and Francis had actually gone all the way yet, because they hadn't. They had, though, come very, very close.

'And so the most lasting of Charles I's innovations were those then most resented,' Miss Fothergill, their history teacher, was saying as she hitched her gown a little further up her shoulders.

Geraldine, her thoughts now on Francis, was indifferent to Charles's political difficulties. She had always wanted to be with Francis. She couldn't remember a time without him. When they were children, she and Francis had been inseparable and they'd known they were going to marry each other from the time she'd been fifteen and he'd been eighteen. That being the case, the temptation to give in to his urgings that they go all the way was becoming almost impossible to resist – or had been, until she'd known of the mess Kiki was in.

'Charles I and Archbishop Laud altered the face of the Church of England,' droned on Miss Fothergill.

She wrote the words CONTRACEPTIVE PILL in her rough book and circled them. If she could get a prescription for the pill, her problem would be solved, but, as Kiki had found, going on the pill wasn't easy when you were seventeen. Horror stories abounded of doctors at family planning clinics informing family GPs and of GPs informing parents. It simply wasn't a step she dared take.

'. . . and, although the restored Anglican Church was not Laudian, but rather Erasmian, it is much due to them that it has since been distinguished by its own particular ambience . . .'

She wondered if Kiki, Artemis and Primmie were

53

listening to Miss Fothergill's biased presentation of Charles I as a martyr, and doubted it. Kiki certainly had too much on her mind and Artemis wasn't much cop at history at the best of times. As for Primmie . . . Primmie would be trying to pay attention, but she'd be feeling too much anguish on Kiki's behalf to be able to write a grade A essay afterwards.

She doodled on the cover of her rough book, wondering whether or not to tell her mother about Kiki's predicament. Unlike her friends' mothers, who, for differing reasons, would most certainly not be helpful, her own mother was fairly unshockable. It came of her being a university lecturer and, like Kiki's parents, being relatively young. Whereas Primmie's mum was in her fifties and Artemis's mother was in her forties, her own mother, like Kiki's, was only thirty-eight. In fact, Primmie's remark about parties to raise money for the Viet Cong was in reference to a party her mother had thrown and which dozens of her mother's left-wing, politically active friends had attended.

So . . . Perhaps her mother would know of a clinic where Kiki could go for an abortion without her having to be referred by her family doctor. There were supposedly going to be loads of such clinics very soon, when the new abortion law really swung into action.

'Charles was also an innovator in the arts,' Miss Fothergill was saying, continuing her eulogy. 'He was a connoisseur of pictures and architecture and of the Baroque culture, of which his court was then the most elaborate expression.'

A tiny ball of paper, thrown from the row behind her, landed on her desk. Miss Fothergill, becoming excited by Charles's patronage of Rubens and Van Dyck, was oblivious.

The note read: *If Cromwell hadn't chopped the boring old fart's head off, I'd have done it for him!* It was from Kiki.

Geraldine grinned and put the note in her pencil case. Somehow, some way, she and Artemis and Primmie would sort things out for Kiki, and if the solution was going to cost a lot of money then Ty would jolly well have to stump up – even if it meant his having to sell his Harley in order to do so.

*   *   *

54

By Sunday morning, she still hadn't spoken to her mother, who had been at a conference all week and was desperately trying to get back from it in time for the demo. Resolving to speak to her that evening, no matter what, and wearing trainers, a denim jacket and jeans, a pair of wool gloves tucked in a back pocket, she set off for Charing Cross station, where she was meeting up with Artemis and Primmie before going on to the rally in Trafalgar Square. Well aware of what probably lay ahead, the gloves were for any barricades the police might have put up outside the embassy and that, along with other demonstrators, she had every intention of pulling down.

On the train from Chislehurst to Charing Cross she had plenty to think about, for not only had she not yet spoken to her mother, she hadn't spoken to Francis, either.

This was because she didn't know where Francis was.

'He's been rusticated,' her Uncle Piers had snapped when, failing to get him on the phone at his university lodgings, she'd telephoned to see if he was at home for some reason. 'He was caught smoking cannabis. Where he is now I've no idea. If he gets in touch with you, Geraldine, let me know.'

She'd said she would, knowing that if, when she saw Francis, he asked her not to tell his father where he was, she wouldn't. That she would see him she didn't have a minute's doubt. He, and a convoy of his friends, would most certainly be at the demo.

She also had Primmie's attitude to Kiki's pregnancy to consider. In the six years the four of them had been friends they had never fallen out – not seriously that is – over anything. Now, however, Primmie was adamant that Kiki shouldn't have an abortion, but should have the baby and then, if she didn't want to keep it, should give it up for adoption. Fortunately, she hadn't said this to Kiki yet, but it was only a matter of time.

Geraldine chewed the corner of her lip. The thing was, even if Kiki wanted to have the baby, how could she? Her mother was in no condition to stand by her and help her through the months of pregnancy. Now in a drying-out clinic there was, for the first time according to Kiki, a real chance that her mother was going to master her alcohol addiction. If, because of her pregnancy, her mother hit the bottle again, Kiki would never forgive herself.

The train rumbled into Charing Cross and she jumped off it alongside a whole clutch of fellow passengers carrying anti-war placards and posters.

Artemis and Primmie were waiting for her as arranged beneath the station clock – and so was Kiki, armed with a Viet Cong flag.

'I thought coming to the rally would take my mind off things,' she said, her face pale and strained. 'I take it you haven't talked to your mother yet?'

'No. She gets back some time today.' Not wanting to create a situation where Primmie might be tempted to tell Kiki exactly how she felt about things, she turned her attention to Artemis, who was, as usual, wrongly dressed for the occasion.

'It's a *demo*, Artemis,' she said exasperatedly, 'not a wedding.'

Everyone, even Primmie, regarded Artemis's plum suede mini-skirted suit and matching high-heeled boots in despair.

'I still wanted to be nicely dressed,' Artemis said defensively.

'Aren't you freezing?' Primmie was very sensibly protected against the brisk March breeze in a windproof jacket and jeans.

'No.' Artemis shivered slightly. 'Now are you three going to spend all day criticizing what I'm wearing, or are we going to Trafalgar Square?'

'We're going to Trafalgar Square.'

As Geraldine led the way, she couldn't help wondering if Artemis had dressed to the nines because she was hoping to run into Francis. Not that she was frightened that Francis might fall for Artemis if he were chased hard enough, because she wasn't. Blue-eyed blondes simply weren't his type. Her concern about Artemis's obvious crush on Francis was that up to now she'd never told Artemis – or Kiki and Primmie – that she and Francis intended marrying when she was twenty-one When she did make her announcement – and it would have to be pretty soon, because it was a secret that was growing harder and harder to keep – she didn't want Artemis feeling that by making a play for Francis she'd made a fool of herself.

'America *out*! America *out*! America *out*!'

56

The chanting from the square was deafening.

'I told you it was going to be big,' she shouted as they pushed and shoved in order to keep moving forward.

'Now I know why people bring placards,' Primmie gasped as a placard-carrying student jostled past her. 'It's so they can use them to push people out of the way.'

Once in the packed square, under her direction and with Kiki's help, they achieved the near impossible. Although Landseer's four lions were already crowded and draped with demonstrators, they managed not only to scramble up one of the plinths but also to squeeze a way on to the lion itself.

'America *out*! America *out*! America *out*!' Kiki shouted triumphantly at full belt, her face still unnaturally pale beneath the sizzling red of her hair.

Only Artemis didn't join in with the spirit of the occasion, and that was because her high-heeled boots and straight suede mini-skirt had meant she'd been unable to do much scrambling and had had to suffer the indignity of being heaved and hauled like a sack of potatoes up on to the lion's freezing cold and slippery bronze back.

Having secured herself a bird's-eye view, Geraldine began scouring the sea of heads.

'How many people do you think are here, Geraldine?' Primmie shouted across to her over the roar of chanting, her eyes bright with zeal, her cheeks wind-stung and rosy.

'I don't know,' she shouted back. 'Seventy thousand, eighty thousand. Too many for me to be able to see where Francis is.'

The chanting died down, placards and Viet Cong flags continuing to wave as Vanessa Redgrave walked to the front of the speakers' platform and launched into a passionate denunciation of United States military involvement in the Vietnam war.

For once, Geraldine didn't hang on her every word. Where was Francis? Why hadn't he phoned her to let her know about his having being rusticated? What if he'd no intention of sitting out his rustication at home in Sussex? What if he decided to do some travelling instead? It had become the in thing to go to San Francisco, the city of love and peace and psychedelic drugs and, knowing how furious his father would be at his having been sent down, he might very well have decided to sit things out in San Francisco for a few weeks.

As Vanessa Redgrave's speech came to an end and the enormous crowd began moving out of the square en route to the American Embassy, Geraldine helped Kiki and Primmie lower Artemis back to ground level, a frown furrowing her brow.

Francis was impulsive to the point of fecklessness. It was one of the reasons her Uncle Piers had always been so pleased about Francis wanting to spend time with her. 'You're steadiness will rub off on him, Geraldine,' he would say, his arm round her shoulders. 'You're the sister he needs and hasn't got.'

Nearly always when Francis did something stupid he would tell her. When he was nine and she was six and the fire he'd started in a nearby wood whilst playing a war game had got out of hand, she'd been the one he'd run to and told. And she, level headed and sensible as always, had climbed on to a chair to reach the phone and had rung for the fire brigade.

'*Ho, Ho, Ho Chi Minh!*' Kiki and Artemis and Primmie were chanting as, with arms linked, they marched in the middle of a procession of thousands towards Grosvenor Square.

Though the crush of the crowd meant they were wedged like sardines, Geraldine was mentally miles away.

When Francis had been twelve and had made himself violently ill after raiding their grandfather's drinks cabinet and experimenting with a mixture of cointreau and crème de menthe, she was the one who had taken the blame, saying it had been her idea and that she'd been trying to make a drink that was a pretty colour and that Francis had drunk it only to keep her happy.

And when she had been fifteen and Francis eighteen and he had taken his father's Lamborghini without permission, running it into one of the trees on the family estate, she had said that she had been the one at the wheel. It had been then, when he'd swung her round and round and hugged her half to death out of gratitude, that things had taken on a new dimension between them.

Suddenly they hadn't been just hugging as they'd always

58

hugged. Suddenly they'd been kissing and touching and rolling round on the floor in a way that had nothing remotely cousinly about it.

From then on, the plan had been that when she was eighteen they would tell everyone that they were in love and that when she was twenty-one they would get married. Nowhere in the plan had Francis haring off alone been mentioned.

'I think things are going to get tricky!' Kiki shouted across to her as they entered the square. 'Have you seen how many police there are? The embassy's surrounded.'

'And we're going to storm it!' a bearded, duffle-coated figure marching nearby them yelled informatively as their section of the crowd launched into a thunderous rendering of 'We Shall Overcome'. 'We're going to give the bastards something to think about!'

Geraldine swung her head towards him. In his hands was a homemade battering ram. Swiftly she looked to her left and her right. Nearly everyone, apart from themselves, was carrying something that could be used to help break through the police cordon.

'You OK, Prim?' she asked, her adrenalin rush touched by a flicker of anxiety.

'Course I'm OK.' Primmie had seen too many photographs of women and children killed or horribly injured as a result of US air attacks to be deterred at the thought of storming the embassy.

Police were now blocking off access to the side streets and Geraldine realized that even if they'd wanted to opt out they couldn't. The crowd was one of scores of thousands – possibly a hundred thousand. It was the biggest – and angriest – anti-war demo in London ever. And they were smack bang in the middle of it.

'*America out!*' she shouted with such force her throat hurt. '*America out! America out!*'

Fighting with police was taking place on the fringes of the crowd and in the area in front of the cordon. Paint cans were being thrown, splattering against the embassy's massive granite-grey façade. The gardens round it were being invaded, daffodils in their hundreds crushed and broken beneath an army of trampling feet.

'Keep close together!' Geraldine shouted as Artemis stumbled. 'If we get separated we'll never find each other again!'

A concerted roar went up as, under a hail of stones, part of the police cordon wavered and then collapsed. For a hysterical moment Geraldine thought they were actually going to do it; actually going to storm the embassy and make a statement to end all statements against America's presence in Vietnam.

'I can't breathe!' Artemis was gasping, buffeted relentlessly forwards by the force of the crush and then, before Geraldine could shout at her not to panic, another roar went up: 'The Cossacks are coming!'

As mounted police began riding into the core of the rally, trying to break it up, and police on foot hurtled in with truncheons raised, Geraldine's common sense kicked in.

'We've got to get out of this!' she yelled, but only Primmie heard her.

Artemis and Kiki were now yards away, trapped in the centre of a group armed with missiles that the police were struggling to reach. The fighting now was wide-scale. Police as well as demonstrators were hitting out bloody faced. Feet away from her a kaftan-clad youth was wrestled to the ground to be handcuffed and hauled, kicking and struggling, to one of the scores of Black Marias crowding the side streets. Ambulance sirens were wailing as the number of injured grew.

Terrified that they were soon going to be numbered among them, Geraldine, with Primmie at her side, tried to fight a way through what had become a full-scale pitched battle, to Artemis and Kiki. It was impossible. A policeman, truncheon raised, made a grab for Primmie, catching hold of her by her hair.

As Primmie, still held only by her hair, was dragged away kicking and screaming, another policeman made a similar beeline for Geraldine. She twisted to evade him and saw, as she did so, that just behind Artemis a path in the crowd was being opened up by mounted police. It wasn't a charge. The horses were backing first this way and then that, in order to force an area of space that the police could occupy. Suddenly Artemis was an island. As the crowd who had hemmed her in scattered before the horses should reach them, Artemis remained dazedly where she was, unaware of what was taking place behind her. Even as Geraldine kicked out at the policeman trying to arrest her, she could see only too clearly what was about to happen. And so could Kiki.

Kiki, much nearer, gave a scream of warning, and then as Artemis continued to stand confusedly in the path of one of the backing horses Geraldine saw Kiki launch herself forward to hurl Artemis out of its way.

Artemis went flying. The rump of the horse barged into Kiki and then, as she tottered, struggling to retain her balance, the horse, still with its back to her, gave a flick of a rear leg, its hoof catching her full in the stomach.

She went down beneath it as if felled by an axe.

Geraldine could never remember exactly what it was she did next. Later, in court, it was detailed she'd bitten the hand of the policeman trying to haul her away so deeply he had needed hospital treatment. All she knew at the time was that she had to get away from him; that she had to reach Kiki.

The horse, aware now that a body was beneath it, was standing absolutely motionless, serving to guard Kiki from further hurt as the battle between demonstrators and police reached fever pitch.

Geraldine fought a way towards her like a wildcat, reaching her at the same time as two ambulance men with a stretcher.

'Is she dead? She hurled the words at them, hysteria a mere beat away. '*Is she dead?*'

Artemis was kneeling in the dust and dirt by Kiki's side, her tights torn and bloodied, her face a mask of fear. 'No,' she said in a cracked voice. 'She's not dead, Geraldine. Her eyes flickered open for a moment a second or so ago.'

As the ambulance men lifted Kiki on to a stretcher, Artemis covered her face with her hands and began to sob.

Geraldine hauled her to her feet. 'We're going with her, Artemis. Wherever they're taking her, we're going with her.'

The main body of the fighting was now taking place on the far side of the square and, as the ambulance men began carrying the stretcher towards one of the waiting ambulances, the remaining demonstrators readily made a pathway for them. Geraldine kept hard on the ambulance men's heels, not letting so much as a yard separate her and Artemis from them. Only at the ambulance doors was she stopped.

'You can't accompany her,' one of the men said curtly as he helped load a still-unconscious Kiki into the ambulance.

'We're her friends,' she said, her voice just as curt as his. 'And we're going with her.'

She never did hear his response. From behind her came the sound of running feet and her arms were yanked backwards with such force she thought they were going to come out of their sockets.

The officer arresting her had egg yolk spattered on his uniform and livid green paint dribbling from his helmet and was in no mood to be messed with. This time there could be no twisting and turning and fighting back. As another officer, hard on his heels, clapped handcuffs on Artemis, she knew that this time they were both most definitely looking at an appearance in court. She didn't care. The only thing she cared about was Kiki.

The ambulance doors were still open, and in the seconds before she and Artemis were frog-marched away she saw that blood, so dark as to be almost black, was seeping through the crutch of Kiki's jeans. Realization slammed so hard that for a moment she could scarcely breathe.

Whatever Kiki's injuries, she was sure of one thing. There was now no need for her conversation with her mother that evening.

If Kiki had been pregnant, she was no longer.

Eight

July 1969

Primmie dressed slowly. First her grey knee-length A-line skirt, then her snowy short-sleeved white blouse. She shrugged her arms into her blazer, wondering if Artemis, Kiki and Geraldine would be wearing school uniform on their last day, certain that, if they were, they would not be feeling nostalgic over it, as she was.

'*Get a move on, Primmie!*' her mother bawled from the bottom of the stairs. '*Yer gonna be late!*'

'*Coming, Mum!*' she yelled in answer, taking a last long look at herself as a schoolgirl.

She was, of course, the only one of the four of them who could still remotely pass as a schoolgirl. Even in school uniform, Artemis, Kiki and Geraldine had long since looked almost bizarre when dressed for school – Artemis, because no school uniform in the world could disguise her voluptuous curves. Kiki, because the knowingness in her green-gilt eyes would have been disturbing in a woman a whole decade her senior and Geraldine ... Primmie paused, trying to hit on what it was about Geraldine that made it impossible to believe she was still – for the next few hours at least – a schoolgirl. Geraldine was just too effortlessly self-confident.

If it hadn't been for Geraldine – and the confidence she inspired – she doubted if her parents would have been happy about her moving into the two-bedroomed flat Artemis's father had provided for Artemis in Kensington.

She ran down the stairs, reflecting that though the last few months had been good ones for her they hadn't been particularly easy for her friends.

For Artemis, the battle about not going on to university hadn't been too bad, because her mock A-level results were so poor no university in the country would have taken her. Kiki's battle, however, had been far different. Ever since the aftermath of the Grosvenor Square demo, when a registrar at St Thomas's had told her father she'd had a miscarriage, Simon Lane had been a different man. Instead of being furious with Kiki – as they had all expected him to be – he had blamed himself for somehow having failed her as a parent. Not wanting to fail her again, he had brought every possible pressure to bear when it had come to the subject of her going – or not going – to university.

Kiki had been absolutely adamant about not applying for a place. 'I've given up two years of my life by staying on through the sixth form to please him,' she'd said fiercely to them all, 'and I've done so on the understanding that I can then do whatever I choose. And I'm choosing to be a rock singer – not a two-a-penny university graduate.'

Geraldine, too, had been stubbornly immovable in her decision not to go on to university. 'I'm getting engaged to my cousin, Francis,' she had told Miss Featheringly, when Miss Featheringly had spoken to her about her decision. 'And after we're married we're going to travel the world – and when we've travelled the world we're going to live at Cedar Court, where our great-grandfather was born and where Francis was born.'

According to Geraldine, Miss Featheringly had been scandalized by such an idle, unproductive attitude towards life. Geraldine, however, hadn't given two hoots. 'At least Miss F. will be pleased with you, Primmie,' she'd said. 'Durham's a top-notch university. Almost as prestigious as Oxford.'

Miss Featheringly *had* been pleased with her. 'And because of your family's financial circumstances, I think it is quite reasonable of you to take a year out in order to save money towards your costs when at Durham,' she'd said when Primmie had told her she wouldn't be taking up the place she'd been offered until September 1970 and that, until then, she would be working as an account handler at a leading advertising agency. Wisely, she hadn't told Miss Featheringly that during her year before beginning university she would be sharing a flat with Geraldine, Artemis and Kiki.

'Come on, Primmie, darlin'' her mother said, pushing a plate of buttered toast into her hand as she walked into the kitchen. 'Yer never late fer school and yer don't want to start now, on yer last day, do yer?'

'No, Mum.' Suppressing a fit of the giggles, Primmie took hold of the proffered plate.

'An' so what 'appens in mornin' assembly on yer last day?' her mother asked, leaning against the sink, her hands wrapped round a mug of steaming tea. 'Is it a bit special?'

'Probably. I know Miss Featheringly has asked Kiki if she'd like to sing.'

'Sing to the school?' Her mum's eyes widened. 'Not one of 'er rock songs, Primmie, surely?'

Primmie bit into her toast. 'No. She was going to, but I think we've talked her out of it.'

'You *cannot* sing a Janis Joplin number,' Geraldine had said to Kiki emphatically, when Kiki had announced that she intended doing so. There'll be school governors in attendance as well as every member of the staff. I may not have a lot of time for Miss F., but even I wouldn't wish her to be publicly embarrassed. And, anyway, how can you sing a heavy rock number with no backing group? Whatever you sing, you're going to have to accompany yourself, and you've only got one pair of hands.'

It was probably that last argument, Primmie thought, that had dissuaded Kiki from opting for her favourite Joplin number.

'Well, whatever darlin' Kiki sings, I'm sure it'll go down a treat,' her mother said, breaking in on her thoughts. 'Now get a move on, Primmie, or yer goin' to miss that bloomin' train!'

'I can't believe this is the very last time I shall ever have to haul myself through the school gates,' Geraldine said to her as, arms linked, they strolled through the usual crush towards Bickley High's front steps. 'Only another few hours and we'll be free at last.'

'I'm going to miss it. I've been happy here, right from my very first day.'

'You'd be happy anywhere,' Geraldine said dryly. 'You have an indecent capacity for being happy. Which is more than can be said for Artemis,' she added as they walked into the cloakroom and Artemis steamed up to them, a pained expression on her face.

'You said *no one* wears uniform on their last day, Geraldine, and look at you! *You* are.'

It wasn't quite true as Geraldine wasn't wearing the cardigan that was obligatory when wearing a blouse and skirt. Not that Bickley High's school skirt looked like a school skirt on Geraldine. Instead of being modestly A-line, it was pencil straight and, as it barely skimmed her knees, her long, colt-like legs seemed to go on for ever. The top two buttons of her blouse were carelessly undone. There was no sign at all of her school tie and her raven-black hair was coiled in a glossily sophisticated knot in the nape of her neck.

'I said it wouldn't surprise me if people didn't wear uniform,' Geraldine said gently.

'And so I didn't! And you are, and Primmie is, and I just *know* everyone else is!'

Primmie regarded Artemis's patchwork maxi-dress with serious misgivings. It was far too fussy. And it certainly wasn't appropriate wear for the last day at school. Only the patchwork's colours – raspberry, bilberry, plum and wine-red – were not completely impossible.

'It will tone with a school blazer,' she said, 'but you're going to have to keep it on all day.'

'But I haven't got one with me!'

'Then borrow mine.' Primmie yanked open her locker door and retrieved the blazer she would never wear again.

Artemis gratefully took it from her. 'Has Kiki said anything to you about what it is she's going to sing?' she asked, painfully aware that she was going to stick out in assembly like a sore thumb.

'No.' Primmie looked round the crowded cloakroom for a glimpse of Kiki's distinctive spicy red hair. 'Has she said anything to you?'

'She told me that as a rock number was out and as she couldn't plug her electric guitar in and would have to accompany herself on her Spanish guitar, she was going to opt for a French song by the actress Jane Birkin. I don't know it, but something French seems an odd choice . . .'

They were now walking out of the cloakroom into the corridor that led towards the assembly hall. Geraldine stopped dead in her tracks.

'Dear God,' she said devoutly, her face paling. 'Not "*Je t'aime, moi non plus*"?'

'I think so. Something like that, anyway. Is it unbelievably sentimental?'

'It's unbelievably sexy! It isn't so much a song as a dirty phone call heavy-breathing number – and Jane Birkin sings it with Serge Gainsbourg. Who's Kiki going to sing it with? The school gardener?'

66

Primmie groaned, knowing Kiki would think singing such a song in assembly hysterically funny.

'Perhaps she was teasing me,' Artemis said hopefully as they filed on to a row at the back of the hall.

On the platform, seated to the left of the school governors and wearing her hated yellow gingham dress, Kiki looked serenely out over the sea of faces, her guitar propped beside her chair. When Primmie caught her eye, she winked.

'Jer-us-al-em,' the school began singing. 'Jer-*us*-al-em.'

Tears pricked Primmie's eyes. It was the last time she would be singing it as a start to her day. The last time she would stand between Geraldine and Artemis, looking at Millet's *The Angelus* and Millais' even more beautiful *Ophelia*.

As 'Jerusalem' came to an end and Miss Featheringly stepped forward to lead the school in The Lord's Prayer, she looked at the posy of flowers in Ophelia's hand, knowing the meaning of every one of them. A poppy, for death. A daisy, for innocence. A rose, for youth. A violet, for faithfulness. A pansy, for love in vain.

'Such a posy of wild flowers used to be known as a tussie-mussie,' Eva, Kiki's mother, had once said when she'd told her how much she loved the painting.

Her heart felt as if it were being painfully squeezed. She'd grown deeply fond of Kiki's parents and, now that she would no longer be sleeping at Petts Wood during the week, she was going to miss them.

'And they'll no doubt feel they same about you,' Geraldine had said when she'd told her how much she was going to miss living half of every week at Petts Wood. 'Mrs Lane can cope with answering calls from patients now, though, can't she? I mean, she hasn't had a drink since coming out of the drying-out clinic, has she?'

'No,' she'd said. 'She's absolutely sober.'

As one of the school governors got up to say a few words she thought, not for the first time, how odd it was that sobriety had made no difference at all to the tensions between Kiki's parents. The major difference was that instead of being so solitary, Mrs Lane had formed a close friendship with a woman who had been a fellow patient, and now was out and about with her, at exhibitions and concerts, all the time.

'And now,' Miss Featheringly was saying in her cut-glass voice, 'one of this year's school leavers, Kiki Lane, is going to sing for us.'

Artemis drew in a deep, ragged breath.

Geraldine said a rare word of prayer.

Primmie felt the fingers round her heart tighten even more painfully.

Kiki moved to the front of the stage, slipped the strap of her guitar over her head and settled the guitar comfortably against her body.

It was the first time Primmie had ever seen Kiki about to sing in public, not wearing a ton of eye make-up, black leather and suicidally high-heeled boots.

In school uniform, and without all the accoutrements of the stage persona she had created for herself, she looked unbelievably young.

Kiki struck a chord on the guitar, looked straight at her and grinned.

'Don't do it, Kiki!' Primmie whispered fiercely beneath her breath. '*Please* don't do it!'

In a rich, husky alto, Kiki began singing the old English folk song 'Greensleeves'. It was a perfect choice. A choice that couldn't, in a million years, offend anyone.

Primmie let out the breath she had been holding and grinned back at her, happily aware that she was living through one of Kiki's finer moments.

Three days later they were all four in the garden at Petts Wood. It was a cloudless day and a heat haze hung over the distant view of the Weald. Nearer, on the golf course that formed the garden's lower boundary, a small group of golfers was walking and every so often they could hear the faint thwack of a club hitting a ball.

'And so your engagement party is definitely going to be held at Cedar Court and not the Connaught?'

The speaker was Artemis and Primmie, lying on her tummy on a travel rug, felt a surge of amusement. Geraldine's forthcoming engagement to Francis was becoming almost as central a topic of conversation with Artemis as it was with Geraldine.

'Yah,' Geraldine responded languidly from a gently

swinging hammock. 'Both Francis and I always wanted the party to be held at Cedar Court. It was Uncle Piers who was holding out for the Connaught.'

'And though Uncle Piers is footing the bill, you're getting your own way?'

This time the speaker was Kiki and Primmie rolled on to her back, throwing an arm across her eyes as a shield against the sun's glare. It was hot. Very hot. The lavender Kiki's mother had planted in lavish drifts amongst Bourbon and Damask roses was alive with bees and scent hung as heavy in the air as smoke.

'Of course I am,' Geraldine said easily. 'Uncle Piers was only rooting for the Connaught because he can't bear the thought of hundreds of guests trampling Cedar Court's lawns.'

'Is that where the main part of the party will be? Outside, in the grounds?'

Again it was Artemis, in a nearby deck chair, who was speaking.

'It's where the dance floor is to be set up.'

'And the stage and sound systems.' This was Kiki.

There came the sound of iced lemonade being poured from the thermos jug into a glass.

'The Atoms aren't going to be playing all night, are they? There is going to be another kind of band, as well? A band that will be playing some nice smoochy music?'

At the edge of anxiety in Artemis's voice, Primmie's amusement deepened. Geraldine and Francis's guest list read like a mini *Almanach de Gotha* and Artemis had made no secret of how high her hopes were of snaring herself a blue-blooded boyfriend.

'There is, but I rather think The Atoms will have a larger share of the evening.'

There was dry amusement in Geraldine's voice and Primmie wasn't surprised. The Atoms was the rock group Kiki had been singing with ever since she had ditched Ty. More professionally managed than the group Ty had been a roadie for, their advert for a singer had been placed in *The Stage* and Kiki had had to go to a rehearsal room in Leicester Square to audition before being taken on with them.

Though they didn't indulge her passion for late-fifties and early-sixties rock songs, they did play some of the hippest clubs

69

in south-east London and Kiki hadn't the least doubt that, now she was free of Bickley High and able to concentrate on her career full-time, the only way she was going was up.

'Geraldine's engagement party is going to be a great showcase for me,' she'd said after seeing the names on the guest list. 'Everyone who's going is the sort of person who throws large parties for anything and everything, and after Geraldine and Francis's party the only band they're going to want to hire is whatever band I'm singing with.'

'And the best thing about *The Atoms* being hired by Geraldine,' Kiki was now saying, 'is that at private gigs the hirer has a say in what is played.'

Primmie opened her eyes and pushed herself up into a sitting-position. 'Don't tell me. All of a sudden, Geraldine's favourites are going to be Brenda Lee and Little Eva numbers.'

'And Cilla's "Anyone Who Had a Heart" and Dusty's "Losing You",' Kiki added gleefully.

'And what about Bobbie Gentry's "Ode to Billy Joe"?' Primmie asked, putting her two-penn'orth in.

'More to the point, what about some more ice? The lemonade is warm.'

'If you want more ice, Geraldine, you go for it,' Kiki said, not stirring. 'I'm too hot to move.'

Equably Geraldine slid out of the hammock and reached for the turquoise wraparound blouse she'd picked up in a flea market and that she'd shed when they had begun sunbathing.

Primmie watched her which a mixture of admiration and disbelief. The white linen trousers Geraldine was wearing were also vintage forties, wide-legged, with turn-ups and very Marlene Dietrich. By rights, she should have looked a ragbag. Instead, she looked incredibly cool – in every sense of the word.

'Has Geraldine told you that she's written a couple of songs for me?' Kiki asked, still lying prone as Geraldine began walking barefoot over the grass towards the house.

Primmie hugged her knees, gazing down the long lawn and over the golf course to where the Kentish Weald shimmered beneath the azure blue bowl of the sky. 'Are they good?' she asked. 'Are you going to use them?'

'They're love songs. More Nina Simone than Brenda Lee. But it's time I was working on a variety of musical styles and if we can get the music and the vocal arrangement right . . .' Her eyes gleamed. 'If we can do that together, if I can come up with my own material, then I'll definitely have an edge where my singing career is concerned.'

'Why didn't you ask me to write some songs for you?' Artemis said, aggrieved. 'I like writing poetry.'

'Song-writing isn't poetry, Artemis, or at least not the sort you have in mind, and you can't read music and Geraldine can.'

Primmie closed her eyes, wondering, if she tried hard enough, whether she could perhaps write songs.

Artemis was obviously being persistent because the next thing she heard was Kiki saying exasperatedly, 'Of course it matters, Artemis! I spend hours debating with Geraldine whether a chord should change to a flat or a sharp.'

Geraldine's shadow fell across her, bringing Kiki and Artemis's conversation to a halt.

Primmie opened her eyes.

'As well as a fresh jug of lemonade I've brought some choc ices from the fridge-freezer. Your mother won't mind, Kiki, will she?'

'No.' At the mention of choc ices Kiki sat up. 'Anything in the fridge-freezer is there for anyone who wants it.'

'Choc ices? Yummy.' Artemis reached for her blouse, which was lying on a pile of magazines, and put it on.

Geraldine handed them round and then, having put the jug of lemonade on the table, sat down cross-legged on the picnic rug beside Primmie. 'You are all OK for what you're going to wear to the party, aren't you? I don't want any last minute flaps – and I want you all in full fig.' She looked pointedly at Kiki. 'This is ball gown time and whatever family jewels you can lay your hands on.'

Primmie licked a piece of chocolate from the corner of her mouth. 'My family jewels will be diamanté, but my ball gown is going to be a knock-out. I'm having it made by Lauren Colefax's aunt.'

Lauren Colefax had been in their form at Bickley from the first year to the sixth and her aunt's reputation as a dress-maker was formidable.

71

'The material is pale lemon taffeta and it's going to have a scooped neckline and huge puffed sleeves.'

She was aware of Kiki flinching and didn't care. 'I'm going to look gorgeous in it,' she said with happy certainty.

'I'm sure you are, Prim.' Artemis looked at her watch and rose to her feet. 'It's nearly six and I have to scoot. My godmother is visiting this evening and I don't want to miss her.'

'And I must go, too,' Geraldine said, rising to her feet in a movement as fluid and graceful as a dancer's. 'Mummy has a meeting with the caterers this evening and I want to be in on it.'

'And I have things to do and people to see as well.' Kiki stood up. 'What about you, Primmie? Do you still want to clear everything out of the bedroom today?'

Primmie nodded. It wasn't something she really *wanted* to do, because she'd been too happy living half of every week with Kiki to be over the moon at finally removing all trace of occupancy from the room they'd shared. It was, however, a task that had to be done.

She picked up the two travel rugs and the thermos that had held the lemonade, glad that Kiki wouldn't be with her when she emptied her drawers and packed her books, sure that, when she did so, she would shed a tear.

Sunlight streamed through the windows as she went through the bedroom's bookshelves, separating her books from Kiki's. No one else was in the house. Kiki's mother was very seldom home, now. Jenny Reece, the friend she had made at the drying-out clinic, was a garden designer. A passionate gardener herself, Kiki's mother took a great interest in Jenny's work, travelling with her whenever she was visiting a new client. Simon wasn't in either, though he soon would be because his evening surgery finished at seven o'clock.

With her books stacked in the sports bag she'd brought with her, she turned her attention to the wall-length shelf of records. Only a few of the vast collection were hers. She removed a Frank Sinatra single and a Julie London single from between a whole raft of Gene Vincent and Little Richard

72

albums and then, hearing a car enter the drive, halted. If Mrs Lane had come home, then she wanted to thank her for all her many kindnesses.

The front door opened and seconds later there came the sound of someone running up the stairs.

Primmie slid the records into her sports bag and walked out of the room on to the wide landing. The door to Mrs Lane's bedroom was open and there was the sound of drawers being opened in a hurry.

Walking across to the open door, she raised her hand in order to knock and announce her presence.

Her hand froze in mid-air.

Mrs Lane was scooping clothes from the drawers of her dressing-table and putting them into a suitcase that lay on the single bed.

'I'm sorry,' she said, confused. 'Are you late for something, Mrs Lane? Are you going away?'

Mrs Lane stood stock-still, a pile of lingerie in her arms. 'Primmie! I didn't know you were here.'

There was such consternation on her face that Primmie moved towards her, certain that someone in the Lane family must have been taken ill and that Mrs Lane was rushing off to be with them.

'What's happened?' she asked, deeply concerned. 'Can I help?'

'No.' Mrs Lane continued what she was doing. 'No, darling Primmie, you can't help. I'm doing something I've wanted to do for ages.'

She dropped another pile of lingerie into the case. 'I'm leaving,' she said starkly. 'I'm leaving for good. Simon knows. I've already told him, but he doesn't believe me. He doesn't think I have the guts.'

Primmie stared at her, aghast. 'But where are you going? Does Kiki know?'

Through the open window there came the sound of a short, sharp toot on a car horn.

'I'm going to live with Jenny.'

As she was speaking she was taking dress after dress out of her wardrobe, laying them on top of the lingerie.

Primmie felt sick with helplessness, wondering what was

73

going to happen when Simon Lane came home; when Kiki came home.

As if reading her thoughts Mrs Lane said, 'I've left a letter on the hall table.' She closed the wardrobe door. 'Please don't look so devastated, Primmie. Jenny only lives in Sevenoaks. I'll still be able to see Kiki whenever Kiki has the time to see me. And Simon will be . . . relieved. It isn't the end of the world and, for me, it's the beginning of a whole new one.'

The car horn sounded again and she clicked the locks of the suitcase shut.

'I've enjoyed having you stay here these last few years, Primmie, dear,' she said, sliding the suitcase from the bed. 'You've been a constant ray of sunshine. Now, though, with both you and Kiki moving out and living in London, it's time for me to move on. Empty marriages make for very unhappy homes and I've taken advantage of Simon's sense of responsibility for me long enough. He needs the chance of a new start just as much as I do.'

She picked the suitcase up, touched Primmie's face gently and walked from the room.

Through the open window there came the sound of a car door being opened and then slammed shut and footsteps scrunching across the gravel towards the front door.

Aware that Jenny was on her way into the house, Primmie hurried out of the bedroom in Mrs Lane's wake.

As she reached the top of the stairs, Jenny Reece strode into the hall, wearing a sleeveless jacket over an open-necked chequered shirt and jeans tucked into muddy Wellingtons. 'Is anything the matter?' she asked as Mrs Lane manoeuvred her suitcase down the last few steps of the stairs. 'I thought I heard you talking to someone.'

'I was talking to Primmie.'

'Thank God,' she said, closing the gap between them. 'I thought perhaps it was Kiki.'

Then, to Primmie's stupefaction, she circled Eva Lane's waist with her arm and bent her head to hers, kissing her deeply, full on the mouth.

Primmie's shock was so great that her legs gave way. As she sank on to the top step in a disbelieving heap, Jenny Reece raised her head, smiled down into Mrs Lane's eyes and said huskily; 'Come along, sweetheart. Let's go.'

Seconds later the door slammed shut after them, and then the only sound was that of the car, speeding down the drive.

Dazed, Primmie remained where she was. Lesbian relationships were something she knew about in theory, but theory – and rather hazy theory at that – was as far as it went. She knew, though, that what she had just witnessed was two women deeply in love.

For a long time she remained seated at the top of the stairs, able to understand, at last, lots of things that had always perplexed her. If Kiki's mother was capable of loving another woman so wholeheartedly it was no wonder that her relationship with her husband had always been tense and unsatisfactory.

Unsteadily she rose to her feet. She had often been in the house before when it had been empty, but it had never before felt as deserted as it did now.

Slowly she walked back into the room she had shared with Kiki, sitting down on the edge of her bed. Kiki, quite obviously, didn't know the truth about the nature of her mother's relationship with Jenny and she had no intention of enlightening her. It wasn't up to her to do so. It was up to her mother to tell her, or Dr Lane.

That Simon Lane knew the kind of dilemma his wife had been battling with was a huge assumption, but knowing how deeply unhappy he'd been for so long, it was one she took for granted.

Though the sun still streamed in through the windows, the heat was no longer fierce. She looked down at her watch. It was seven fifteen. With a heavy heart she continued to sit, waiting for Dr Lane to return home from his evening surgery.

It was seven forty-five when she heard the sound of his car easing its way up the gravelled drive.

Her hands tightened in her lap.

The car came to a halt; the driver's door opened, was closed.

There came the familiar sound of his footsteps crossing the gravel to the house.

Still she didn't move.

75

The heavy oak front door opened and she could hear him stepping into the hall, closing the door behind him.

Then there was silence and she knew he was reading the letter that had been propped on the hall table. At last, after what seemed an age, she heard him walking slowly towards the kitchen.

On legs that felt like jelly she rose to her feet. She needed to let him know that she was still in the house; that she, too, had packed her bag and was about to leave.

Reluctantly she walked downstairs and towards the kitchen.

He was standing at the window, his back towards her, his shoulders tense, his hands thrust in his pockets, his misery so palpable her heart hurt.

She cleared her throat.

'There's no one else in,' she said awkwardly as he spun round. 'Just me.' And then, even more awkwardly, 'I was here when . . . when Mrs Lane left.'

'Did she tell you that she was leaving for good?' he asked, the sun streaming in the window behind him, turning his fair hair to gold.

She nodded.

'And was her friend with her?' he asked.

'Yes,' she said, having no intention of increasing his hurt by telling him what she had seen. 'Would you like a cup of tea?' she asked, offering the comfort her mother always offered in times of crisis.

He nodded. 'That's a very kind offer, Primmie. Thank you.'

Silence fell between them as she crossed to the sink and filled the kettle, painfully aware that, once Kiki had moved into the flat in Kensington, he was going to be living in the large house completely on his own.

As she waited for the kettle to boil he turned to look out of the window again, his hands still in his pockets, his shoulders still tense, his misery making him look much younger than his thirty-nine years.

'Would you like a couple of biscuits with the tea?' she asked, inadequately.

He didn't answer her, instead he said, 'And are you leaving for good, too, Primmie?'

'Yes. I should have taken my things home days ago – when it was the last day of term.'

'I shall miss you.'

His voice was bleak and she walked across to him, standing by his side at the window. Though it was now the end of July, the garden was still overflowing with roses in full flower. A Kiftsgate rampaged in a pear tree, clouds of creamy-white, semi-double flowers tumbling down through its branches in a mass of blossom. In the herbaceous borders pale pink roses mingled with lupins and delphiniums and everywhere there was lavender and the sweet scent of thyme.

'I shall miss you, too,' she said, wondering if he would ever know just how much.

'You will still visit, Primmie, won't you?'

'Yes.' There was a catch in her voice. 'Yes, of course I will.'

'That's good,' he said quietly, the tension in his shoulders easing.

The kettle began to boil and she stepped away from him to make the tea, knowing that their relationship had shifted and changed and that from now on, in some way she wasn't yet sure of, things were going to be different between them. Different and very, very special.

Nine

Wearing the dark glasses that made her feel like an American superstar, Kiki strolled down the King's Road in high spirits. Bickley High was now a part of her past. She'd stuck out the last two years in the sixth form only because Artemis, Geraldine and Primmie had been sticking them out with her. She sidestepped a couple of orange-robed, bell-carrying Hare Krishna devotees and mentally corrected herself. Primmie hadn't been sticking things out in the sixth form. Primmie had been perfectly happy – and hardworking.

It was, she thought, deeply ironic that the only one of the

four of them who wanted to go to university – and who was going to go – was the only one for whose family it would be a financial burden.

The up side, of course, was that Primmie wasn't going to Durham till she had spent a year in London, working and saving money towards her living costs – which meant that their unity as a foursome was preserved for another twelve months at least.

And in another twelve months she, Kiki, intended to be a star as big as Lulu or Dusty.

It was a quarter to seven in the evening and the heat was still beating up from the pavement in waves. The guy she was on her way to have a drink with was a copywriter whose best buddy just happened to be the manager of Fleetwood Mac and, a week ago, he'd passed one of her demo tapes on to him.

A shop window filled with gorgeous mini-skirts and slinky thigh-high boots caught her eye. She came to a halt in front of it, wondering whether a mini-skirt might be a better bet than the mock lizard-skin hipsters she was wearing. The thing was, she didn't really like skirts. What she felt comfortable in were skin-tight pants, teeteringly high-heeled boots and jackets with the collars flicked up, Elvis style. That it was a style a decade out of date didn't bother her in the slightest. It was *her* style and just as Geraldine's vintage look was inimitably her own, so was hers.

Deciding against a mini-skirt, she took off her dark glasses and went in the shop to buy a pair of the hooped brass earrings that had also been in the window, well aware that what she should have been shopping for was a dress to wear to Geraldine's engagement party. Not to wear on stage, of course. On stage she wore black leather in the same way the Beatles always wore collarless jackets. Geraldine, however, expected her to mingle as a guest when her set with The Atoms was over and had made it quite clear that, as a guest, she should dress accordingly – which meant, apparently, a ball gown.

Well, Geraldine could go whistle. There wasn't enough money in the world to lure her into a county-set tulle or taffeta ball gown. What she might be lured into, though, was a pair of silver sequinned hipsters worn with a skin-tight sleeveless top and a pair of stiletto-heeled, ankle-strapped shoes.

Walking out of the shop, the earrings swinging in her ears, she wondered where to find what she was after. Walton Street had dozens of seductive boutiques and was only a hop and a skip from the King's Road. And there was Kensington Church Street – but Kensington Church Street would mean a cab ride if she wasn't to be late for her date.

She shrugged her shoulders. The party wasn't for another two weeks and there were more important things to think about than what she was going to wear when in guest mode at Geraldine's party.

Her demo tape, for one thing. With her earnings from The Atoms, she'd bought herself a four-track recorder, a mixer and some effects and had started over-dubbing her voice. Harmonization had never really been her thing, she'd always preferred simply belting out a song with a hot band behind her, but with the songs Geraldine had helped her put together she'd done over-dub harmonies, doing three- and four-parters.

The result had been a revelation, for she'd realized that she didn't have to work harmonies out, that she had the ability to hear them in her head. The discovery had reminded her of how, when she'd begun piano lessons at six years old, she'd almost immediately had the ability to play by ear. Even better had been the guitar lessons when she was nine. By the time she was ten she knew how to play all the diminished chords and had spent hours in her bedroom with the door closed, creating and playing riffs and practising her autograph.

Once she'd started going to Bickley High and had made friends with Artemis, Geraldine and Primmie, piano and guitar lessons had taken a bit of a back seat. Music hadn't, though. The first single she'd bought for herself had been Elvis Presley's 'Good Luck Charm'. It was never her favourite Presley number – 'All Shook Up' had that honour – but Presley was definitely Number 1 where she was concerned. Another favourite, that first summer at Bickley High, had been the Everley Brothers 'Walk Right Back'. She'd spent hours in her room singing along to it, pretending to hold a microphone, pretending she was on stage.

She continued down the King's Road, thinking back to the time when she'd been eleven and her dream of becoming a rock star had first taken serious hold. It had been Helen

Shapiro who had been the catalyst. Helen Shapiro who had had a hit record at fourteen. How had she done it? Whom had she known? And if Helen Shapiro could become a school-age pop star, why couldn't she? The question had tormented her endlessly, and if anyone had been responsible for her going to the Two Zeds and so tenaciously latching on to a member of the band playing there, it had been Helen Shapiro.

Not that Ty had been a musical member of the band, of course. All he had been was their road manager. He had, though, been her ticket to singing with the band. Because she'd become his girlfriend she'd gained the invaluable experience of singing in public one, and sometimes two, nights a week.

There'd been other aspects, too, to the couple of years she'd spent as Ty's lady. For one thing, she'd begun dressing like an Angel's mamma – wearing tight slacks, sleeveless sweaters and bright lipstick as opposed to the floppy hats, mini-dresses and pale, pale mouths beloved of dolly birds.

The black leather that Ty had suggested she always wear on stage had become a uniform, too. At first, until she cottoned on to the fact that Hell's Angels never, but never, wore leather jackets, she'd assumed that black leather trousers and jackets were standard biker's gear.

Even when she found out differently, she didn't care. Black leather had become her image. Audiences at their gigs perceived her as being a badass chick – and until the hideous moment when she had realized she was pregnant, a badass chick was how she'd liked to think of herself.

She paused at an ice-cream stall and bought herself a giant cornet. Those few weeks of pregnancy had brought her down to earth big time, and when the nightmare had been over she'd never wanted to see Ty again.

She hadn't missed him, but she had missed his Harley. Straddling the pillion, jamming crazy through traffic at 90 miles an hour, other Harleys in front, abreast and behind them, beards and bandanas flying, was an adrenalin rush like no other.

Riding pillion had been the up side of her time with the Angels. The down side had been that their girlfriends had to

80

know their place – and knowing her place had never been her style.

She crossed the pavement to where a street trader was selling dazzling coloured scarves decorated with signs of the zodiac. What had suited her style, she reflected as she flicked through the scarves, was growing up fast. She'd been fifteen when she'd lost her virginity to Ty and not much older when she'd begun smoking pot.

What Artemis, Geraldine and Primmie would have made of it if she'd told them she still didn't know. At a guess, Geraldine would have been very laid back about it and unshocked to the point of disinterest. Artemis would have squealed in affected horror and Primmie . . . Primmie would have been deeply anxious that she was going to come to grief. Which, in becoming pregnant, she had.

Deciding against buying a scarf, as the only one with Leo, her birth sign, was in red and red was a colour she never wore, she continued with her summer-evening stroll. Within minutes she was passing the Chelsea Antique Market and, as it was one of Geraldine's favourite haunts, her thoughts automatically swung to Geraldine.

Close as she was to Geraldine, she didn't understand her. Geraldine was rich, seriously beautiful, totally unshockable and utterly fearless. Where men were concerned, she could have had whoever took her fancy simply by crooking her little finger. And yet she never did so.

Unlike a year ago, when going on the Pill for anyone still in their teens was nearly impossible, more and more family doctors were now prescribing for the young and single, and even if they were stuffily refusing to do so there was the Brook Advisory Centre, where the Pill was provided, no questions asked. The Brook Clinic had been her saviour after the Ty debacle, and shortly after she had gone there so had Geraldine. Geraldine's reasons had, though, been a little different to hers. She had wanted the freedom of being able to enjoy sex as easily as enjoying sweets. Geraldine had simply wanted to be able to sleep with Francis without getting pregnant.

That none of her three friends slept around – as everyone else she knew now did – was something she simply didn't

understand. The ability to have sex without disastrous consequences was, after all, the ultimate freedom – a freedom women
had dreamed of throughout history. Now, thanks to the Pill,
they were the first generation of women able to live their
sexual lives with the same freedom men had always done.
And what were Geraldine, Artemis and Primmie doing with
that freedom? Absolutely nothing. The permissive society was
totally lost on them. They might just as well have been living
in the Middle Ages.

The pub she was heading for came into view and she quick-
ened her stride, still brooding on the mystery as to why, when
the rules had all changed, her friends weren't taking advantage of the fact and living their lives with the same heady
liberation she was living hers. Geraldine, of course, had her
explanation ready made.

'I'm in love with Francis,' she always said as if stating the
obvious. 'I've always been in love with Francis. Hard though
that may be for you to understand, Kiki, we were born to be
together. That's just the way it is – OK?'

Grudgingly she'd said that it was OK – though she didn't
really think it was OK at all. She thought it bizarre and knew
that even Artemis, who had got over her crush on Francis
once she knew Geraldine was in love with him, thought
Geraldine's fixation on him odd. The difficulty in assessing
whether Geraldine and Francis's relationship really *was* odd
was that none of them really knew Francis. Whenever he was
in London he and Geraldine went out together on their own
or with Francis's friends. During his years at university
Geraldine had gone up to Oxford to see him, and now he'd
graduated most of their time together was spent in Sussex, at
Cedar Court.

Tall, lanky and fair-haired he was, as far as she was
concerned, a prime example of the upper-class, chinless-
wonder brigade – and what Geraldine saw in him, she couldn't
fathom.

At least, though, Geraldine had a reason for not being one
of the sexually liberated. The same couldn't be said for Artemis
and Primmie. Artemis's problem was that she so longed to
be perceived as having true class, the kind she believed came
from being born of a family who'd had wealth and titles for

generations, that she couldn't allow herself to behave in a way that might be construed as common and remind people that her father was a nouveau riche from Rotherhithe.

Geraldine had pointed out to her that if she really wanted to pass as a member of the landed classes she should be sleeping around like a rabbit. Artemis had merely said that she didn't see Geraldine sleeping around and, when Geraldine had mildly protested that she'd been sleeping with Francis since she was seventeen, had said that as Geraldine was going to marry Francis, her having sex with him didn't count. That Artemis would eventually begin seeing things differently she didn't doubt. For the moment, though, Artemis was preserving her virginity as if it were some kind of star prize.

As for Primmie . . . She stepped into the packed interior of the Prince of Wales, reflecting that Primmie doing anything unconventional or reckless was impossible to imagine. Primmie would fall in love with a fellow student when she went to university and have an utterly boring and traditional white wedding followed by a honeymoon in Spain if she was lucky – and Clacton if she wasn't.

The Prince was heaving with teens and early twenties and she weaved a way through the throng, making for a group standing at the near corner of the bar. At the centre of the group was Howard Phillips, the copywriter who'd passed her demo tape on to Fleetwood Mac's manager. The two dudes drinking with him were unknown to her and her heart began thudding. What if one of them was Fleetwood Mac's manager? What if he'd been so bowled over by her demo tape that he'd asked to meet her? What if this was IT? The night when her stratospheric rise to fame began?

'Hi,' she said laconically, stepping round a doe-eyed girl wearing mauve thigh-high boots, a mauve mini-dress and very little else. 'Am I late?'

'Kiki, baby,' Howard Phillips shouted over the deafening din of conversation going on all around them. 'Nice to see you!' Somewhere a jukebox was playing Fleetwood Mac's 'Black Magic Woman' and she wondered if it was by chance or design.

'This is Kit Armstrong, he runs a studio in Courtfield Road.' Still bellowing, Howard caught hold of her hand and pulled her into the centre of his little group. 'And this is Wayne Clayton, one of the best creatives in town.'

'Studio? A recording studio?' Disappointment that neither of them was Fleetwood Mac's manager slammed hard, but if one of them was seriously in the music business she might still be on to a winner.

'Yep. I run it out of a basement,' Kit Armstrong said, nursing a gin and tonic. He was sporting one of the most luxuriant Zapata moustaches she had ever seen, plum velvet hipsters, a white linen jacket, and beneath it nothing but bare flesh and hair. 'It isn't RCA and I'm not Phil Spector, but small is sometimes smartest. Scottie of Fleetwood Mac rated your tape and thought I should hear it. Having done so, I'd like to hear you at the studio, in the vocal room. Are you up for it?'

She shrugged, not wanting to look desperately eager. 'If you like. I'm with The Atoms, you know that, don't you?'

'Yeah, I know you're a professional,' he said, getting the point she'd wanted to make. 'But any interest I have is in the kind of R&B ballad numbers that are on the tape. Howard tells me you wrote the songs yourself.'

She hesitated, tempted to take all the credit, and then said with another careless shrug, 'Half and half.'

He nodded, not asking which half, lyrics or music, had been her input, saying only, 'What are you drinking?'

'Vodka and kahlua.'

'I've heard The Atoms,' Wayne Clayton said as Howard Phillips turned towards the bar and tried to gain the attention of a barmaid. 'Their sets are full of dated rock numbers as I remember.'

Kiki regarded him stonily. If he was a creative, he was in advertising with Howard and therefore of no account. 'Rock doesn't date,' she said tightly. 'And the old numbers are the best.'

Wayne Clayton grinned. 'Not if you want to be more than the front singer of a band playing gigs at weddings and working men's clubs. If you want the big time you have to move with the times. Not stay in a sixties groove.'

'I'm my own person,' she said witheringly. 'I don't follow the crowd – though as you're in advertising, I don't suppose you know much about that.'

He cracked with laughter and Kit Armstrong passed her drink to her, saying, 'Wayne's the advertising world's great white hope. Keep in with him. You never know when he'll be useful.'

'Kit's got musicians booked in for later tonight,' Howard said, slipping his arm round her waist. 'Piano, drums, bass and guitars. They'll be there to finish off something they've been working on for days, but Kit's had a word and they're going to keep him happy and stay on. I reckon it'll be dawn before you're all out of there.'

'And is all this for Fleetwood Mac's manager?'

'Who knows – and does it matter? I've got you in at one of the best small studios around – and all for free. Free studio time, free musicians, free engineer, free tapes. I deserve a big thank you, don't you think?'

Knowing exactly the kind of big thank you he was thinking of – and having already made up her mind that she was going to disappoint him, she said, 'I think it's time I found out what Kit's going to want from me in the studio,' and stepped away from him, turning her attention to the man who mattered.

'Which song really caught your ear?' she asked, standing so that her back was towards Howard and Wayne.

'The funkiest.' He scratched his chest. '"White Dress, Silver Slippers". It has a beat like a sledgehammer.'

The beat had been all down to her and Kiki felt excitement coiling tightly in the pit of her stomach. If he liked the music she had written to Geraldine's lyric – if he liked her arrangement of the song – then maybe he would record it and she would at last be on her way as a solo artist.

'D'you reckon this?' he asked as 'Purple Haze' by the Jimi Hendrix Experience blasted their eardrums.

Her gamine grin nearly split her face in two. 'He's from outer space,' she said, wishing the demo tape had had a pyschedelic rock number on it, hoping Armstrong wasn't going only to be interested in Geraldine's rhythm and blues ballads.

'He's a wizard,' he agreed, a pint of lager again in one hand, the thumb of his free hand hooked into his trouser belt.

It was going well between them and Kiki knew it. She wondered what the chances were of his trying to score with her and of how she would react if he did. The bare chest was nicely muscled but a trifle too hairy. He had good hands, though, strong and well shaped – and his leather belt sat attractively low on snake-thin hips.

Deciding that his advantages – not least his recording studios – far outweighed the disadvantages of his tightly curling body hair, she was just about to move a little closer to him when out of the corner of her eye she saw someone at the far side of the pub trying to attract her attention.

She narrowed her eyes, unsure who it was.

The person in question began shouldering his way through the crush towards her, an equally tall and gangling friend in his wake, and, with a flare of irritation, she recognized Francis Sheringham.

'Bugger,' she said beneath her breath and then, as she was thinking of how best to give him the brush off, she heard Kit Armstrong say dryly, 'A couple of aristos are coming our way, Wayne. I thought James was in 'Frisco.'

Seconds later, as Jimi Hendrix gave way to Janis Joplin, Kit slapped James on the back and she was again the centre of attention as James said he'd only crossed the pub to be introduced to her.

'She's a friend of Francis's soon-to-be fiancée,' he said, draping an arm round Kit's shoulders as he regarded her appraisingly. 'Francis says she's the hottest singer in town – and she's certainly got the hottest eyes.'

There was general laughter and, with great difficulty, Kiki let the remark ride. If James was a close friend of Kit Armstrong's there was no sense in making a caustic comment. She didn't want to make even the tiniest of waves where she and Kit were concerned – not if he was going to be instrumental in bringing her to the attention of people in the business who mattered.

'I didn't know you'd ever heard me sing,' she said to Francis as his friend got a round of drinks in.

'I haven't, but your reputation goes before you, Kiki.' He shot her a down-slanting smile, looking for all the world like a courtier of Charles II, his fair hair tumbling to his shoulders in glossy waves, his exquisitely tailored velvet suit a rich electric-blue, a black cameo ring on the fourth finger of his right hand.

To Howard, he said, 'Kiki and her band are to be the lead band at my engagement party in two weeks' time. As you're a friend of James's – and as he's going to be my best man one day – why not come along?'

'You'll hate yourself if you don't,' James said, retrieving two pints of lager from the bar and passing one to Wayne and the other to Howard. 'Francis's pile, Cedar Court, is an Elizabethan gem, and unlike Penshurst or Sudely isn't open to the public. You see it as a private guest or you don't see it at all.'

'James is heir to a dukedom,' Francis said in Kiki's ear. 'It's not supposed to count these days, but believe me, it does. It's the reason Kit will be asking him round to the studios if he's got anyone interesting in there. The last time we dropped by, so did the Stones. Their pad is in Courtfield Road. Mick Jagger loves decadent aristos – they have something he wants – and he certainly has something aristos want. All in all, it makes for a nice little mutual admiration society.'

For the second time that evening Kiki's heart began pounding like a piston. The Stones! Dear God, if she could only meet the Stones in a situation where they would hear her sing!

'Kit *is* having someone interesting in the studios tonight,' she said, no longer irritated by his presence, and forcing herself to sound very offhand. 'Me.'

With satisfaction she saw she'd taken him completely aback.

'Wow!' His eyes widened and, for the first time, she noticed that there were extraordinary flecks of gold in them. 'Really? What a blast!'

He turned to James. 'Kiki's doing a session for Kit later this evening. What say we hang around?' And then, to Kit, 'Is that OK with you?'

'Sure, no problem. It's going to be an all-night number and Kiki and the session musicians will be working their butts off. It isn't going to be party time. Understand?'

'Clear as a bell.' He turned his attention back to Kiki, shooting her his disarming, down-slanting grin.

'You don't mind me muscling in on this, Kiki, do you?

Nervous tension fizzed in her throat. 'No,' she said truthfully. 'I'll be glad to have you around, Francis.'

It was true. Over the last half an hour or so she had become acutely aware of just how important her performance for Kit Armstrong was going to be. He had major connections – the casual mention of the Stones dropping in at his studios was evidence enough of that – and suddenly she was cripplingly nervous. Though not a major friend, she had known Francis indirectly for almost as long as she'd known Geraldine, and suddenly he seemed wonderfully familiar and she wanted him with her in the studio as fiercely as if he were a good luck charm.

A thought suddenly hit her and she downed the last of her Black Russian in a hurried swallow. 'If we're going to be there all night, what about Geraldine? Are you supposed to be meeting up with her later?'

The sudden smile came again and, with a slam of shock, she realized just why Geraldine found him so attractive.

'She's sitting in on a meeting between her mother and the party caterers,' he said, taking her empty glass from her hand, 'and as I'm thinking of going into the music business as a manager, tonight is just up my street. It could be the start of the big time, Kiki.' His smile deepened and he gave her a conspiratorial wink. 'For both of us.'

'I hope so.' The blood tingled along her veins in the way it always did when she was about to do something very, very reckless. 'I really do hope so, Francis.'

Ten

August 1969

Geraldine whistled her Uncle Piers's two Labradors to heel and, with her hands in the pockets of her Indian-embroidered cotton skirt, strolled out of the grand drawing room, that had been added in Queen Anne's reign, and on to the terrace.

Far away, beyond the vast manicured lawn and formal

gardens, workmen were erecting the stage on which, in ten hours time, Kiki and The Atoms would be strutting their stuff. As she paused at the top of the stone steps leading down to the lawn she could see that there were other workmen, sound engineers and electricians, beavering away with them. Further to the right a series of elaborate tents had already been erected and dozens of catering staff were busy ferrying equipment into it from a massive van parked on rough grass near to the ha-ha.

Though she couldn't see her mother, Geraldine knew that she would be somewhere at the centre of the fevered activity, directing operations with all the efficiency of an army commander. There was no sign of her widowed uncle, which wasn't surprising. Pleased as he was by her and Francis's engagement, his only involvement where the party was concerned had been his insistence that the music and dancing take place as far away from the house and gardens as possible.

'If we site the stage too near the ha-ha there'll be casualties,' Francis had pointed out, reasonably. 'There's going to be a lot of champagne drunk and by midnight most of my friends will be high on dope. If they take a tumble into the ha-ha, they won't be able to clamber out.'

'If they're high on dope, the ha-ha will be the best place for 'em,' her uncle had retorted, unfazed at the thought of marijuana, worried only that his ancient lawn should remain unsullied.

With the dogs at her heels Geraldine walked down the shallow steps and turned to the left on the pathway that skirted the lawns' perfect edges. There were going to be three hundred guests that evening and, no doubt, several gatecrashers. There was a mass of things to do and for the next half an hour or so she was going to do none of them. She was simply going to enjoy her delicious sense of anticipation. The coming evening was, after all, one she had looked forward to ever since she was a little girl.

Though other childish daydreams had come and gone – becoming a nun, a trapeze artiste, a vet – the dream of becoming engaged to Francis and of celebrating their engagement at Cedar Court in the blissful knowledge that she would one day become mistress of it was one that had never wavered.

It was, she had once told Artemis, her destiny. Artemis hadn't hooted with laughter as Kiki would probably have done if she'd said the same thing to her, nor had she looked faintly troubled as Primmie tended to do whenever she told her she couldn't possibly contemplate falling in love with anyone other than her cousin. Unexpectedly, Artemis had suddenly become her closest confidante – and she had every intention, at the party, of making her idyllically happy by introducing her to as many eligible young men as possible.

Mature yew hedging framed the south-facing borders, and the path, now flanked by carnations, led her beneath an archway draped with a waterfall of white roses. The fevered activity down by the ha-ha was now lost to view, the sound of the hammering so muffled by the high hedging that it could scarcely be heard.

She continued thinking about Artemis, and how nice it was that Artemis was finally beginning to lose the puppy fat that had plagued her for so long. With her barley-gold hair and corn-flower-blue eyes, she was fast becoming a classic English beauty.

Primmie, too, seemed, in the space of just a couple of weeks, to have a lustre about her. Ever since the four of them had made friends, Primmie, months older than both Kiki and Artemis, had always looked the youngest by at least a couple of years. Now, for some reason she couldn't fathom, Primmie no longer looked as if she was someone's younger sister. There was a glow about her that was almost palpable.

As she walked past a Greek-inspired fountain into the grey and white garden that opened on to the parkland, she wondered if the change in Primmie was due to her having started work as a junior account handler at BBDO, an advertising agency in Hanover Square. From her first pay packet she'd bought herself a plum velvet waistcoat and matching skirt from Biba, the waistcoat edged with the same flower-patterned braid that trimmed the hem of the skirt. Though she wore her new outfit with a puritanically high-collared white blouse, the overall effect was still exotic-looking enough to be almost hip.

The thought of Primmie being hip brought a smile to her lips. Primmie simply didn't have it in her to be unconventional. When she'd told her that she and Francis intended hitting the hippie trail she'd been more appalled than envious.

'But I thought we were all going to be living together in London for a year?' she'd said, looking stricken. 'Wasn't that the plan, Geraldine? Please say you're not going off to India until I go to university.'

Because of Francis's sudden enthusiasm for entering the music business, which, if it lasted as long as previous enthusiasms, would take approximately eight or nine months to get out of his system, she'd been able to reassure Primmie that their year together in the Kensington flat was still on.

She was out of the garden now and walking across the parkland towards a giant oak. How old it actually was was impossible to tell, but she liked to think it had been planted by the Francis Sheringham who, having found favour and riches under Elizabeth I, had, in 1603, built Cedar Court.

As the two Labradors raced ahead of her, she reflected wryly that at least she would be kept busy during Francis's latest enthusiasm. 'Kit Armstrong is keen on recording Kiki singing the songs the two of you have written,' he'd said when telling her that Kiki was on the verge of going solo and that he was going to manage her. 'So we need more songs, Geraldine sweetheart. It won't be a problem, will it?'

As, hampered by her skirt, she climbed up into the tree towards the gigantic branch that was her favourite perch, she fought down a stab of impatience. Without his latest enthusiasm they could have set off any time they wanted for India – enjoying lots of other places en route.

The light breeze blowing across the parkland was lifting her hair and it was getting caught on the twigs and leaves of the branch above her. Deftly she swirled it round her hand and wound it into a sleek knot in the nape of her neck, seeing, as she did so, that a car was turning off the little-used road that flanked the far edge of the parkland.

It was a red E-type Jaguar and her heart gave a lurch of joy. It was Francis and he would know exactly where to find her. As the dogs finally gave up hope of a walk and settled down on the grass, she thought how odd it was that Cedar Court seemed to be hers already and that it was as if Francis was the one who was visiting.

Ever since coming down from Oxford he'd had a bachelor pad in town, not far from the flat she, Kiki, Primmie and

Artemis had just moved into. In three years' time, when they married, they would have to find somewhere much bigger, but whatever they found it wouldn't be their main home. Her uncle had already told them that from the day of their marriage they would be able to regard Cedar Court as their marital home.

'That's because he wants to offload all the hassle of looking after it,' Francis had said dryly.

'*I'll* be doing the looking after,' she had said, knowing full well that was the situation her uncle intended and that he was looking forward to it, just as she was.

For the moment, though, she was without any kind of routine, unlike her three friends. Primmie left their Kensington flat at eight thirty in order to reach Hanover Square by bus for nine o'clock. Some nights she would then return by six thirty, other nights it would be ten thirty or eleven o'clock before they saw her again – presumably because she was busy socializing with her new work colleagues at the agency. Artemis left at nine fifteen for the Lucie Clayton Modelling School, which was just a short walk away, and invariably came straight home for a long, lingering bath, before going out somewhere with her and, if Kiki was around, Kiki. Kiki rarely surfaced until eleven o'clock and then always had somewhere important to her career to go, or someone it was important she see, seldom returning until whatever gig she and The Atoms were playing was over. Of the four of them, only she, Geraldine, had no kind of structure to her day.

She turned on the branch she was straddling in order to be able to catch the first glimpse of Francis as he emerged on to the parkland from the high-hedged grey and white garden. The last couple of weeks, of course, ever since they'd moved into the flat, she'd been kept busy arranging the party taking place that evening. Once the party was over, though, and with Francis haring around Tin Pan Alley making contacts, time was going to hang heavy on her hands unless she got herself a job of some kind.

The problem was, it was hard to be enthused about a job when she didn't need one financially and when she wasn't remotely ambitious – and she certainly didn't want a job that would interfere with Francis's and her social life. Idly she wondered about becoming a photographer's rep or assistant – Bailey was coming to the party that evening and he'd be bound to know someone who would be happy to employ her. Or maybe she could do as lots of debutantes did and get herself an undemanding job as a receptionist in an advertising agency.

Francis strolled unhurriedly out of the grey and white garden and, as the dogs sprang to their feet and bounded to meet him, she shelved all thoughts of how she was going to occupy her time until they went to India.

'Hi! I'm here!' she called out unnecessarily as he walked over the grass towards the tree. His hands were in the pockets of crushed velvet, ruby-red trousers. His shirt was equally magnificent – purple, with pink paisley motifs – and his fair hair hung in rippling waves to his shoulders, as glossy as a girl's.

The tree had been a regular meeting place since their childhood and he usually swung himself up into its branches, making himself as comfortable as he could beside her. Today he remained at its foot as the dogs circled him, barking furiously in fresh hope of a walk. 'The trousers are new,' he said explanatively. 'Ossie Clark made them for me. I'm not risking them clambering up to you. You'll have to clamber down.'

'Is Ossie coming tonight?' she asked, adjusting her position so that, instead of climbing down, she could jump and let him catch her.

'He is, and so is Celia and so is Alice.'

Ossie was haute couturier to the swinging elite. Celia was his wife, and Alice Pollock his business partner. If they were definitely coming, it meant their close friend David Hockney would also show – and if he did she was going to ask him if he would do a portrait of her and Francis.

'That's good,' she said and, without a word of warning, slid off the branch.

It was an action he hadn't been expecting, and though he successfully broke her fall he didn't do so without reeling and toppling backwards, taking her with him.

He lay, winded, his arms still around her, making no move to get to his feet. Geraldine, in exactly the position she wanted to be, made no move to get to her feet either.

'I love you, Francis,' she said as the Labradors nuzzled at them, anxious to know they weren't hurt.

'I know,' he said, pushing one of the dogs away, a smile spreading to his eyes. 'I love you too.'

As the dogs mooched off a few yards and settled down to sleep, he rolled her on to her back, kissing her long and deeply.

When he finally raised his head she smiled up at him. 'How long have we been meeting beneath this tree?' she asked, her mouth still only millimetres from his.

He frowned, pretending to think. 'Twelve years? Thirteen years?'

'And have we ever made love beneath it?'

He chuckled. 'No – and thirteen years ago that was because you were five and I was eight.'

'Ah,' she said on a long sigh. 'But that was then – and making love beneath our very special tree, on our engagement day, would be wonderfully symbolic, Francis, wouldn't it?'

'It would indeed,' he said, and the next moment his hair was coarse beneath her fingers, his hands were hard upon her body and his mouth was dry as her tongue slipped past his lips.

The official moment of their engagement – the moment when he slid what was always known in the family as 'the Sheringham rock' on to her finger, was not completely private.

'It fits quite nicely, doesn't it?' her uncle said, regarding the thirty-two-carat pink diamond with satisfaction. 'Amazing that it hasn't had to be altered. Francis's mother had to have the shank made smaller and I remember my grandmother telling me that when she was first given it she had to have it altered to fit as well.'

'And it hasn't been remodelled since your great-grandmother's day,' her mother said, putting her champagne flute down so that she could take a closer look. 'I did suggest to Francis that perhaps it might be an idea to have it re-fashioned in a modern setting, but he said you didn't want him to.'

'And I didn't – and don't,' Geraldine said, one arm linked through Francis's, a glass of champagne in her free hand. 'I love the idea that the ring looked just like this when Francis's mother wore it, and my grandmother and great-grandmother before her.'

'It was uncut when John Francis Sheringham brought it back from India in 1858.' Her uncle looked round the vast drawing room in order to locate John Francis's portrait. 'And which Indian prince he filched it from, no one knows.' Through the open windows, on the early evening air, there came the sound of heavy rock music. Piers Sheringham flinched as if he had been struck. 'What, in the name of Creation, is that?'

'The band,' Francis said, grinning. 'They'll be tuning up or whatever it is rock bands do pre a concert. Guests are already arriving and it's time we put in an appearance and greeted them.'

Geraldine was well aware that she looked sensational. Her hair hung waist length, as shiny as black silk, held away from her face by two heavy tortoiseshell combs. Her dress was starkly simple. A white velvet gown, the top cut halter-fashion, the skirt falling to her white, satin-clad feet, in a pure straight line. What she wasn't quite prepared for was just how sensational Artemis and Primmie looked. They had travelled down to Sussex together in Artemis's father's chauffeur-driven Rolls because, though Artemis had passed her driving test and was the proud possessor of an MG sports car, she had no intention of ruining her hair – or her dress – by driving it.

'You look absolutely gorgeous, Artemis,' she said, meaning every word, 'and *thin.*'

For months past, knowing she would soon be going to the Lucie Clayton Modelling School, Artemis had worked ferociously hard to lose weight and they'd all known that she'd successfully lost her chubbiness. What Geraldine hadn't realized, though, until she saw Artemis in a dress that was, for once, both appropriate to the occasion and stunningly beautiful, was that she had become catwalk model slender.

The dress was ice-blue silk and skimmed her body voluptuously, the neckline daringly low, a deeply cut V at the back reaching to her waist. Instead of looking anxious or flustered, as she had so often done in the past whenever the occasion had been special, she looked nervously exultant. 'I *am* thin, aren't I?' she said, her gold hair coiled into an elaborate chignon, her eyes alight with happiness. 'And you are going to introduce me to *hordes* of blue-blooded young men, aren't you?'

'Everyone I put purposely across your path will have a title or be heir to one and have squillions of cash!' she promised as Primmie, who had been greeted by Piers, hurried up to them, radiant in a traditional, full-skirted ball gown of pale lemon taffeta, the neckline gently scooped, the sleeves huge and puffed and old-fashioned.

'Ooh, isn't this just *magic*?' she said, as acres of fairy lights that had taken weeks to put into place lit up the house and the gardens. 'And doesn't Artemis look simply *staggering* and – oh gosh – your engagement ring, Geraldine! I've never seen anything so beautiful. It looks like the Koh-i-noor!'

Kiki, too, had done her best, by her own lights, to dress for the occasion. She wasn't wearing a ball gown – that would have been too much to expect. Her silver sequinned hipsters and silver bandeau top were, however, worn with an exquisite white organdie silver-trimmed ankle-length coat that, worn unfastened, floated round her in sumptuous splendour. Her silver ankle-strap shoes sported four-inch-high, lethal-looking stainless steel heels. Her talon-like nails were painted silver and her eye shadow was silver. 'It's my moon-girl look,' she said, drinking champagne with them before The Atoms's first set. 'Don't you think my Cleopatra eye make-up looks even more dramatic with silver eye shadow than it did with purple eye shadow?'

'It looks . . . mesmerizing,' Primmie said, wondering just how many pairs of bat-wing false eyelashes Kiki was wearing. 'But why are you wearing your hair dragged so tight to your scalp and worn in that uncomfortable-looking knot on the top of your head?'

'So that I look even more extraordinary, of course. Honestly, Primmie. Sometimes you're so *dim*.'

'She looks totally futuristic, doesn't she?' Francis said as he escaped from greeting more of their guests and joined them. 'I'm seriously considering pursuing this moon-girl image now that I'm managing her. And don't breathe a word, but this is her swan-song with The Atoms. From now on, Kiki Lane is a solo artiste.'

A pleased-as-Punch look flashed between him and Kiki and

then Kiki began making her head-turning way down towards the ha-ha and the stage and Francis gave a whoop as he recognized Ossie Clark and his entourage making their way towards them.

'I didn't know Francis had become Kiki's business manager,' Artemis said, her heart pounding as she became aware that David Bailey was making a beeline towards her and Geraldine. 'Will they get on, do you think? You know how difficult Kiki can be.'

'They're getting on like a house on fire,' Geraldine said, flashing the Sheringham rock in Bailey's direction. 'How perfectly brilliantino that you're here, David, darling. Do let me introduce you to two of my closest, closest friends, Artemis Lowther and Primmie Surtees. The third closest, closest is going to be on stage in another few minutes. Have you heard Kiki Lane sing? She's unbelievable. Absolutely fabulous.'

For the next hour or two, she and Francis were so busy circulating amongst their three hundred guests that she caught only fleeting glimpses of Artemis and Primmie. She did, however, manage to steer some highly eligible young men in Artemis's direction and, considering how mesmerizingly beautiful Artemis was looking, none of them had needed any heavy-handed persuasion. Primmie, too, was quite obviously having a wonderful time. She saw her dancing with Kit Armstrong; dancing with Wayne Clayton; dancing with a far-distant Sheringham cousin.

When The Atoms were on stage, though, Kiki commanded all their attention. She kicked off with Connie Francis's 'Stupid Cupid', followed by a whole host of other old, classic rock numbers, finishing with her favourite of favourites, 'River Deep, Mountain High'.

'She's going to do her rhythm and blues numbers and 'White Dress, Silver Slippers' in their second set,' Francis shouted to her over a roar of applause for 'River Deep'. 'Have you seen the expression on Kit Armstrong's face? Kiki's going to be big, Geraldine. Big. Big. Big. And when she's earning millions, I'll be right there, taking a very healthy percentage!'

'I hope so,' she shouted back, meaning that she hoped Kiki would make it big time, clapping for all she was worth, the Sheringham rock glittering and flashing like fire.

*   *   *

97

Later, when the mood had mellowed and a small dance band was playing George Gershwin tunes and she was in Francis's arms, dancing barefoot on the grass, she knew she had never been happier. 'This is a moment I'm going to remember all my life,' she said dreamily as they swayed gently to 'Night And Day'. 'It's a moment I'm going to tell our children about, and our children's children.'

'And then they will want parties in the garden with a cast of hundreds,' he said, shooting her his dearly familiar, down-slanting smile. 'And we'll be middle-aged grouches like Pa, complaining about the noise and the damage done to the lawns.'

'We'll be happy,' she said, pressing even closer to him, 'and that's all that matters, Francis. It's all that ever matters.'

Eleven

Artemis was deliriously happy. For the first time in her life she was attracting the kind of attention she'd always longed for. The Lucie Clayton Modelling School had given her confidence and polish. Left to her own devices, when it had come to choosing her dress, she would undoubtedly have opted for a traditional taffeta ball gown, floor skimming and full skirted. Instead, having sought advice at the school, she had screwed up her courage and bought a silk dress of stunning simplicity. Aquamarines, loaned to her by her mother, danced against her neck, and her buttercup-blond hair, scooped into an elaborate chignon, shone like satin.

Why had she never realized before that if she only lost weight – and learned how to move gracefully– she would be stunningly beautiful? Even Kiki had been gratifyingly complimentary.

'You look sensational, Artemis,' she had said before going on stage for her first set. 'Absolutely stunning. It's a pity Prince Charles isn't here; you'd bowl him over!'

Though Prince Charles wasn't on the guest list, droves of

other young men were and Geraldine was doing a brilliant job of giving her the information she wanted about them.

'You'd be wasting your time there,' she said as the devastatingly handsome young man she had been dancing with went off to get her champagne glass refilled. 'Sam has tons of charm, but no cash and not much hope of any – unless he marries it. Now the Hooray Henry fast coming your way in order to take advantage of Sam's absence is a very different matter. Money, breeding and – I know how important this is to you, Artemis – a title when daddy dies.'

When Artemis danced with him, she discovered that he also had bad breath. It was a pity, because he was obviously dazzled by her, but bad breath was an unforgivable failing and she discarded him as speedily as she had discarded Sam.

By the time dusk had merged into night, Cedar Court's gardens and grounds were thick with dancing and champagne-drinking couples, and seeking Geraldine out in order that she could whisper vital information about whomever it was she was with was growing increasingly difficult.

'Nine thousand acres in Northumberland,' Geraldine said in her ear as they squeezed past each other in the crush. 'Bent as a five bob note. Sorry, Artemis.'

Soon, even Francis was in on what was going on.

'Let me introduce you to Charlie Moffat,' he said, steering a goggle-eyed young man her way and then, when the introductions were over, saying out of the side of his mouth as he walked away, 'Heir to a baronetcy. Five thousand acres in Wiltshire. Good luck!'

By the time fireworks were let off in a staggeringly beautiful display at the far side of the ha-ha, she was enjoying herself so much she even abandoned her search for Mr Right – Charlie had clammy hands – in order to share a bowl of strawberries with Howard Phillips.

'I'm only here because Kiki introduced me to Francis a couple of weeks ago,' he said, raising his voice in order to be heard over the whoosh of rockets, showers of golden stars cascading in their wake. 'Who is it you're a friend of? Francis or his fiancée?'

The display was building to a crescendo and, in order to

heighten the spectacle, *Ride of the Valkyries* thundered from the sound system.

'I'm one of his fiancée's best friends,' she shouted over the music as fireworks shot and swooped and crackled and blazed. 'But I know Francis as well. Do you know that they are cousins and that they were childhood sweethearts? It's all very romantic, don't you think?'

'Or incestuous, depending which way you look at it,' a voice said from behind them. Artemis turned to see who was speaking and her heart jarred. He was tall and thin and, unlike most of Francis's friends, who were wearing velvet suits or even satin ones, he was wearing a traditional white dinner jacket. His dark hair skimmed his collar, sleek and straight, a lock falling over his forehead in a way she found so sexy she didn't care that he didn't look hip in the way that most of Francis's friends did.

'That's a horrid thing to say,' she said, aware that her voice sounded very odd and high.

He shrugged. 'They're first cousins.' There was a drawl in his voice that reeked of class. 'It's a blood relationship too close for comfort in my book.'

'Knock it off, whoever you are.' Howard, annoyed at having his tête-à-tête with Artemis interrupted, allowed Lancashire vowels to show. 'It's their engagement party and as you're presumably here because you're a friend, the least you can do is to act like one.'

'Oh, I'm a friend all right.' A winged eyebrow quirked slightly. 'But are you? I rather think not. You're certainly not a fellow Oxonian.'

Howard, who had attended a secondary modern, flushed. 'You're an offensive sod,' he said tightly, and then, turning to Artemis, 'Another glass of champagne, Artemis?'

'Yes,' she said, wanting him to go away as quickly as possible. 'Thank you, Howard.'

As a discomfited Howard saved face by stalking off in search of champagne, Mr Satanically-Handsome lifted a finger and a young girl from the caterers, bearing a tray of glasses and Bollinger, was instantly at their side.

'Francis tells me you're a fashion model,' he said as Artemis wondered how many more points, in just a few minutes, he could possibly score.

'Yes,' she said, sending silent thanks Francis's way and not letting on that she was still at Lucie Clayton's and had yet to brave a catwalk professionally.

'I saw David Bailey a minute or so ago. You're not with him, by any chance?'

She had just been about to place her empty strawberry dish on to the waitress's tray, but that he might seriously think she was with David Bailey so disconcerted her that she dropped it. Disconcerted even further and allowing her new-found poise to go to the winds, she was about to bend down and retrieve it when he caught her wrist, his eyes meeting hers.

'Allow me.'

As he scooped up the dish she was aware that his eyes were green – not cat-green, like Kiki's, but water-deep green. Feverishly she looked round, desperate for a glimpse of Geraldine. She needed information and she needed it fast, before another look straight into her eyes made her heedless of whether or not he met the requirements she was determined any boyfriend – and potential future husband – must have.

'I take it no response means that you're not,' he said, placing her strawberry dish on the waitress's tray and handing her a brimming flute of champagne. 'It was out of order to think that because you're one of his favourite models you might also be officially with him this evening.'

She tried to speak, but nothing came.

He didn't seem to notice her difficulty. 'I'm Rupert Gower,' he said, not bothering to take a glass of champagne for himself. 'I've known Francis ever since we went to Ludgrove together.'

'Ludgrove?'

'Ludgrove Prep. It has a tradition of sending pupils to Eton. Without it, I doubt Francis would have made the grade.'

'Artemis Lowther,' she managed in a cracked voice, her heart racing so fast she could hardly breathe, knowing that Francis would only have spun him the line about her being a favourite of David Bailey's if he'd wanted to attract him to her side – and that he wouldn't have done so unless Rupert met requirements. 'I've been one of Geraldine's best friends ever since I was eleven.'

'One of them?' The winged eyebrow quirked again. 'How many best friends does Geraldine have?'

'Three,' she said, hiding sudden, crippling shyness behind the barely discernible, aloof smile all would-be models at Lucie Clayton practised. 'Primmie, Kiki and me.'

'Kiki Lane, the lead singer with The Atoms? The singer Francis is going to manage?'

She nodded, aware, for the first time, that the firework display had come to an end and that the crush of guests, who had come down to the ha-ha to see it, was now thinning. Fairy lights still twinkled, though, and the night sky was thick with stars.

'I believe she's about to do another set,' he said, glancing down at an expensive-looking wristwatch. 'What would you like to do? Listen to her or have supper?'

'Have supper,' she said, knowing that Kiki wouldn't notice that she wasn't in the crowd round the stage and wanting to be alone with Rupert Gower – or as alone with him as it was possible to be at such a huge party.

They strolled over the grass in the direction of the refreshments marquee. The flower-decked tables were candle lit and, with Kiki and The Atoms now the main focus of attention, the earlier crowd of people dining had dwindled to a handful.

The food hadn't dwindled, though. There was clear soup in cups, mousse of chicken, mayonnaise of turbot, lobster patties, quenelles of pheasant, rose cake, biscotins of pears, compôte of fruit, meringues, trifle, apricot choux.

'And knowing Geraldine's mother, there'll be another soup served just before everyone begins leaving,' Rupert said, as, their plates full, he led the way to a small table for two. 'She used to hostess balls for the local hunt for Francis's father, after Francis's mother died, but then Francis's father got iffy at having a hundred or so people milling about the house and garden and we had to go back to holding them at our previous venue. Hopefully, when Francis inherits, we'll return to having our hunt ball here.'

'I didn't know Francis hunted.' Artemis felt a little queasy.

'Of course he hunts. We're in the middle of excellent hunting country. Didn't you know that?'

She took refuge in the aloof expression she'd been taught to adopt when sweeping down a catwalk. 'No,' she said, terrified that things were about to go wrong between them; that he was going to realize she wasn't true county set, but the daughter of a man who had started life in a Docklands terrace house.

'I'm a town girl, not a country girl,' she said as uncaringly as she could manage, wondering if when Geraldine was at Cedar Court, she, too, hunted. If she did, she'd never made any mention of it – which wasn't too surprising considering what Primmie's reaction to such an activity would have been. She, too, felt quite ill at the thought of a fox being torn apart by a pack of hounds.

The situation was saved by the muted sound of Kiki launching into 'White Dress, Silver Slippers'.

'She's good, isn't she?' Rupert speared a piece of chicken. 'What is it she's singing now? I don't recognize it.'

Vastly relieved that the subject had turned to something non-controversial that she knew something about, she laid down her fork and said, 'It's a song she and Geraldine co-wrote. She's going to record it. Francis thinks it will launch her as a solo artist.'

'Does he, indeed?'

There was wry scepticism in Rupert Gower's voice and she blinked, not knowing quite how to respond.

'Francis knows sod all about the music business – or any kind of business. Managing Kiki is just something he's amusing himself with. It's merely a whimsical lark. Proper commitment to anything would bore him rigid.'

'Would it?' she said faintly, wondering just how Francis's desire to marry Geraldine fitted into the picture Rupert was painting. It was hardly something she could ask about and she said instead, 'And what about you, Rupert? What is it you do?'

'I'm a merchant banker in a bank founded by my father. Would you like some dessert now? Meringues with another bottle of champagne? Or perhaps the apricot choux?'

'Meringues, please,' she said, mindful of her diet, relief at the information he had imparted flooding through her. A banker. A *merchant* banker. And in a bank founded by his father! It was enough. He might, or might not, be heir to a title, but even if he wasn't, everything she now knew about him was enough. She had attended the party with every intention of finding herself a suitable boyfriend, a boyfriend who would, hopefully, become the husband of her dreams, and Rupert Gower – who had gone to Eton with Francis and who was tall, dark and handsome – fulfilled her criteria perfectly.

There came the sound of a storm of applause and then Kiki launched into the Martha Reeves and the Vandellas 1966 hit, 'I'm Ready for Love'.

'So am I, Kiki,' she whispered beneath her breath as Rupert strolled across to the vast buffet table for the meringues. 'Oh, so am I!'

'You do realize that your south London accent is now very fashionable, don't you, Primmie?' Kiki said.

It was Monday evening three weeks later and they were all four of them at home.

'I'd give anything to have a legit "sarf" London accent,' Kiki continued, sprawled on the sofa in a scruffy dressing gown, a mud pack on her face and cucumber slices over her eyes. 'It's practically obligatory in the music industry – either that or a Liverpudlian accent.'

Artemis, in a white towelling robe, an equally pristine white towel wound turban-style over wet hair, shuddered. 'Well, *I* wouldn't adopt a south London accent,' she said emphatically, filing her nails. 'Rupert would hate it.'

'Just as well you feel like that, Artemis,' Kiki said dryly, 'because you'd never get the hang of it.'

Artemis drew in her breath, about to make an indignant response. Not wanting a squabble, Geraldine intervened.

'How are things going between you and Rupert?' she asked, tossing the *Private Eye* she'd been reading aside. 'He's taken you nightclubbing twice this week – things must be going well.'

'They are.' Her happiness was so obvious it glowed.

'Which clubs did you go to?' Kiki took the cucumber slices off her eyes and dropped them into a cup of coffee that had gone cold.

'Annabel's.' Artemis was unable to keep the satisfaction out of her voice. Annabel's was the most aristocratic of nightclubs – Prince Charles had been there on one of the nights they'd gone.

Kiki snorted and sat upright, her legs crossed Buddha-style. 'Trust it to have been Annabel's! Why don't you go somewhere kinky and uninhibited for a change?'

'Because I don't want to – and besides, all Rupert's friends go to Annabel's. It's fashionable.'

'It's elitist – packed full of debs, aristos and Guards officers. You'd have much more fun at the Flamingo where the music is blues and black soul.'

Artemis was caught, and knew it. If she said she didn't like blues and black soul Kiki would go off on a rant that could last all evening.

'Talking of bluesy stuff,' Geraldine said, coming to her rescue, 'let's play some Billie Holiday and open a bottle of Chablis to celebrate our all being home together.' Wearing wine-red velvet trousers and a loose silk shirt she crossed the room barefoot, heading for the kitchen and the fridge.

Kiki looked across at Primmie, who was trying to read Boris Pasternak's *Doctor Zhivago*. 'You're nearest the gramophone, Primmie. Put Billie on, will you?

Primmie, ever accommodating, put her book down and obliged.

Artemis stopped filing her nails and watched her. There was something odd about Primmie lately. Usually she chattered away ten to the dozen, but almost from the moment she'd moved into the flat she'd become oddly reticent. Finding out what her colleagues at BBDO were like – colleagues she now spent a lot of her free time with – was like getting blood out of a stone.

'Where do your BBDO friends hang out, Primmie?' she asked as Billie's 'Long Gone Blues' filled the room.

Primmie flushed slightly. 'A local wine bar.'

'What? Every night?' Geraldine asked, walking back into the room with the bottle of Chablis and glasses.

'I'm not out *every* night. I stayed in and did my laundry last night – and Kiki's laundry, because she lets it pile up till I can hardly see the bedroom floor – and Saturday night I visited my mum and dad.'

'Oh, well, if you were in glorious downtown Rotherhithe on a Saturday night, I, for one, am not envious.' Kiki rose to her feet. 'Do you think this mud pack should come off now? My face is beginning to sting.'

'You have a mud pack on?' Geraldine said in mock surprise, beginning to pour out the wine.

Kiki threw a cushion at her head. Billie's inimitable voice continued to magically dip and glide and Artemis continued to regard Primmie thoughtfully.

Primmie was still slightly flushed and it wasn't because she was annoyed at Kiki's meant-to-be-funny dig about Rother-hithe, it was more as if she were embarrassed and uncomfortable because she was concealing something. Though she may have been speaking the truth about visiting Rotherhithe on Saturday night, the bit about her evenings being spent with her work colleagues in a wine bar local to Hanover Square was definitely not the entire truth. With a flash of intuition, it occurred to her that Primmie might have a boyfriend – a boyfriend she didn't want them to know about.

She took a glass of wine from Geraldine, wondering if Primmie was being reticent because her boyfriend was a workman, not a colleague. Perhaps he was a carpenter who was refurbishing the offices, or an electrician. Or – her eyes flew wide at the thought – perhaps he *was* a colleague, but was married!

'Primmie, you're not involved with a mar—' she began, perturbed.

Kiki, who cut across people's conversations all the time, said, 'Hasn't anyone been checking the time for me? Half an hour this face pack had to be on for. I was *relying* on someone to tell me when the time was up.'

'It's up now.' Primmie rose briskly to her feet. 'As we're all in tonight I'll make something to eat. Do Eggs Benedict sound OK?'

With an odd, set expression to her face she marched out of the room, into the kitchen.

Artemis bit her lip, her concern escalating, certain that Primmie had known *exactly* what it was she, Artemis, had been going to say – and that she'd waltzed out of the room before she should be given a second chance of saying it.

As there came the sound of a pan being put on the stove and a cupboard being opened, she said tentatively to Geraldine, 'I'm a bit worried about Primmie. I think she may have a boyfriend.'

'Well . . . it wouldn't be before time, would it?' Geraldine took a sip of her wine. 'I may only have had one boyfriend in my life, but he's been my boyfriend since childhood. Kiki was fifteen when she began going around with Ty. You and Primmie have been very slow off the mark where boyfriends are concerned and if Primmie is finally dating someone, it's something to be pleased about, not worried over.'

'Y-e-s,' Artemis said doubtfully, not sure she liked being bracketed in a 'slow off the mark' category with Primmie. 'But what if he isn't suitable?'

'In what way, for goodness sake? Primmie isn't you, Artemis. If she's attracted to someone, she's not going to worry about his family's social status, his bank balance or his prospects. All that is going to matter to her is what he's like as a person – and whether she fancies him or not.'

'But what if he's . . . he's . . .' She hesitated. She couldn't very well say, 'What if he's a carpenter or an electrician,' because Geraldine would get seriously cross with her if she did. 'What if he's married?' she said.

Geraldine's eyes flew wide and Artemis felt an unworthy stab of satisfaction at having taken her so aback.

'Married?' She put her wine glass on to the coffee table as if afraid she might spill it. 'What on earth put an idea like that in your head? Primmie's far too open and straight to get involved with a married man. Stop worrying about her, Artemis. It's your own love life you should be giving thought to. According to Francis, Rupert thinks you're the last thing in cool sophistication – which makes me think he's fallen for the person he thinks you are, not the person you really are.'

'But I *am* sophisticated now! I did my first fashion show last week and I've got *three* work engagements this coming week.'

'And you were wonderful last week,' Geraldine said truthfully. 'I barely recognized you, you were so soignée and self-confident.'

'Well, then?'

'But that's just a veneer you've learned to adopt at Lucie Clayton – and if it's the same veneer you're dazzling Rupert with, what happens when he discovers the real you? Won't there be problems?'

107

'Problems?' Kiki asked, swinging back into the room. 'Who and what are we talking about?'

'Geraldine thinks Rupert can't possibly have fallen for the real me and that when he discovers what the real me is like, he's going to dump me!' Though her voice was wobbling, Artemis managed – with effort – to hold back the tears that were threatening to spill. 'And I think she's being very cruel and totally out of order.'

'I just want you to be aware of how stunningly successful you've been at creating a very cool, very sophisticated image,' Geraldine said soothingly. 'So successful that, according to Francis, Rupert thinks the image is the real thing.'

'I told him that Francis had been fibbing about my being one of David Bailey's favourite models. If I'd been intent on leading him up the garden path, I wouldn't have done that, would I? And he was absolutely uncaring about it. He said I probably soon would be one of Bailey's favourite models and that I was far more lovely than Jean Shrimpton.'

'That's because despite all the weight you've lost you still have tits and Jean Shrimpton doesn't,' Kiki said, taking up a cross-legged position on the sofa again.

'OK, I back down.' Geraldine reached for her wine glass. 'Rupert *does* know the real you and, though I would never have teamed the two of you together in a million years, I should bear in mind that opposites attract. Where is he taking you at the weekend? Annabel's again?'

'The Hurlingham. He's playing polo.'

Kiki made a rude noise

Artemis was uncaring. Opposites *did* attract. Rupert was wild about her – and that was all that mattered. 'I've never been to a polo match,' she said with a trace of her old uncertainty. 'What should I wear?'

'Your Mary McFadden coffee-coloured silk with the tiny, tiny pleats would look wonderful. And wear a big white straw hat with a floppy brim. Polo is dressy.'

'And expensive,' Kiki said, as Primmie came back into the room carrying a tray.

'Do you want your Eggs Benedict in here or in the kitchen?' Primmie asked. 'And what is expensive?'

'Polo – and we'll eat in here.' Geraldine began clearing the papers and magazines from the low glass table so that they could picnic off it.

'What is it that makes polo so expensive?' Primmie asked, settling the tray down. 'Is it having to have your own horse?'

'Pony, Primmie,' Geraldine corrected, vastly amused. 'In polo, the mounts are always referred to as ponies. And you can't get by with one pony. You need to change your mount every two or three chukkas and have a couple in reserve if poss.'

'And how many ponies does Rupert have?' Artemis took the towel off her head and shook her hair loose so that it would dry. 'And how many chukkas are they in a game?'

'I've no idea how many ponies Rupert has, but there are six chukkas in a game.' Geraldine took a mouthful of egg dripping with hollandaise sauce. 'There are eight players in every game and you have to be a very, very experienced rider to play.'

'And is Rupert a very experienced rider?' Mindful of her diet, Artemis was ignoring the egg and sauce and nibbling at a small piece of crisp pancetta.

'He carries a six-goal handicap.'

'And is that good?'

Geraldine gurgled with laughter. 'Yes, Artemis. It's very good. Superlatively good. It makes him one of the best players in the country.'

Artemis sighed rapturously, her pique of a few moments ago completely forgotten. 'Wonderful,' she said dreamily. 'Absolutely and utterly wonderful!'

Twelve

May 1972

Primmie walked through Soho with a song in her heart. It was a gorgeous day. The sky was a heavenly blue. She'd just been given a new, very important account to handle – and she was on her way to have lunch with Simon.

She looked down at the wristwatch her mum and dad had bought her for her twenty-first birthday and saw that she was going to be at the restaurant way too early instead of being late, as she usually was. It didn't matter. It was a wonderful day and she had never been happier.

Ever since her birthday in April, she and Simon had been unofficially engaged. The difficulty about announcing their engagement was that Kiki was in Australia, on tour, and it wasn't news Simon wanted to break to his daughter over the phone. She was, however, due home at the end of the week, and Simon would then have the heart-to-heart with her – a heart-to-heart he should have had months and months ago.

His reluctance to put Kiki in the picture as to the nature of their relationship had put her under great pressure. Geraldine, Artemis and Kiki knew, of course, that ever since the break-up of Simon and Eva's marriage, she and Simon had been extraordinarily close. Kiki had said she thought it bizarre that one of her best friends was also a friend of her father, but otherwise had been uncaring about it. Neither Geraldine nor Artemis, who had always liked Simon, had thought it at all odd, but that had been because they didn't know that she'd always had a crush on him, that she'd been in love with him since she was eighteen – and that he was the reason she'd stayed on at BBDO instead of taking up her place at university.

The trees in Soho Square were in full leaf and the park seats were full of office workers enjoying picnics and sunbathing. She squeezed her way on to one of the seats, raising her face to the glorious heat of the sun. She knew, of course, why Simon was so reluctant to tell Kiki that the two of them were in love. It was the same reason he'd been so hesitant about first making love to her. He was twenty-one years her senior – and he was her friend's father.

'You lived in my home, Monday to Friday, from the time you were eleven years old to the time you left school at eighteen,' he'd said once, when she'd wanted to tell the whole world that they were in love. 'Can't you see how that will look to people, Primmie? They may wonder just *when* I became sexually interested in you. I'm a family GP, I can't afford the slightest whiff of scandal – and if the word paedophile is ever bandied about, I'm finished.'

She had understood, but keeping their love affair a secret from Geraldine, Artemis and Kiki had been the hardest thing she had ever done. Sometimes she'd had the feeling that Geraldine had long ago guessed the true nature of her feelings for Simon – and of Simon's for her – but if she'd guessed, she'd never said anything.

Another few days, though, once Kiki was home and Simon had spoken to her, then everyone could know and congratulate her – her parents included.

'But they'll be *appalled*,' he had said, running his fingers through his fair hair when she had asked if she could, at least, tell her parents. 'They trusted you in my care for seven years! They, of all people, have every reason to wonder what sort of man I am – and for just how long I've had designs on you.'

'You're a good, kind, gentle, wonderful man,' she had said, her head resting against his shoulder. 'And no one could ever believe differently. *I* know you never thought of me in any way that was inappropriate when I was a child and no one else will believe you did, either.' She'd begun to giggle, thinking of the long two years between Eva having left him and their becoming lovers. 'And if they *don't* believe me, I shall have to tell them that in the end it was virginal me who seduced you!'

Whether anyone would believe her last remark – which was a perfectly truthful one – was doubtful and a wide grin split her face. Geraldine and Artemis were going to be staggered when they learned that she and Simon were lovers – and they were certainly going to have to stop teasing her about what they had always thought was her boyfriendless state.

She glanced down at her watch again and saw that it was five to one. The restaurant where she was meeting Simon was in Greek Street, on the far side of the square and, unhurriedly, she rose to her feet.

Breaking the news to Geraldine and Artemis – and Kiki, too, of course – was something she had longed to do for so long that now the time was nearing she was on tenterhooks.

111

It would certainly be great news to break at what was to be a reunion for them all. Kiki had been away for two months, touring Australia, and Geraldine had been away for nine months, trawling through northern India and Kashmir with Francis. Artemis hadn't been in circulation of late, either. Married to Rupert and living in the Cotswolds, she now used the flat only as a pied-à-terre. With Kiki always flying off to gigs abroad and Geraldine satisfying her wanderlust now that Francis was no longer Kiki's manager, the only person permanently resident in the flat they had all shared was herself.

As she strolled out of the square, it occurred to her that she wasn't likely to be living in it for much longer either. Once Simon's and her engagement was announced and happily accepted by everyone there was absolutely no reason for delaying their marriage. Unlike other engaged couples, they didn't have to save for a home. Simon hadn't wanted to move from the house at Petts Wood and, as it was a house she had always loved and she had no troubled feelings about his life there with Eva, she hadn't asked that he do so.

As she crossed the road into Greek Street she could see his dearly familiar figure walking up it from the opposite end. He was wearing grey flannel trousers and a tweed jacket, just as he had been the first time she had seen him. With a stab of déjà vu she remembered the moment when she had stood with Geraldine at the entrance to Bickley High, watching in appalled fascination as Artemis's father had pitched into him for having clipped his wing mirror.

Even then, without even having met him, she had liked him. He had been so quietly polite in the face of Mr Lowther's aggressive rudeness that it would have been impossible *not* to have liked him. He had been attractive, too. His slim build and fair hair had reminded her of a painting she had once seen of St George.

As he saw her coming towards him, a smile creased his face. With love for him flooding through her, she ran towards him. He caught hold of her hands, squeezing them tightly, not hugging her and kissing her, as she would have liked him to do. Public displays of affection were not Simon's style.

'Hello, sweetheart,' he said, releasing hold of one of her

112

hands so that they could walk along the pavement side by side. 'How long have you got for lunch today?'

'An hour and a half. Howard is in Birmingham, seeing a client.'

That Howard Phillips had moved from the creative side of advertising into management and was her account director at BBDO was something she had found far more interesting than Kiki had. 'He's a wanker,' Kiki had said, uncaring of the fact that he had been instrumental in introducing her to Kit Armstrong – and that without Kit Armstrong she would never have had a hit record with 'White Dress, Silver Slippers'.

'Smashing.' Simon pushed open the door of the Hungarian restaurant that was their favourite eating place. 'It means we don't have to keep looking at our watches.'

As Simon didn't work in town – and because of the nature of his work – weekday lunches together were prized occasions. Today, a locum was taking his surgery and home visits for him. Today she was doing a rare thing – taking an extended lunch break in order to be with him as long as possible.

'Good afternoon, madam. Good afternoon, sir,' the elderly waiter who seated them said in greeting.

Primmie always had to fight the urge to giggle when addressed, in The Gay Hussar as 'madam'. For Simon's sake, it was an impulse she kept well under control. He liked the restaurant's old-style service and ambience: the stiff white cloths on the tables, the unchanging but satisfying mid-European menu, the snug intimacy that was worlds removed from the brash and noisy Italian trattorias thronging the rest of Soho. Another advantage of it, for him, was, she knew, that they were unlikely to run into any of her work colleagues there.

'You can't possibly want them to know that you're going out with a man old enough to be your father,' he said whenever she suggested they meet up somewhere her work colleagues would also be.

His sensitivity where their age difference was concerned troubled her because she found it so unnecessary. He was forty-two and forty-two wasn't old. Her father was in his sixties. Now that *was* old – and if Simon had been in his sixties she'd have been able to understand his constant anxiety about how people would view their relationship.

'It just isn't anyone else's business,' she had said, time and time again. 'I love you, and you love me, and that's all that matters. If anyone has any comment to make about it, why should we care?'

The waiter broke in on her thoughts. 'We have wild cherry soup today, madam,' he said, 'or perhaps you would prefer the duck pâté as a starter?'

'The wild cherry soup would be lovely,' she said, and then, so familiar with the menu that she didn't need further help, 'and could I have the fish dumplings with dill sauce as my main course?'

'You may indeed, madam.'

As Simon ordered bean soup, paprika chicken and a bottle of Merlot, she wondered if the waiter was aware that she and Simon were not father and daughter, nor uncle and niece, but lovers. Always, when they were out dining, she wanted to hold hands with Simon across the table; to make an outward display that would leave no doubt in the eyes of anyone seeing them that they were in love. Simon, though, would never be drawn into behaving in a way that might draw attention to their relationship – and to their age difference.

'I've been thinking about the tête-à-tête I'm going to have with Kiki, Primmie,' he said when the waiter had retreated out of earshot. 'And I've decided to postpone it for a week or two.'

'Postpone it?' She stared at him, bewildered. 'But why? I don't understand. You've bought me a ring and I want to wear it. I can't bear being with Geraldine, Artemis and Kiki, pretending that the two of us are just friends and nothing more. It makes me feel as if our being in love is something to be ashamed of – and it isn't.'

The wine waiter brought the bottle of Merlot to the table. Simon tasted it, waited until their glasses had been filled and then said gently, 'I know how hard the situation is for you, Primmie, believe me I do, but what if Kiki doesn't react as we hope she will? What if there is a knock-on effect that will spoil other things?'

She laced her fingers together in her lap. 'I'm sorry,' she said, fighting down a rising sense of panic. 'I don't understand. A knock-on effect on what? What difference is there in telling her at the weekend when she arrives home and

114

telling her in a few weeks' time? The sooner we tell her, the sooner we can tell everyone else, and people are going to be happy for us. There aren't going to be any problems. Why should there be? And what are the other things you think could possibly be spoiled?'

'There's the wedding.'

'The wedding? Our wedding?'

'No,' he said patiently. 'Geraldine's wedding. That's why Geraldine and Francis have come home, isn't it? To get married?'

'Yes, But I don't see . . .'

'And both you and Kiki are to be bridesmaids?'

'Yes, but—'

'And if Kiki isn't as rapturous about our engagement as you think she will be, then it will make for a difficult atmosphere when you are bridesmaids at Geraldine's wedding and that would be grossly unfair to Geraldine. So I think it best that . . .'

The waiter approached their table again and served them with their first course.

Ignoring it, as Simon ignored his, Primmie said, 'But Kiki *isn't* going to have problems about our becoming engaged. She's the most *liberated* person I know. She's . . . she's . . .' she struggled as to how best to convey to him that where sexual relationships were concerned, his daughter was an 'anything goes' liberal whose sex life was promiscuously freewheeling. It wasn't something that could be said without causing him a great deal of hurt.

She said instead, 'Kiki is a major pop star – and pop stars aren't conventional and they don't have old-style values. When you tell her about us she'll simply roll her eyes to heaven and ask if we want her to sing at the reception.'

He gave a faint smile. 'I wish I could believe that, sweetheart, but I don't. I know you're her friend, but I'm her father. I know a side to her you've never seen. Behind her couldn't-care-less attitude to life, Kiki is deeply insecure and, for reasons I don't understand, I'm responsible for that. She was deeply traumatized when Eva set up home with Jenny Reece and, unlike you, I think there's a chance our news will affect her the same way.'

Primmie pressed her lips together tightly. Even as a teenager she had never been able to understand why he took so much upon himself where Kiki was concerned. And he was wrong in thinking Kiki had been traumatized over her mother's relationship with Jenny Reece. Kiki had been shocked – not an easy thing to achieve – but it had been a shock she had soon come to terms with. Spelling this all out to him would, though, be pointless. He simply wouldn't believe her and they would end up having an argument that would distress them both.

Knowing that unless she took their conversation on to dangerous ground she was going to have to accept the decision he had made, she said, 'And you'll tell her immediately after the wedding?'

Hearing the flicker of fear in her voice he leaned across the table towards her. 'Immediately,' he said reassuringly. 'I love you, Primmie. I want to marry you and spend the rest of my life with you. Never doubt that. Promise?'

'I promise.' Her voice was thick with emotion. 'And I love you with all my heart, Simon.'

A shadow fell across them. 'Excuse me, sir.' The waiter looked concerned. 'Your soup is all right, yes? There isn't a problem?'

Primmie felt a near hysterical giggle rise in her throat.

'Everything is fine.' Simon's eyes held hers. 'I and my fiancée are just taking our time over things, that's all.'

It was the first time he had ever acknowledged their relationship in public.

Primmie's cheeks flushed rosily, all her anxieties quelled. She had waited two years from first knowing she was in love with him to their becoming lovers. A further two weeks of secrecy until their engagement was announced was going to make no difference to their life together. Free of any sense of impending catastrophe, she turned her attention to her wild cherry soup.

The next morning she was sick. Hoping she wasn't about to go down with gastric flu or a viral infection, she drank a glass of lemon barley water and hurried off to work.

'Buses up the creek as usual?' Howard said sympathetically as she made an entrance at the agency, twenty minutes late.

'No. Tummy bug. Nothing to worry about.'

116

Throwing her jacket over the back of her chair, she glanced down at her diary. 'Is everything in place for this morning's eleven o'clock meeting in the conference room, or is it still to do?'

'It's all in place, but it won't do any harm to give everything a once-over – and check that Creative have got their act together. I'd like Steve to run his story board past me one more time before I do the pitch to the client – and make sure that when Bayers arrive there's lashings of hot coffee.'

Later, once again at her own desk, she studied the list she had made for herself the night before and began on the most urgent of her phone calls. She had just finished chasing Production for proofs she was waiting for when the phone rang.

'Yes?' she said peremptorily, hoping to goodness the Production boys weren't phoning to say that the proofs were lost.

'Primmie, thank *God* I've made contact with you!' It was Artemis, and as Artemis tended to be theatrical Primmie didn't immediately assume that there was a disaster. 'I was petrified you wouldn't be in the agency,' Artemis continued as if it was an absolute miracle that she was even in the country. 'I thought you'd be out, wining and dining a client.'

'At ten in the morning? And only account directors get to do the wining and dining bit – though I had lunch in Soho yesterday, with Simon.'

'Simon?' Artemis sounded bewildered. 'Kiki's father?'

'The same.' Primmie kept her voice light, determined not to become irritated just because Artemis hadn't reacted as she would have liked on hearing Simon's name.

'That was very sweet of you,' Artemis said, as if having lunch with Simon was an act of kindness. 'Is he retired now?'

Primmie's good intentions went to the wind. 'No,' she said vehemently, 'Simon is *not* retired. He's only forty-two and he's a very attractive man.'

'Oh!' Disconcerted by her reaction, Artemis's bewilderment deepened. 'Well, yes,' she said uncertainly, quite obviously trying to be placating. 'If you say so, Primmie.'

Primmie bit back another sharp retort and, signing off a set of proofs, said, 'What's the emergency? I haven't much time to chat, Artemis.' She tossed the proofs into her out-tray and turned her attention to some artwork for her cosmetic account.

117

'Geraldine's mother rang me this morning to say that my matron of honour dress and Kiki's and your bridesmaid's dresses are ready for their final fitting. She knows how difficult it is for you to get time off work and so has arranged that we all three go to the dressmakers together, on Saturday afternoon.'

'Kiki doesn't get back from Australia till Saturday morning. And what is going to happen to fittings for the wedding dress? Geraldine isn't back till some time next week.'

'Tell me about it,' Artemis said dryly. 'How she can leave *all* the wedding preparations to her mother is beyond my understanding. It isn't as if it's going to be a small wedding. It's going to be huge.' She paused slightly. 'Even bigger than my wedding was.'

Dutifully Primmie came in on cue. 'Nothing could be bigger than that, Artemis. Or more beautiful.'

'It *was* beautiful, wasn't it?' she said dreamily. 'And the bridesmaids' dresses were so much prettier than the ones Geraldine has chosen for us. I know Geraldine has unusual taste when it comes to clothes – but narrow-skirted gowns in gun-metal grey silk aren't very bridal.'

Primmie grinned. The dresses she, Kiki and Geraldine had worn at Artemis's wedding at St Margaret's, Westminster had been confections of layer after layer of pale peach organdie sprigged with tiny embroidered roses and seed pearls, the crinoline skirts so wide it had been all they could do to squeeze down the aisle. Persuading Kiki into hers had been a major achievement.

'I must go, Artemis,' she said, catching sight of Howard pointing frantically to his watch. 'I'll see you Saturday. Should we go to the dressmakers separately or meet up first?'

'We'll meet up first. I'll pick you up at the flat.'

'Fine. Bye.' Hastily she tossed proofs and artwork she hadn't yet checked back into her in-tray and left her desk, heading off in Howard's wake towards the conference room. Artemis wasn't often right about things, but she had a point where the bridesmaid's dresses were concerned. Gun-metal grey *was* an unusual choice of colour – but Geraldine's sense of style was unerring and their silver-grey dresses, set off by posies of white roses, would, she was sure, look sensational.

* * *

118

When Artemis arrived at the flat early Saturday afternoon she looked as washed-out as Primmie felt.

'What's the matter,' she asked as Artemis put the MG into gear, heading for Kensington High Street. 'Have you got a touch of gastric flu as well?'

'Flu?' The car veered slightly. 'No, of course I haven't. And what do you mean "as well"? You're not ill, are you, Primmie?'

'No. I'm not ill. I just keep feeling a little queasy.'

Artemis, who was usually full of concern if people were even the teeniest bit under the weather, didn't respond. Primmie looked across at her. Artemis was, as always, immaculately made-up, but, as well as looking ill, she looked as if she had been crying.

Waiting until the nightmare of the traffic in Kensington High Street was behind them and they were in the marginally less congested area of Fulham, she said hesitantly, 'Are you sure you're OK, Artemis? There's nothing wrong, is there?'

Artemis made an odd sound in her throat and Primmie wasn't sure if it was a cough or a stifled sob.

A motorbike veered in front of them and Artemis avoided running into him – but only just.

'Is it the bridesmaid's dresses?' Primmie persisted, knowing that with Artemis, anything was possible. 'You're not seriously upset about having to wear grey, are you?'

This time there was no mistaking the sound that Artemis made. It was definitely a stifled sob.

'It's Rupert!' she said, tears beginning to run down her face. 'I so want a baby and he told me last night that I mustn't keep on about wanting to be pregnant.'

'Well, you have only been married for a year. I suppose he thinks it's a bit soon . . .'

'No. No, it's not that, Primmie. It's . . .' Uncaring of the right of way of the traffic around her, she cut across the busy inside lane and brought the sports car to an abrupt halt on a No Parking spot. 'It's because he says I *can't* become pregnant!' She was sobbing in earnest now, her words coming in gasps. 'He had mu-mumps when he was twenty-one and ever since he's been ste-sterile – and he didn't tell me! He ma-married me and didn't tell me that I wouldn't be able to have children! Can you believe that, Primmie? Can you *believe* it?'

119

Thirteen

Kiki looked out of the plane window and viewed the hotch-potch of green fields and scatterings of red-brick houses with relief. Ten more minutes and she'd be on the tarmac at Heathrow. She stared down at what, at a rough guess, was the outskirts of Slough.

Part of her couldn't wait to be back in the Kensington flat with Primmie – but there were going to be problems. Primmie hadn't a clue about the kind of lifestyle led by people in the music business. She'd never been happy about having marijuana in the flat. A bathroom cabinet full of uppers and downers would cause huge ructions. As for cocaine . . . cocaine would be a complete no-no. She chewed the corner of her lip. She could book into a hotel and look round London for a flat of her own, but living on her own held no appeal whatsoever. After two months on the road, she needed her friends around her – and Primmie was a friend in the very fullest sense of the word, as were Artemis and Geraldine.

Artemis, although no longer living in the flat, regularly stayed overnight when making a trip up from the Cotswolds to shop at her favourite boutiques. As for Geraldine . . . Geraldine was due back from India any day, and until her wedding at the end of the month she, too, would be living at the flat.

Though it was a domestic situation that suited her, it incensed her present manager, Aled Carter. 'Sharing a flat with three old school friends is not a pop star lifestyle,' he'd ranted at her time and time again. 'It doesn't project the right image, Kiki.'

Well, maybe it didn't, but it was what she wanted. It was

what felt right. As for darling Primmie . . . where the coke was concerned, she'd have to be discreet, that was all. It wasn't as if she snorted lines of it morning, noon and night. Coke was for when she was too exhausted to give a performance without a bit of help, or for when she was partying. It wasn't something Primmie would ever have to know about.

They were coming in to land now and she scooped her distinctive hair beneath a baker-boy beret and slipped a pair of dark glasses on. She wasn't expecting to be met by fans or members of the press, but it was always a possibility and she wasn't in the mood.

She thought with relief of the chauffeured white limo that would be waiting for her. It was a touch Aled insisted upon, irrespective of whether or not members of the press were there to see it.

'Behave like a star, think like a star, and you'll be a star,' was his mantra and it had brought him success with a whole gamut of pop groups and solo artists.

The first single she'd recorded under his aegis had stayed in the charts for thirteen weeks. Success like that was one of the up sides of having him as her manager. A down side was that he was a slave driver who planned her weeks down to the last minute. Sometimes she would be up at six in the morning and be singing by nine – and this was after not getting home from a gig until the early hours. There were no such things as weekends off. Even though she'd just flown in from Australia, she knew he would have a full day planned for her for tomorrow.

As she disembarked she reflected on how different it had been when Francis had been her manager. Then, every gig had been fun and there had never been acrimonious disputes about what she should or shouldn't record. Acrimonious disputes with Aled were, unfortunately, plentiful. The current dispute was over material for her new album. Aled wanted it to be composed mainly of songs written by Geraldine and herself – which was understandable considering how big a hit 'White Dress, Silver Slippers' and another song she'd co-written with Geraldine, 'Twilight Love', had been.

The problem was, Geraldine hadn't been around to write

songs with. For the past nine months she'd been on the hippie trail with Francis, seeking nirvana in India and Tibet.

Once out of baggage reclaim she pushed her trolley into the arrivals hall, seeing with a mixture of relief and disgruntlement that there were no members of the press waiting to greet her, only Albert, Aled's driver.

'Aled says welcome back and he'll meet up with you later today,' he said, dealing manfully with her luggage.

'Yeah. Well. He will if he can get me out of bed.'

She flung herself into the limo, knowing why Aled was impatient to see her. He wanted to know what the timing was going to be on the delivery of new songs, and until she met up with Geraldine she couldn't tell him.

She frowned, aware that even when Geraldine hit base again there was going to be little opportunity for her to put in the kind of time needed for an album. From now until her wedding day Geraldine's life was going to be one hectic whirl – a whirl that would have no time in it for lyric writing.

'Put a music station on, Albert,' she said, wanting distraction.

A second later the sound of The New Seekers' 'I'd Like To Teach The World To Sing' filled the limo. It was a sharp reminder of the kind of lightweight pop numbers Aled might drum up for the album if she failed to come up with anything herself.

'Dear God,' she said devoutly. 'That was number one in January. I can't believe it's still being given airtime. What's at the top of this week's charts?'

'"Amazing Grace" by the Pipes and Drums and Military Band of the Royal Scots Dragoon Guards.'

'You're kidding me?'

'Nope. There ain't been anything decent in the number one slot for ages, apart from T Rex's "Telegram Sam".'

Kiki said a rude word and lapsed into silence. The nitty-gritty of the problem was that of all the things she had written only the songs co-written with Geraldine had ever been real successes – and motivating Geraldine into songwriting was hard work, because Geraldine only ever did something if it amused her to do so. During the time Francis had been enthusiastically involved in the pop world, Geraldine had amused herself by being a stylist for a photographer friend, and, when the amusement of being a stylist had waned, by doing an antiques appreciation course at Sotheby's. In between times she had occasionally co-written songs with her and then, when the antiques appreciation course had come to an end, she had decided that Francis and she had delayed their trip to India for long enough – and the next thing she, Kiki, had known, was that Francis was off on the hippie trail and she was without a manager.

She chewed the corner of her lip again, still not knowing quite how she felt about it all. As it had happened, Aled had taken over managing her career and no great harm had been done, but the outcome might have been very different and, if it had been, Geraldine would have had a lot to answer for.

They were speeding through Chiswick now and she glanced down at her watch. It was five past three and for the first time it occurred to her that, as it was a weekday, Primmie wouldn't be at the flat to welcome her home.

'Mr Carter has left a schedule for you to look over,' Albert said, breaking in on her thoughts. 'It's tucked in the rear seat-pocket.'

With bad grace, Kiki removed the large white envelope, not bothering to open it. There'd be time enough later, when she was in a scented hot bath and not feeling so grumpy.

She tried to remember if she'd ever felt grumpy about any of the things Francis had ever arranged for her, and couldn't. She and Francis had got along famously and though he'd been brand new to the business he'd launched her solo career with all the expertise of an old pro. Her anger when he'd told her he was going off to India had been monumental.

'India can wait! India's always going to be there!' she'd raged. 'Building up my career *can't* wait! And how can I write more songs with Geraldine if she's meditating with Tibetan monks or sunning herself in Kathmandu?'

Raging had made not the slightest bit of difference. To her stunned disbelief, once Geraldine had decided that she'd waited long enough to hit the hippie trail, Francis hadn't even put up a fight about it.

She hadn't understood his behaviour then, and she didn't understand it now, because Francis had *loved* being part of the music business. As the limo pulled to a halt, she found

123

herself hoping that he'd missed it so much he'd be on his knees, begging her to ditch Aled Carter so that their old business relationship could be renewed.

And what of their other relationship? The one that no one knew about? What was going to happen to that once Geraldine and he were married?

She got out of the limo, taking the envelope with her. Ever since her Hell's Angels days she'd been promiscuous. If she wanted to sleep with someone she slept with them, whether or not she was in a relationship with them, or even likely to be in a relationship with them. Spending so much time with Francis had inevitably meant that there'd been occasions, usually when they were on an adrenalin high after a successful gig, when they'd fallen into bed together.

It had been something neither of them had tortured themselves over. Francis always spoke of Geraldine as if she were, quite simply, his best friend, and they were marrying because it was something his father and her mother had planned for them since the cradle. 'Geraldine loves Cedar Court passionately – far more passionately than anyone else I might marry ever would,' he'd said. 'What's more, she'll run the estate like clockwork, which is all to the good, because I've no interest in doing so.'

Kiki, who hadn't a romantic bone in her body, hadn't been overly shocked at such a prosaic approach to marriage. If that was how Geraldine and Francis wanted to arrange things, it was fine by her – as was the great sex she and Francis enjoyed whenever there was no other outlet for post-concert adrenalin highs.

The first thing she saw as she entered the flat was a large card propped on the telephone table on which was written: *Welcome home! There's a bottle of bubbly in the fridge and I've left the water heater on, so there'll be lashings of bath water. I'll be home as soon as poss. Love you. Primmie.*

Feeling immediately cheered, she tossed her beret on to the nearest chair and, leaving Albert to hump her luggage into the hall and to see himself out, she went into the bathroom and turned the hot tap full on.

While the bath was filling, she went in search of the champagne. It was Louis Cristal. Mentally giving Primmie full marks, she opened it with expertise born of long practise then, the champagne bottle in one hand, a glass in the other, Aled's envelope tucked beneath her arm, she went back into the bathroom.

Half an hour later, soothed by champagne and deep, scented bathwater, she stretched a hand over the side of the bath and reached for the envelope. The sheet of paper inside was headed: *Schedule Week Commencing 3rd May.*

Tuesday 5th
1000 – Urgent meeting my office re material for new album.
1300 – Lunch with Kit, Mr Chow's.
1500 – Interview with *New Musical Express.*
1600 – Photo shoot.
1800 – Rehearsal *Top of the Pops.*

Wednesday 6th
1000 – Meeting with producer *Juke Box Jury.*
1300 – Lunch San Lorenzo with Dick Shields, EMI.
1530 – Rehearsal with new session musicians.
1900 – *Top of the Pops.*
2200 – Party at Ad-Lib.

Thursday 7th
0800 – Meet with choreographer for Birmingham gig 29th.
1000 – Meet re next month's gigs in Milan, Pisa and Rome.
1230 – Interview for *TV World.*
1300 onwards – Song material discussion with Kit.
1800 – Rehearsal with new session musicians.

Friday 8th
0830 – Flight to Newcastle. Tyne Tees TV.

Saturday 9th
0800 – Return London. Morning meet new album issue.

At the bottom, by hand, was scrawled: *Great offer star spot Saturday night TV* Arthur Haynes Variety Show. *Will talk asap.*

She dropped the schedule back on to the floor, ran the hot tap to heat the cooling water and closed her eyes. A variety show. A *variety* show? Was Aled mad? She was a rock singer, not a bland all-round family entertainer. What kind of a career path was he trying to push her down?

The sound of the flat door slamming open and Primmie shouting 'Welcome back!' as she ran down the hall towards the bathroom banished Aled from her thoughts.

The bathroom door crashed open and Kiki's grin split her kittenish face in two. 'I'm already halfway through the Louis Cristal,' she said, raising her champagne glass. 'Thanks for the thought, Prim. It was a lifesaver.'

'Gosh, but it's good to have you home, Kiki!' Primmie fell on her knees beside the bath, radiant faced. 'The flat was quiet as a tomb without you!'

Kiki gave her a damp, loving kiss on the cheek.

'It's good to be home, Prim. Australia was exhausting. When we weren't performing we were travelling God alone knows how many miles to wherever it was we were performing next. The road crew were a nightmare and I haven't had a day to myself since I left England. What's been happening here? Any news of when Geraldine is back? How's Artemis? When I left she said she was hoping to become pregnant. Has she?'

'Geraldine will be back by Saturday. We all have dress fittings for the wedding Saturday afternoon. As for Artemis . . .' There was no longer a beaming smile on her face. 'Artemis isn't pregnant.' She rested her arms on the edge of the bath. 'And she's not going to become pregnant, either.'

Kiki's eyebrows rose.

'Rupert is sterile. He had mumps as an adult and there's no question of Artemis being able to have a baby.'

Sending scented bubbles surging, Kiki pushed herself sharply upright. 'Then why was Artemis so full of how she wanted a baby straight away? That's why she's no longer interested in modelling, isn't it? Because she wanted to fall pregnant as soon as possible? Didn't she realize what his having had mumps as an adult could mean?'

Primmie's face was grave, her eyes troubled. 'He didn't tell her, Kiki. Not until a few days ago.'

Kiki opened her mouth to speak, but no words came. At

126

her second attempt, she said, 'What a bastard! What an absolute, utter *bastard*!'

It was so true that Primmie had nothing to say. At last she said, scraping round for a mitigating circumstance, 'Perhaps Rupert didn't tell her before they were married in case Artemis would no longer want to marry him and he was frightened of losing her.'

Kiki slid back down in the bath again, bubbles rippling up round her shoulders. 'That doesn't make things better, Primmie. It makes things worse. It means he was *deliberately* deceptive – and deceptive about something he must have known would be whackingly important to Artemis. It's not as if she's one of life's career girls, is it? The modelling was just something very Chelsea set for her to do until she married.'

This again was so true that Primmie again remained silent. Kiki put her champagne glass down on the edge of the bath, swirled the water and the bubbles round with her hand and then said meditatively, 'Do you think she'll leave him because of it? She could work as a model again and move back in with us – it is her flat, after all.'

Aware that it was possibly a scenario that Kiki, who had always thought Rupert Gower an upper-class wanker, would like to see happen, Primmie said, 'Artemis won't leave him. She's in love with him – and if she begins to believe that he didn't tell her before they were married because he was terrified of losing her, she'll forgive him absolutely.'

'But at the moment she's grief stricken about it. Right?'

'Oh yes,' Primmie said, remembering the way Artemis had cried and cried and cried. 'She's devastated. She's heartbroken about not having children. I don't think she's ever going to get over it.'

'And you, Primmie? What about your love life? What's happening there?'

Primmie flushed, wishing with all her heart that Simon had telephoned Kiki with the news of their pending engagement. Knowing it would be out of order for her to say anything until Simon had had the chance to break the news to Kiki himself, she said, 'My love life is wonderful, but I can't talk about it just yet. Maybe in another couple of days . . .'

Kiki eyed her in amusement. That Primmie had had a secret

relationship ever since her early days at BBDO was something she had cottoned on to long ago. As Primmie wasn't secretive by nature, the only conclusion she'd been able to come to was that the guy in question was married. And, if the flush of excitement in Primmie's cheeks was anything to go by, wasn't going to be married for too much longer.

'Is he older than you?' she asked, voicing another long-held suspicion.

Primmie's flush deepened. 'He's forty-three,' she said and then, as if terrified of giving away any more, she stood up, saying, 'Shall I put some pasta on? You must be starving.'

'Pasta would be super – and don't worry about the age difference between you and your bloke, Primmie. As long as he makes you happy, go for it!'

'Thanks, Kiki.' Primmie paused at the bathroom door and shot her a blinding smile. 'I'm going to.'

The next morning as Kiki backed her oyster-pink Mini Cooper out of the flat's communal underground garage she was still seethingly angry at the thought of Artemis's heartache. She'd realized when Artemis and Rupert had first become a couple that Rupert had little knowledge of the real Artemis. He'd fallen in love with a soignée, beautiful, blue-eyed blonde, who sexually had played very hard to get and whose outward demeanour was the last thing in cool, sophisticated chic.

In reality, of course, the cool, sophisticated chic was merely a façade learned at modelling school behind which Artemis skilfully hid her many insecurities. Rupert thought he had netted himself a model destined to become as well known as Twiggy or Jean Shrimpton – models as famous as the pop stars and actors they associated with. Instead, he had netted someone who, now she had gained impeccable social standing, was totally uninterested in being anything other than an indulged wife and a doting mother.

Right from the very beginning it hadn't been a marriage made in heaven. Now it seemed a marriage destined for disaster.

She pulled out into the busy traffic of Kensington High

Street, the sun roof open. Denied the pleasure of speeding she turned on the eight-track tape player that took up most of the dashboard, and the sound of Little Richard giving vent to 'Baby Face', blasted from the speakers. As pedestrians turned their heads to see just where the cacophony of noise was coming from, Kiki grinned. Where rock was concerned, the old numbers were the best. She just had to convince Aled Carter of it.

'You're not listening, Kiki.' Aled Carter, short, fat and full of frenetic energy, stubbed a cigar out in a giant glass ashtray and sent his swivel-chair revolving, as if doing so would give him time to control his temper. When he was again facing her, he slapped a hand down on his oversized desk. 'A star appearance on Saturday night TV is a gift. It's absolutely non-negotiable. And you should be on your knees thanking me for it.'

'Well, I'm not. Variety shows are crap TV and *The Arthur Haynes Show* is barely one up from the Black and White Minstrels.'

Mutinously she stood at the far side of his desk. She was wearing tight-fitting jeans tucked into lizard-skin boots and a T-shirt covered in royal-blue sequins. Her lipstick was sporting pink, her eyeliner jade, her eye shadow fuchsia.

The rainbow of colours left Aled unimpressed. He tightened his lips and breathed in hard. 'Don't push me, Kiki. You're not a big enough star – and you never will be if you don't start doing as you're told. I indulged you in holding off recording an album until you had enough Lane/Grant material to go into a studio with, even though it caused havoc with your recording contract. Now you're telling me there *is* no material – and not likely to be until some unspecified date. You've only had two hit records, Kiki. They were big, but not so big they won't swiftly be forgotten if an album isn't released pretty damn quick. I've been busy liaising with Kit, putting together a package I think we can go with.'

With pudgy fingers, he held a sheet of paper towards her. 'Cast your eye over the songwriters and here's a tape. Eight of the tracks are brand new. The rest are covers. And this is

129

the way it's gotta be, Kiki. Lane/Grant tracks are gonna have to be for album two.' He paused and then said meaningfully; 'That is if there *is* an album two.'

Not remotely unnerved, Kiki handed him back his type-written list, slid the tape into her back pocket and eyeballed him stonily. 'You haven't come up with one decent name.'

'Whom were you hoping for?' he shot back sarcastically. 'Burt Bacharach and Hal David?'

'Maybe. At the very least Carol King or Don Black.'

He breathed in hard. 'The day will come, Kiki, but it isn't today.' As if the subject had been satisfactorily resolved, he spun his chair round again and this time, when again facing her, said, 'As for *The Arthur Haynes Show.* You'll do it. The exposure is huge.'

With rare self-control, she remained silent, knowing that argument would be a complete waste of time.

He wasn't fooled into thinking that she was now seeing things from his point of view. 'Rock stars have a short shelf-life,' he said bluntly. 'All-round family entertainers stay the course. Don't be your own worst enemy, Kiki. Don't think you know best where your career is concerned, because you don't.'

She gave an ungracious lift of her shoulders. Choosing to take it to mean she was now OK with things he flashed his teeth in what passed for a smile. 'And your one o'clock lunch date with Kit is off. He has summer flu.'

'Has the table been cancelled?'

'No. Not yet. Why?'

'Because I haven't seen my father in over three months and if Kit's cancelled I might as well meet up with him, instead.'

She swung out of the office, knowing she was doing so for what was near to the last time. Aled might genuinely believe he knew what was best for her, but lightweight songs and variety shows were not the way she wanted to go – and that meant that he and she were going to have to split up.

'Bye, Kiki,' Aled's secretary said to her as she marched through reception.

Kiki raised a hand in response and seconds later was in the street. Quite simply, she didn't have to put up with all the shit Aled was dishing out. He hadn't been responsible for the

130

success of her first two records. Francis had been managing her when she'd achieved her breakthrough successes. All Aled had done was to capitalize on the success she and Francis had achieved – if sending her off to Australia for two months and thinking that getting her a spot on *The Arthur Haynes Show* could be called capitalizing.

Knowing what it was she was going to do the instant Francis returned to London, she didn't head immediately for her parked Mini, but for the nearest phone box.

'I'm back, Simon,' she was saying three minutes later. 'How do you fancy lunch at Mr Chow's?'

A group of American tourists descended on her as she walked across the pavement towards the restaurant.

'Kiki! *Kiki!*' they whooped, surrounding her in a flurry of excitement, searching in pockets and bags for something she could autograph.

She obliged them with gusto, seeing, with a real buzz, that her father was approaching down the street and was witnessing the adulation she was receiving.

He hung back until her fans finally allowed her to continue across the pavement.

'My goodness, does that sort of thing happen often?' he asked as they walked into the restaurant together.

'Fairly,' she said, trying to sound cool about it and not give away the thrill it had given her for him to see her in pop star mode.

Once they were seated at a table, he said, 'How was Australia? Did you get to see much of it?'

'I saw dusty small-town airports, dusty dressing rooms and scores of hotel bedrooms that all looked the same,' she said, doing a recce of the restaurant. 'I didn't have a day off – or not one when I wasn't travelling from one town to another – in the entire two months I was there. The road crew were hell and the weather was worse. I don't like sun, not day in and day out with temperatures zooming off the scale.'

'Oh!' he looked disconcerted.

He also, she noticed, looked very out of place in Mr Chow's. He was wearing grey flannels and a tweed jacket with elbow patches. As he pushed a lock of floppy fair hair away from

131

his forehead, she found herself looking for signs of grey. There weren't any, and neither was he going bald. If only he didn't dress like an old fogey he would still, she thought, be passably attractive.

'So when did you arrive back?' he was saying. 'Yesterday?' She nodded, still recce-ing the room. Dudley Moore was seated with a young woman at a nearby table but, as she didn't know him, there was no kudos to be gained from his proximity. An agent she knew slightly was having lunch. He caught her eye, briefly acknowledging her presence. It wasn't quite the in-crowd atmosphere her ego needed. Then the door opened and Davy Jones of The Monkees breezed in, Peter Tork, Mike Nesmith and Micky Dolenz behind him.

She'd been on the same bill with them at a concert at Wembley Arena and, as heads turned and the atmosphere at their presence became electric, she simply made eye contact with Davy and enjoyed the next few minutes with almost orgasmic pleasure.

'Kiki!' Davy hollered, ignoring the headwaiter, who had rushed towards him, and heading straight towards her table. 'How was Aussie-land? Great to see you. Now you're back we'll have to meet up. We're staying at the Savoy and heading back to the States in a week.'

Every eye in the room was on them, as well it might be. The Monkees' last album had sold over three million copies. They were as big as the Beatles. Bigger than the Rolling Stones. What was more, they were greeting her as a fellow performer and her father was there to see it. It was a high better than anything she'd ever experienced on cocaine or LSD.

When the mini-reunion was over and the headwaiter had steered Davy, Peter, Mike and Micky to a reserved table at the back of the room, Simon said bemusedly, 'Who are they?'

She stared at him.

'Are they a pop group?' he asked helpfully.

'They're The Monkees,' she said at last, in a strangled voice. 'Don't you know *anything*, Daddy?'

It was the first time she'd called him 'Daddy' in years and was a sign of just how truly shocked she was by his ignorance.

'Surely you've seen their TV series?' she said, regaining her breath. 'And don't you remember seeing them on the TV when they first arrived in England? There were thousands of screaming fans at Heathrow to meet them.'

A young man stepping up to their table interrupted them. 'I know this is a very uncool thing for me to do when you're dining,' he said, handing his menu to her, 'but would you sign it for me?'

It *was* an uncool thing to do, but Kiki didn't mind. Flashing him a brilliant smile she signed the menu with a flourish.

When they were on their own again Simon said, bewildered, 'Does this sort of thing ever let up?'

'No,' she said. 'I'm a pop star.' She remembered her confrontation with Aled. 'I'm a *rock* star,' she amended, deciding it was high time she began making the distinction.

'And you're happy?'

Her eyes widened fractionally. It was a question she could never remember him having asked before. 'Yes.' Being forced to think about it made her realize that she wasn't one hundred per cent happy – and wouldn't be until she'd ditched Aled and was again being managed by Francis. That, though, was now only a matter of time. 'Are you?' she asked, to take the heat off herself.

'Yes.' He leaned across the table towards her, his hands clasped in front of him. 'I'm very happy, Kiki. Happier than I've ever been before in my life.'

'Great,' she said, embarrassed by his unexpected intensity. 'Shall we order?'

'Not until I tell you why I'm so happy.'

He looked nervous as well as intense and suddenly she knew what was coming. He'd found himself a girlfriend. Was perhaps even thinking of getting married again.

'Do we have to have this conversation here?' she said, her stomach coiling in knots. 'Won't it wait?'

He shook his head, his grey eyes holding hers steadily. 'No, Kiki. It won't wait. It's waited too long.'

'You've got yourself a girlfriend,' she said, wondering why the idea was so repugnant to her. 'And you want to introduce me to her.'

'I've got myself a fiancée,' he said, a pulse throbbing at

the corner of his jaw. 'And I don't have to introduce you to her. You already know her.'

She stared at him blankly, wondering if he was speaking of one of her mother's friends, or one of his patients. Dozens of them were divorced or widowed ladies of a certain age, but no one likely came to mind.

'As I don't know anyone over the age of twenty-five,' she said, 'it isn't likely that I do.'

His hands, on the stiffly starched tablecloth, were clasped so tightly that the knuckles shone white.

'She isn't over the age of twenty-five.'

She stared at him. 'I don't think I heard you correctly,' she said at last, in a voice that seemed to come from a great distance.

'She isn't over the age of twenty-five.' He shot her a sheepish grin, took a deep breath and said, 'It's Primmie.'

She continued to stare at him, this time blankly, truly not understanding. 'Primmie? The woman you're engaged to works with Primmie?'

He shook his head. 'No, Kiki,' he said gently. 'It's Primmie I'm in love with. It's Primmie I'm going to marry.'

She opened her mouth to speak, but no sound came. Struggling to breathe, beginning to hyperventilate, she clumsily pushed her chair away from the table. 'Oh God!' she gasped, struggling to her feet. 'Oh Christ!'

His grin vanished to be replaced by agonized concern. 'Kiki, please don't be so distressed!' He rose abruptly, painfully aware that every eye in the room was now on them. 'I know it must be a shock to you, but it isn't anything sudden. It isn't something Primmie and I are rushing into.'

'How long?' She was shaking as if she had a fever, her brilliantly bold make-up no longer dazzlingly eye catching, but bizarrely garish on a face drained of blood. 'How long have you and she . . . have you and she . . .'

She couldn't finish the sentence. It conjured up too many ghastly images. Primmie and Simon in love and in bed together. Primmie and *her father* in bed together. When had it started? After the four of them had moved into Artemis's flat? Or had it been before? Had it been when they'd still been in the sixth form and Primmie had been at Petts Wood from Monday to Friday? Had it been going on before her mother had left home?

'You can't do it! I won't let you do it!' She felt as if she were plunging into a bottomless pit. 'I will never, ever, speak to you or see you again, not as long as I live, if you marry ... marry ...' Appallingly she found she couldn't say Primmie's name. 'It's indecent!' She was crying now, oblivious to the embarrassed waiters hovering nearby. 'It's obscene. And the press will think it's obscene, too. There'll be "Rock star's GP father marries her best friend" headlines. And if they get to know that Primmie lived with us weekdays from the age of eleven ...'

The horror in her eyes was now equally matched by the horror in his and suddenly she knew that the pit wasn't bottomless; that there was hope.

She sucked in a deep, shuddering breath. 'Can't you see what the press will make of it?' she said urgently. 'There'll be ugly rumours. The General Medical Council may get involved. You could be struck off.'

For a second he merely stared at her like a man poleaxed and then, ashen-faced, he began propelling her out of the restaurant, pushing her past the waiters, desperate to be out of earshot of their fellow diners.

On the pavement she swung towards him with such force she nearly fell, her face made childishly clownish by runnels of tear-streaked mascara and jade eyeliner. 'Don't you see now how wrong it would be?' she persisted passionately. 'It would mean Primmie would be my stepmother! Promise me you won't do it. Promise me.'

'I have to have time to think, Kiki.' A fit forty-three-year-old when he'd entered Mr Chow's, he now looked sixty. 'Primmie has brought me so much happiness ...'

'But you're old enough to be her father!' She saw him flinch and didn't care. 'You're not being fair to her. You're not being fair to me.' Tears rolled mercilessly down her cheeks. 'Mummy running off with that Reece woman was bad enough, but this ... this will emotionally *destroy* me!'

He'd never known her cry before, not even when she'd been a little girl, and he couldn't bear it. As if she were a child again he put his arms round her, swamped by doubts and suspicions held at bay for months.

'You may be right,' he said at last, thinking of the press attention Kiki now attracted. Thinking of the way his neighbours and patients would react to the news that he was marrying a girl they regarded as being a close member of his family. Thinking of how if he broke off his relationship with her Primmie would have the opportunity of falling in love with someone of her own age. Thinking of how Kiki would be spared hurt that was, quite obviously, intolerable.

He closed his eyes, not wanting to think of the lonely years ahead or of the expression on Primmie's face as he broke the news to her.

'You won't marry her, will you, Daddy? Promise me. *Promise* me!'

It was her use of the childhood diminutive that finally finished him.

'No,' he said defeated as a bus rattled past them. 'No, Kiki. I won't marry Primmie.'

'Promise?' she said again, her voice so tense it was easy to believe that her life depended on his answer.

'I promise,' he said heavily, wondering how, in the name of all that was holy, he was ever going to be happy again.

Fourteen

May 1972

Geraldine curled her naked feet beneath her as she settled herself comfortably on the sofa in the Kensington flat. She was wearing an ankle-length kaftan embroidered in red silk roses and, low across her forehead, a broad bandeau of intricately patterned jet and turquoise beads. Her sleek black hair was waterfall straight and waist-length, her skin golden.

'Nepal and Kathmandu were heaven, Primmie, but it's good

to be home,' she said, swirling ice cubes round in a glass of gin and tonic. 'Francis has taken up the sitar and I've learned a few words of Hindi. Neither ability is going to be of much use to us, but it's been fun. Francis was suspected of being a CIA agent in Afghanistan and nearly converted to Buddhism in Tibet.'

Instead of collapsing into giggles, Primmie smiled. Coming from Primmie it was a rather lacklustre response.

Geraldine put her glass down and pushed herself a little further upright against the cushions. 'Is anything wrong, Primmie?' she asked, 'or have I just been away too long? When I phoned Kiki from the airport she only wanted to speak to Francis, and when I phoned Artemis she sounded as if she'd been crying, though when I asked she said she had a cold and that you'd fill me in on what's been happening. By which I assume she means between her and Rupert. What gives?'

Primmie, seated on the floor in front of the fireplace, its grate empty save for a jug crammed with white carnations, hugged her knees. 'I've barely seen Kiki since she got back from Australia on Monday. Where was she when you phoned her?'

'Aled Carter's office.'

'Umm. She isn't too happy at the moment with the way he's managing her career. I expect that's why she's so keen to speak to Francis. She'll want his advice. As for Artemis . . .' She paused. She appreciated that Artemis found it a difficult subject to talk about, but, even so, she wished Artemis had felt able to tell Geraldine herself. 'She and Rupert aren't able to have a family,' she said at last. 'He had mumps some years ago and has been sterile ever since.'

Geraldine's jaw dropped. 'And he didn't *tell* her? Before they were married, I mean.'

'No. She only found out a couple of weeks ago.'

Geraldine's eyes held hers, horrified. 'Dear God,' she said at last. 'No wonder Artemis sounded as if she had been crying.' She regarded Primmie sombrely. 'Is that why you're in such an odd mood, Prim? Because you're distressed on Artemis's behalf?'

Primmie hugged her knees a little tighter. 'I *am* distressed on Artemis's behalf. Who wouldn't be? But I'm also on edge because I thought I was going to be making the most wonderful

137

announcement this week – and now it's going to have to be put off because Simon is ill and has gone away to recuperate and so hasn't told Kiki – and Kiki needs to be told first . . .'

'Whoa, girl.' Geraldine shifted position, sitting bolt upright and cross-legged. 'Why has Kiki to be told first? And where does Simon come in? And why are you looking as if you're about to burst if you don't get it all off your chest?'

'Because I *am* about to burst if I don't get it all off my chest. I'm so happy . . . I've been happy for so long, and yet I've never been able to tell anyone and now, when I thought I *would* be telling everyone, I'm on hold again because Simon's gone down with a viral infection and has gone away for a few days to get over it.'

Geraldine stared at her. 'Are you telling me that your being happy has something to do with Simon?'

Primmie bit her lip, her eyes glowing.

Geraldine sucked in a deep, unsteady breath. 'Dear heaven, Prim. You've been a bit of a dark horse, haven't you? You and Simon?'

Primmie nodded.

'And Kiki doesn't know?'

'No one knows. That's what's been so hard, Geraldine. Simon never wanted anyone to know. Now, though, it's different. We're going to get married and Simon has been waiting for Kiki to get back from Australia so that he can finally put her in the picture.'

'And now he's ill and can't do so?'

Primmie's radiant glow ebbed. 'He rang me Monday evening to say that he wasn't well and was going to go away for a few days. He sounded terrible, really ill, so ill he forgot to tell me where he was going. I rang him back when I realized, but he'd already put his phone on answer. As he didn't ring me again, I can only imagine he went away that night.'

'And Kiki doesn't know?'

Primmie looked despairing. 'No. Not that I've been able to talk to her properly since Monday, because I haven't. She's been in meetings of one kind or another all week. On Wednesday night she was on *Top of the Pops*. On Thursday she was in rehearsals with new session musicians until way past midnight and then she flew off to Newcastle to record a

138

pop programme for Tyne Tees TV. She only got back in town this morning – and then she went straight to see Aled Carter without coming here first.'

'There are telephones,' Geraldine said gently, as if Primmie might have forgotten about them.

'Getting hold of Kiki on the phone is impossible. If she's in a meeting or in a studio or in rehearsals the calls are never put through.'

'I wasn't thinking of Kiki. I was thinking of Simon.'

'Simon?'

'When Kiki was in Australia. Couldn't Simon have phoned her then, and told her about you and him?'

'Well, he could, but he didn't want to do it that way. He wanted to tell her face to face. After all, it is pretty momentous news, isn't it?'

'Yes.' Geraldine reached for her gin and tonic. 'Yes,' she said again, keeping her voice studiedly neutral. 'In fact, "pretty momentous" is something of an understatement.'

'And you're pleased for me?'

Aware that she hadn't yet congratulated Primmie, Geraldine flashed her a blinding smile. 'Of course I'm pleased for you, Prim,' she said sincerely. 'Simon is a wonderful person and, if you love him, he's a very lucky man. Do we have any champagne in?'

Primmie nodded, her face radiant, her anxiety over Simon's health put on hold as she was able to indulge in the sheer joy of being congratulated on her pending engagement.

'Great. Let's crack a bottle open and celebrate.'

As Primmie sprang eagerly to her feet and headed for the kitchen, Geraldine's smile faded. Primmie's news *was* great, because despite the age difference she felt sure Primmie and Simon would make each other very happy. The problem was Kiki. What was Kiki's reaction going to be when her father told her he was going to marry Primmie? Primmie didn't seem to be anticipating it as a problem, but she, Geraldine, wasn't at all sure that she was right in not doing so. Kiki was totally promiscuous where her own sex life was concerned, but that didn't mean to say she wouldn't be surprisingly old fashioned when it came to her father's. Though it clearly hadn't occurred to Primmie, she thought it possible Kiki would take huge

139

exception to the idea of her being her stepmother – and if she did, how was Primmie going to handle it?

'Goodness, aren't you gloriously suntanned?' Artemis said enviously as she and Geraldine drew apart after an enormous hug. 'Even if I'd been to India, my skin would never go such a gorgeous honey colour. It would just go an ugly red and peel.'

'That's because you're a natural blonde and have the type of skin that looks best English rose pale.'

Even as she said the last word, she regretted it, for Artemis's beautifully etched face was far too pale and there were dark shadows beneath her eyes.

'Has Primmie told you?' Artemis said, as if reading her thoughts.

Geraldine nodded. 'I'm sorry, Artemis. Terribly, terribly sorry.'

'We'll adopt, of course. We'll have to, won't we?'

Her eyes were overly bright and it was obvious she was near to tears. As they were at the dressmakers, with the bridesmaids' dresses and Geraldine's grandmother's wedding dress spread all around them, ready to be fitted for the last time, it wasn't the best place to give in to crying.

'Did Kiki say how she would be getting here, Primmie?' Geraldine looked down at her watch, giving Artemis a moment or two to get herself under control.

Primmie, lovingly admiring the cobweb-delicate, French lace wedding dress, turned reluctantly away from it. 'She didn't say. When I told her about it, on Monday, she said she'd be back from Newcastle mid-morning and I just assumed she'd be at the flat by the time Artemis called by and that we'd all three come here together.'

Geraldine turned to her patiently waiting dressmaker. 'We'll just have to start without her, Antonella. Whom do you want to fit first? Me or my bridesmaids?'

'The bridesmaids, I think,' Antonella said, a large pincushion strapped to her left wrist. 'Miss Surtees's size has been constant right from her first visit and I think there will be very little adjustment to make to her dress, but Mrs Gower's weight looks as if it might have gone up a little.'

Artemis flushed, well aware she'd begun comfort eating. 'It has,' she said bleakly. 'But not for any nice reason.'

No one said anything. The dressmaker was silent because she was busy taking Artemis's dress off its padded hanger and Primmie and Geraldine were silent because they knew to what Artemis was referring and there was no appropriate response they could make.

When the long process of the final fitting of Primmie's, and Artemis's dresses was over, Geraldine said, 'There's no need for you both to stay whilst my dress is adjusted. It's bound to take an absolute age. Are you able to stay at the flat tonight, Artemis? It would mean we could all go out for an Italian this evening.'

'I'd love to,' Artemis said sincerely, 'especially if there was a chance of Francis being with us as well, but I can't. Rupert and I have had an awful week. He just can't seem to understand why I'm so upset. He says having babies isn't the be-all and end-all of everything and that if he'd known I was only getting married in order to become pregnant he wouldn't have married me.' Her voice wobbled. 'He doesn't mean it, of course, and he knows I didn't really only get married so that I could become pregnant, but I did think that when I was married I'd be able to have babies. Surely everyone who gets married thinks they can have babies?'

'You will have babies,' Geraldine said positively. 'You'll adopt lots and lots of the most adorable babies imaginable.'

Artemis managed an uncertain smile. 'Will it be the same, do you think? And I don't need lots and lots of babies. I'd be over the moon with just one.'

'It will be your baby and you'll love it and it will love you. And look on the bright side. It won't have inherited Rupert's total lack of simpatico. The more I think of it, Artemis, the more I think adoption will be a blessing in disguise.'

She'd been trying to make Artemis giggle and she succeeded. 'You're right, Geraldine,' she said, looking much cheered. 'I hadn't looked at it that way before. And I'll be able to choose whether I have a boy or a girl, won't I?'

'Probably. I don't have a clue about adoption procedures. Now scoot, I have a wedding dress to be fitted – and if you or Primmie run into Kiki, tell her to get over here pretty damn quick.'

Ten minutes later, standing immobile before a three-way

mirror as Antonella adjusted the seams of the Edwardian wedding dress, Geraldine was pondering two things. One was the mystery of why, having gone off on Monday to recover from a viral infection, Simon Lane hadn't been in touch with Primmie by telephone – and he hadn't, because she'd asked. And though Primmie hadn't indicated that she thought it odd, or a problem, she had been unusually quiet. The other thing occupying her mind was more important. Primmie had said Kiki wasn't happy at the way Aled Carter was managing her and that she wanted to speak to Francis about it. Primmie's assumption had been that Kiki merely wanted his advice. She, however, wasn't so sure.

Kiki had behaved as if it had been the ultimate betrayal when she'd had to find another manager and, now that she and Francis were back from India, she was primed for Kiki suggesting to Francis that he become her manager again.

And she, Geraldine, didn't want him to.

There were many reasons why. One was the drug-ridden lifestyle of the music industry. She'd always been laid back about dope. Cannabis had been a part of her life, and Francis's, since they'd been teenagers and had never, as far as she could see, done either of them any harm, but that had probably been because their lives hadn't centred around it. On the hippie trail, things had been different. There had been an uncontrolled abundance of drugs and, though she hadn't taken any of them, Francis, adopting the attitude that it was all part of the hippie experience, had indulged in them all. On the trail it had all seemed quite normal, because so many other travellers were behaving the same way. Now, however, they were back in London and about to embark on a quite different lifestyle at Cedar Court and she was determined that drugs of the hard variety were going to have no part to play in it.

Another reason for her not wanting Francis to immerse himself in Kiki's career again was the amount of time he had given to it. Back then, it hadn't mattered so much. Now, however, when she had so many plans for Cedar Court, it was very different, because what she was going to do was huge and couldn't be done alone. She was going to open the house and grounds to the public.

A rare jewel of an Elizabethan manor house, it would, she

was sure, be a great draw. The work, though, would be colossal. The overgrown gardens, though poetically lovely in their wildness, weren't the kind of gardens the public could be expected to admire. There would have to be vast re-furnishing, too, so that as much of the house as possible was in keeping with its Tudor style. And she and Francis would have to drum up as much Elizabethan family history as possible – and search out mementos of it.

All in all, it was going to be a colossal amount of work and it was work she and Francis would have to do together and that she passionately wanted them to do together. However unhappy Kiki was with Aled Carter's management of her career, she would either have to endure it or find someone else. But that someone else was not going to be Francis – of that, she'd made up her mind.

'There, I'm through,' Antonella said with satisfaction.

Geraldine looked at her reflection and knew she'd been right in opting to wear her grandmother's wedding dress instead of a fashionable mini style or a traditional crinoline-style dress. She didn't weigh a hundred pounds soaking wet and the exquisite handmade lace clung sinuously to her high, small breasts and slender hips, falling arrow-straight to skim her feet and drape into a small train. The coronet of seed pearls and hip-length veil she was to wear with it were the coronet and veil her mother and her grandmother had worn. She wouldn't look fashionable, but looking fashionable had never been her style. What she would look was distinctive and very, very Geraldine.

'Wow! You look sensational!' Kiki said, bursting into the room, wearing a black top, black pencil skirt and motorcycle boots, her legs bare.

'Are you back with Ty again?' Geraldine asked dryly, regarding Kiki's outfit with a mixture of despair and amusement. 'All you're short of is a death's head motif and an Apache headband!'

'And a Harley!' Kiki said with a grin, flinging herself down on one of the sofas Antonella provided for clients. 'I'm just back from Geordie-land. Naked legs and motorcycle boots are the in thing up there.'

'Remove them before Antonella has heart failure. This is

a dust-free zone. And while Antonella helps me out of my dress, fill me in with all the gossip. It's been nine months since I last saw you. What's new?'

'I'm a star,' Kiki said with a self-satisfied grin. 'But then, thanks to Francis, I was a star before you went away. I've just done a two-month tour of Australia. I'm off to Italy to do another tour – much shorter – the day after your wedding. Aled Carter sucks and I can't crack on with an album because we haven't got our heads together over songs.'

As she stepped free of her wedding dress and as Antonella, white-gloved, lifted it away from her, Geraldine grinned. 'Well, if that's all, I haven't missed much. Get your Gothic-looking garb off so that Antonella can give your dress a last fitting!'

'Joking apart, Geraldine, we *have* to work on some more songs,' Kiki said, tugging her black top over her head to reveal that she was bra-less. 'Because we haven't done so, Aled Carter is going to be able to make me go in a studio and record absolute tosh.'

She yanked off her motorcycle boots and tugged her skirt down. 'The new tracks Aled's come up with for my album are about as hard-edged as "I'd Like To Teach The World To Sing".'

Geraldine stepped into a flower-patterned georgette dress she'd bought in the Chelsea Antique Market and said sympathetically, 'Poor you. What are you going to do about it?'

As Antonella slid the grey silk bridesmaid dress over her head, Kiki said, 'First of all I'm going to pin you down to doing some serious songwriting and secondly I'm going to dump Aled and have Francis as my manager again.'

Geraldine smoothed the bias-cut skirt of her dress over her hips. 'That may be what you'd like, Kiki, but you're going to have to think of other options.'

As Antonella began her work of tucking and pinning, Kiki's eyebrows rose nearly into her flame-red hair. 'Just what do you mean? There *are* no other options. I need more songs in the style of "White Dress, Silver Slippers" and "Twilight Love" and I need Francis as my manager again.'

Geraldine slid her feet into a pair of gold sandals. 'The songs aren't that much of a problem – or they aren't if Aled has others in mind for the album you're about to record. By the time there's a follow-up album, we'll have songs for it. Where Francis is concerned, though, the problem isn't so easily solved.'

Kiki sucked in her breath, her nostrils whitening. 'You'd better explain why quickly to me, Geraldine, and it had better be good. You're not dragging him off on another bloody hippie trail, are you, to South America or Tibet?'

'No.' Geraldine's beautifully boned face was grave. 'Francis and I are going to live at Cedar Court after the wedding. You've always known that was our plan. And we're going to open the house and grounds to the public.'

'So?' Kiki stepped out of reach of Antonella's ministrations. 'Just because Francis will be living at Cedar Court instead of in town, doesn't mean he can't manage me. He won't be giving up his flat in town, will he? And if it really comes to it, he could have a helicopter. The parkland at Cedar Court is big enough to land a jumbo jet!'

Antonella, unable to continue with the fitting, began tapping a foot impatiently.

Geraldine knew just how she felt.

'There's no need to fly into a tantrum, Kiki,' she said, keeping her voice steady with difficulty. 'Francis never intended being your manager long term. It was just something that it suited him to do at the time. From now on, all his time and energy are going to be taken up with turning Cedar Court into a miniature Penshurst or Hever Castle. It's something I can't do on my own. I need him to help me do it.'

'Well, I jolly well need him too!'

Eyes blazing, Kiki yanked the dress up and over her head with such carelessness that Antonella shouted in horror and rushed forward to lift it away from her.

'Everything in my life is going haywire at the moment,' Kiki continued explosively, dragging on her skirt. 'I have to record an album and do you give a shit that there are no decent songs for it?' She pulled her black top any old how over her already tousled hair. 'No. You couldn't care less. As for Francis . . .' She thrust her feet into the motorcycle boots. 'Cedar Court is your obsession, Geraldine, not his. Francis *loved* being in the music business. He *loved* being my manager. And he wants to be my manager again.'

She stormed across to the door and yanked it open. 'And do you know how I know?' she demanded. 'I know because I've already asked him and he's already said there's nothing he'd like better!'

The door slammed behind her with such force the whole room seemed to rock.

After a long, embarrassed silence, Antonella cleared her throat. 'The dress,' she said, Kiki's bridesmaid dress still in her arms. 'I'd hardly begun the fitting . . .'

'Don't worry.' White-lipped, Geraldine picked up her handbag. 'Kiki will come back so that you can fit it properly or, if she doesn't, and if the dress isn't perfect, it will be her fault, Antonella, not yours.'

She didn't drive back to the flat. Instead, she headed out of London, towards Sussex and Cedar Court. At Horsham she drew up near a telephone box and phoned Primmie.

'Kiki and I have just had words,' she said, knowing it was an understatement but wanting to keep it brief. 'I've got a million and one wedding plans to verify and check and as it will be easier to do it all from Cedar Court, that's where I'm going. Bye, God Bless.'

Ringing off before Primmie could ask what the angry words had been over, she rang Francis at his Chelsea flat, which was where she had left him. There was no reply.

With a headache of major proportions beginning to build up behind her eyes, she returned to her car and continued driving towards Sussex, well aware that she had a problem of major proportions on her hands.

Kiki's temper had always been explosive, but she could never remember ever having had such a nasty exchange with her. Even worse, the issue they were over had been serious, because Kiki had been right when she'd said that Francis had loved the music business and being a part of it as her manager. Rubbing shoulders with rock stars like The Stones and The Beatles had given him an enormous buzz, and when it had come to launching Kiki's solo career he'd shown a natural talent for promotion and networking. But that wasn't what she wanted. All their lives she'd either kept Francis out of trouble or got him out of it, and with instinct she trusted implicitly she knew that the music industry – and the hard drugs so freely available in it – was no place for Francis to be.

Once at Cedar Court, where her uncle, knee-deep in the wedding preparations her mother was frantically making on her behalf, was deeply relieved to see her, she rang Francis again.

Again, there was no reply.

'Why would he be at his flat?' her Uncle Piers asked, mystified. 'I know he spent last night there, but that was because you'd both landed at Heathrow disgustingly late. I haven't seen the wretched boy for nine months and I expected him to be here by now. Where the devil is he?'

If Kiki really had asked him to be her manager again, then she could only have done so that morning. Had he, instead of either remaining at the flat so that they could meet up after her visit to the dressmakers, or driving down ahead of her to Cedar Court, arranged to meet up with Kiki so that they could talk things over further? And if he had, was he going to be so hyper at the thought of being part of the rock world again that talking him out of it was going to be a real problem?

With a level of anxiety that was completely foreign to her, she rang the Kensington flat.

Primmie answered the phone.

'Hi, Prim. Is Kiki with you?'

'No. Are things seriously wrong between you and her?'

'I'm not sure.' It was, Geraldine reflected, the stark truth. 'Is anything wrong your end, Prim? You're voice sounds odd and I've never known you be as quiet as you were this morning when your dress was being fitted.'

There was a slight pause and then Primmie said, echoing her, 'I'm not sure. It's just that Simon still hasn't returned home. He phoned me last night to say that he's not going to be back until the wedding.'

'My wedding, or his and yours?' Geraldine said, making the effort to put a bit of their usual banter into the conversation.

'Yours.' Unusually for her, Primmie didn't giggle. 'He says whatever the bug that's laid him low, it's left him feeling whacked and he doesn't want to put himself back into circulation too quickly. And he says that when he comes back there are lots of things he wants to talk to me about.'

'Well, yes. I suppose there will be. Wedding preparations can be pretty hectic. I don't know how I would have managed if it hadn't been for my mother doing everything for me whilst I was away.'

There was no chirpy response.

'Is there something else, Primmie?' she said at last. 'Something you're not telling me?'

'Yes. I didn't mean to break the news like this – before I've even told Simon – but I'm pregnant, Geraldine.'

Geraldine sucked in her breath sharply and Primmie said hurriedly, 'It isn't a problem, Geraldine. I'm happy about it – in fact, I'm overjoyed about it, but it has happened at a bad time. It isn't news I want to break to Simon over the phone – and I'd much rather not be telling him until he's spoken to Kiki and set his mind at rest that she's going to be happy for us. Then there's Artemis. How can I tell Artemis that I'm having a baby when she's so distraught about not being able to have one of her own?'

It was a question Geraldine didn't have an answer for. She was too busy trying to get her head round the fact that Primmie's baby would be Kiki's half-sister.

The sound of Francis's sports car, speeding towards the house through the parkland, brought her concentration smartly back to her own problems.

'I must go, Prim. I can hear Francis's car. I'll ring you again this evening. Love you. Bye.'

'Not before time, boy,' her Uncle Piers said minutes later, striding out of the house ahead of her, to greet his only child. 'It's a miracle to me you didn't come to grief in the Khyber Pass, or the Himalayas, or whatever other godforsaken place it is you've been to – and I suppose I've Geraldine to thank for the fact you haven't!' He hugged Francis tightly. 'And why is your hair on your shoulders?' he demanded irascibly. 'You can't get married looking like that. You'll be mistaken for the bride!'

'Don't worry, Dad. I'll be wearing it in a ponytail on the great day.' He winked at Geraldine. 'I knew you'd be here, Ger. I came as soon as poss.'

Geraldine walked across to them and slid her arm round Francis's waist. 'Have you been having a meeting with Kiki?' she asked, not allowing a trace of tension to show in her voice.

'You're a witch. How did you guess?'

His father was now stomping back into the house and, with his arm round her shoulders and hers still round his waist, Francis began walking her across the courtyard towards the gardens and the parkland that lay beyond them.

'She told me she'd spoken to you when I saw her at the dressmakers this morning.' For the first time in her life, Geraldine found that keeping her voice casual was an enormous effort. '

'And so it's not going to come as too much of a shock to you when I tell you that I'm going to be managing her again?' He was looking down at her as he spoke, and he was smiling.

They had only reached the grey and white garden – but Geraldine came to an abrupt halt.

'She did tell me, but I didn't believe her.'

'Because it clashes with our plans for Cedar Court?'

'Because it isn't what we'd planned.'

He made an awkward grimace. 'It won't make too much difference. I won't be managing a whole stable of singers and bands. It will only be Kiki. And she's good, Geraldine. Aled Carter is trying to present her as an all-round family entertainer, and for Kiki that's the kiss of death. Wholesomeness isn't what she's about. She's a British Janis Joplin. A hard-edged, badass chick!'

Geraldine bit back a tart response with difficulty.

His grey eyes pleaded for her understanding. 'My managing Kiki and your organizing things here at Cedar Court could be run in tandem. And think of the pop parties we could have. If we started the organizing now we could hold a huge pop festival here next spring. The Duke of Bedford's Festival of the Flower Children at Woburn attracted twenty-five thousand people. Even if entry was kept down to a pound apiece, the sums are magic.'

At the thought of thousands of hippies, out of their brains on dope, ploughing up Cedar Court's gardens and parkland and trashing them into a quagmire, Geraldine went paper white.

'It isn't what I want, Francis. You said yourself that when

149

Kiki appeared at the Shepton Mallet Festival the place was a mudslide . . . and all festivals attract Hell's Angels. The thought of droves of them descending on Cedar Court is unbearable. It isn't what Cedar Court is about.'

'OK,' he said ruefully, tilting her face to his and kissing her. 'No pop festival.'

'And no managing Kiki's career?' Her arms were round his neck, her mouth still only a fraction from his.

He winced, as if in pain. 'Kiki's a hard lady to say no to.'

'Then don't,' she said huskily, pressing close against him. 'Let me do it for you.'

With a deep sigh of acquiescence, he slid his hand over the thin material of her dress, cupping a small breast in his hand. 'Are you always going to fight all my battles for me?' he murmured, amusement as well as desire in his voice.

'Always,' she whispered, in the second before his mouth closed on hers in a long, deep, arousing kiss.

For the next week she was rushed off her feet as she helped her mother finalize all the wedding arrangements. Francis opted to stay in his Chelsea flat as, once again, the caterers moved in to Cedar Court and a magnificent, medieval-looking marquee was erected and fireworks were set in position all along the banks of the ha-ha. The wedding itself was to take place in the nearby village church, and there, too, decorations were under way.

'How you managed arranging a wedding at St Margaret's, Westminster, is beyond me,' she said to Artemis, over the phone. 'The choirboy who is singing the solo has gone down with flu. The vicar has suddenly informed me that he isn't happy for confetti to be thrown in the churchyard and Primmie's bridesmaid dress still hasn't been delivered.'

'Well, mine has,' Artemis had said, pacifyingly. 'The main thing is, has Kiki's dress arrived? And does it fit?'

'Yes, to your first query. I don't know, to the second.'

Kiki, in many more ways than one, was proving to be a major problem. As she hadn't returned for a final fitting of her dress, Antonella had simply finished it off without any of the last-minute fastidious attention Artemis's and Primmie's dresses had received.

'Are you telling me you haven't seen her all week?' she asked Primmie when she phoned her for what was their ritual nightly chat.

'No. She's begun recording her album and is working, eating and sleeping at the studio.'

'And Simon? Have you heard from him?'

'Yes. He'll be back the night before the wedding, so we're going to meet up at the church.'

'And Kiki? Has he broken the news of your engagement to her yet?'

'No.' Primmie sounded bewildered. 'It isn't something he'd ever do over the phone, Geraldine. Just as I'm not going to tell him about the baby over the phone.'

'Yah. Right. Of course. Bye, Primmie. I'll speak to you tomorrow.'

It had been a phone call Geraldine had pondered over for quite a long time. Kiki 'working, eating and sleeping' at the studio sounded very much to her as if Kiki were avoiding Primmie. If she were, there could only be one reason for it: that unknown to Primmie, Simon had already told Kiki their news and Kiki was having problems with it. Worse, the problems were such that Simon was having second thoughts, hence his disappearance off the scene – not because he was ill, but because he was giving himself time to reconsider Primmie's and his future. All in all, the scenario didn't bode well for Primmie's happiness and nor did it help with her own patience levels where Kiki was concerned.

Every phone call she made trying to contact her ended in failure. Kiki was either recording or not at the studio – and if she wasn't at the studio, no one at the studio knew where she was. Not until the following Wednesday, three days before the wedding, did she finally succeed in reaching her, via Kit.

'Hi, Geraldine,' Kiki said laconically when she came to the telephone. 'I hope you're not phoning fussing about the dress, because it's going to be fine.'

'Great. It isn't what I'm phoning about, though. I know Francis told you he'd take over managing you again, but he hadn't thought it through when he said it. It just can't be done, Kiki.'

There was a short, tense pause, and then Kiki said in a

151

voice dripping ice, 'Are you telling me that you've strong-armed him into changing his mind, Geraldine?'

'I'm telling you Francis has changed his mind, Kiki.'

'If he has, you've changed it for him!'

As denying it would have been untruthful, Geraldine said with all the patience she could summon, 'It isn't the end of the world, Kiki. You'll find someone else. It will be easy, now you have so many contacts in the business.'

'I don't want anyone else!'

Geraldine could almost hear Kiki stamping her foot.

'Stop being so childish,' she said, exasperated. 'All Francis's thoughts and efforts are going to be directed towards opening Cedar Court to the public. He simply isn't going to have the time for other things. You're going to *have* to find someone else.'

'Oh no I'm not.' There wasn't a fraction of give in Kiki's voice. ' I want Francis, Geraldine. And you're making a huge mistake if you think I won't get him!'

She slammed the telephone receiver down with such force that Geraldine winced.

'Oh no you won't, Kiki,' she said beneath her breath, wondering just what the chances were of Kiki having got over her rage by Saturday. Somehow, she didn't think they were too good. Usually, Kiki's explosive temper tantrums were over in the blink of an eye. This time, though, the issue was so serious there was a definite risk that when she walked down the aisle on Saturday there would be a gloweringly sullen-faced bridesmaid walking in her wake.

She woke early, at Cedar Court, on the morning of her wedding. It certainly wasn't traditional for a bride to leave for her wedding from her bridegroom's home, but she had never had any intention of starting the day differently. Cedar Court was her family home, it was what her life was about, and Francis hadn't slept under its roof since their return from India.

'I'll stay in Chelsea until the big day,' he'd said on their first morning back in London, 'then I won't be underfoot while you and your mother are tearing your hair out getting things ready for the wedding.'

It wasn't either in her or in her mother's nature to panic unnecessarily, and they hadn't done so. Francis absenting himself from Cedar Court had, however, meant that she'd been able to enjoy her wedding preparations with total concentration.

Pushing herself up against the pillows, she looked across the room to where her grandmother's dress was hanging in layers of protective polythene. Had her grandmother, on her wedding day, felt so utterly certain of her future happiness as she now did?

With a shiver of joyous anticipation she swung her feet to the floor and padded barefoot across to the windows with their decorative leaded tracery. The sky was already blue, the dew sparkling.

Ten minutes later, in jeans and a T-shirt, she was running through the gardens towards the parkland and the oak tree.

In its high, familiar branches, she could view Cedar Court and its surrounding estate in their glorious entirety. It was hers and Francis's now – and one day would be their child's. In the year before they'd gone off on the hippie trail, and whilst Francis had been managing Kiki's career, she had spent her time with her uncle, studying every aspect of how to care for the house.

'The sooner you take over doing it, the better I shall like it, Geraldine,' he had said, heavily. 'A house this age needs constant vigilance and maintenance. Nothing is permanent. Lead on the roof wears thin, a hole the size of a pinhead lets in rain which can soon turn it rotten. Woodworm is a constant nightmare. Deathwatch beetle a torment. Francis simply won't accept just how much effort is necessary to preserve the house. If it were up to him, it would be a ruin by the time his heirs inherited it. You, thank God, will see to it that it isn't.'

She lifted her face to the already warm, early morning sun. The bough she was seated on swayed gently, creaking like the timbers of a ship. Her uncle had lived in only a few of Cedar Court's many rooms. She and Francis were going to live in them all, opening them up for the purpose for which they were built; having paintings made indistinguishable by layers of treacle-dark varnish cleaned and made beautiful again; having ceilings restored and old and beautiful carpets mended.

Her eye was caught by movement at the end of the quarter-mile long drive. A second later she recognized the caterer's van and, twenty yards or so behind it, the florist's van. Soon, Primmie, Artemis and Kiki would be arriving. Her day was beginning. The most wonderful, splendid, *joyous* day of her life.

'But why isn't Kiki already here?' Artemis queried, smoothing the sophisticated silver-grey silk of her dress over hips that had once again become quite plump. 'It's not long before we have to leave for the church.'

'She'll be here,' Geraldine said confidently, refusing to let anything spoil the spellbinding pleasure of the feel of her grandmother's wedding dress against her skin.

'But the two of you have fallen out, haven't you?' Artemis continued, fidgeting with her bouquet as Primmie adjusted Geraldine's veil. 'What if she doesn't turn up?'

'Of course she'll turn up.' Geraldine didn't know whether to be amused by Artemis's typical pessimism or annoyed. 'Even Kiki wouldn't let a falling-out spoil my wedding day.'

With the veil adjusted, Primmie had stepped towards the window.

'Is she coming yet, Primmie?' Artemis asked, still anxious. 'Can you see her car?'

'No, but I'm sure I just saw Simon's.' Primmie's face was radiant. 'Perhaps he's dropping her off before he goes on to the church.'

Before she could rush to the door and run down downstairs and throw herself into his arms, Geraldine said, 'Don't even think about it, Primmie. He'll crush your dress, muss your hair, ruin your lipstick. Wait till after the ceremony for your reunion.'

'Excuse me?' Artemis was staring at them in stunned bewilderment. 'Excuse me, but why would Kiki's father be mussing Primmie's hair and ruining her lipstick? What on earth is going on here? You're not telling me that Primmie and Kiki's father are . . . are . . .'

As she struggled for an appropriate, tasteful word, Geraldine's mother came into the bedroom.

'Simon Lane has just called by to drop a wedding gift off. The vicar has telephoned to say that guests are already arriving. I didn't tell him that one of the bridesmaids still hasn't arrived here. What *is* Kiki thinking of? Doesn't she know that my nerves will be stretched to breaking point without her making matters worse by being late?'

The minute she'd gone, Artemis said, her eyes the size of gobstoppers, 'Primmie Surtees! You're not telling me that you and Simon Lane are . . . are . . .'

'Yes,' Primmie said, eyes shining as she put Artemis out of her misery. 'And so you'll soon be a matron of honour again, Artemis.'

'I don't believe it! I simply don't believe it!' Artemis sank down on the nearest chair, uncaring as to whether or not her dress would be creased. 'Does Kiki know yet? And if you have me as your matron of honour, will you be having Kiki as a bridesmaid?'

Geraldine saved Primmie from answering a question she knew Primmie hadn't yet thought through. '*I* shan't be having her as a bridesmaid unless she arrives here pretty quickly,' she said, noting the time on the bedside clock. 'And once it's two o'clock, if she's not here, I shall leave for the church without her. Brides are allowed to be late. Bridesmaids are not.'

The next person to burst in on them was Francis's father.

Geraldine stared at him in bewilderment. 'Why haven't you left for the church, Uncle Piers? Shouldn't you and Francis be there by now?'

'I've just come *back* from the church. His best man and the ushers are there – and so are many of the guests – but he isn't. I thought he might have called by here.'

'But why should he? We're trying to follow tradition. We're not to see each other today until we meet at the altar.'

With a snort of exasperation, her uncle stomped back downstairs.

After a moment's awkward silence, Primmie said, 'I shouldn't worry about Francis not being at the church yet. He's like Kiki. He can sometimes be terribly badly organized unless he has someone chivvying him all the time.'

Geraldine, acutely aware of just how much she organized

155

things for Francis, bit back any sort of comment. Leaving for the church cross at Francis was absolutely not in her plans. There were still twenty minutes to go before it was two o'clock. By then Francis would be there. And if, when she arrived, Kiki wasn't part of her entourage, then that was something Kiki would just have to live with. She wasn't going to let Kiki's mean-spirited behaviour spoil her day. She wasn't going to let *anything* spoil her day.

The telephone on the bedside table rang. Primmie, who was standing the nearest to it, answered it.

'It's Kiki,' she said with blinding relief, passing the receiver to Geraldine.

'Hi, Kiki.' With difficulty, Geraldine kept her voice unstressed. 'Where are you? Have you got stuck in traffic in the village?'

'I'm not in the village, Geraldine.'

The minute she heard the timbre of Kiki's voice, Geraldine knew she would be going down the aisle without her. Kiki had been smoking dope. A lot of dope.

'Where are you?' she asked, fighting a disappointment she knew would take a long time to recover from.

'I'm in Rome. I'm starting a series of concerts here this coming week.'

'Great,' she said, not thinking that it was great at all. 'And I'm about to get married. An occasion you seem to have forgotten about.'

'No, I hadn't forgotten. I just can't manage to be there.'

There wasn't an ounce of apology or regret in Kiki's voice and Geraldine sucked in her breath, stunned by her rudeness.

'And, perhaps more importantly, Francis can't manage to be there, either.'

For a second Geraldine didn't take on board what she was saying and then, so that there could be no possible mistake, Kiki said, 'Francis is with me in Rome. We may get married, we may not. Sorry, Geraldine.'

The line went dead, and for a paralysing, stupefying moment Geraldine continued to stand, the telephone receiver still in her hand. As if from a far distance, she heard Primmie say, 'What's the matter, Geraldine? Has Kiki been delayed? Is she not going to get here?'

156

Not answering her, not turning her head, she dropped the receiver like a stone and, with a howl that was primeval, flung herself headlong on to the bed, sobbing and sobbing for the love she had lost and the future she would now never have.

Fifteen

It was a moment Primmie knew she would never forget. A moment when life, for all four of them, changed, never to be the same again.

Geraldine's mother, white faced, informed the guests assembled at the church that the wedding would not be taking place. A doctor was called and Geraldine was given a sedative that did little to ease her grief and rage. Francis's father aged visibly as he took on board the consequences of his son's action. Artemis gave way to hysterics and she, Primmie, struggled to comprehend what the repercussions of Kiki's monstrous behaviour were going to be.

Not, in a million years, could she envisage Kiki and Francis as a happily married couple. They were both too selfish, thoughtless and reckless. Francis needed Geraldine for the stability she gave him and to take from his shoulders all responsibility where Cedar Court was concerned. It was a responsibility Kiki would most certainly never take on. Responsibility, of any kind, was not in Kiki's vocabulary.

Hard on the heels of the realization that Francis had destroyed Geraldine's happiness – and his own – for a relationship Primmie was sure would be shallow and short-lived, was the devastating realization that she was going to have to tell Simon exactly why the ceremony had been called off. So far, none of the bewildered guests had been given any details. Simon, however, was going to have to be told – and she would have to do the telling.

It was going to be a hideous start to their reunion and, as the sedative given to Geraldine began to take hold and Artemis

157

slid her white satin pumps from her feet and covered her, still in her wedding dress, with an eiderdown, Primmie left the room and made her way downstairs with a heavy heart.

He was still at the church, as were lots of other guests. Whereas they were milling in groups in the churchyard, speculation rife as to why the bridegroom hadn't shown up, he was leaning against the lychgate, his legs crossed at the ankle, his arms folded.

It was so long since she had seen him, over three weeks, that despite all the shock and distress and anger that she was feeling, her heart leaped with joy at the sight of him.

'Simon! *Simon!*' Her slim-fitting, ankle-length bridesmaids' dress made running difficult, but she ran all the same, hurtling towards him, registering with a stab of shock how deeply unhappy he looked.

Slowly, almost reluctantly, he uncrossed his arms. She threw herself into them, certain that somehow he knew about Kiki and Francis.

'You've been told?' she gasped. 'Isn't it terrible? Isn't it absolutely awful?' The tears she'd been holding back began streaming down her cheeks. 'I've missed you so much, Simon, and now, when everything should be so wonderful for Geraldine and Francis – and for you and for me – it's just all so . . . so . . .'

She couldn't think of a word that would sum up her feelings. Geraldine's life was ruined. Though it was just conceivable that Geraldine might, one day, get over losing Francis, she could envisage no scenario where Geraldine would get over losing Cedar Court and of not having her child inherit it.

With all her heart she now wanted to tell Simon about *their* child, about the baby she was expecting, but it was news for a joyous moment and the present one, filled with grief at Kiki's wanton and treacherous behaviour, was not remotely suitable.

She felt him gently touch her hair and, as she raised her tear-streaked face to his, she saw, with a fresh slam of shock, that he was looking completely bewildered.

'What's happened?' he asked quietly, his face still looking oddly harrowed. 'Has there been an accident?'

158

'No.' She took a deep, shuddering breath. 'Kiki phoned Geraldine at twenty minutes to two to tell her that she was in Rome and that Francis was with her. She said that they might get married, or they might not. And then she rang off.'

'Dear Christ!' Since the moment he'd put his arms round her he hadn't been leaning against the lychgate. Now he tottered back against it, his face ashen. 'Dear Christ,' he whispered again, devoutly. 'How could she *do* such a thing? When did their relationship begin? Why was it *she* who telephoned Geraldine, and not Francis?'

He was no longer holding her. With his back to the gate, his hands were clamped on to it as if, were he to let go, he would fall.

'I don't know, darling.' Some last remaining thread of loyalty to the friend she had grown up with as a sister prevented her from saying what she felt in her heart – that Kiki hadn't so much taken Francis from Geraldine because she wanted him as a long-term lover or husband, but because she wanted him to manage her career.

'I need a drink.' He looked ghastly and, remembering how he always felt personally responsible whenever Kiki behaved badly, she wasn't surprised.

Wiping tears from her cheeks, she was just about to suggest that they go back to Cedar Court so that she could change out of her bridesmaid's dress and he could get the drink he so obviously needed, when he said, 'And I need to talk to you, Primmie. It's no use my putting if off because this has happened.'

'Putting what off?'

A joker of a wedding guest, cheated of throwing his confetti on Geraldine and Francis, had emptied his box of confetti into the air and the light breeze was now blowing it towards them. She could see it settling on Simon's hair and feel it on her own.

He let go of the gate and took hold of her hands. 'It's over between us, Primmie,' he said tautly. 'It has to be. Our being apart has given me plenty of time to think and I'd be doing you a great disservice if I married you. The age difference is too great. There'd be ugly talk. You lived in my

159

home as a child and the gossip . . . the gossip would be horrendous.'

She opened her mouth to speak, but no words would come. Flakes of confetti settled on her mouth and her eyelashes. The blood was drumming in her ears so loudly she thought she was going to faint.

'But I love you!' she managed at last, her voice cracking and breaking. 'I don't care about the age difference! I've never cared!'

'I know.' Very carefully he let go of her hands. 'But I care, Primmie. I'm sorry, darling. It won't work and I should have seen that it wouldn't far earlier. You'll get over me, just as Geraldine will eventually get over losing Francis.'

'But I won't! How can I possibly ever get over you when . . . when . . .' She choked on the words she was about to say, knowing that if she told him about the baby he would feel duty-bound to marry her. And she didn't want him to marry her out of a sense of duty. She wanted him to marry her because he loved her deeply; because he couldn't envisage life without her – as she couldn't envisage life without him. ' . . . When I love you so much,' she finished, fighting back the sobs that clutched at her throat.

'You're twenty-one,' he said gently. 'When you're twenty-one, life goes on. You'll find happiness with someone else, Primmie dearest. Someone your own age. Someone who, like you, will want children. I'm too old to begin parenting again. Kiki . . .' He winced with pain. 'Kiki is as much as I can cope with.'

'What will you do?' she whispered, wondering how she was going to live with her hurt, wishing that the ground would stop tilting so crazily.

He took a deep breath and braced his shoulders. 'First, I'm going to fly out to Rome and speak to Kiki. It won't make any difference to what has happened, but when realization dawns as to just how monstrously she has behaved, she's going to need someone – and when she does, she won't be able to call on her friends, because she's lost them, hasn't she? I can't imagine Geraldine ever wanting to see her or speak to her again, and neither you nor Artemis are going to be lending her a shoulder to cry on over this, are you?'

160

With her heart hurting, she shook her head, unable to even envisage offering Kiki sympathy over her selfish, reckless action, wondering how it had happened that, on a day that should have been so joyous, both her world and Geraldine's had come crashing down around them simultaneously.

What, she wondered, was life going to be like, now that it was no longer the four of them, but the three of them? Close as all their relationships to each other had been, Kiki's and her relationship had been, perhaps, the closest, because for seven years they had shared a bedroom and lived, Monday to Friday every week, as sisters. And they still did live together. What was going to happen when Kiki returned to London and to the flat? How could things ever be the same between them when Kiki had so treacherously and callously ruined Geraldine's life?

'I'm going, Primmie.' His voice was bleak, and if it hadn't been for the tears running relentlessly down her face she would have seen that his eyes were full of pain. 'Though I know you don't believe me, you'll be happy again, Primmie dearest. Goodbye. God bless.'

Without reaching out to her again, without touching her or kissing her, he turned away from her and, his shoulders hunched, his hands deep in his pockets, began walking down the narrow lane towards his parked car.

Other people were leaving the churchyard in his wake, the thrown confetti sprinkling their clothes and blowing in little flurries along the ground. Not caring as they looked curiously towards her, she stood at the lychgate, weeping, the tears spilling down on to the pale grey silk of her bridesmaid's dress. Then, as she heard the familiar sound of his car engine rev into life, she hugged her breast as though holding herself together against an inner disintegration and slowly began to walk back towards Cedar Court.

Artemis took her back to London. It was an almost silent journey, with both of them being too heartsick to talk. Only when they neared Kensington did Artemis say, 'You still haven't told me about you and Simon, Prim. How long have the two of you been in love? What does Kiki think about it? You do realize that if she comes to your wedding – and she'll have to, won't she, seeing as she's Simon's daughter? – Geraldine won't come. It's the end of it being the four of us. Kiki has destroyed that for good.'

'There won't be a problem about who to invite to the wedding, because there isn't going to be a wedding, Artemis. What there was between Simon and me is now all over.'

'And does it matter?' Artemis asked, turning her head towards her, her eyes wide.

'Yes, Artemis.' Her eyes were bruised with grief, her face pale. 'It matters very, very much.'

Artemis was silent again for a few minutes as she continued to drive through the busy traffic in Kensington High Street and then, turning into the side street towards the flat, she said awkwardly, 'But you'll get over it, Prim, won't you?'

As Artemis brought the car to a halt at the kerb-side, Primmie clasped her hands tightly in her lap. 'How?' she asked, her voice thick with pain, knowing that it was pointless keeping her pregnancy a secret any longer. 'I'm having a baby, Artemis. I'm nearly two months pregnant.'

Artemis had, of course, wanted to come into the flat with her, to make her a cup of tea or pour her a stiff drink and to give what comfort she could. It was comfort Primmie couldn't cope with.

'I'll speak to you tomorrow, Artemis,' she said, stepping out of the car. 'All I want to do now is to go to bed and to sleep.'

It was only half the truth, for what she did when the door of the flat closed behind her, was to throw herself on her bed, and sob and sob until she could sob no more.

Two days later, early in the evening, Geraldine let herself into the flat. 'I've heard,' she said bluntly, looking a ghost of her former self. 'Artemis rang me.'

Primmie, who had been relying on Artemis to do just that, hugged her tightly. 'He couldn't cope with the difference in our ages,' she said brokenly, her face buried in Geraldine's hair. 'And he was frightened of the talk.'

'Talk?' Incredulously Geraldine pulled away from her, to look into her face. 'What kind of talk?'

Primmie gave a helpless, despairing shrug of her shoulders.

'That perhaps there'd been something going on between us when I was still at Bickley High and living in his home. That, being so much older than me, he'd taken advantage of me. He's a family GP, Geraldine. It's understandable his being so scrupulously careful.'

She knew she didn't sound convinced and, when she saw the expression in Geraldine's violet-dark eyes, she knew that Geraldine wasn't convinced either.

'And all this has just occurred to him, out of the blue? I don't think so, Primmie. Kiki's got to him. She's either emotionally blackmailed him into not marrying you – which would be easy considering the ridiculous guilt he's always felt where she's concerned – or she's threatened there'll be an absolute stink of publicity about it, because of her being who she is.'

Primmie's eyes widened disbelievingly.

'Oh, come on, Prim! Don't tell me you hadn't worked it out for yourself? I know you said Simon and Kiki hadn't met up before he became ill and vanished off to recuperate, but I don't believe it for a minute – and nor do I believe he was ever ill, apart from perhaps being ill with the guilt he so likes to saddle himself with. And this time his guilt would have been over deciding to break off his relationship with you in order to keep Kiki happy.'

Her voice was totally unlike her usual voice. Instead of being husky and affectionate, it was harsh and full of vitriolic bitterness.

Still disbelieving, Primmie shook her head vehemently. 'No,' she said, lifting up a hand as it to physically ward off Geraldine's words. 'No. That isn't possible, Geraldine. Why would Kiki do such a thing?'

'Because she wouldn't want the world to know that her father was in love with her best friend!' Geraldine erupted explosively. 'Dear God, Primmie! Didn't you ever look at your relationship with Simon from Kiki's eternally selfish point of view?'

She threw herself down on to the sofa, one arm stretched out along its back, her long legs crossed.

'The chances of Kiki absolutely *loving* the fact that you would be her stepmother were always nil,' she continued, her eyes continuing to hold Primmie's fiercely. 'She would hate it. It wouldn't accord with the image she's so carefully constructing for herself where her public is concerned. And she wouldn't think any further than that, Primmie. *She* wouldn't like it, and so she'd take good care that *she* didn't have to put up with it. And to hell with you and your feelings.'

'No.' Primmie felt as if she were back at the lychgate again; as if the ground were shelving away at her feet. 'No,' she said again, her throat tight. 'I can't believe Kiki would do that to me. She wouldn't. She couldn't.'

Geraldine gave a harsh, mirthless laugh. 'Oh yes she would! If she'd take Francis away from me, on our wedding day, then you'd better believe that she'd take her father away from you! Kiki's a bitch, Primmie – a selfish, unfeeling, cold-hearted *bitch!*'

In the hideous days and weeks that followed, Primmie never openly acknowledged to herself that Geraldine's reading of the situation was correct, but doubts were sown and doubts remained. She could, she knew, have telephoned Simon and asked him if he and Kiki had had a meeting and if Kiki had pressurized him into not marrying her. Though the temptation had been strong, it had been one she had resisted. For one thing, hearing his voice, when he no longer wanted to hear hers, would have been more than she could bear, and for another, if Kiki *had* brought pressure to bear on him, his succumbing to it showed that he had never loved her in the way she'd believed he had.

With the acceptance that their relationship was utterly over, all her thoughts turned to the baby she was carrying. How were the two of them going to manage on her salary? Even more of a problem, how was she going to be able to continue working at BBDO, when there were no affordable nursery facilities within even a bus ride of the agency or the flat?

It was a problem she couldn't talk over with Geraldine, for within days of visiting her at the flat she had gone to Paris.

'And not for a holiday, Prim. For good,' she had said, her voice still hard and barely recognizable. 'London is too small a city for me and Kiki both – and now that Cedar Court will never be mine, I have to put distance between it and me. If I don't, I shall go mad.'

Her last remark had, Primmie knew, been quite literal.

Hard on the heels of Geraldine's phone call had been a phone call from Kiki. 'Hi,' she had said laconically, as if nothing very much had taken place since the last time they had spoken. 'I shan't be coming back to the flat, Primmie. Francis and I are going to be making Cedar Court our British base. You can empty my room and give the contents to Oxfam.'

And then, before Primmie had the chance to respond, she'd severed the connection.

At the beginning of August, it had been Artemis's turn to drop a bombshell. 'Daddy wants to sell the flat,' she had said, unhappily. 'I've tried to get him to change his mind, and I've tried to persuade Rupert to buy it from him, so that you could still stay on in it, but Daddy's realizing all his assets so that he can move to Portugal with a bimbo he's left Mummy for, and Rupert says he simply can't afford the asking price. What will you do, Primmie? Will you move into a flatshare or will you move back in with your parents for a while?'

Artemis had sounded so distressed on her behalf, that Primmie had assured her that it wasn't a problem and that she would soon find herself another flat.

The problem was, of course, that she couldn't do so, because what she was looking for was a flat not just for herself, but for herself and her baby. Up until now she had never had any money worries, for the rent she paid to Artemis's father was ridiculously low. The rents being asked for other flats in the area were so astronomical as to make even looking at them a complete waste of time. Flatsharing, which she could have happily done under normal circumstances, was now impossible. No single girls sharing a flat together would want to be kept awake at night by a baby crying and by having their flat full of baby paraphernalia.

Aware that she didn't have to vacate the flat for several weeks yet, she extended her search to south-east London, only to find the experience a grim one. There were some nice flats, but their rents were always stratospherically beyond her means and the flats she could afford were poky, dingy disasters.

She was now four and a half months pregnant and still hadn't told her parents.

'What are you doing with yourself, gel?' her father asked on one of her regular telephone calls to him. 'We ain't seen sight or sound of yer fer yonks.'

She'd promised to visit at the weekend, knowing that when she did so she would have to tell them about the baby and knowing that the news would hit them hard.

Making things even more difficult was that when she broke her news she wouldn't even be able to tell them who the father of her baby was. The repercussions if she did so would be too dreadful.

'Have you thought of having the baby adopted?' Artemis asked hesitantly, when she told her how much she was dreading speaking to her parents. 'It might be the best thing, Primmie.'

'No.' The word came unhesitatingly. 'No, I couldn't do it, Artemis. I couldn't hand my baby over to people I didn't know, never to see it again. I absolutely couldn't. Not ever. Never.'

There was a short, tense silence, and then Artemis said carefully, 'It might not have to be like that, Primmie. Not if . . . not if . . .'

'Not if what?' she asked, not sensing where Artemis was going.

Artemis took a deep, steadying breath. 'Not if the adoptive parents were Rupert and me.'

Primmie heard herself gasp as if she had been slammed hard in the stomach.

'Please don't be angry, Primmie!' Artemis's words came in an absolute rush now the issue she'd been longing to broach for weeks was finally out in the open. 'It's just that I know you may not have thought of having the baby adopted, and for Rupert and me – and for you and for the baby – it would be the most perfect solution. We wouldn't have any worries about hereditary defects or . . . or anything like that. Not that *I'm* worried about that side of adopting, but Rupert is. He keeps saying that if we adopt we won't know what kind of genes our baby will have inherited, but this way he wouldn't have to worry, because nothing inherited from you or Simon could possibly be bad and . . .'

166

'No.' This time the word was a croak. 'No, Artemis. I couldn't possibly . . . I want to keep the baby . . . .I can't even begin to imagine giving it up.'

'But this way . . . this way you won't be giving the baby to people you don't know.' Artemis was crying now. 'You know how much I would love it and cherish it and . . . and if you don't let us adopt it, I don't think Rupert will adopt at all and then I'll never have a baby . . .' She was weeping so earnestly now that Primmie could barely hear what she was saying. ' . . . And I do so want a baby, Primmie! I could give it everything. All the love in the world, a beautiful home, a privileged education, holidays abroad, *everything*. Please, please say you'll think about it, Primmie. Not just for your sake and for my sake, but for the baby's sake, too.'

With tears streaming down her face, Primmie had hung up the phone, unable to say a word in response.

Later, thinking again about the visit she was about to make to Rotherhithe, she decided that when her mum and dad had got over their initial shock, she would ask if she could move back home. And that she would also ask if after the baby was born her mother would look after it for her, so that she could keep on working at BBDO. It was, after all, the standard solution to her kind of problem.

She was at work when she made the decision, and within seconds of making it her telephone rang.

'Sorry to ring you at work, petal,' her dad said, sounding most unlike his usual cheery self. 'But your mum's bin taken badly. She's 'ad an 'eart attack. Could you get down to St Thomas' as quick as possible?'

She'd got there in twenty minutes and the instant she'd seen her father's terrified face and realized just how ill her mother was, she'd known that she wouldn't be telling them her news. It was distress they didn't need, and if and when her mother recovered it was obvious she wouldn't be fit enough to look after a baby.

For the next few weeks, between work and hospital visits, she flat hunted, without success. Several times she thought she had found a flat she could afford, only to be told by its

167

landlord that it wouldn't be suitable for her if she was having a baby. 'No dogs, no children' was the refrain, and she met with it time and time again.

By the beginning of September it was so obvious that she was pregnant that Howard called her into his office to ask her about it. 'Will you be staying on here, after the baby is born?' he asked, struggling not to look at the very naked third finger of her left hand.

When she had told him she would, he had looked even more uncomfortable, pointing out to her that, though he would like to make exceptions for her, he wouldn't be able to, and that there was no way he could allow her time off work if the baby were sick.

'If the baby is sick, I'll make arrangements,' she had heard herself say in a voice far more confident than she felt.

Later, in her own office, she had stared blankly at the wall, wondering just what those arrangements would be. So far, because she couldn't do so until she knew where she would be living after the baby was born, she hadn't even found herself a registered childminder.

'Are you OK, Primmie?' someone from Creative asked as he popped his head round her open door.

'Yes,' she had lied, looking wan, knowing very well just how much gossip was flying round now that her condition was so obvious.

In mid-September there was no avoiding the fact that Kiki and Francis were back in London. With a new record out, Kiki was on *Top of the Pops* and posters advertising her record were everywhere. She didn't get in touch, though, and Primmie couldn't bring herself to telephone Cedar Court, to get in touch with her. After all, if she did, what could she say to her? It would be impossible to talk to her as if her running off with Francis had never happened, and equally impossible to talk to her about it.

At the end of September she discovered that the general gossip at BBDO was that her baby was due in the new year, and that she would be having it adopted and returning to work.

'But I'm not going to have it adopted,' she had said explosively to one of the secretaries when they passed the gossip on to her.

'Aren't you?' The secretary had looked perplexed. 'But don't you think it would be better for the baby if you did? Bringing up a baby on your own isn't easy, you know. My father was killed in the war and all I remember about my childhood is that there was never enough money for anything. No nice clothes, no ballet lessons, no music lessons, nothing.'

She had breezed on her way, but it had been an encounter Primmie could have well done without.

At the beginning of October Artemis's father informed Primmie that he had sold the flat and that he would be obliged if she could vacate it by the end of the month. Hastily she had moved into a top-floor flat in Catford.

'Catford? *Catford?*' Artemis said in disbelief when she came to help her move her things. 'But it isn't on a tube line! It will take you *ages* to get to work in the morning. And a top-floor flat? How will you manage getting a pram up and down the steps? It will be a nightmare, Primmie. An absolute nightmare.'

'It will be affordable,' she had said grimly. 'Besides, I'm used to living south of the river. I'd have looked for a flat in Rotherhithe if it weren't that it would be too close to my mum and dad.'

'They still don't know?'

'No. Mum's had a second heart attack and whenever I visit St Thomas' I always wear a coat. They'll have to know eventually, of course. But I don't want them knowing now, when they have so many other worries.'

Artemis had tightly clasped together hands that were becoming plump again. 'They needn't know at all, Primmie. Not if you let me adopt the baby. Rupert says if it's a boy he will put his name down at Eton and if it's a girl she can go to Benenden.'

'No.' Adamantly Primmie shook her head. 'No, Artemis. No, I couldn't. I'd never be able to live with myself.'

'But *why?*' Artemis's voice was again thick with tears. 'You'd always know what was happening to the baby, you'd know that it was happy and loved. It's the *right* thing to do Primmie, can't you see that?'

All through November, in the most miserable late-autumn weather possible, she toiled cumbersomely backwards and forwards from Catford to Kensington, taking a train up to Charing Cross Station from Catford Bridge, and a tube from Charing Cross. At seven and a half months pregnant she was already enormous and on her return home the three flights of stairs to her flat seemed as steep as a mountain.

Exhausted, she would lie on the bed, staring at the ceiling, knowing that she had to find a more suitable home – a home in which she could bring up a child.

She was lonely, too. So lonely that it was a physical burden. Shattered as she was by Kiki's heartless behaviour, she missed her fizzing vitality and mercurial changes of mood. Not being cross at Kiki, or irritated by her, or laughing helplessly with her left a gap in her life that stunned her by its enormity.

She missed Geraldine, too. Geraldine had always been such a calming, relaxing influence. If Geraldine had still been living at the flat when Artemis's father had given notice that he was selling it, then their finding another flat – a flat suitable for a baby as well as themselves – would not have been a problem. Geraldine wouldn't have minded the noise and mayhem of a baby. Geraldine would have been supportive and practical and upbeat about the situation. But Geraldine wasn't with her, to assure her that she was doing the right thing in not giving her baby up for adoption. Geraldine was in Paris and, totally out of character, had hardly been in touch since leaving London.

There was Artemis, of course, and she valued Artemis's friendship just as much as she had always valued Geraldine's. The problem was that in all their meetings and phone calls – and Artemis made the journey from the Cotswolds on an almost weekly basis in order to have a 'girlie' lunch with her, and telephoned her nightly – the word 'adoption' lay, spoken or unspoken, like a heavy weight between them.

Night after night, unable to sleep despite bone-tiredness, she would think of all that Artemis and Rupert could offer her baby, questioning herself as to whether her longing to bring up her baby herself was nothing but selfishness on her part and not in her baby's best interest.

When December came, and there were only a few weeks before the baby was due, Artemis invited her to spend Christmas with Rupert and herself.

'I can't, Artemis,' she said as the baby kicked with such force it completely winded her. 'Mum is still in hospital and I'll be spending Christmas Day with her. And with Dad, of course.'

'And in your coat?' Artemis asked mildly.

Primmie bit her lip, well aware that her coat was no longer capacious enough to disguise her condition.

'Course I don't mind yer 'opping off dahn to Artemis's fer Christmas,' her dad said when she tentatively broached the idea to him. 'Tell yer the truth, gel, it'll be a bit of relief knowing you're somewhere 'aving a proper Christmas. I reckon me and your Mum are just goin' ter forget abaht it this year. Next year, though, we'll 'ave a real old knees-up!'

Christmas with Artemis and Rupert in their Cotswold home had been super-traditional. The house had once been a vicarage and, with a be-ribboned holly wreath on the front door, was chocolate-box pretty. There was a ceiling-high tree festooned with glittering baubles in the large square entrance hall, and their Labrador, a puppy the last time she had seen it, rushed to greet her, a scarlet bow tied jauntily round its neck.

On Christmas Eve they tore themselves away from a roaring log fire to go to a local carol service, returning from it with several of Artemis and Rupert's neighbours, and their neighbours' children, for a fork supper at the house. The conversation had revolved around local matters: the problems being caused by hunt saboteurs, a rehashing of the year's polo victories, the chance one of Rupert's friends stood of winning a parliamentary seat for the conservatives at the next election.

It wasn't her kind of milieu, but she enjoyed herself more than she had done for ages and ages, and what was extra nice was seeing Artemis so happy in the home that she and Rupert had created for themselves.

The next morning they all three exchanged presents and then, after Artemis had put the turkey in the oven, they went to morning service in a little Norman church, festive with candles and crib. On their return home she helped Artemis set the lunch table and, to a huge storm of barking from the dog, Rupert's parents arrived. 'Where is your mother this

171

Christmas?' she asked Artemis a little later as Artemis laid chipolatas on an oiled baking sheet and rolled rashers of bacon and threaded them on long flat skewers.

'On a cruise ship somewhere in the West Indies.' Artemis laid the finished skewers of bacon next to the sausages. 'Daddy's insisting on a divorce in order to marry the little fortune-hunter he's living with in Portugal and Mummy is trying to line herself up a new husband as quickly as possible.'

At the bleakness in her voice, Primmie said awkwardly, 'I'm sorry, Artemis.'

'So am I, Primmie darling, but it's no use being glum about it, especially not on Christmas Day. Have you ever made bread sauce? And if not would you like to learn how?'

As they continued working companionably together in a kitchen larger than her Catford flat, Rupert's parents occasionally drifted in for a few words, glasses of sherry in hand.

Rupert, who in the past had never been chatty towards her, was charm itself and it was obvious that Artemis was still head over heels in love with him. Though Geraldine's private life, and her own, had crashed into smithereens and Kiki's future love life was clearly destined for disaster after disaster, Artemis's seemed idyllic – the only thing lacking in it children.

It was a subject that was carefully never mentioned directly, but that was ever present obliquely. On Boxing Day morning the sun had shone and, leaving Rupert's parents indoors, they all three went for a short walk in nearby woods.

In a kingfisher-blue coat, her gold hair falling loosely to her shoulders, Artemis slid her arm through Primmie's and, as they returned towards the house via a paddock and a stables, said, 'I want to introduce you to Ben, Primmie. He's one of Rupert's Christmas presents to me and he's absolutely gorgeous.'

In the end stall of the stables stood a stocky Shetland pony.

'Isn't he just too lovable for words?' Artemis cooed ecstatically.

Primmie nodded, knowing full well why Ben had been bought; why Artemis and Rupert had gone out of their way to show him to her.

He was a pony any child would fall in love with. A pony simply waiting for a small owner.

*   *   *

Later, back in her dingy flat in Catford, the contrast between the type of home she could offer her child and the type of home Artemis could offer it was so stark her heart hurt. For hour after hour she lay in bed, staring into the darkness, struggling with a decision that was the hardest she'd ever had, or hopefully ever would have, to make. Then, just as the sky was beginning to lighten, she got out of bed and telephoned Artemis.

'You're right, Artemis,' she said quietly when Artemis, still half asleep, came on the line. 'You can give my baby far more than I can and I want Rupert and you to adopt it.'

There was a gasp and then Artemis burst into tears of relief and gratitude. At last, when she could finally speak, she said thickly, 'You've made me so happy, Primmie – and the baby will be happy, too. It will always be happy – I promise you that on my life.'

From that moment, things moved fast. Within days a social worker from her local authority had visited her.

'You'll have to be counselled about your decision,' she had said, poo-pooing her reaction that counselling was unnecessary, 'and the prospective adoptive couple will have to undergo the same type of a home study they'd have to undergo if they were adopting in the usual manner.'

'Our assigned social worker wants to assess our motivation for wanting to adopt,' Artemis said over the telephone, comparing notes. 'And she doesn't like the fact that we are friends and that it's a private adoption. I spent all day yesterday being questioned about my background and what she called my "relationship history". That covered my relationships with my parents, with boyfriends before I married, and my relationship with Rupert.'

'Now they want to know all about my lifestyle,' she said on a flying visit to the flat, a few days later. 'Rupert has to make a statement of all our finances, past, present and projected, and we both have to be checked out by the police and the NSPCC.'

* * *

173

Artemis wasn't the only one suffering lengthy questioning.

'And are you happy, Miss Surtees, as to the religion Mr and Mrs Gower propose bringing your child up in?' Primmie's social worker asked, reading from a list a yard long.

'Church of England?' Primmie nodded, hating the whole ghastly procedure. 'Yes. Perfectly happy.'

Artemis's next telephone call to her was one of near-hysterical distress. 'We've just been told that it's going to take *four to six months* to get approval and that even when we do get approval our dossier has to be sent to the Department of Health and that it could be another few months wait before the adoption can be finalized!'

Horrified, Primmie lowered her ungainly weight on to the nearest chair. 'But the baby is due in a couple of weeks, and once I begin looking after it myself . . . once I begin doing that, Artemis, I won't be able to part with it, I just know I won't!'

Artemis and Rupert had known it too and, at a financial cost she could only speculate about, had put the arrangements into the hands of one of the most high-powered lawyers they could find.

The results had justified their actions.

'With the help of a sworn statement from you, we're going to be allowed to take the baby home the day you leave hospital,' Artemis told her, her voice weak with relief. 'And you still want me there with you when you go into labour, don't you?'

'Yes, Artemis,' she said, trying not to think how different things would be if only it were Simon who was going to be with her. 'Yes. Of course I do.'

On her last day before taking maternity leave, her colleagues at BBDO presented her with a lace baby shawl from Harrods and two exquisite layettes, one in pink and one in blue.

'So one of them will be the right colour,' her account director had said jocularly as he made the presentation to her, 'and if you have twins, and they are a boy and a girl, they'll both come in handy!'

Her waters broke that evening on the train mid-way between Charing Cross and Catford. Damp and in great discomfort she

174

walked from Catford Bridge Station to the flat and then phoned
Artemis.

Artemis's immediate reaction was to panic.

'But why aren't you at the hospital?' she shrieked. 'Why
didn't you get a cab? Who's with you now?'

'No one,' she said placatingly, 'and I'm fine. It will probably be hours yet before I need to go to the hospital.'

'You can't take the risk, Primmie! Not when you have no
one with you! I want you to phone for a cab and go there
now, right this minute. If I set off immediately, I should be
there in a little over three hours.'

Knowing that it was useless to argue, Primmie hung up,
made herself a cup of tea and seated herself on the edge of
her bed to time the pains she had begun having.

They were coming quite strongly, every twenty minutes,
and she realized that Artemis had been quite right in demanding
that she got herself to the hospital as soon as possible.

'Blimey, love. Don't yer 'ave anyone wiv you?' the cab
driver asked, eyeing her enormous bulk with nervous eyes.
'Coming now, is it?'

'Yes, but not *right* now,' she said, trying to sound reassuring.

By the time they reached the hospital, she wasn't sure
whether she'd been speaking the truth or not.

'Don't worry love,' a hospital porter said cheerily as she
gasped in pain. 'I'll have you in Gynae in three seconds
flat.'

'I didn't think the pains would get so bad so quickly,' she
said as he seated her in a wheelchair and began pushing her
towards a lift. 'It's my first baby and first babies usually take
ages to come, don't they?'

'Well, some do and some don't,' he said, as he wheeled
her into the lift. 'Which means some people are lucky, and
some aren't.' He was ginger-haired and freckled and looked
to be all of eighteen. 'And you're probably going to be one
of the lucky ones, see?'

His opinion was backed by the more knowledgeable opinion
of the midwife who examined her.

'My goodness, dear. You're dilating nicely already,' she
said, taking off her thin rubber surgical gloves and binning

them. 'Now let's get you shaved whilst you're still relatively comfortable.'

All Primmie had been able to think of was that if her present condition was relatively comfortable she wasn't remotely looking forward to what was to follow.

An hour later, as she was transferred into the delivery room, she knew she'd been right to be worried. The pains were so frequent, and so deep, that it was impossible to breathe normally through them – and impossible not to cry out.

'Come along, dear,' a different midwife was now saying to her. 'You're almost fully dilated. There's not long to go now. Just imagine there's an orange in your vagina and that with every pain you're pushing it a little further out.'

It wasn't an image she found helpful. The pain was so intense, so unlike anything she had ever previously experienced, that she knew she was fast losing control.

'Here's a little gas and air,' another voice said, putting a mask over her nose and mouth. 'Now when the next pain comes, try and work with it.'

She tried to work with it and heard someone groaning as if they were being racked. As she realized that the person was herself, she became dimly aware of Artemis's voice some distance away, saying frantically, 'But I *am* the husband! Or, at least, I'm here *instead* of the husband, because there isn't one and I promised Primmie I'd be with her!'

Whether Artemis was with her or not, Primmie neither knew nor cared. She was being split apart. Split in a way she knew she couldn't possibly survive.

'Pant,' someone was saying urgently to her. 'Pant! *Pant!*'

Seconds later she heard herself scream and then there was a rushing, slithering sensation and instead of screaming she was crying with relief and joy as one of the midwives helped her to raise her head and she was able to look between her blood-smeared, sweat-sheened legs and see her baby.

Covered in mucus, it was kicking and crying, its blond hair clinging wetly to its skull.

'Oh! Is it all right? Is it all right?' she demanded in a frenzy of anxiety.

'*She* is perfect,' the midwife attending to the baby said.

'Now just let me check her air passages and then you can hold her for a minute or two while we wait for the placenta to come away.'

Wrapped in a towel, her still bawling daughter was placed in her arms, and as she felt the weight of her against her breast, and looked down at her little crinkled face, she was filled with such love it seemed impossible to contain it.

There came the sound of someone entering the delivery room and seconds later Artemis was saying to her in reverent awe, 'Is it a boy or a girl, Primmie?'

'It's a girl, Artemis.'

With tears of emotion streaming down her face, Artemis looked down at the baby and said, 'Please, may I touch her, Primmie? Please?'

Primmie nodded and Artemis bent down to gently cradle the now quiet baby.

'And now you'll have to leave the room,' one of the midwives said to her, briskly. 'We don't usually allow husbands to hold the baby at this stage, let alone girl friends.'

As Artemis reluctantly stood upright again, Primmie said in a voice raw with emotion, 'Her name is Destiny, Artemis.'

'Destiny?'

Incredibly, naming the baby had been something they had never discussed.

Primmie nodded. 'Naming her is the one thing I can do for her, Artemis. And I like the name Destiny. It's unusual and special'

'It's a beautiful name, Primmie.' Tears continued to stream down Artemis's cheeks. 'And she's beautiful, Primmie. She's perfect.'

'And you now *have* to leave,' the midwife said, running out of patience. 'This is a delivery room, not a private ward.'

As Artemis finally did as she was told, the other midwife said chattily, 'It's most unusual for anyone to have their best friend in the delivery room with them. Have the two of you always been so close?'

'The four of us were always close,' Primmie said, too exhausted to care that she wasn't making much sense. 'But now things are different.'

The midwife, accustomed to the disorientating effects of

177

gas and air on her patients, lifted Destiny from her arms without asking her to explain herself.

Primmie, watching as Destiny's umbilical cord was cut, thought of just how different things now were. She thought of Kiki, at Cedar Court with Francis. She thought of Geraldine, in Paris. And she thought of Artemis, with whom her relationship would never be the same now that Destiny would grow up calling her 'Mummy'.

Things were not merely different now – they had changed beyond all recognition. An era had ended and another era – one she found impossible to imagine – was about to begin.

Sixteen

March 1978

It was the first day of spring and Primmie was making a mug of tea for the carpenter/odd-job man who was fitting new kitchen units for her. The units were a present to herself and one she had wanted for a long time, for years, in fact. When she had first moved back into her childhood home in order to look after her mother, the upheaval of having new kitchen units fitted had been more than her mother could face, and after her death Primmie simply hadn't had the heart to begin the refurbishment the run-down terraced house so badly needed.

Another reason she hadn't done so had been lack of money. New kitchen units, even bottom-of-the-range ones, weren't cheap. She switched on the radio as she waited for the kettle to boil, reflecting that, if she'd stayed on at BBDO, she would have been earning a very healthy salary by now and would have been able to buy solid wood units, not merely the functional plywood ones now being installed. Staying on at BBDO, gaining promotion to account director level, hadn't been an option, though, not once her mum's health had deteriorated to the point where she needed full-time nursing.

Afterwards, when her mother had died, she hadn't approached BBDO to see if they would re-employ her – and she hadn't approached any other advertising agencies either. Instead, she had taken a job as general office manager in a small import/export company five minutes walk from her Rotherhithe home. It was a far cry from the glamour of advertising, but it suited her. Though not ill, her father was growing increasingly infirm and she preferred to go straight home after work, to make him a meal and to keep him company, rather than frequent glitzy wine bars with colleagues as she had done in her BBDO days – or as she had done if she hadn't been meeting Simon.

'I like this song.' Ted Dove, who had been measuring a unit and the space it was to fit into, leaned back on his heels and stuck the pencil he had been using, behind his ear. 'It's very gentle and somehow folksy.'

The interruption was both unexpected and deeply welcome. Over long, painful years she had schooled herself not to dwell on thoughts of Simon, and she refused to allow herself to do so now. Instead, she zeroed in on what was being played on the radio. It was 'Mull of Kintyre' by Wings.

'Yes,' she said, aware that the kettle was boiling and had probably been doing so for several minutes. 'I've always liked Paul McCartney. I was a real Beatles fan when I was a teenager.'

'Were you?' he began rifling through his battered tool-bag. 'I was more of a Frankie Laine fan, myself. But then, I was a teenager in the early fifties, when teenagers weren't yet called teenagers – if you follow what I'm saying.'

She smiled to acknowledge that she did know what he was saying and poured boiling water into an already warmed teapot.

He withdrew an electric drill from his tool bag. 'My late wife was the last person I saw do that,' he said, watching her. 'Most ladies now use tea bags.'

The flare of shock she felt at his being a widower tempered her amusement at his use of the word 'ladies'. He didn't look like a widower – his shirt was far too crisply ironed – and she wondered if he was living with a girlfriend. One thing she did know was that though he was engagingly friendly there was also something reassuringly respectful about him.

179

As she'd contacted him via a card he'd placed in a sweetshop window, the latter realization had come as something of a relief.

'Yer want ter be careful who you're getting, gel,' her dad had said to her, when she'd told him of how she'd found the carpenter who was going to put their kitchen in for them. 'What if 'e's one of these 'ere cowboys?'

She'd had doubts herself, but his hourly rates had been so reasonable that she'd overcome them. Then, after she'd telephoned him and he'd come to the house to have a look at the size of the kitchen and to estimate how long the job would take him, she'd felt reasonably sure that she was safe in employing him.

He'd *looked* trustworthy, for one thing. And he'd had a nice manner.

He hadn't gone round her kitchen tut-tutting and shaking his head, saying that for a job such as hers he'd have to put his hourly rates up, and nor had he made her uncomfortable by trying to flirt with her. He'd simply told her how many days he thought the job would take and asked her when she would like him to start. Even more breathtakingly, he hadn't let her down. Two days ago he'd been there on the agreed morning and, as chunkily built as a boxer, his hair a thatch of thick curls, dressed in a short-sleeved chequered shirt and faded corduroy trousers, he had also looked remarkably neat and tidy.

Now, after the remark about her pleasantly old-fashioned way of making tea, he got on with his work without further chat, obviously happy at having the radio on for company.

As she got on with some ironing, doing it in the living room whilst her dad watched snooker on the television, it occurred to her that though she'd taken three days of her holiday time to be at home whilst he was putting the units in for her she really hadn't needed to do so.

'Penny fer 'em,' her dad said, as Cliff Thorburn potted a blue into the centre pocket.

'I was just thinking that I needn't have taken three days' holiday to be at home whilst the kitchen's being done – and that set me to thinking that we haven't made any arrangements for a holiday this year. What would you like to do, Dad? Would you like to go to Whitstable again, for a week?'

'I'm 'appy anywhere, gel, you know that. But what about you? Don't yer want to go off somewhere exotic, with a couple of friends from work or somefink?'

'My friends at work are all married, with families.'

Wryly she was aware that it sounded as if she had a host of married friends, when in fact there were only another five office staff at Perrett & May Import and Export and, though she was on friendly terms with all of them, she wasn't friends with any of them. Not in the way she had been friends with Geraldine, Artemis and Kiki.

She folded the pillowcase she had been ironing and put it to one side, wondering if such intense, urgent, passionate friendships were only ever forged in youth. Certainly, she couldn't imagine making such close friendships again. They had been friendships she had believed would last a lifetime and that, for reasons she knew in some cases and was mystified by in others, were now nothing but ghosts of what they had once been.

Geraldine, for instance. As she began ironing her father's pyjamas and as the sound of David Bowie's 'Space Oddity' came mutedly from the kitchen, she pondered on the mystery of why Geraldine had, ever since moving to Paris, remained so firmly out of contact. There was always a birthday card and a Christmas card from her, though never with a return address so that she could respond in kind. Why, when they had never had a cross word over anything, had Geraldine cut herself off from her with almost the same finality with which she had cut herself off from Kiki?

It just didn't make any sense to her – and Artemis had not been able to throw light on it, either.

'A couple of cards are all I get from her, as well,' she'd said the last time they had mulled the hurtful mystery over. 'Perhaps she just doesn't want any reminders of her old life – the life that included Francis. He and Kiki are living in America now, according to an article in a magazine I read at the hairdressers. Apparently, she's huge over there. Almost as big as Gloria Gaynor.'

Kiki was also big in Britain. As *The Jimmy Young Show* continued to be audible from the kitchen, Primmie knew it was only a matter of time before a Kiki Lane record was played. Even her early records, 'White Dress, Silver Slippers' and 'Twilight Love', continued to get plenty of airtime. Kiki had written both songs with Geraldine and, whenever Primmie heard them, she wondered how Geraldine felt about receiving her share of royalties from their collaboration.

For all she knew, of course, Geraldine's bitterness towards Kiki could well be a thing of the past. Ten months ago, in a newspaper gossip column, she had seen a photograph of Geraldine. Wearing a halter-necked evening gown, she'd looked stunningly elegant and had been on the arm of a French cabinet minister. A week ago there'd been another photograph, this time in a different newspaper and with a different escort. The occasion had been a reception at the French Embassy, in London, and her escort had been André Barre, a major European industrialist.

The photographs had left Primmie in no doubt that Geraldine was leading the kind of high society life that came so naturally to her and, with all her heart, she hoped that Geraldine was happy again.

Although Geraldine hadn't kept in touch – apart from the occasional card – Kiki had, or at least she had for a short while.

'Hi,' she would say over the telephone, uncaring of the time difference between Britain and America and waking her in the middle of the night. 'How ya doin', Primmie? How's tricks?'

There was usually a cacophony of noise in the background. Laughter and music and glasses clinking. Valiantly Primmie would try and rouse herself into full consciousness in order to hold a sensible conversation with her. Even when she succeeded, it was generally to no very good purpose, for Kiki was always high on drink or, Primmie often suspected, drugs, and meaningful conversations were impossible.

Still, the phone calls had always been very welcome. They had been a link, however inadequate and tenuous, with a part of her life that was now firmly in the past.

'Will that young chap be needin' another mug of rosie?' her father asked, breaking in on her thoughts. 'Yer mustn't neglect him, Primmie. Workmen need reg'lar mugs of tea. It's what keeps 'em going.'

'I've just made him one, but I'll make him another, if it will keep you happy. And he's not a young man, Dad. He was a teenager in the fifties and he's a widower.'

'Is he indeed?' For some reason she couldn't fathom, her father seemed to find this information interesting. 'So the two of you 'ave got chattin', 'ave yer? That's nice. And bring me a mug of tea as well, Primmie, will yer? This snooker's thirsty work.'

Going back into the kitchen, this time to the sound of Abba's 'Take A Chance On Me', had been a relief, because the way her thoughts had been going Artemis would have been the next person to dominate them.

'My Dad thinks you might be ready for another mug of tea,' she said, filling the kettle again, wondering if the day would ever dawn when she and Artemis would be able to be friends again without there being the most unbearable tensions between them.

'Blimey!' Ted Dove didn't pause in what he was doing. 'The last lot isn't cold yet, Miss Surtees.'

'Primmie,' Primmie said, her thoughts still on Artemis. 'Please call me Primmie.'

The difficulties between Artemis and herself had kicked in from the day Artemis had left Greenwich Hospital with Destiny in her arms. The pain of parting with Destiny had been indescribable, her only comfort her certainty that the parting was in Destiny's best interests.

The first harsh reality she had had to come to terms with was that on-going contact with Destiny just wasn't possible. The emotional trauma of playing auntie to her own child was simply too much. It was easier to follow Destiny's progress via regular lunch meetings with Artemis in London and by their frequent telephone calls to each other and the photographs Artemis constantly sent her.

For nearly a year, it was an arrangement that, oiled by the fact they both loved Destiny fiercely, treasured every minute of talking about her and trusted each other completely, had been as successful as any arrangement could be, under the circumstances.

Then had come the thunderbolt that had turned her world upside down. Rupert made it known that he found the

183

arrangement emotionally unhealthy and that he wanted it to end.

'And that is what all the adoption societies advise as well, Primmie,' Artemis had said to her, ashen faced. 'They say it's much better for the birth mother to make an absolutely clean break with the child she's given up for adoption – and in most cases, of course, that's what happens automatically.'

'But I don't visit Destiny! I don't have her here to stay with me, or take her out for the day! I don't have the contact with her that even an aunt or a godmother would have! All I have are photographs – and lunches and phone calls with you, when you tell me how she's progressing and what she's been doing, when I can at least talk about her!'

The conversation had taken place at their usual meeting place for lunch, a Greek restaurant in St Martin's Lane.

'I know, Primmie, I know.' Artemis, wearing a Jean Muir pink wool crêpe dress, its matching swing-coat disguising a figure that was way overweight again, began silently weeping. 'It's just so *hard*, Primmie,' she said, the tears streaming down her beautifully made-up face. 'Rupert can be quite . . . quite *fierce* about things he feels passionately about, and he feels passionately about this. He doesn't want me to continue giving you a blow-by-blow report of Destiny's progress, especially as the little darling is a little late in doing some things. It's nothing to worry about, of course, because some babies are walking at a year old and others stay very firmly on their bottoms for ages longer than that – but Rupert thinks there's a situation where, as she gets older, you might begin questioning some of the decisions we make about her . . . that you might . . . might . . .' The expression in her china-blue eyes was agonized. 'That you might begin to *interfere*.'

Primmie had been so aghast, so devastated, that she'd thought she'd been going to faint. 'You mean that you're not going to meet me for lunch any more, so that we can talk about her?' she'd said, disbelievingly. 'That we're not to phone each other to talk about her? That we're not to be *friends* any more?'

'Of course we'll still be friends, Primmie!' Artemis was openly crying now, her mascara beginning to streak. 'How could we not be friends? And I'll still send you photographs and phone you to talk about Destiny, it's just that I won't be able to do so as often as I do now . . . and we won't be able to meet for lunch any more. It would cause far, far too many problems for me with Rupert. Don't dislike him for feeling as he does, Primmie. All he wants is the best for Destiny and to feel that . . . to feel that she's really *ours* and that we're not sharing her.'

With legs that had felt as if they were going to give way any moment, Primmie had risen to her feet and stumbled out into the street. She, too, had been wearing pink. A dusky pink silk polo neck and raspberry-coloured tweed skirt that she'd bought in the winter sale at Marks & Spencer's.

It was an outfit she never wore again; an outfit she couldn't look at without remembering Artemis's hideously searing words.

'Excuse me, Primmie.' Ted Dove sounded a little amused as well as a tad concerned. 'But though I said I didn't want another mug of tea yet, you've put the kettle on and if you don't switch if off pretty soon, the steam will be so thick I won't be able to see what I'm doing.'

With a start, Primmie came back to the present moment, saw that the kettle was on the point of boiling dry and switched it off. 'I'm sorry,' she said. 'I was miles away.'

'Somewhere nice?'

She shook her head. 'No, not very. Could you change your mind about not having another mug of tea? I'm making one for my dad, so it's just as easy to make two.'

'Well, if you're bending my arm,' he said, shooting her an extraordinarily sweet smile. 'But better make this the last one, eh? Any more, and I won't get finished by this evening.'

He had been finished by that evening and Primmie was very happy with both the work done and the price charged. Three days later he was on her doorstep again, this time without his tool bag and looking a little sheepish.

'I wonder if you'd do me a favour, Primmie?' he said. 'I've just done a quote for a lady further down the street and she'd like a reference before giving me the go-ahead. Would you mind very much giving me one?'

'No, of course not.' She opened the door wider, so that he could step inside whilst she went to find a pen and paper.

When she came back into the narrow hallway, it was to find her father chatting to him.

'Nice bloke, that,' he said, when Ted Dove had gone on his way, her reference in his shirt pocket. 'He's the sort of chap you should be givin' the eye to. How old are yer now, Primmie? Twenty-seven? If yer don't get a move on, I'm never goin' ter be a granddad!'

There was no way he could know the storm of emotions his words aroused and, knowing that what had been said had been said innocently and as much in fun as in seriousness, she forced a tight smile and announced she was going for a walk.

Destiny was five now. The birthday photograph Artemis had sent her – presumably without Rupert's knowledge – showed a fair-haired, blue-eyed, shy-looking little girl. What would her father say if she showed it to him? If she were to tell him he'd been a granddad for five years now? She headed in the general direction of the Thames, wishing she had never kept her secret from him, hating the weight of its burden.

The following Saturday morning, Ted Dove was on her doorstep again.

'Yes?' she said, beginning to suspect he was calling by for no other real reason than that he wanted to keep seeing her and, if her assumption was correct, wondering how she felt about it.

'I was just passing and thought I'd ask you if you were pleased with your units,' he said. 'If there's anything not quite right . . . if you want any adjustments making . . . it's no problem. I've got a couple of free evenings next week and . . .'

'They're fine, thank you.'

'Ah.'

Her reply seemed to take the wind out of his sails a little bit. 'Good,' he said, rallying, obviously thinking of what next to say and making no attempt to take his leave.

In growing amusement, Primmie didn't help him out. She was wondering if he had some Irish in him, for his colouring was typical of a certain type of Irishman. His curly hair was true black – almost blue-black – and his eyes were a quite startling shade of blue. Though his features could only be described as homely, there was charm in his long, mobile mouth – and his hair and eyes were enough to make any woman look at him twice.

Under her gaze he began colouring slightly and it occurred to her that he wasn't aware of his own attractiveness, which, where she was concerned, only made him more attractive.

'Well, then,' he said at last, 'if there's ever anything else you'd like doing around the house, you'll get in touch, Primmie, won't you? I don't only do carpentry work. I can turn my hand to plumbing and electrical work as well.'

'Would you like to come in for a minute or two and take a look at the kitchen now it's in use again?' she said, taking pity on him and coming to the major decision that, if he were to ask her out on a date, she would go. 'Then you can see for yourself how absolutely perfect it is.'

With an assenting grin, he followed her down the hallway and she was aware of how comfortable she felt with him.

'Who's that yer've got with you, Prim?' her father shouted out from the sitting room, where he was watching a Saturday-morning cartoon.

'Ted Dove,' she shouted back, knowing her father would make no objection at all to her having Ted Dove in the house again. 'He's just going to cast an eye over his handiwork in the kitchen.'

As she opened the kitchen door, they were met by the smell of a freshly baked loaf.

He breathed in deeply, as if on the seafront at Brighton.

'Would you like a slice?' she asked, glad she'd started the day in a bread-making mood.

'I'd love one,' he said fervently. 'I haven't had a slice of fresh home-baked bread for years.'

Standing with her back to him, she began slicing the crusty loaf.

He cleared his throat.

She reached for the butter dish, a smile tugging at the corners of her mouth.

'I didn't only call round to make sure you were happy with the units I put in,' he said awkwardly as she took a knife out of her cutlery drawer. 'I really came round to ... to ...'

187

Still with her back to him, she began spreading butter on to the thick slice of bread she had cut, her smile deepening.

'... to ask if, perhaps, you'd like to go to the cinema with me one evening?'

Biting her lips to prevent herself from grinning, she slid the buttered slice of bread on to a plate and turned to face him.

'W-e-ll,' she said, trying to sound doubtful. 'I'm not sure ...'

The agony in his blunt, black-lashed eyes was so intense she didn't have the heart to tease him any further.

'I'd like to,' she said, aware of a sensation of excitement deep in the pit of her tummy; an excitement she hadn't felt in years. 'I'd like to, Ted. I'd like to very, very much.'

They went to see *Star Wars* at a cinema at the Elephant and Castle, had a fish and chip supper afterwards and enjoyed every minute of their evening together. A week later, they went to the cinema again, this time to see Sylvester Stallone in *Rocky*. Afterwards, as Ted walked her home, she asked him if he fancied seeing a French film that was on at the National Film Theatre.

'Is it one of those highbrow, intellectual films?' he asked in alarm.

'It's had good reviews,' she said cautiously.

'Well, if you want to see it, Primmie, of course I'll be happy to go. The only thing is ...' He hesitated, looking deeply uncomfortable. 'The only thing is,' he said again, 'if it's one of those foreign films with sub-titles I might not be able to follow it very well.'

'Of course you will.' She hugged his arm reassuringly. 'The subtitles will be in English, not French.'

'Yes, well ... that's just it, Primmie.' They were about to turn off Jamaica Road into a side street and he came to a halt beneath a street lamp. 'You see, Primmie love, I don't read very well.' Beneath his thick thatch of curly hair, his eyes were apologetic. 'In fact, I can hardly read at all.'

'Oh!' For a second she was so taken by surprise that she didn't know what to say. Then she saw that, besides apology, there was also fear in his eyes – fear that she would now think less of him; that she would no longer want to go out with him.

'It doesn't matter,' she said swiftly, not wanting him to think for a second his not being able to read very well meant her feelings towards him had altered. 'Or, at least, I know that it *does* matter, in lots and lots of ways and especially to you, but it doesn't matter where you and me are concerned. Do you understand?'

His relief was so obvious and so intense that it brought a lump into her throat.

'That's good to know, Primmie,' he said thickly.

Her arm was still in his, her face upturned.

He cleared his throat. 'You mean the world to me, Primmie. You know that, don't you?'

She nodded, aware that in the short time they had known each other he'd come to mean the world to her, too.

For a long moment their eyes held and then he drew her closer towards him, wrapping strong arms round her, lowering his head to hers, kissing her with exquisite tenderness.

She knew then, with his first kiss, not only that he loved her – really loved her – but that she loved him; that she would always be able to trust in the strength of his gentle, compassionate nature; that, unlike Simon, he would never let her down and that one day, in the not too distant future, they would marry.

All that summer their courtship continued. In July, when she went to Whitstable for a week with her father, Ted drove them there and brought them home again In August they went to Brighton together for a few days. In September, on her birthday, he asked her if she would marry him.

It was then that she told him about Destiny.

He was appalled.

He was appalled not at her having had a child out of wedlock, but at her having given Destiny up for adoption. And when she told him of her relationship with Artemis and how she had believed that with Artemis as Destiny's adoptive mother she would never lose contact with Destiny, but would always know how she was progressing and what she was doing – as well as having the reassurance that Destiny was happy – and of how those expectations had been crushed into extinction, he'd been more than appalled. He'd been horrified.

'It isn't Artemis's doing,' she'd said, leaning against him as he'd hugged her tight. 'Artemis is deeply distressed about it, but she has the kind of marriage where her husband makes all the decisions and expects her to abide by them. Causing waves over something Rupert feels strongly about is something she'd never have the nerve to do. She'd be too fearful of the long-term consequences. '

'Things will be different when Destiny is a young woman, Primmie,' he'd said, his voice full of love and certainty. 'And until she is, we'll have children of our own to love and care for. My Sheila couldn't have children and it was always a deep sadness to us. Now, though, you and me . . . . why, we'll have hordes of children, Primmie darling. Ten at least.'

'I think ten might be a few too many.' Her head had been against his chest, her voice still wobbly from the emotion that talking about Destiny always aroused in her, but there had also been relieved laughter in her voice. With Ted by her side, she could cope with anything. Life was good again, and when they were married it would be even better. There would be children, a whole houseful of them. In imagination, she could already feel their arms around her neck and their kisses on her cheek.

They married on the fourteenth of September, exactly six months to the day after they had met. It wasn't the kind of wedding she had once imagined she would have. Instead of taking place in an Anglican church at Petts Wood, the service took place at Woolwich Registry Office. Instead of an elegant champagne reception at the Bromley Court Hotel, there was to be a traditional south-east London knees-up for friends and family in the Territorial Drill Hall, Rotherhithe. And instead of her future home being a large detached house in Petts Wood, its enormous garden merging into a golf course with, beyond, nothing but a glorious vista of rolling fields and trees, she and Ted were going to start married life in a council house only a stone's throw from busy Jamaica Road.

As she made her vows and as Ted slid a plain gold wedding ring on to her finger, Primmie's only pang of regret was that Kiki, Artemis and Geraldine were not sharing the day with her. As for the far-off dreams of youth, they were as dust in the wind. What mattered – what would matter for the rest of her life – was the love she and Ted shared.

And she was deeply, profoundly grateful for it.

Seventeen

September 1978

Kiki rolled over in bed and groaned. She was in London, bloody London, and the only ameliorating factor was that, for the next three days, Francis wasn't. She tugged off her eyeshades and peered venomously at the hotel clock. It was 10.15 a.m. Her flight from New York hadn't landed until 02.00 a.m. and so she'd had five hours sleep – maybe five and a half, at a pinch.

What time was she due at the studio? She rolled on to her back again and stared up at the ceiling. 'Kit's expecting you to show by midday!' Francis had shouted after her, when, following another of their ferocious quarrels, she'd stalked out of their New York apartment and down the stairs to her waiting taxi.

Without moving off her back, she reached for the phone, waited for room service to answer and, when someone did so, said peremptorily, 'Coffee, please. Gallons of it.'

Then she pushed herself up against the pillows, swung her legs from the bed, reached for an emerald silk kimono and, slipping her arms into it, walked across to the window and opened the curtains.

The view was of Marble Arch and near-gridlocked traffic crawling down Bayswater Road towards Lancaster Gate. Away to the left were the grassy green vistas of Hyde Park, its trees just beginning to turn russet and gold. Further left, on the southern side of the park, lay Kensington.

She chewed the corner of her lip. Even though she knew

that the flat she had shared with Primmie, Artemis and Geraldine had long ago been sold, that Primmie was living in a council house in Rotherhithe, Artemis living in the Cotswolds and Geraldine . . . She tasted blood on her tongue and realized that she'd bitten her lip. She licked it away. That Geraldine was in all probability still living in Paris, the pull of the old flat in Kensington was almost palpable.

If Artemis's father had still owned it and if Primmie had still been living in it, then she would be staying there now and . . . and . . .

She tried to finish her train of thought and couldn't. All she knew was that if the flat and Primmie had still been in her life, she wouldn't find London quite as hateful as she did.

For a start, she had no friends in London. She never even saw Primmie. How could she, when Primmie was an office clerk living in a Rotherhithe council house and she was a rock star? There was just no point of contact between them. It would have been different – just – if Primmie had still been living in a spacious Kensington flat and been a high-flyer in an advertising agency – or even if Primmie had married Simon.

She tried to thrust the last guilt-ridden thought away.

Because she was in London, face to face with the obligation of meeting up with her father, it wouldn't go.

Still looking down at the crawling traffic she brooded over whether or not she had done Primmie a disservice when she had emotionally blackmailed Simon into not marrying her. At the time, it had seemed the only possible course because she hadn't been able to even begin imagining her father and Primmie having sex together – and the thought of Primmie becoming her stepmother had, five years ago, been horrific. Now it no longer seemed so very dreadful. Primmie as her stepmother would have been a hell of a lot better than the middle-aged nightmare he had married some months ago. And if Primmie had married Simon, she and Primmie would still have been in contact and her childhood home would still have been somewhere she wanted to visit.

There came a knock on the door and, without turning her head, she called out, 'Yeah. Right. Come in.'

Behind her, the door opened and a waiter entered. Crossing to the sitting area of the room he set a tray bearing a percolator, cup and saucer, sugar and cream, on to a coffee table.

Kiki didn't acknowledge his presence. Her thoughts were too far away and too dark. Why was it that, though her life was now packed with people – fellow pop stars, bands, backing singers, hangers-on, fans – she had no friends? That Geraldine was no longer her friend was understandable, but Artemis, too, was now out of her life – and she missed Artemis just as intensely as she missed Primmie.

The problem between her and Artemis was, of course, Francis. Artemis had been totally unforgiving about her having, in Artemis's words, 'stolen' Francis from Geraldine.

Having given up her modelling career to devote herself to family values deep in the heart of rural Gloucestershire, Artemis had behaved towards her as if her sexual relationship with Francis was a capital crime.

'Surely it's better that we've come out into the open about it?' she'd stormed back at her in their one and only telephone call after the wedding day that wasn't. 'Or would you have liked it better if Francis had gone ahead and married Geraldine and we'd simply carried on shagging each other as if his marriage made no difference?'

Artemis's response had shocked the socks off her. The friend she'd saved from the hooves of a police horse had called her a cow, a bitch, a whore – and had said that she never wanted to see her, or speak to her, again.

And hadn't.

As for Geraldine . . .

She bit the corner of her lip and tasted blood again. She'd had no contact with Geraldine since the telephone call she had made to her, from Rome, on the morning of the day Geraldine was to have married Francis.

The waiter had long gone and she turned round, crossed to the table and poured a coffee, bitterly reflecting on how much she had lost, and for how little. The heady excitement of her sexual relationship with Francis had palled once it was no longer illicit. Bored, she'd run true to form, finding additional excitement elsewhere. Francis had been insultingly unconcerned, but then, as she had speedily come to realize, Francis skimmed across the surface of life, never letting anything affect him too profoundly.

They'd stayed together as a couple because, with his being her manager and her being his one and only client, it had been as easy to do so as to split up.

She sipped her black coffee, eyed the clock, knew that she should telephone Simon to let him know that she was in London – and made no move to do so.

His reaction, when he'd realized she'd been having an affair with Francis through most of the time that Francis and Geraldine had been engaged, had been almost as extreme as Artemis's.

Francis's family problems had been even worse. His father had informed him he no longer wanted any communication with him and that as far as he was concerned he no longer had a son. Hopes she'd had of mammoth pop concerts at Cedar Court, with herself headlining, had been ground into dust and, even after all this time, just thinking about that unfulfilled expectation made her seethingly, spittingly angry.

Her eyes narrowed. Just because she was in London again, she wouldn't give in to what she had long since come to term her 'London demons'.

Primmie, Artemis and Geraldine were all in her past. None of them had made out of their lives what she had made out of hers. She was famous. She was a rock star.

She slammed her now empty coffee cup back down on the tray, well aware that though she was a rock star, she wasn't a rock superstar. None of her clutch of hit records had been a number one hit. When she toured, she always took second billing. True, the second billing was always to someone who was massive and the venues were prestigious, the arenas vast – but she didn't *want* to be second billing to Rod Stewart or Abba or Wings. *She* wanted to be the draw. *She* wanted to be massive. *She* wanted to be the superstar.

In deep depression she took off her kimono and, leaving it where it fell, walked into the en-suite bathroom and stepped into the shower, turning it on to full power. Where her career was concerned, she was at yet another crisis point. Francis simply wasn't big-league enough to represent her in the way she now needed to be represented. And nor was he ever going to *be* big-league enough – not now his main concern was cocaine.

Since they'd been in New York, Francis's use of cocaine had escalated sky high. At first she'd been indifferent about it, and then she'd become aware that his judgement and his sense of what worked musically was being affected. It was then, when she'd realized he was becoming a hindrance to her career, not a help, that she'd made up her mind that he had to go.

And that was why she was in London without him. She wanted time alone to gear herself up before the final, inevitable scene.

The professional reason for her trip was a benefit concert she was appearing at, in five days time, at the Albert Hall. Every rock star and band worth their salt was taking part and she'd been desperate to be included. Once confirmation had come that she was to be part of the package, Francis had suggested she take advantage of being in London by spending some time with Kit, playing around with ideas for new arrangements. Working informally at Courtfield Road was a habit of long-standing. Only when she was convinced that a song was really workable would she suggest it to the recording studio she was contracted to.

'I want some shopping time to myself,' she'd said to Francis when, in New York, he'd said he would be attending the benefit. 'I'm not going to trumpet the fact that I'm in London until the day before the concert when I turn up at rehearsals. I'm not in the mood for meeting up with people and partying.'

Francis, who never did anything but party, had shrugged, happy in the knowledge that there'd be parties and action enough once the benefit was over. With such a large collection of rock stars and bands, all gathered at one prestigious venue, how could the aftermath not be an orgy of wild times?

She'd read his mind as clearly as if he'd spoken aloud. Now, as she stepped from the shower and towelled herself dry, she wondered how he would find his wild times without her. He was, after all, only at the parties of the famous because of his position as her manager. As she was the only person he managed, once she dropped him, he'd be on no one's A

195

list. There'd been a time when – on the back of managing her – he could have picked up other clients with ease. With his managerial and creative judgement now shot to pieces by prolonged use of charlie, that was no longer the case.

Still naked, she began putting on make-up, not overly caring about Francis's future partying problems. Her own problems were what concerned her. After nine years in the business, twelve if she dated the start of her singing career to when she was fifteen and had begun singing with the group Ty managed, she still wasn't a superstar – and, over the years, she'd tried everything. She'd fronted a group and she'd gone solo. She'd written and recorded her own material and she'd done ace covers of other people's material. She'd given it her all in Britain and she'd done her damned best in the States. She'd done clubs, festivals and toured until she never wanted to see a tour bus again. She'd recorded hard rock, soft rock, even punk rock – and she *still* wasn't where she wanted to be.

The American manager she had arranged would handle her career once she'd given Francis the heave-ho had told her she'd been mismanaged. 'I've seen you a bunch of times,' he'd said. 'You've not captured what you do live on a record yet. Not truly. And you've been spreading yourself too thin. Your career's been unfocused, but with me at the helm it sure as hell isn't going to be so any longer.'

She pulled on skin-tight leather trousers and a clinging white Stars and Stripes T-shirt. With new management she would, at last, be where she should have been seven years ago. She would be a diva. An icon. Francis had been a mistake. He was a loser. In retrospect, she thought that he probably always had been a loser and that only his Prince Charming handsomeness and upper-class confidence had, until his overindulgence on cocaine, hidden the fact from her – and from other people.

Thirty minutes later Kit Armstrong was greeting her at his Courtfield Road studio, a mug of steaming black coffee in one hand, a cigarette in the other.

'Hi, Kiki. You look great. Where's Francis?'

'Francis is history,' she said, as he kissed her on the cheek. 'Or he will be once the Albert Hall benefit concert is over.'

His eyebrows rose and he pursed his lips.

'And don't look at me like that,' she said crossly. 'Instead of furthering my career he spends all his time off his tits on coke.'

Kit grinned. 'And when has that been a sin?' he asked, leading the way down the corridor that led from the deceptively ordinary front door to the enormous studio that lay at the back of the house. 'How else do you get through after-show parties and endless schmoozing?'

'He doesn't only use it to be sociable.' They stopped off in the kitchen and she dropped her tote bag on to the first convenient chair. 'And his judgement has gone. He suffers mood swings. He's aggressive. Paranoid.'

'Whoa!' Kit held up both hands. 'Aggressive? *Francis?*

'You betcha.' Her green cat-eyes glittered. 'And I don't have to put up with it. Not when it's my career he's flushing down the pan!'

Kit frowned, his lazy good humour ebbing. 'But that's not happening, Kiki, is it? Word around town is that though you're not top of the tree in Britain you're near to being so Stateside.'

Kiki made a snorting sound. 'That's thanks to a London-based publicist earning his wedge.' She ran a hand through her hair, her shoulders slumped. 'I'm doing OK in America, Kit, but I'm not as big there as publicity articles here have led people to believe. And that's between you and me and no one else, OK?'

He nodded, well aware he was probably the only person in the world to whom she would speak with such truthfulness.

'So what's the plan?' he asked, knowing very well that with Kiki there would be one.

She perched on a high stool and kicked off her sandals.

'First, I get Francis out of my life. He may have been great for my career in the early days, but he's lost it, Kit. Well and truly. Though I'm not as big as I want to be in America, I'm bigger there than I've ever been here – so I'm going to continue to make New York my base. I have a hotshot American manager lined up. I'm already in a recording contract . . .'

'Which Francis negotiated?'

She nodded, unabashed, ' . . . and I want to persuade the powers that be that it's time I changed my sound from hard rock to . . .'

'Lighter, more commercial fare?'

' . . . to beat-heavy urban funk.'

Kit put down his mug of coffee and opened the door of a giant fridge. 'Extreme is never a good idea,' he said, reaching for a bottle of vodka and a bottle of kahlua. 'You've still got your London fan-base to think about – and take it from me, London isn't yet ready for the sort of gritty lyrics and tunes you've been hearing on the streets of New York.'

He mixed a Black Russian and added ice. 'My advice . . . if you're going to re-package yourself . . . would be to hone in on the dance scene and release a series of dance-orientated singles.' He handed her the cocktail. 'You couldn't go wrong. John Travolta and Olivia Newton-John were number one in June with "You're the One That I Want". And what is top of the charts as we speak? "Summer Nights", by the same squeaky-clean duo.'

Kiki pulled a face. 'Yeah, well, I'm not squeaky-clean.'

Picking up his coffee mug again, he guffawed with laughter. 'You never spoke a truer word! Shit, Kiki. You're not even *nice*. You're a manipulative egomaniac who doesn't give a damn about anyone but herself.'

Her feline face split into a grin. 'Yeah, well, I have an agenda,' she said, totally unoffended. 'And nice people don't become world-famous rock stars.'

Kit opened his mouth, about to say that Lulu had managed pretty OK, and then, knowing her jealous streak, thought better of it. 'So let's get to grips with today's agenda,' he said. 'I've blocked out the rest of the day in the diary, so what say we make a start?'

Still holding her glass of vodka and kahlua, Kiki slid from the stool. 'Fine with me,' she said, and, in a far better mood than the one she had arrived in, she followed him out of the kitchen and into the studio.

Later, when she was leaning against the end of the console, her head down on her forearms, listening to playback, Kit said, casually 'By the way, Geraldine Grant was in one of the gossip columns last week. Some kind of a bash at the French Embassy. She looked very swish.'

'Did she?' She raised her head sharply. The unexpected

mention of Geraldine's name left her feeling as if she'd been punched in the chest, but her voice was as casual as his. 'Who was she with? A husband? A boyfriend?'

The playback came to an end. Neither of them commented on it. Instead he was staring at her, eyebrows raised. 'A boyfriend, I think. Doesn't Francis know if she's married? I know his running off with you estranged them, but as they are cousins I'd have thought news as to whether she was married or not would have filtered along the old family grapevine.'

Kiki gave a rude snort. 'There isn't a family grapevine – not one that extends to Francis. None of his family has anything to do with him. It's why there have never been any rock concerts at Cedar Court. We were forbidden to show our faces there from day one.'

'How very prehistoric.' Kit's black silk shirt was half open to the waist and he toyed with a shark's tooth hanging round his neck. 'Will things change when the two of you are no longer together, d'you think?'

Kiki shrugged. 'I don't know. I don't care.' This time she didn't have to try to sound indifferent, because she was.

Kit looked down at his outsize wristwatch. 'The musicians I've booked will be here in a minute. D'you want me to try and dig out the newspaper while we wait for them?'

'Sure. Cool.'

She fought the desire to begin biting her nails. Why was she so fussed by the thought that, only a week ago, Geraldine had been in London? She probably lived in London again now. Had probably been living in London for years.

She chewed the corner of her lip again. If Geraldine were moving in the kind of circles that reached the gossip columns, would she still be in touch with Primmie? Did Geraldine, Primmie and Artemis all meet up regularly for girlie, giggly lunches? Did Geraldine and Primmie stay weekends in the Cotswolds with Artemis and Rupert? Did Artemis and Rupert and Primmie and her husband perhaps all spend weekends together at Cedar Court? And if they did, was her name ever mentioned? Did any of them ever wish that they'd somehow stayed friends with her?

'Here you are.' Kit slapped a crumpled newspaper into her hands. 'It's a brilliant photo, isn't it?'

It was. Geraldine was wearing an evening gown that looked as if it had been designed by Givenchy or Saint Laurent. Her night-black hair was swept high in an elegant chignon. Her long, glittering earrings looked to be composed of nothing but diamonds. The man with her was middle aged and distinguished looking, his hair silver-grey at the temples, his dinner jacket a dream of masculine tailoring. They were arm in arm and there was a caption beneath the photograph. *After talks with the Prime Minister, the European industrialist Monsieur André Barre attended a reception at the French Embassy with his regular companion, London-born Miss Geraldine Grant.*

'Yes,' she said to Kit, her voice as indifferent as before. She handed him back the newspaper and changed the subject. 'If the musicians you've booked don't turn up pretty pronto we're not going to be able to play about with the backing and I may as well not have bothered coming.'

'They'll be here.' He tossed the newspaper into a rubbish bin. 'So who's the latest man in your life, Kiki? Spill the beans.'

'It's no one you need know about.' Leon was a twenty-three-year-old, light-skinned black American. As handsome as sin, he was really a jazz drummer and could make the beat take off like no other drummer she'd ever heard. Having no intention of allowing Kit to get his rocks off by feasting on details of her love life, she began thinking about the newspaper photograph again.

Geraldine was quite obviously not yet married and, as she wasn't described as being André Barre's fiancée, was apparently not about to be. She looked good, though. She looked a million dollars.

There came the distant sound of a doorbell ringing. 'We have lift-off,' Kit said, striding past her. 'And remember, Kiki. We're going to try an 8-string base on "Nightline". If it doesn't work, we'll go to 12. Just be sunny.'

She made another rude noise. Being sunny, the way she felt right now, was impossible. She had too many things on her mind. She took a packet of Rizlas and a small polythene envelope out of the rear pocket of her jeans and began rolling a joint. What she needed, to restore her equilibrium, was some good sex. In three days' time Leon, as part of the band backing her for the benefit, would be flying in with Francis – but three days' time wasn't soon enough.

As there came the sound of loud voices and laughter, she looked towards the door Kit had left open with interest. With luck, one of the musicians would be a hunk. Life couldn't be all problems and disappointments. She was a rock star, about to appear at one of the most prestigious venues in Europe alongside the biggest names in the business. Casual sex went with her territory – and she had no quibble about casual sex. Absolutely none at all.

Four days later, she was in seventh heaven. The rehearsals at the Albert Hall had been going on for most of the day and the fevered activity – the rubbing shoulders with fellow rock stars, the sense of being a player, of being where the action was, of being wonderfully special – was meat and drink to her. Or it was until her old buddy Davy Jones wandered over to have a chat whilst she was watching Boney M go through their paces.

'Hiya,' he said, nursing steaming coffee in a paper cup. 'I'm disappointed in you, Kiki. You know that, don't you?'

'What for?' Davy was one of the few guys who had never made a pass at her and so she knew he wasn't referring to an occasion when she hadn't come across.

'The Cocoanut Grove date in Los Angeles. When our manager asked Francis if you'd like to second bill on it for us we thought you'd jump at the chance. As it is we had to make do with a singer so bad, if his performance had been a fight it would have been stopped.'

She didn't laugh. She couldn't. She felt frozen inside. 'Are you telling me that Francis was approached with an offer for me to perform at the Cocoanut Grove with The Monkees?'

His eyebrows rose as he cottoned on to the fact that she hadn't known about it. 'For four weeks, two shows a night.'

'When was this?' She could hardly get the words past her lips, her jaw was clamped so tight. The Cocoanut Grove, Los Angeles. It would have meant the chance of being reviewed in the *Hollywood Reporter,* even, perhaps, the *Los Angeles Times.* There would have been celebrities in the audience.

201

Movers and shakers. Hell, it might even have led to a stint in Las Vegas!

'Six months ago. Are you telling me Francis never told you the offer was on the table?'

Twenty yards or so away from them, on stage, Boney M were going through 'Rivers of Babylon' for the third time as the lighting for it was adjusted and re-adjusted.

'No,' she said, white to the lips. 'It obviously slipped his mind.'

Because he was only her height, Davy's eyes met hers straight on. 'Then get yourself another manager,' he said sagely. 'Slips of memory like that are no help to anyone's career. Is he with you now? Here at the Hall?'

Somehow, she managed to unclamp her jaw. 'He should be. He should have arrived today, but he hasn't shown yet. But when he does . . .'

She didn't finish her sentence. She didn't need to. When Francis finally showed he would be doing so for the last time.

'The Cocoanut Grove!' she screamed at him as he lounged against the door of her otherwise empty communal dressing room, looking jet-lagged and the worse for wear. 'The Cocoanut Grove, and you didn't even *tell* me about it! Why? Were you off your head on charlie, or was it simply that you couldn't be bothered?'

It was the next day and the concert was already under way. In five minutes, perhaps less, it would be time for her to strut on to the stage and to give it all she'd got. At the moment, though, she could think of nothing but unleashing her pent-up fury.

'You *know* how important America is to me! You *know* how prestigious the Cocoanut Grove venue is. If I'd once successfully fronted for The Monkees, then I'd probably have been able to do more and more with them – perhaps even record with them and appear on their TV show! You're my manager and yet you blew it for me! Well, you sure as hell aren't going to blow anything else! I've had it with you, Francis. I want you out of my life every which way there is!'

'So I forgot,' he said wearily. 'It isn't the end of the world, Kiki. And don't let's row when we're within hearing of nearly

202

every group that's appearing. Go on stage, do your stuff, and then we'll talk.'

'Like hell we will!' She was wearing a boldly coloured neo-psychedelic jacket with nothing beneath it but a black bra, skin-tight black trousers and four-inch-high silver-heeled stilettos. 'I want you to get the fuck out now, Francis! As far as you're concerned, I'm a memory, got it? If we're ever in the same room again, you don't see me. Got it?'

He blanched, suddenly aware that this was no ordinary row – that she was deathly serious.

'What's the matter, Kiki?' he asked tightly. 'Have I outgrown my usefulness? Are you going to move on to someone with more to offer you? Are you hungry for another victim?'

'Yes,' she said brutally, noting dispassionately how his looks were beginning to go. His fair-haired, Prince Charming hand-someness had once been his redeeming grace. Now, though he was only thirty, the waving hair he still wore shoulder-length was beginning to thin and looked dull – and he was too thin. There was now no longer anything sexy about his narrow hips. They merely looked bony. They'd been together for six years when they should have been together for a year – if that.

'Yes,' she said again, no longer shouting, but tightly in control. 'Yes, I have outgrown you and yes, I am going on to the next person who will be useful to me. As for your being a victim, if that's how you see yourself, then that's what you are. But I didn't make you one. That's been down to you, Francis. No one else.'

There came a hammering on the door and Leon's voice shouted: 'Get the hell outta there, Kiki! We're on next!'

She strode towards the door and Francis moved out of her way. 'I don't want to find you here when I come back,' she said tersely as she opened the door. 'You're not my manager any more. Got it?'

'Oh yes,' he said bitterly. 'Where you are concerned, Kiki, I got things a long time ago.'

She hesitated, about to at least throw him a final goodbye.

Leon seized hold of her arm. 'What the fuck d'you think you're playing at, babe?' he demanded, beginning to propel her down the stone-floored corridor at top speed. 'It's a five-minute hike from here to the stage. Get your ass moving *now.*'

Without looking back at Francis, she broke into a run.

Six minutes later, she was prancing on stage for her 'Twilight Love' opening number. The vast audience, already well warmed up by previous acts, roared approval for a song that had first been a hit for her six years ago. Her surge of adrenalin was cataclysmic. This was all that mattered. This was where she wanted to be. And with Francis now part of her history and a new hotshot American manager all set to re-package her image and take her to new heights, she'd soon be headlining concerts as a bona fide rock phenomenon.

Behind her, she could hear Leon really taking off on the drums. The rest of the six-member band were top-notch, too. As she went into her next number, she maintained the heart-pounding pace; the applause was thunderous. Sweat was pouring off her, but she didn't care. This sensation of being the centre of the universe was all she wanted. It was all she'd ever wanted. And as she gloried in the spotlight, no one was further from her thoughts than Francis Sheringham.

Eighteen

September 1978

Geraldine let herself into her ground-floor Parisian apartment. The house, with Palladian columns decorating its main façade, was set on a bend in the road, near to the Madeleine. In a previous age it had been one of many prestigious mansions, now it stood a little isolated, uncomfortably at odds with the busy, twentieth-century traffic hurtling past its paved courtyard frontage.

Nothing hurtled past at the mansion's rear, though. As Geraldine closed the door to her apartment behind her and looked ahead through the hall and into the salon she could see, through the arched French windows, the small garden that had motivated her into signing the lease and agreeing to an astronomical rent.

There was none of the vibrant colour of Cedar Court's magnificent herbaceous borders, no spectacular vista of lawns and rolling parkland. What there was, though, was an intricate, classical box-hedged parterre, so dramatic that it looked as if it were a stage set.

Dropping her lizard-skin shoulder bag on to a gilded reproduction Louis XVI salon chair, she walked over to the windows, opened them and stepped outside.

When she had moved into the apartment, five years ago, the spaces enclosed by the box hedges had been rank with weeds. Now they were planted with white flowers from spring to autumn. In April the delicate lockets of white dicentra swayed in gentle movement. In summer Iceberg roses were a sea of foaming blossom, and now, in September, wax-white Japanese anemones fluttered and stirred above the dense green of the box.

She leaned against the jamb of the French windows, wishing she had a drink in her hand. The rosewood credenza that served her as a drinks cabinet was only a dozen steps away but she didn't have the energy to turn round and walk back into the room. She felt too melancholy; too deep in thoughts of her recent, unsettling trip to London.

The temptation to get in touch with both Primmie and Artemis had, when she had been there, nearly overwhelmed her. Only the thought of the lies she would have ended up telling them had deterred her. After six years of no real contact – apart from the birthday and Christmas cards she had sent them – they would have wanted to know why she preferred Paris to London, what it was that was keeping her there; what it was she did for a living.

Lies, of course, would have been easy. When she'd first arrived in Paris she'd built on the antiques course she'd taken at Sotheby's by taking a fine art and antiques course at the Louvre, and she could have said that on finishing it she'd begun working at a gallery, or that she was a PA to an art dealer. She could, in fact, have told them anything – that she was a secretary, a receptionist, or a stylist again – and they would have been none the wiser. It wouldn't, though, have explained why she'd made no direct contact with them and why, on the cards she had sent, she had never given an address to which they could have written back.

It was late afternoon and the sky was smoking to dusk. The immaculately clipped box parterre was surrounded by pale gravel and beyond the gravel was a profusion of less geometric planting. Cistus, white hydrangeas, choisya, the pale grey leaves of Jerusalem sage. She watched the late summer light play on the restricted green, white and grey colours of her carefully thought out, restrained planting scheme and tried to imagine what Artemis's and Primmie's reactions would have been if she had told them that she was a high-class call girl.

She couldn't do it. Her imagination simply wouldn't take her that far. She could, of course, have dressed up the description of what she did by saying that she worked for an escort agency, but what would have been the point? Even Artemis would have known what was meant by that.

'You are a sex worker,' her friend Dominique would say with a Gallic shrug, her English heavily accented. 'So what ees ze problem?'

The answer was that there wasn't one – apart from the fact that she didn't want Artemis and Primmie to know that she was a sex worker.

The longing for a drink overcame her disinclination to move and she turned and walked back into the salon. The temptation to meet up again with Artemis and Primmie hadn't been the only reason her trip to London, with André Barre, had so unsettled her. There had also been another temptation. The temptation to drive down to Cedar Court and to never, ever leave it.

Her hand trembled slightly as she poured Rémy into a cut-glass tumbler and added a cube of ice.

'Cedar Court is always here for you, my dear,' her Uncle Piers had said to her in the indescribably hellish hours after Kiki's telephone call from Rome. 'You needn't fear finding Francis here. This is an outrage too far and I shall be telling him so. From now on, I don't want to see him. He's never had a sense of responsibility towards his heritage. You're the only one who's ever valued the house and our family history. It's your family home and, as always, you are welcome to live here whenever you want and for however long you want.'

She'd been so slaughtered with grief at all she had lost that she'd barely been able to thank him for his kindness. And he had been kind. Everyone had been kind. But she hadn't wanted kindness. She'd wanted Francis and she'd wanted Cedar Court. She'd wanted it not just as her family home, but as her marital home – the home where her children would have been born. The home her eldest son would have inherited.

At the thought of Francis marrying Kiki and having children, and of Kiki's son inheriting after Francis, she had vomited until all she had been able to bring up was bile.

She hadn't taken up her uncle's offer. To be at Cedar Court, without Francis would have been a pain beyond enduring.

Instead, she had fled to Paris, returning to England only twice. The first time for her mother's funeral, the second time because André Barre had wanted her on his arm when he attended the reception at the French Embassy in London – and because she had thought that she could at last make a visit to London without subjecting herself to memories she preferred to suppress.

She'd been wrong in thinking she could do so.

The very first thing that had met her eyes as André Barre's chauffeured car paused at traffic lights en route to London from the airport had been a giant poster advertising a rock concert to be held at the Albert Hall. Kiki's name hadn't been headlining the bill and hadn't been printed in very large letters, but she had seen it all the same.

It was then that her stomach had begun churning, for she'd known that if Kiki was in London, or about to come to London, then so was Francis. What if she ran into the two of them? What if she saw him, his arm around Kiki, happy with her? London wasn't a village, and such a meeting wasn't likely, but stranger things had happened.

Seated in the back of the limousine, André's heavy thigh close against hers, she had felt beads of sweat break out on her forehead. It was too late now for her to head back to

France, but if she'd known Kiki and Francis were to be in London, not America, then she would never have accepted André's invitation. Never. Not in a million years.

Nursing the Rémy, she went back outside, this time walking down the broad shallow steps that led on to the gravel. At the far end of the small garden was a trellised wall thick with ivy, and in front of it, beneath the boughs of a silver birch, was a small wrought-iron table and a single chair. Still cradling the Rémy, she sat down, looking back over the dark green density of the box-hedged parterre and its infill of white anemones, wondering if Kiki had contacted Artemis and Primmie when she was in London.

In the hideous hours after the telephone call from Rome, Artemis, still in her matron of honour dress, had vowed that for as long as she lived she would never have anything to do with Kiki. Primmie hadn't echoed her, but Primmie's shock at Kiki's action had, she knew, been deep and it was impossible to imagine her ever condoning it. That, though, had been six years ago, and six years was a long time.

She took another deep swallow of cognac. Perhaps, by now, Artemis and Primmie were again on speaking terms with Kiki. Perhaps they and their husbands would be attending the concert at the Albert Hall and afterwards perhaps they would have dinner with Kiki and Francis or, as Kiki and Francis's guests, go to a glamorous showbiz party with them.

A blackbird flew down from the silver birch and began searching the ground beneath the choisya for worms. She watched it, knowing she was making a huge assumption where Primmie was concerned. Primmie might not be married. She might be quite content to be a high-flyer at BBDO. She was very likely a senior account director by now, or perhaps even on the board.

At the thought of how much she missed Primmie, a spasm of pain crossed her face. If only she could visit Primmie and have Primmie visit her – but she'd known from the moment she had embarked on escort work that she couldn't possibly remain in contact with Primmie and Artemis. It simply wouldn't have been fair to either of them to have her world touching theirs in any way, shape or form.

The blackbird, a worm in its beak, flew back into the tree.

The light was changing now, deepening into the spangling blue dusk of mid-evening. She rose to her feet. She hadn't played back her answerphone messages yet and there would, as always, be a long stream of them to listen to and to respond to.

Fifteen minutes later, seated at her Empire-style secretaire, listening to the messages with a pen in one hand and a large diary open in front of her, she was every inch a career woman running a highly successful business. And a career woman was how she thought of herself.

'It ees a business, yes?' Dominique, a fellow student on the fine arts and antiques course she'd been attending, had said to her after breaking the astounding news that she was funding her way through the course by working for an escort agency. 'How else could I afford such expensive fees?'

Geraldine hadn't known, because it was a question she'd never had to address. Her place on the course had been paid for out of an allowance that came from family money.

The knowledge of how Dominique was financing herself hadn't interfered with their casual friendship. They generally spent their lunch-times together, buying a baguette at one of the many cafés near to the Louvre and then walking the short distance to the Seine to sit and eat. Only when Dominique had realized that she didn't have a boyfriend had their casual friendship turned into something a little deeper.

'That is very strange, *n'est-ce pas*?' she had said, taking it for granted that a girl with Geraldine's striking looks would have no trouble finding a boyfriend if she wanted one.

Previously in such circumstances Geraldine had kept her thoughts to herself. This time, to her great surprise, she had found herself telling Dominique all about Francis and Cedar Court – and all about Kiki.

It had forged a bond between them. From then on, though Dominique never took the place that Artemis, Primmie and Kiki had once held in her life, she had become someone she spent time with, both at the Louvre and away from it.

Then had come the day when, just as they were about to go in to a lecture on eighteenth-century ceramics, Dominique had been told there was a telephone call for her.

Half an hour later, they had met up at their usual lunchtime café. '*Merde*!' Dominique had said, her part pixie, part Joan of Arc face stressed. 'My father is going to be in Paris overnight and wants to spend the evening with me – and I'm scheduled to meet a client at eight o'clock at the George V.'

'Tell the agency you can't make the appointment. Another girl will have to go,' she'd said, buying baguettes for them both.

'It is not so simple, Jerraldeen.' As she had softened the g and rolled her r's, Dominique's dark eyes had been despairing. 'It is a first-time client – a very important first-time client – a sheikh. If I tell the agency I can't meet with him, they won't give me the chance of such a good offer again. I was very lucky to get him in the first place – and I was hoping he would become a regular. Then I wouldn't have to spend so many evenings with boring fat businessmen.'

Geraldine had made a sympathetic noise and handed Dominique her baguette.

'You just don't know how competitive agency work is,' Dominique had said glumly as they walked out of the café and began walking towards the Seine. 'I'm not regarded as being very committed, because it's known I'm only working to fund my studies. And a sheikh! He was probably only assigned to me by accident and now I can't capitalize on it! It simply isn't fair! *C'est un crime*!'

'Couldn't you get another girl to take your place without letting the agency know?' she had suggested, trying to be helpful.

Dominique had pondered the suggestion for a moment or two and had then shaken her head. '*Non.* I've told you, this is a very competitive business. If I did, I'd never get him back again.'

They sat down on a bench beside the river, looking across its glittering surface towards the turrets of the Conciergerie and the spires of Notre Dame.

'Then I have no more suggestions,' she had said, thinking of the ground-floor apartment she had just viewed near the Madeleine, and wondering if she had the front to ask her father if he would increase her already substantial allowance so that she would be able to afford its exorbitant rent.

'Ah! But I have one!' Dominique's flawless-skinned face

was no longer glum, but radiantly alight. 'If *you* took my place, there would be no such problem. It is a perfect solution, *n'est-ce pas*? You simply tell him that you are me – and if he asks for you again, when I turn up I will explain to him and keep him happy.'

'And if he's disappointed that it is not me he is seeing again?' she had asked teasingly.

'Once I am with him, there will be no chance of that,' Dominique had said smugly. 'I am a professional – or, at least, a semi-professional. And I am French,' she had added, as if that settled the question.

Laughter had risen in Geraldine's throat. Dominique was quite right in assuming herself to be streets ahead in sexual experience where numbers of partners were concerned, but she rather felt she could make quite an impression, if she so wanted – and the assumption that French women were far superior to English women in the sexual expertise stakes rankled.

'Would you like to take a bet on it?' she had said good-humouredly.

'I would love to take a bet on it, *chérie,*' Dominique had responded, vastly relieved that her problem was solved.

Sheikh Abdul Mustafa was Eton educated and an erudite man and, much to her chagrin, Dominique had lost her bet.

With the last appointment nearly pencilled in her desk diary, a corner of Geraldine's mouth tugged into a smile as she continued responding to her many answerphone messages and reflecting on how shamelessly easily she had slipped into her new lifestyle.

She had never been on the books of any agency. She hadn't wanted to be. At first she had merely continued to be the sheikh's paid companion whenever he was in Paris – which was often – and then, when her course at the Louvre came to an end and she had been faced with the prospect of finding a job, she had decided that any job would be too restrictive.

She enjoyed her free time. She enjoyed not having to be up in the morning at seven or eight o'clock. She enjoyed being able to choose when she would work and when she would not. And she enjoyed the company of wealthy men.

If she had been on the books of an escort agency, she would, she knew, have found herself spending most of her time with men she would never, under normal circumstances, ever want to spend time with, let alone go to bed with. Abdul had been an exception, and it was only exceptional men she was interested in. He'd had friends. There had been introductions. With nine out of ten introductions, it had never gone any further, because she'd been very, very picky as to whom she added to her client list.

That she wasn't reliant on the income she earned from selling her body and companionship infuriated and bewildered Dominique. 'Then why do it, Jerraldeen?' she had demanded. 'Why not just find a rich boyfriend and marry and be happy?'

Dominique had long ago given up escort work. The instant she had her qualification from the Louvre beneath her belt, she had found herself a job in a small gallery on the Left Bank and couldn't understand why Geraldine didn't do the same.

'Because I don't want to have to be up early every morning and be at someone else's beck and call all day,' she had said with blunt honesty. 'And I'm not in the market for a husband. People only have one soulmate in a lifetime – and I've known the identity of mine since before I could walk. I won't find another soulmate, Dominique. It isn't possible.'

Aware that Francis was beginning to fill her thoughts and not wanting him to, she pushed her diary to one side and rose to her feet.

She had no appointments to keep. The evening was hers, to do with as she pleased. She put an LP on to her record player and, as the sound of Maria Callas singing Verdi filled the apartment, went into her bedroom to take off the cream linen suit she was wearing.

The suit was a businesswoman's suit and it was typical of the way she now dressed. The floaty, vintage clothes she had once loved so much were a thing of the past. They gave out the wrong image. The key to frequenting hotel lounges and bars without attracting the unwelcome attention of the management was to dress as if for an executive meeting.

The telephone rang. She waited for the answerphone to click on.

'*Chérie*,' Dominique said impatiently. 'Pick up the phone. I need to talk to you.'

212

Switching the answerphone off, she picked up the receiver and settled herself comfortably on her king-size bed.

'*Soir*, Dominique,' she said affectionately. 'What is it you need to talk about?'

'I have an old school friend who wants to do escort work, but doesn't want the hassle of doing it via an agency – and who hasn't the connections to sort it for herself,' Dominique said, not beating about the bush. 'Would you take her under your wing, Jerraldeen? Make some introductions for her? She's only interested in the "if you have to ask the price, you can't afford it" end of the market – and she's happy to pay you a hefty commission.'

Geraldine's lips twitched in amusement. 'I thought you were upset that I was still doing escort work myself, Dominique? Don't you think beginning to pimp is even worse?'

'*Non*.' Dominique's voice was quite decisive. 'Pimping is the way you should go, *chérie*. You are a great organizer and you know many, many rich men – especially rich Englishmen.'

Geraldine's mouth twitched again. When Dominique had first realized the kind of social background she came from she had been over the moon with delight. 'But these men – these polo players and these friends of your father's and your uncle's – they will *love* to be introduced to beautiful, upmarket French escort girls whenever they are in Paris!' she had said when she had realized Geraldine's connections. 'You have contacts too good to ignore!' Aware that Dominique was still waiting for a response from her, she said, 'Does your friend have her *baccalauréat*?'

'*Merde*!' Dominique's voice rose several decibels. 'Yes! But what does it matter? She wants to earn money as a call-girl, not as a brain surgeon!'

'Because the kind of clients I cultivate are the kind who expect intelligent company as well as glamorous company. I've got my own reputation to consider here, Dominique.'

'Then you will do it? *Merveilleux*! I will get Veronique to ring you.'

Later, relaxing in a deep, foam-filled, scented bath, Geraldine reflected on how easy it would be for her to run her own escort business. The girls would have to be very carefully selected, but as she knew from her client list, she was good at careful selection.

The sound of Callas singing 'O Don Fatale', from Verdi's *Don Carlos* permeated the lamp-lit apartment and she closed her eyes, enjoying Callas's interpretation of the imperious and strong-willed Princess Eboli, about to be banished from court for betraying the Queen. As Callas's stupendous voice expressed passionate anguish, Geraldine reflected that if she were to run an escort agency she was going to have to expand her client list dramatically.

She didn't envisage it being a problem. She had, as Dominique had previously pointed out, plenty of excellent contacts, all of which could be quarried hard. She slid a little lower beneath the scented bubbles. And she could run classified ads in the *International Herald Tribune*. As long as the ads were worded in such a way that glamorous 'company' was all that was being offered, she wouldn't run foul of the law.

The more she thought about the idea, the better she liked it. The building up of a successful agency would be a challenge. It would satisfy her well-developed business instincts and would keep huge amounts of money flowing effortlessly into her bank account.

As 'O Don Fatale' ended, she opened her eyes, her decision made.

She was going to move from the shop floor into management.

She was going to become a madam.

Nineteen

September 1978

Artemis sat back on her heels in front of the opened suitcase. On either side of her were piles of clothes, all neatly folded, all waiting to be packed.

'Me, Mummy. Me.' From a nearby drawer Destiny was

dragging underwear Artemis had no intention of taking with them to Spain.

'That's lovely, darling, but Mummy only wants the clothes that are here, on the floor in piles,' she said lovingly.

Destiny beamed at her seraphically, hoisted the clothes across to the suitcase and dropped them in it. 'Me, please,' she said, giving Artemis a sticky kiss on the cheek. 'Me please, Mummy.'

Artemis felt as if her heart were being squeezed. Destiny's speech and understanding were those of a three-year-old and yet she was now five. Why, when she was able to accept that Destiny was a little slow for her age, couldn't Rupert accept it? Why had he to be so nasty about it and make so many difficulties?

'She isn't just slow, Artemis. She's backward!' he had shouted at her the previous evening when she had told him that she'd offered the use of their home to the local Women's Institute for their annual Autumn Fair. 'Do you want everyone to know our daughter is never going to be able to keep up in a normal school? Nearly all of those silly women you make jam with are married to men I socialize with! I'm not going to have everyone speculating about whose side of the family her mental slowness comes from! I still have some pride, even if you don't!'

It had been a hideous scene. An absolute nightmare.

Their shouting had woken Destiny who had then gone into a distressed crying jag. By the time she'd soothed her it had been midnight and, when she'd finally slid into bed beside Rupert, she'd lain awake for hours.

He hadn't reached out to her, to take her in his arms, to whisper that he was sorry, and to comfort her. Being a comfort, at any time, was not Rupert's forte.

She placed a pile of sarongs and a clutch of swimsuits into a corner of the suitcase. Married life was not the bowl of cherries she had expected it to be.

One of her first actions as Mrs Gower had been to give up working as a model and, instead, to channel her energies into being a supportive wife and, as they entertained on a large scale, an excellent hostess.

To her amazement, it had been a decision Rupert had hated, not because there was any great loss of income – she'd never been the kind of fashion model who'd earned squillions every time she stepped on to a catwalk, but because he felt she was robbing him of the kudos of having a fashion model for a wife. That he felt like this – that he had been living in the unrealistic belief that she would one day be a Twiggy or a Jerry Hall – had shocked her inexpressibly, because it had shown how little he really knew about her.

And he had certainly married her without realizing that his father-in-law was not a man he could socialize with without embarrassment.

She picked up a pile of brilliantly coloured T-shirts and held them close against her chest. Why couldn't he be more tolerant about things? Her father now lived in the Cayman Islands and they hardly ever saw him. And Destiny wasn't seriously handicapped. The educational psychologist they had seen had said that she had a slight learning disability and that, though there was a possibility it might grow worse as she grew older, necessitating her attending a special needs school, there was also the chance that with time there might be improvement.

'What kind of improvement?' Rupert had asked tightly as Destiny had played happily on the floor with different coloured spoons. 'Improvement enabling her to become well educated? To go to university?'

'I think those aims would be overly ambitious, Mr Gower. Destiny is never going to be a high academic achiever. What you can be grateful for is that she doesn't also have a specific learning difficulty, such as dyslexia. She doesn't have a hearing impairment. She isn't autistic. She doesn't have excessive emotional and behavioural difficulties.'

'But she may well need to go to a special school?' A pulse had begun beating at Rupert's jaw.

'It's a possibility. A lot will depend on the yearly assessments that are made over the next three or four years. Certainly I see no reason why she shouldn't attend a local primary school. However, by the time she is eight, there may be a case, for her own happiness, of her attending the kind of school where her obvious ability difference will not put her at risk of being bullied. And we wouldn't want that, would we?'

216

Parting Destiny from the spoons, Artemis had lifted her on to her knee. 'No,' she had said fervently, hugging her close. 'We want her to go to schools where she can realize her full potential and be happy. We want what is best for her, don't we, Rupert?'

He hadn't even looked towards her. His handsome face had been taut with barely controlled emotion. 'People will know, won't they?' he had said. 'When we take her out with us, people will guess she's retarded.'

'The word retarded is totally inapplicable, Mr Gower,' the psychologist had said icily. 'You have a daughter who is, and probably always will be, a slow learner. You also have a daughter who is beautiful, emotionally responsive and loving. The majority of parents who step into this room would consider you an exceedingly lucky man.'

It was then that Rupert had catapulted to his feet, his nostrils white, the pulse at his jaw line pounding. 'The majority of parents who step into this room didn't adopt the child they brought with them, did they?' he'd shouted with such unleashed passion Artemis had thought she was going to faint. 'When you adopt a child, you expect a healthy child, an intelligent child!'

He'd marched towards the door and yanked it open.

'What I didn't expect,' he'd stormed at the appalled psychologist, 'was a child who wouldn't be able to go to the school her name has been down for since she was born. And so you'll forgive me if I don't count myself lucky – if what I count myself is bloody, bloody, *un*lucky!'

He'd slammed the door after him with such force it had rocked on its hinges.

Destiny, alarmed by the noise, had let out a distressed wail. Artemis had lowered her to the floor and, holding her hand tightly, had stumbled to her feet. 'I'm sorry . . .' she had said, her voice so wobbly it hadn't even sounded like hers. 'My husband is upset . . . he expressed himself badly . . . he didn't mean . . .'

She hadn't been able to continue. She'd been crying too much.

She felt like crying now as she continued packing her suitcase for Spain. Destiny's suitcase was already packed, as was

217

Rupert's. Destiny loved their holiday home in Marbella. She loved the pool and being able to spend all day every day in a swimming costume. At Marbella, she had a friend, the gardener's six-year-old son, who regarded her as his best buddy. Because Destiny was always so happy in Spain, she, Artemis, had always looked forward to the times they spent there. She wasn't looking forward to it this time, though – not when Rupert was being so viciously unreasonable.

The Women's Institute Autumn Fair, for instance. Why shouldn't it be held at their home? What difference did it make if a wider circle of people met Destiny and realized that she had learning difficulties? It wasn't as if they could keep the fact that she was slow for her age a secret. And she didn't understand why Rupert should want to try to keep it a secret. Destiny was, after all, an enchanting child. She wouldn't ever gain a place at Oxford, but so what? And anyway she, herself, had never been overly bright academically. Yet Rupert had fallen in love with her. So, if he loved her, why couldn't he love Destiny?

Destiny, tired of ferrying clothes from drawers, had curled up on the sheepskin rug by the side of the bed and gone to sleep, her thumb in her mouth.

Looking at her, tears burned the backs of Artemis's eyes. More than anything else in the world she wanted Rupert to love Destiny in the same way that she did. To have a daddy that loved her and was proud of her was what every little girl deserved. Her own father had many faults and his nouveau riche brashness had often mortified her, but he'd always loved her, just as she'd always loved him.

She closed the lid of the case, passionately wishing that she could talk to Primmie – knowing that if she gave in to the temptation Rupert would never forgive her.

Careful not to disturb Destiny, she walked across to the window. Primmie didn't know that Destiny wasn't as bright as she should be for her age. In the early days, before Rupert had absolutely forbidden contact between the two of them, she had sometimes mentioned to Primmie that Destiny was being a little slow in learning to talk or to walk or to potty-train. Way back then, it had never occurred to her that it was something that would develop into a cause for concern – and

Primmie had never seemed to think it a cause for concern, either. The anxieties had come later and she'd been quite unable to talk to Primmie about them.

'Your husband is quite correct in his view that maintaining contact between yourselves and the birth mother is undesirable,' a woman from the Adoption Advice Service had said forcefully.

And so, because persisting would have put her marriage in danger, she had ended her frequent contact with Primmie. It hadn't stopped her constantly thinking about Primmie, though, for Destiny looked so like her.

Occasionally – just occasionally – usually when Destiny was throwing one of her rare temper tantrums – she also saw glimpses of Kiki. The reminder that Destiny was Kiki's half-sister always came as a slam of shock.

'Kiki doesn't know,' Primmie had said at the time of the adoption. 'And if she did know, it would complicate matters dreadfully.'

Her telling Kiki that Destiny was adopted had never been remotely likely. She'd had one telephone call from Kiki, shortly after Kiki had run off with Francis, and she had made it clear to Kiki then that she never wanted to speak to her again. Nor, apart from their parents, did she and Rupert tell anyone else. Only when Rupert had realized that Destiny wasn't progressing as she should had he begun mentioning to friends and extended family that she was adopted.

She knew why he'd begun telling people, of course. It was because her limited vocabulary embarrassed him.

She gazed broodingly down at her magnificent, rain-sodden garden. 'Embarrassed' was too coy an expression for what Rupert really felt. The bottom line was that he was ashamed of Destiny. She knew it. The psychologist had known it. And one day Destiny would probably know it, too.

'There are residential schools,' he'd said to her the previous evening, before their discussion had grown ugly and heated. 'The sooner she goes to one, Artemis, the better it will be for her.'

'But she's happy at her primary school!' she'd protested, fighting back tears. 'She'd hate to be away from home – away from me – she's *five and a half*, Rupert. To send her to a residential school would be cruel. It would be *barbarous*!'

219

It was then that he'd stormed from the house, driving away at criminally high speed.

It was now twelve hours later and he still hadn't returned.

Fighting back tears, she wondered where he had spent the night and if he would be home in time for them to catch their flight, late that evening, to Malaga If he weren't, it wouldn't be the end of the world, for they could always book on another, later flight.

Or she and Destiny could fly out without him.

Her last thought was so untypical of her, it made her feel quite giddy. The way she organized her life was around Rupert. As a banker, the demands on his time were enormous and making arrangements so that they fitted in with his busy schedule – and rearranging them if his schedule changed – was second nature to her.

This time, though, was different. This time holiday plans weren't under threat of having to be rearranged because of Rupert's banking commitments. This time she would be quite within her rights to carry on with them regardless.

The logic of her reasoning didn't make her feel any happier. If Rupert returned home to find that she and Destiny had left for Marbella without him he would be furiously angry. So angry it was quite possible he wouldn't fly out to Spain at all – and then where would she be? The answer was that if she weren't very careful, she would be in a marriage heading for the rocks. And she didn't want that. Not in a million years did she want that.

'Don't think that your husband's reaction is unique, Mrs Gower,' the psychologist had said to her after Rupert's obscenely abrupt departure from his office. 'Many parents – especially fathers – find the path to accepting their child as he, or she, is, and not as they had expected them to be, difficult. Acceptance needs time . . . and patience.'

He had, she knew, been talking about her having patience with Rupert. Well, patience was something she had in abundance. She hated rows and confrontations – which was one of the reasons the scenes of the last few weeks had been so hard for her to handle. When her world had consisted simply of Kiki, Geraldine and Primmie, she had always been the placid member of their tight-knit foursome, a follower, not a leader. She didn't possess an iota of Kiki's mercurial mood swings, or Geraldine's single-track strength of mind, or Primmie's brave stoicism. She'd always needed someone to lean on and, without her friends around her, the person she leaned on was Rupert.

And she couldn't envisage ever doing otherwise.

Behind her, still curled on the sheepskin rug, Destiny made a little snuffling noise in her sleep. Turning away from the window and stepping towards her, Artemis slipped off the cashmere cardigan she was wearing and laid it gently over Destiny's shoulders. She was going to behave for the rest of the day just as she would have done if the hideous row between herself and Rupert had never taken place. She was going to leave Destiny in the care of Kirsten, their Austrian au pair, and drive into Cirencester to buy the remaining few articles she wanted to take with her to the villa.

With a last, loving look towards her soundly sleeping daughter she left the room, went downstairs, told Kirsten that Destiny was asleep on the rug in the bedroom and, pausing only to pick up a jacket and her shoulder bag, left the house.

The rain that had fallen earlier was no longer in evidence and the fields and hedgerows on either side of the A436 were dappled in sunshine. As she drove through the loveliness of the familiar scenery, she began to feel less desperate about Rupert's attitude towards Destiny. It was an attitude that would change, when acceptance came. And acceptance would come – eventually.

She was so deep in her thoughts that she didn't register the oil slick in the road as she approached the sharp bend – and the trees and bushes were so dense that she wasn't forewarned of the lorry that was heading towards her from the opposite direction.

One minute she was deep in thoughts of Rupert and Destiny and the next she was crying out in alarm as the back wheels went into a skid – feverishly she spun the wheel, trying to drive into it. In three seconds of mounting terror she registered that she was totally out of control of the car, that she was careening backwards into the opposite lane and, last and finally, that an enormous lorry was rounding the bend, about to slam broadside into her.

221

Restrained by her seat belt, the impact hurled her sideways across the front passenger seat at an ugly, almost impossible angle. For a beat of consciousness she heard metal screech and tear; was aware that the bodywork of her car was buckling in on her; aware of indescribable pain and of her own screams.

And then nothing.

Even when rescue workers cut her free, she still didn't regain even partial consciousness. Only eternities later, through a fog so thick she couldn't penetrate it with either speech or movement, was she aware that she was still alive.

'Thank God, but you're so lucky, darling,' she could hear Rupert saying to her over and over again in an anguished voice, a voice so unlike his normal voice that she'd wondered if it really was Rupert. 'You could have died. That you're still alive is an absolute miracle.'

With enormous effort she'd managed to move her hand, bringing pressure to bear on his.

There'd been a great deal of activity around her after that.

'She's coming round from the anaesthetic,' she heard a woman's voice say.

A different voice, this time male, asked her if she'd like a piece of ice to suck.

As she'd made a movement, assenting, she'd felt Rupert's hand tighten on hers and gratitude for his nearness had swamped her like a tidal wave. She was alive, when she could very easily have been dead. Destiny hadn't been with her in the car. Destiny wasn't hurt. And Rupert was half out of his mind with worry and was at her side. Everything was going to be all right. Her little family wasn't falling apart. The three of them were going to win through. All that was needed was time.

'Your recovery to mobility is going to be a lengthy process,' her surgeon said, standing by the side of her bed.

Artemis managed a brave smile. 'I know.' She turned her eyes away from him to the array of pulleys that were holding her right leg, heavily encased in plaster from hip to ankle, at an improbable angle. Her right arm was also encased in plaster and her left shoulder and her chest were bandaged and strapped.

'How long a time is it going to be?' she asked, her thoughts on Destiny; wondering how Destiny was going to manage without her.

'Five months. Six months. It's difficult to tell at this stage. You will walk again, though due to your pelvic bones having been so badly damaged it's likely you will be left with a slight, residual limp. As to the other long-term damage . . .'

'There's no need for that to be in words again,' she said swiftly. 'My not being able to have a baby isn't the huge blow it may seem. My husband is sterile. Our daughter is adopted and, when we want more children, we'll adopt again.'

'Good.' He smiled with relief. 'Then all that remains, Mrs Gower, is for your bones to knit together – and for you to survive the next few months of immobility without too much impatience.'

Her first thought, when she'd known she was going to be hospitalized for a long period, had been that Rupert was going to have to engage a nanny to care for Destiny. Kirsten was well able to dress her and make her breakfast and drive her to and from school. She couldn't, however, take over caring for Destiny full time. She simply wasn't trained for such responsibility.

'Norland, darling,' she said to Rupert when he visited her. 'It will have to be a Norland-trained nanny – and it will have to be one who specializes in looking after children with slight learning difficulties.'

When he visited her the second time, he brought Destiny with him. It was a hideous experience. Destiny screamed in anguish at the plaster casts, refusing to believe that they weren't hurting Artemis. Artemis, unable to take Destiny in her arms and to comfort her, had become so deeply distressed her blood pressure had soared. Rupert, mortified at having a screaming, hysterical child in his care in a public place, had looked, and felt, as if he were about to have a stroke.

'It would be hard enough explaining to any five-and-a-half-year-old why Mummy is trussed up in bandages and plaster,' he had said despairingly when he'd returned to the ward after depositing Destiny in Kirsten's care, 'but it's even harder trying to explain to Destiny. I should never have brought her.'

223

It was so true that tears had streamed down Artemis's face. How was she going to manage months immobile and in plaster if she couldn't see Destiny? And what effect was their separation going to have on Destiny?

'Take her to Spain for a long holiday,' she said to Rupert after much thought. 'She loves it at the villa and she'll have Luis to play with and I don't think she'll be so constantly aware of my absence there.'

'I can take her and the new nanny there, but I can't stay there with them. I'd cleared the decks at work for the duration of the month we intended being there, but now that's been and gone there are issues I simply have to be on the spot to deal with.'

He looked haggard. Though she wouldn't have admitted it to anyone but herself, Artemis rather liked the fact that he was taking her accident so hard. It showed how important she was to him – and she quite understood about his not being able to take weeks and weeks away from the bank, now that the summer was over and he was up to his eyes in work.

'Destiny and Marielle have made good friends with each other, haven't they?' she said, after having had their newly employed nanny visit her several times in hospital in order to satisfy herself that she was absolutely the right sort of person to be caring for Destiny. 'And though it's school term again in Spain, Luis finishes school at two o'clock. It means he and Destiny will still be able to spend lots of time together. I think things will be all right, even if you aren't there all the time, though you will keep flying out at weekends whenever you can, won't you?'

He promised to do so, setting all her fears at rest in a way that was quite new for him. Suddenly, he wasn't being as self-centred as usual. Suddenly he really was putting her – and Destiny – first in his thoughts.

Her private room looked out on to a vista of trees, their leaves beginning to turn yellow and crimson. In Marbella, though the weather would no longer be hot, it would still be warm and Destiny would be able to spend the greater part of the day playing out of doors with Luis. Her being absent from school for a long period would no doubt upset the local educational authorities, but that couldn't be helped. The circumstances were, after all, exceptional. In Gloucestershire Destiny would be constantly aware of her absence. In Marbella she would have Luis as a companion and wouldn't pine for her quite so much.

All that now remained was to say goodbye to her.

'Do you think you should, Artemis?' Immaculately city-suited, Rupert looked more like a visiting consultant than a visiting husband. 'She's going to scream the place down when she sees you're still encased in plaster. I'm going to have to then remove her, kicking and struggling, from the building and you're going to be so distressed your blood pressure is going to leap off the Richter scale. It might be best for you not to say goodbye to her at all.'

She'd known he was right, but she hadn't been able to bring herself to agree to his suggestion.

'I'm not going to see her again for *months*,' she said unsteadily. 'I have to see her, Rupert. Perhaps if Marielle comes with her when you bring her, she won't be so frightened by the plaster casts.'

It had been a vain hope. Destiny had been just as bewildered and frightened as on her first visit.

'Which is why, on the wards, patients aren't allowed to have children under the age of eight visit them,' Rupert said in exasperation as Marielle did her best to soothe Destiny and Artemis lay as helpless as a trussed chicken, tears rolling down her face.

With a great effort at patience, he turned his attention to Destiny. 'Now be a big, brave girl and kiss Mummy goodbye,' he said, unable to keep exasperation from his voice.

Destiny did her best to do as he asked. Her body heaving with suppressed sobs, she threw her arms round Artemis's neck, kissing her with wet, sticky kisses.

A nurse entered the room and Rupert moved towards Destiny, lifting her away from the bed.

'Mummy!' she shrieked hysterically as he handed her to Marielle. 'Mummy! Mummy!'

Holding her hand, Marielle tried to lead her from the room, but Destiny twisted away from her, rushing back to the bed

225

and crashing into it with such force that the hoist supporting Artemis's right leg juddered dangerously.

White-faced, Rupert yanked her up into his arms.

'*Mummy!*' Destiny shrieked again, her arms stretching desperately out over his shoulders towards Artemis as he headed out of the room, a distressed Marielle at his heels. '*Want Mummy! Want Mummy! WANT MUMMY!*'

The door swung shut behind them, but her cries could still be heard. Not until Rupert stepped into a lift with her, and the lift doors closed, did Destiny's heartbroken sobs cease ringing in Artemis's ears.

The tears she had not given way to when Destiny had been with her streamed down her face for a long time. The last thing she wanted was to cause Destiny distress, and yet, because of her accident, that was exactly what she was doing.

'But I'll make it up to you, cherub,' she said to the photograph standing on her bedside locker. 'When I leave hospital, I'll make all these months of separation up to you. I promise.'

Four days later, first thing in the morning, one of the nurses who regularly attended her put her head round the door of the room, a very odd expression on her face. Instead of coming into the room and wishing her a cheery good morning, she ducked back out again, leaving Artemis wondering if the ward was short staffed and people were under strain.

Five minutes later the ward sister came into the room. Sister's round was carried out every afternoon at four o'clock and, at the sight of her even before breakfast had been served, Artemis's eyebrows rose.

'What on earth is the matter, Sister?' she asked good humouredly. 'Am I about to be transferred to another hospital or something?'

The sister shook her head, her face so grave that all Artemis's good humour vanished.

'What is it?' If she had been able to move, she would have sat bolt upright. As it was, the only way she could express her growing alarm was by her voice and her eyes.

'I'm afraid I have very bad news for you, Mrs Gower.'

Other people were entering her room. A nurse with a kidney

bowl and a syringe. The Anglican vicar who visited those of the Anglican faith once a week, if they so wanted.

At the sight of him, Artemis's alarm turned to terror. 'Is it my husband?' she demanded, desperately trying to remember what day it was; whether it was today Rupert was flying home from Spain, leaving Destiny in Marielle's care. 'Has there been a plane crash? Is he hurt?'

Both the sister and the vicar seated themselves by the side of her bed. 'There's been a fatal swimming accident, Mrs Gower,' the sister said, taking hold of her hand. 'It occurred yesterday evening, but by the time we were informed you were asleep and the doctors deemed that you shouldn't be woken.'

'Rupert's dead? Rupert's drowned?' She couldn't make sense of the information she was being given. How could Rupert have drowned? He was a polo player. He was fit and strong.

'Not your husband, Mrs Gower,' the vicar said gently, speaking for the first time. 'Your daughter.'

She tried to speak, and couldn't. She opened her mouth to scream, and couldn't. Immobile in plaster, she felt herself spinning into a world so bleak and empty and bereft that it was beyond imagination.

It was a nightmare world.

A world she was never going to be able to escape from.

A world without her child.

A world without Destiny.

Sedatives, administered for the first twenty-four hours by injection and then orally, kept her sane – or at least she later presumed they had.

A telephone trolley was brought into her room so that she could speak to Rupert.

'Where were you when it happened?' she demanded in a voice no longer recognizable as her own. '*How* did it happen?'

'She was in the paddling pool. She should have been quite safe. Juanita was with her . . .'

'Juanita?' She felt as if she was in a place with no footholds. 'Who is Juanita? Where was Marielle? *Where were you?*'

She could hear him clearing his throat, swallowing hard. 'Marielle's mother was taken sick the day we visited you at the hospital. I arranged that I would fly out with Destiny and engage a nanny on the spot, in Marbella. Marielle was going to fly out and take over from her when her mother was no longer so acutely ill. It was a quite sensible arrangement, Artemis . . .'

'Sensible? *Sensible?*' She felt as if she were in an airless room from which there was no escape. 'You left our daughter . . . you left Destiny . . . in the care of a Spanish nanny you had only engaged that day . . .'

'The day previously. The day we arrived.'

' . . . and she was so negligent . . . she was so blind . . . that she allowed her to drown in a paddling pool no more than a foot deep!'

'She only left her for a minute, Artemis. She went back into the villa for sun-cream. As you so rightly say, the water in the paddling pool is only a foot deep. It should have been quite safe. It was just a horrible, hideous, tragic accident, darling.'

'*And where were you?*'

She didn't want to hear him explain the accident away as if it were something that couldn't have been helped. She didn't want him to be emotionally together and controlled. She wanted him to be destroyed with grief, as she was destroyed. She wanted him to realize that what had happened was his fault – his fault for having left Destiny in the care of a nanny about whom he knew nothing whatsoever.

'I was playing golf,' he said, and then, at last, his voice gave way. 'I'm so sorry, darling. So very sorry. We'll adopt other children. You'll be a mother again, I promise.'

It had been more than she could bear hearing. How could he not understand that no amount of other children would ever replace the child they had lost? Dropping the phone, she covered her eyes with her free hand, crying as if she would never stop.

Unbelievably, there was a moment of fresh agony. The moment when she realized that there was no way she was going to be able to attend Destiny's funeral, not even if Destiny's body were flown home to England.

'And so as that is the case, Artemis, I really think it best that the funeral take place out here,' Rupert had said, as rational as always. 'Once it's over I'll come straight home and we can begin building our lives again.'

He made it sound so easy – and it was, she knew, going to be so hard. Impossibly hard. He was also not taking into account that nothing was going to be over until the most hellish task of all was undertaken.

Primmie still had to be told.

And she was the one who would to have to tell her.

PART TWO

Twenty

K iki toiled up the stairs of the digs her agent had booked for her, a large, heavy shoulder bag bumping against a mock-snakeskin-trousered thigh, a bulging sports bag in one hand. In high ill humour she kicked open the door at the top of the stairs. The room beyond was just as bad as she had expected it to be. There was a bumpy-looking bed covered in a red candlewick bedspread that had seen better days, a dressing table and wardrobe that looked as if they'd come from a car boot sale, and the lampshade on the bedside light was scorched.

She dropped the sports bag to the floor and slung the shoulder bag on to the bed – which creaked beneath the weight. She winced. Once again, when it came to accommodation, no one had done her any favours. It was an easy bet that no one else on the Grantley Working Men's Club Rock Star Fiesta was holing up in such a dump. Mervyn, the latest in a line of agents so long even she couldn't remember half of them, had been adamant, both about the gig and her accommodation arrangements.

'They're grade-A showbiz digs and Grantley's a new club on the outskirts of Leeds. It's cost a million and they want to open with a bang. There'll be some big names on the bill and to pad things out a little they want some faces from the past. Rock stars from the sixties and seventies. Dusty Springfield. Adam Faith. That sort of thing.'

'Dusty Springfield and Adam Faith are dead,' she'd said through gritted teeth.

'So they are, doll.' Mervyn had grinned at her across his cluttered desktop. 'But you're not. Are you?'

She'd known then that the grandly named Grantley Rock

Star Fiesta was going to be yet another humiliating debacle. She wasn't going to be heading the bill; she wasn't going to be put up in a decent hotel; she wasn't going to get any rock star treatment. 'So what's new, Kiki?' she'd said to herself as, furious at Mervyn's last crack, she'd stormed out of his office. 'What's bloody, bloody new?'

'Reinvent yourself, babe,' her last lover, who had just ditched her, would say whenever he drummed up enough energy to be interested in her problems.

Thinking about that remark now made her snort derisively. No one, in the history of show business, had ever reinvented herself with the frequency with which she had. With every decade someone, manager or agent, had announced that if only she'd adapt her style to the latest trend she'd make the leap from middling success to superstardom. Punk, funk, rap, jazz, avant garde, new wave – all had gone into the blender at one time or another. And the result was always the same. The leap was never made. It was thirty years since she'd been the latest hot item, storming the charts with the two songs she had co-written with Geraldine. Even now, at Grantley, 'White Dress, Silver Slippers' and 'Twilight Love' were the nostalgia numbers that would be wanted from her.

She frowned, wondering if it would have been any different if, way back in 1972, she hadn't been so dismissive of the way Aled Carter had wanted to route her career. If she'd done the ghastly *Arthur Haynes Variety Show*, if she'd allowed Aled to mould her as a family entertainer in the style of Lulu, would she have become a lasting big name, as Lulu had?

It was impossible to tell. From then on, though, she had been on a downward spiral. True, it hadn't seemed like that during the years she'd been with Francis. In those days, she'd enjoyed all the trappings of stardom, confident that superstardom was only a whisker away. Well, it hadn't come. The new hotshot American agent she'd ditched Francis for had proved not to be so hotshot after all – at least, not where she'd been concerned.

He'd been another very wrong turning. Thanks to him, she'd spent years in America when she should have been concentrating on the British pop scene. After endless incarnations, she'd finally returned to her roots – a British public and, for material, good old-fashioned rock.

She'd kept herself in work – just. There'd been a Rock Revival Festival at St Austell in Cornwall earlier in the year, where she'd featured top of the bill alongside Eric Burden and Marty Wilde. Both of them were old buddies. Both of them had given her the respect she felt she deserved and now so rarely received.

The St Austell gig had been an isolated high spot. Everything she'd done since then had been at a third-rate venue, with a third-rate audience. She was fifty-two and, where her career was concerned, hope was dead. The problem was, if her career was dead then so was she, because she didn't have anything else. If she wasn't Kiki Lane, a rock star, then she wasn't anybody. She was a nobody. And she'd long ago made up her mind that she'd rather be dead than be a nobody.

Not wanting to follow her thought process to its logical conclusion she moved sharply away from the window, forcing herself to think instead of the shit-awful band that was presently backing her, wondering when they were going to arrive. Of all the errors of judgement she'd made in her career, not being part of a decent band had been the most catastrophic.

It had been an error various managers had, over the years, tried to put right. For three years, whilst in America, she'd been the lead singer of a group with the name Kiki and the Wild Boys. It hadn't prospered. The drummer, lead guitarist and bassist had lived up to their names with such fervour that the drummer had had an alcohol-induced brain seizure, the lead guitarist had exposed himself on stage and the bassist had died from suffocation, having inhaled vomit as a result of barbiturate intoxication.

Next, she'd been lead singer of the Shamans. The keyboardist was in a long gay relationship with the slide guitarist. She'd embarked on a hot sexual relationship with the keyboardist. The slide guitarist had attempted suicide. It hadn't made for a brilliant working atmosphere on stage.

Bands she'd formed for herself had sometimes been good, but had always broken up. She'd acquired a reputation for being difficult to work with, of being a mediocre rock singer who had a diva attitude. Now her reputation was fast becoming that of being a performer who was over the hill.

She flopped on to the bed, shuddering at the mere thought of the words 'over the hill' and of the unfairness of it. She looked – and sounded – just as good as Lulu. Lulu was her age, perhaps even a tad older, and she'd never heard anyone referring to Lulu as being over the hill. The difference was, of course, that Lulu had always had excellent management. Lulu hadn't lost her way early on, flitting between being a solo artist and being the lead singer of a band; moving from rock to soul to jazz to funk, so that in the end no one knew what type of music she stood for.

Well aware that if her mood plummeted any further she'd never summon the motivation to rehearse at Grantley later that evening, she thrust a pillow between her back and the bed head, hauled her shoulder bag a little nearer and slid her lap top from out of it.

For the last six months, she'd been writing a novel – or at least, she supposed it was a novel. It was such a bizarre assort-ment of fact, fiction and psychedelic experiences that it was hard to tell just what it was. All she knew was that the mental effort of putting words on to the screen was therapeutic to her.

FRIENDS REUNITED – THE WEBSITE WITH THE HIGHEST NUMBER OF HITS SO FAR THIS YEAR read a flyer as, before opening her Word file, she went on the net to see if she had any emails from her agent.

She knew all about Friends Reunited, of course. Who didn't? She'd always thought it such a naff idea that checking it out had never entered her head. Now, for the first time, it did so. It would be interesting to see if anyone from Bickley had registered on it.

As she logged on to the website, she tried to remember the names of some of the girls who'd accompanied her through her years at Bickley. Not Geraldine, Artemis and Primmie, of course. Geraldine, Artemis and Primmie had been part of her life in a way that was quite unforgettable. There'd been other girls, though. Girls she'd never made friends with. Samantha Wade-Bembridge and Lauren Colefax, who, with the benefit of hindsight, had been budding lesbians. Snobbish Mirabel

Des Vaux, who'd infuriated her year after year by always pipping her to the post in the school marathon. Sophie Menzies, who'd been academically brilliant. Beatrice Strachan, who had always saved Artemis from being bottom of the class.

Once on the website it took her mere minutes to find Bickley High and to enter the year she had left. Seconds later a whole host of long-forgotten names were staring her in the face.

As was Primmie's.

She gasped, catapulted back into the past with such speed and unexpectedness that she felt as if she'd been hit in the chest. There was an envelope icon beside Primmie's name, indicating that she'd like to be contacted, and a message icon. Never, in all her life, had Kiki wanted to access anything so much as that message icon.

And she couldn't, because she wasn't registered as a Friends Reunited member.

Feverishly she began registering: filling in boxes, waiting for her application to be validated, waiting to be able to access Primmie's message. When it finally flashed on to the screen, it was tantalizingly brief.

Hi, Primmie here. As I'm now widowed and my four children have long ago left home, I've said goodbye to Rotherhithe and taken up an opportunity I've been given of living on a smallholding on the outskirts of Calleloe, on the beautiful Lizard Peninsula. There's plenty of room for guests and I'd love to hear from, and be visited by, any old friends from my Bickley High days. Love to everyone who knew me back in the sixties. Primmie.

That was all. There was no photograph to access – just the envelope icon if she wanted to contact Primmie via the website.

Making no move to do so, she dug into her shoulder bag for Rizlas and weed and began rolling herself a spliff. What on earth had taken Primmie to a smallholding in Cornwall?

She lit her spliff, readjusting her thoughts, aware that it wasn't, perhaps, quite so extraordinary after all. Primmie may have been born and bred in Rotherhithe, but she'd always been a country girl at heart. She remembered how much Primmie had loved the spacious garden at Petts Wood, with its views over the golf course to the North Downs.

It was a garden that, if she, Kiki, hadn't interfered and if her father had married Primmie, Primmie might be tending now.

Her widowed status would still have been the same, though.

She inhaled deeply, not wanting to think about her father's death, not wanting to think about her complete lack of family life. True, her mother was still alive, but her mother had lived for the last twenty years in Vancouver with Jenny Reece – which didn't make for frequent contact. And, apart from her mother, she had no one. No husband, not even an ex-husband. No brothers and sisters, nieces and nephews. No children.

And no friends, or at least, not real friends. Not friends as Artemis, Geraldine and Primmie had been her friends. Darkly she wondered if, since the days when it had been the four of them, she'd ever had any friends. During the days when her career had been on the up and up, the days when she was a somebody, she'd always been surrounded by hordes of people she had assumed were friends. People who were now nowhere to be seen.

With a last look at Primmie's message, she exited the site. She couldn't afford to sink into a depression she couldn't claw her way out of. She had a show to do tomorrow night and rehearsals to get to grips with tonight, and – who knew? – the Grantley Rock Fiesta could well be a blast, with her the high spot of the programme.

Her brief surge of optimism was short lived. When the band backing her collected her in the their minibus they warned her to take a deep breath before reading any of the billboards for the concert.

She soon saw why.

Kiki Laine – '70s rock star was fourth down on the hoarding outside the club.

Rage roared through her veins. It was bad enough that she was fourth down and that her name was spelled wrongly, but why '70s rock star? Why not just Kiki Lane? Did her future lie only in exploiting her earlier successes? Was she ever again going to be booked for anything other than nostalgia concerts?

'Are you the lighting girl we're expecting?' a harassed-looking young woman asked her as she strode angrily into the club ahead of the band.

Hardly able to contain herself, Kiki whipped off her dark glasses. 'No, I'm bloody not! I'm Kiki Lane! Now which way are the bloody dressing rooms?'

It hadn't been an auspicious beginning. For the first time in her life, she felt exhausted. More than exhausted, she felt hammered. This wasn't how it was supposed to be. She was supposed to be a huge icon, a major player on the celebrity circus circuit. Instead, she was fast becoming a laughing-stock. There had definitely been sniggers from the band member hardest on her heels when the stupid bitch in the foyer had asked her if she was the lighting girl.

'Hi, Kiki, I'm Shania Lee,' an emaciated girl with blue hair and a metal stud in her lower lip said to her as she walked into a large communal dressing room. 'How ya doin'?'

Kiki didn't answer her. She was too busy digesting the fact that she was going to be sharing a dressing room.

'I'm the drummer with Dog Days,' the girl said helpfully.

Dog Days were a punk nostalgia band, well known enough for the girl not to have needed to explain who she was. That she'd done so, so unpretentiously, deserved a response.

'Hi,' she said, making an effort. 'Nice to meet you. How many numbers are Dog Days pencilled in for?'

'Four. We're doing The Ramones' "Don't Come Close" and "Howling at the Moon". I don't know about the other two numbers. Probably The Sex Pistols "Pretty Vacant" with an Eddie Cochran number thrown in for good measure.'

'Wicked.'

The girl grinned. 'It's really great to be on the bill with you, Kiki. My mother's a great fan of yours. She says I used to gurgle along to "White Dress, Silver Slippers" when I was in my pram.'

Kiki didn't even try to smile. When Shania Lee had been in her pram, 'White Dress, Silver Slippers' would have already been a nostalgia number.

'I need a drink,' she said abruptly, having seen all she wanted to see of the dressing room situation. 'There must be a bar open somewhere in this million pound dump.'

As she swung out of the dressing room to find it, Shania

fell into step beside her. 'It's an eyesore, isn't it?' she said as they were assailed by the smell of fresh paint and new wood.

Kiki grunted agreement, her mind still on the dressing room scenario. A newly built club this size would have star dressing rooms – and she hadn't been allocated one. It was a public humiliation and she didn't see any way out of it, because if she made a scene, demanding a star-status dressing room, and was refused, the humiliation would simply escalate.

'Nick says the days of clubs like this are so long over it simply isn't true,' Shania was saying.

Kiki tried to rustle up some interest. 'Who's Nick?'

'My partner, but he also manages my career. It's a great arrangement, because it means he really does have my interests at heart.'

For the second time within hours Kiki was plummeted into her past. Shania's set-up with Nick was the same set-up she'd had with Francis. Francis, too, had had her interests at heart – or he had until he'd self-destructed on cocaine.

As she walked into a bar area crowded with musicians and lighting men, she wondered where Francis was now. It occurred to her, not for the first time, that he could have died twenty or even thirty years ago. People with drug habits like Francis's didn't make old bones.

The wall behind the bar was mirrored and she was staring at her reflection. In her mock snakeskin trousers and sequin-decorated black T-shirt, she was still as whippet-slender as Shania. Thanks to professional help, her spikily cut and gelled hair was still fox-red – and her cheekbones looked sharp enough to slice through metal. She still looked what she was – what she'd always been – a rock singer. But she was a rock singer on the skids. She was on a downhill curve that was never going to straighten out and climb to dizzy heights. Any dizzy heights there had been were all in her past. If she exited the scene now she would be remembered as a rock chick of the '70s and '80s who, in 2003, was a necessary adjunct to any rock nostalgia concert going.

If she continued, she would begin to be perceived as a pathetic has-been – and it would then be as a has-been that she would be remembered.

The time to bow out was now.

She was going to quit just as soon as this godawful week's gig was over. She was going to drive to the coast and find a high cliff – and then she was going to throw herself from the top of it.

Instead of it being the kind of wild, rash decision that was soon forgotten about, it was one that took deep root.

When she strutted on stage the following night wearing disco diva shoes with high Perspex heels studded with rhinestones, prepared to yet again give it all she'd got, the applause was embarrassingly thin.

Not for the first time in her life she hated an audience. Feeling as if she was on a treadmill she belted out all her old hits and near hits.

And then came the ultimate nightmare. Then came the moment she had never, in a million years, thought she would ever have to endure. Impatient for the headlining band to make an appearance, part of the audience began to slow handclap her – and within seconds the rest of the audience joined in with them.

Though her backing band continued playing, she stopped singing. Tears stung the backs of her eyes. This was it, then. This was what it felt like to die on stage. Well, she bloody well was never going to do it again. She was going to drive to the only part of the country she knew that had high cliffs. She was going to drive to Cornwall and put an end to the miserable charade that was now her life. She was going to drive to Cornwall, because in Cornwall there was someone to say goodbye to.

In Cornwall, there was Primmie.

Twenty-One

July 2003

Following a steward's directions, Artemis drove her Volvo over rough grass to the far corner of a huge field. As she

241

parked between a Range Rover and a Mini Cooper, she was nervous. She'd never felt comfortable at polo matches, not even in the early days of her marriage when she'd been thrilled at incorporating such an upper-class, elitist activity into her life. The rules of the game had always been beyond her and when the wives and girlfriends of Rupert's fellow players realized she didn't have a clue as to what was going on – and worse, that she didn't even ride – they'd ceased treating her as a member of their privileged circle.

She slipped her feet out of her driving shoes, exchanging them for a pair of high-heeled, open-toed court shoes. She'd put on so much weight that if she didn't wear high heels she looked as broad as she was tall. It wasn't a figure fault that would be troubling many of the other female spectators. From bitter experience she knew they would all be slender and supple – and young.

Slamming the car door behind her, she began walking with difficulty over the uneven ground. Nearly every one of Rupert's friends had dispensed with the wife they'd been married to when she had first met them and opted for a newer, slimmer model with an age range of early twenties to late twenties. It didn't make for peace of mind when you were fifty-two and a size eighteen. Not that anyone knew she was a size eighteen, because she religiously cut all sizing labels from her clothes and sewed size fourteen labels in their place.

Rupert hated her being plump – though he didn't call her plump. He called her fat. The problem was that the unhappier he made her about her weight, the more she sought comfort in chocolates and cakes. It was all a hideous vicious circle and it wasn't as if she'd ever *naturally* been slim. She'd been plump as a child. The only time she hadn't been plump was when she was at Lucie Clayton and the short period afterwards, when she was modelling.

She reached the end of the field that had been sct aside for surplus cars and saw, ahead of her, that a chukka was in progress. With increasing nervousness she smoothed the skirt of her white polka-dotted navy silk dress and checked that her pearls were lying at the right depth in the V of her neckline.

Rupert would most definitely not be expecting to see her – not after their row of the previous evening. She'd been right to object to his plans, though. A month away, playing polo in Brazil, was absolutely out of order when they hadn't, this year, spent any time at their holiday home in Corfu.

She was nearing the first of the jeeps and horseboxes parked round the edge of the ground and she pulled her tummy in as far as it would go, plastering a falsely bright smile on her face. Dozens of casually dressed girls were draped over the bonnets of the jeeps, their dark glasses making it difficult for her to know if she knew any of them or not. She couldn't see anyone dressed stylishly, as she was, and realized too late that she'd committed a fashion wobbly by dressing for a casual match as if for Hurlingham.

A couple of the girls turned at her approach and one or two of them gave her a laconic wave. She smiled brightly back at them, desperately wishing she'd worn something a little less garden-partyish. No one else was wearing high heels. Absolutely no one.

She scanned the players. Rupert's team was wearing pink shirts and his lean, still muscular figure was immediately identifiable.

'Have you only just arrived?' a middle-aged woman standing a few feet away from her said, lowering her binoculars. 'Because if you have you've missed a brilliant first couple of chukkas.'

'Yes, and have I?' Artemis moved nearer to her, grateful at no longer standing so conspicuously alone.

'And have you seen the rogue player?' the woman continued, amusement in her voice. 'It's not often you see a woman playing, but Serena really is something special, isn't she?'

Artemis's carefully shaped eyebrows rose. There were women's polo teams, of course, but she'd never known Rupert play against one – or with a female team member.

She raised a hand to shield her eyes, squinting into the sun to where Rupert was playing with flamboyance, throwing himself out of the saddle in an impressive display of gung-ho horsemanship. As he bent low, thwacking the ball, she saw that he was passing it to a fellow player who was, most definitely, female.

'Who is she?' she asked, as the girl galloped unmarked down the field.

'Serena Campbell-Thynne – her father is a former chairman of the Guards Polo Club. Oh, golly! Look! She's going to score! Go for goal, Serena! *Go for goal!*'

To Artemis it suddenly seemed that everyone was shrieking Serena's name. As Serena whacked the ball straight through the posts there were screams of near hysterical delight from the girls clustered round the jeeps.

Artemis wasn't looking at the girls, though – or at Serena Campbell-Thynne. She was looking at her husband. He was standing in the stirrups, his polo shirt soaking wet, whooping like a schoolboy. She tried to remember when she'd last seen him looking so vividly alive and couldn't. Was it because he was where he liked to be best – on a polo field? Or was it something else?

The chukka ended and the players began cantering off the field to change their lathered ponies for fresh ones. 'Brilliant, Serry!' she heard Rupert shout as, both of them still mounted, he pulled her towards him, giving her a smacking kiss. 'Absolutely top-hole!'

'They make a wonderful pair, don't they?' the woman at her side said fondly.

Artemis didn't make any response. She couldn't. She was too busy fighting a hideously familiar, sickening sensation deep in the pit of her stomach. Serena Campbell-Thynne was laughing across at Rupert, tugging off her riding hat. A sheaf of pale blond hair, tied into a ponytail, tumbled free. She said something to him, but what it was she couldn't hear. Then, as Serena dismounted, Artemis heard her call across to Rupert: 'Don't get too complacent, Ru. There are still three chukkas to go!'

Ru? *Ru?* In all the years she'd known him, she had never known anyone to shorten Rupert's name. Nor had she ever known him to affectionately shorten her name. He'd never called her Tem or Temmie. He'd always called her Artemis. But he'd called Serena Campbell-Thynne Serry and he'd kissed her in full view of everyone.

'I first saw them playing in the same team a couple of months ago and was struck then by how beautifully they pass the ball between each other,' the woman was saying informatively. 'It's not surprising they've both been chosen for the

244

team that's off to Brazil next month, is it? Perhaps they intend having a beach wedding out there. That would be nice, wouldn't it?'

'No,' she said, through lips that felt frozen. 'I don't think so. He's married. He's been married for thirty-two years.'

'So long? He must have married very young. He only looks to be in his late forties.'

The two teams of four were cantering back on to the ground, Rupert and Serena's ponies shoulder to shoulder.

'He's fifty-six,' Artemis heard herself say, her voice sounding as if it were coming from a great distance. How many other spectators were assuming that her husband and Serena Campbell-Thynne were an item? And how long had their behaviour led to such an assumption being made?

She looked at the small groups of people nearest to her. Were they not coming up to her, acknowledging her presence and greeting her because they were embarrassed at her having put in an appearance when Rupert and Serena were playing together? Or, like the woman still standing by her side, were they completely oblivious to her identity? She hadn't, after all, attended a polo match in years. She'd never set eyes on Serena Campbell-Thynne before. And Serena Campbell-Thynne hadn't, as yet, set eyes on her.

In the fourth chukka Rupert's team failed to score and the opposing team scored twice.

In the fifth they were lagging behind by two goals.

Artemis didn't know why she was still standing watching Rupert and Serena shout frenzied encouragement to each other as they galloped and turned at dizzying speed. It was as if she were rooted to the spot. As if she couldn't turn away no matter how much she wanted to.

Why did she always think that it wouldn't happen again? Why was she always taken by hideous, ghastly surprise? His first affair had taken place only months after Destiny's death. His last – and most serious – had ended three years ago. It had been with Lydia Gerard, the wife of one of Francis Sheringham's old friends. Lydia was the daughter of a duke and, knowing Rupert as she did, she had been convinced that if James Gerard had divorced Lydia, she, too, would have found herself in the divorce courts. The prospect of

245

having a duke for a father-in-law, rather than a construction magnate, would have been more than Rupert could have resisted.

The eight players were cantering off the field again for a brief respite before the final chukka. Artemis had lost track of the score. Rupert's team could be winning, she didn't know. She only knew that if, as well as being a superb horsewoman, Serena Campbell-Thynne was listed in *Burke's Peerage,* then she, Artemis, could well be facing another huge threat to her marriage.

Her family background had always mortified Rupert. In their early days together he had managed to gloss over it, but as time had gone on he had found it a social liability to have a father-in-law whose name was synonymous with building sites. And though her not being keen on horses and riding hadn't been an issue in the years when he'd thought her the most beautiful girl he'd ever seen, they'd soon became an issue when she began putting on weight.

'Here we go again,' the woman at her side said, with satisfaction. 'Last chukka and the pinks are going to have to score twice to win.'

Dimly, through her misery, Artemis was aware that as the riders rode back on to the field the atmosphere was electric. Why, when all that was happening was that eight players, on eight ponies, were whacking a ball about, she couldn't begin to imagine.

'Oh! Shame!' the woman cried out passionately. 'Did you see how Serena was ridden-off then?'

Artemis had seen a member of the opposing team barge his pony against Serena's, drastically altering the direction in which she was galloping. She hadn't known the technical term for what he'd done, but she had fiercely hoped he would send her flying out of the saddle.

Seconds later Rupert was hooking mallets with the offending rider, shouting insults at him as he did so.

Another four or five minutes and the chukka – and the match – was going to be over. What was she going to do then? Walk back to her car and drive home, pretending that nothing had been said to her? Or was she going to walk over to Rupert and remind Serena Campbell-Thynne – and anyone else who might be watching – that Rupert was a married man?

'To your left, Serry!' she suddenly heard Rupert shout.

'He's got a clear ride to goal,' the woman beside her said, informative as ever. 'Is she going to pass to him? Oh, yes! Good girl! I said they made a brilliant team, didn't I?'

Everyone else watching seemed to think the same. No one was lounging against the bonnets of cars or jeeps now. Everyone was on their feet and as Serena passed the ball to him and Rupert cantered after it, there was a roar of approval.

From the urgency of it, Artemis gathered that there must have been goals that she hadn't registered and that, if Rupert scored now, his team would have won.

She saw him raise his mallet, hitting the ball with every ounce of his strength. As it went flying between the posts and as the whistle blew to end the match, there was a storm of cheering.

'Well, that was a spectacular finish, wasn't it?' the woman said, beaming across at her. 'My name is Olwyn Kent, by the way. My son, Lance, was in Rupert Gower's team.'

'And mine is Artemis Gower,' Artemis said, her eyes on Rupert as he cantered triumphantly up to Serena, leaning across so that he could hug her shoulders, her mind made up as to what it was she was going to do. 'I'm Rupert's wife.'

Olwyn Kent's jaw dropped in appalled horror.

Artemis didn't wait to hear any clumsy attempts at damage limitation. She began walking away, towards where the presentation to the winning team was to take place, aware that, even though she stood out like a sore thumb in her polka-dotted navy silk dress, Rupert still hadn't registered her presence.

He'd dismounted and, in his pink shirt, white jodhpurs and riding boots, he looked spectacularly handsome. Olwyn Kent had been right. He did look to be in his mid-forties, not his mid-fifties. True, there was a flash of silver at his temples, but the rest of his hair was still raven dark and constant sporting activity had kept him lean and supple. She could well understand why young women kept falling for him.

There was a fresh burst of applause as he walked across to accept the trophy. Artemis watched, as if watching a stranger.

This was a side of his life she had excluded herself from years ago when they had adopted Orlando and Sholto and she'd again become a full-time mother. Because of Rupert's position as a merchant banker, they had always entertained on a massive scale and, because she had wanted to do so, she had always done the cooking herself, just as she had always looked after Orlando and Sholto herself. It had been a way of life she'd found great satisfaction in, but the debit side had been that she hadn't had the time or inclination to be an adoring supporter at polo matches.

Over the years there had been numerous young women who, where Rupert was concerned, had fulfilled that role for her. Finding out about them had always caused her intense misery, but none of them had proved to be a serious threat to her marriage. Only Lydia Gerard, with her near royal family links, had achieved that.

And now there was Serena Campbell-Thynne, whose father was a former chairman of the Guards Polo Club – and whether Serena would be a major grief to her or not was impossible to tell.

For the moment, though, she was going to behave as if Serena didn't exist. Avoiding emotional showdowns where Rupert might be pushed to make a choice between her and the girlfriend of the moment was how she had survived. It had kept her thirty-two-year marriage intact when the marriages of nearly every other woman she knew of her age, had long ago ended in divorce.

As Rupert lowered the trophy he'd been holding high, she took a deep, steadying breath and stepped directly into his line of vision.

If he was appalled or embarrassed at realizing she must have seen his over friendly behaviour towards Serena, he did a spectacular job of not showing it.

'Just what the hell,' he said through gritted teeth, as she walked up to him, 'are you doing here?'

'It's so long since I saw you play and . . . and I wanted to make up for our having such a nasty row last night,' she said, uncomfortably aware that if she'd known last night that one of his reasons for wanting to go to Brazil was so that he could spend time with Serena Campbell-Thynne she would have been even more adamant that he should, instead, be spending his month's holiday with her, in Corfu.

A youth walked a lathered pony between the two of them. Artemis, who had never been able to come to terms with just how big a pony could be, stepped back quickly, going over on the same ankle that had let her down earlier.

Holding the trophy with one hand, he hooked the thumb of his other hand into the waistband of his very snug-fitting jodhpurs, saying exasperatedly, 'You'd have done better to have worn boots or trainers, Artemis. This isn't Windsor Park or Hurlingham.'

'Yes.' She was well aware of her fashion faux pas. 'So I'd noticed.'

The pony no longer separated them, but he didn't make a move towards her. The gap between them was only three or four feet, but to Artemis it was a chasm she felt completely unable to bridge.

Why couldn't he be nice to her? Why did she always have to try to please him and placate him? When she'd first fallen in love with him, she'd thought his olive-skinned good looks and offhand, saturnine manner very Heathcliff and romantic. Now, at moments like this, she found his manner both confusing and intimidating.

'I thought perhaps we could spend the rest of the day together,' she said, trying to sound happy and unconcerned. Trying to sound normal.

He looked vaguely amused. 'At the stables?' his eyes flicked over her fussily stylish dress. 'I don't think so, Artemis, do you?'

As she struggled to find an answer that might lighten the atmosphere between them, she saw, out of the corner of her eyes, that a tall, lithe, blond-haired, jodhpured figure was strolling towards them.

She sucked in her breath. Serena must have guessed, or been told by now, that Rupert was talking to his wife and her walking across to join them was shockingly bad manners.

She rearranged her smile, preparing to launch into a freezingly cool 'I'm Rupert's wife and I'm very pleased to meet you' speech that would, hopefully, take the wind completely out of Serena's sails.

She wasn't given the opportunity, because Serena didn't so much as give her a glance. 'What a great match that was, Ru,' she said, walking directly up to Rupert and slipping her arm through his. 'I'm soaking with sweat, absolutely dripping.'

She ran a finger down Rupert's perspiration-sheened neck and then, turning to face her, she very slowly and very provocatively licked the perspiration from her finger.

Artemis made a strangled sound deep in her throat.

Serena smiled lazily at her. 'And you are Artemis?' She tilted her head quizzically, obviously finding it amusing that Rupert was married to someone overweight, inappropriately dressed and old enough to be her mother.

The nervous tension in the pit of Artemis's stomach was replaced by anger so all consuming she thought she was going to explode.

'I'm Mrs Gower to you! And don't *ever* touch my husband like that again in front of me!' Absolutely convinced that Rupert would be as appalled at Serena Campbell-Thynne's brazenly crude behaviour as she was, her eyes flew to his, expecting support.

To her stunned disbelief, there was none forthcoming.

Without troubling to remove Serena's hand from his arm or to crush her with a look, as he could crush most people, he merely said, 'You can see the situation, Artemis. This isn't the place I would have chosen to come out into the open about things, but you'd have had to know some time, and so it might as well be now. I'm in love with Serry, and I'm going to marry her. The best thing you can do is to go home. I'll tell the boys, there's no need for you to do that.'

Artemis stared at him goggle eyed, not trusting her ears. He couldn't have said what she thought he'd said. He couldn't possibly be ending their life together – ending thirty-two years of marriage – on a polo field, in full view of hundreds of people!

He was.

The way he and Serena were facing her, standing together as a couple, told her he was.

She felt her head swim and knew she was on the verge of fainting. Aware that if she did she was too heavy to be picked up and carried and would, instead, be left lying in an undignified heap until she should recover consciousness, she sucked in deep gasps of air.

'You *bastard*!' she hissed, when the world steadied enough for her to speak. 'You complete and utter *bastard*!'

He breathed in hard. 'For God's sake, Artemis,' he said, impatiently. 'There's no need for such over-the-top drama. We came to the end of the road years ago. Stop behaving like a fishwife. This isn't your father's birthplace. You're not in Rotherhithe now.'

The contempt in his voice completely undid her. She was making a spectacle of herself in public, and all for no good reason. The only way to deal with the nightmare scene she'd found herself in was to exit from it fast. That way, something might still be salvaged.

As her eyes met his, she knew she was fooling herself. Rupert had meant everything he had said about their marriage being finally over. She'd lost him and, as she turned blindly away, stumbling in her distress, she wondered wildly if she'd ever had him in the first place, or if her entire marriage had been nothing but a long, pathetic sham.

People were making way for her, but she couldn't see clearly and then, seemingly out of nowhere, Olwyn Kent was at her side.

'Tell me where you live and I'll drive you home,' she said, taking hold of her arm as she stumbled yet again, this time on a divot kicked up by a pony.

'Thank you.' She was crying, not desperately or tragically, but silently and without hope. 'How could he do it?' As Olwyn steered her steadfastly towards the field of parked cars, tears spilled down her cheeks and on to her dress. 'How could he do it here? In front of everyone? In front of *her*?'

'Because when you said he was a bastard you were right. And because he wants to pretend that he's years younger than he really is and having a wife in her twenties will enable him to achieve his fantasy.'

For the first time Artemis attempted to wipe the tears from her face with her fingers. 'You too?'

'Oh yes,' Olwyn Kent said, as they mercifully left the polo field behind them. 'Mine left me for a lapdancer. All too trite and pathetic for words. She's only interested in him as a slap-

251

up meal ticket and he, stupid fool, thinks he's found a love only Shakespeare could do justice to.'

She opened the passenger seat door of a Citroën Xantia and helped Artemis into it.

'What you need now,' she said, walking round the car and opening the driver's door, 'are friends. Real friends. Have you got many?'

Artemis thought of all her Women's Institute and Conservative Party friends and nodded. 'Yes, but only friends who have known me as Mrs Rupert Gower and who are Rupert's friends as well.'

Olwyn turned the key in the ignition and revved the engine into gear. 'Friends whose loyalties are divided aren't the best sort at moments like this. What about old school friends? Have you any of those?'

Artemis fumbled in her handbag for a handkerchief and blew her nose noisily, tears still dripping down on to her dress.

'Yes,' she said at last. 'I have three. But I've lost contact with them.'

Olwyn careened off the grass of the parking area and bucketed on to a tarmacked lane. 'Then find them,' she said forcefully. 'Check out Friends Reunited. And try to stop crying, Artemis. You're ruining your lovely dress and he isn't worth it. No man is.'

Twenty-Two

September 2003

It was early morning and the air was damp with dew. Geraldine wrapped her cream silk dressing-gown a little closer round her racehorse-lean figure and then folded her arms, leaning against the jamb of the open French doors, looking out over her immaculate garden.

The roses were already in flower. Snowy-white Boule de

Neige and blush-tinged Comtesse de Murinais edged the gravel pathways and luminous Purissima tulips infilled her box-edged parterre. It was a very Parisian garden, restrained in colour and formal in structure. She, too, after thirty years of living in the city, had become very Parisienne – which was probably why she was being so phlegmatic about the appointment written in her diary for ten o'clock.

Aware that the morning was getting into its stride she reluctantly turned her back on the view of the garden. She needed to check her emails before leaving the house for Neuilly, and she didn't want to run out of time. Today, of all days, she needed to remain calm and unhurried and perfectly in control.

At nine thirty, not troubling to tell her housekeeper when she would be back, she left the house by its classical-pillared front entrance and, minutes later, hailed a taxicab in the busy Boulevard de la Madeleine.

'The American Hospital, 63 Boulevard Victor Hugo,' she said to the taxi driver in French, her accent flawless.

He turned left into Rue Caumartin and, amid a familiar reek of Gauloises, she sank back against cracked leather, suddenly tired with nervous strain. What was her consultant, Mr Zimmerman, going to say to her? Were the results of her last lot of blood and bone marrow tests going to be negative or positive? And if they were positive, just how was she going to come to terms with such a verdict? What plans was she going to have to make?

Not able to come to an answer she stared out of the window as the taxicab swerved to avoid a pedestrian. Rue Caumartin was, as always, a hive of activity. Cafés throbbed with life, smart boutiques were thronged with shoppers, tourists crowded the pavement.

She'd always loved the fact that such activity took place so near to her home. It made the green oasis of her garden seem very special. On her rare trips back to London, she'd never been able to understand why Londoners, instead of aspiring to live in the heart of their city, as Parisians did, preferred living on the outskirts, in places like Bickley and Bromley.

As the taxicab crossed the Boulevard Haussmann, she

thought back to her school days at Bickley and the long, sun-filled afternoons she'd spent with Artemis and Primmie in Kiki's parents' garden.

She didn't think of Kiki, because she never did. Not ever.

She often thought of Primmie and Artemis, though. She knew that twenty-five years ago Artemis and Rupert had lost a child in tragic circumstances, because she'd seen notification of the death in *The Times*. And she knew that Primmie had married. For three decades, that had been all she had known about Primmie, and then she had accessed Primmie's message box on the Friends Reunited website.

It had meant registering, of course, but she hadn't registered under her own name. In her line of business, real names were a handicap and using a false name was second nature to her. Besides, there was always the chance that Kiki would access the website – and she didn't want to hear from Kiki. She just wanted to know how Primmie was, if life had treated her well and if she was happy.

A ghost of a smile touched the corners of her mouth as the taxi driver turned right, heading straight as an arrow for Montmartre. Primmie had a great capacity for happiness and if she was living on a smallholding in beautiful countryside then she would be in her element. She wondered what kind of lives Primmie's adult children led. She wondered if Primmie had remained in contact with Artemis.

And because she was thinking about the past she thought, as always, of Francis.

Throughout the years he had been with Kiki, in America, he had intermittently made contact with his father by phone, and whenever he did so her Uncle Piers would telephone her and let her know that Francis was still in the land of the living.

All such telephone calls had ceased after Kiki had ditched him, replacing him with a hotshot American manager and, if the music magazines were anything to go by, a black lover several years her junior.

As time had passed without any kind of contact from him, her uncle had backtracked on his decision to disown him and had flown to Los Angeles to try to track him down. It had been an abortive exercise.

'Kiki Lane has no idea where he's gone, and isn't interested,' he'd said to Geraldine grimly. 'And everyone I've spoken to who knows him says his drug problem is way out of hand. They reckon that's the reason he's dropped out of sight – that he's given up the effort of living anything approaching a regular way of life. All we can do, Geraldine, is wait until he surfaces.'

The taxicab was in the much broader Avenue de Clichy now, the vast Cimetière de Montmartre on their right-hand side. Cemeteries had never held an attraction for her and most definitely didn't do so today.

She focused her thoughts once again on Francis. Her uncle had long ago resigned himself to the fact that Francis was dead. 'And if he is, and if he hasn't fathered any children that can be traced, you are my next of kin, Geraldine. You can either keep Cedar Court, battle with the death duty and pray that the various money-making activities I've been reduced to implementing – the business convention, wedding receptions, clay-pigeon shooting weekends, craft fairs, et cetera – continue to provide for it, or you can hand it over to the National Trust. I don't care,' he had said wearily. 'To tell the truth, my dear, I've tired of the battle. I've lost interest.'

So, too, had she. Her obsession with her family home had been fuelled by the prospect of living there with Francis and of raising a family there. Thanks to Kiki, she hadn't done so. She was now fifty-two and, without a child to inherit from her, ownership of Cedar Court seemed pointless.

The taxi dived beneath the Boulevard Périphérique, emerging at the Porte de Clichy. Her fingers tightened on the silver handle of her Gucci handbag. After her meeting with Mr Zimmerman she might well have to arrange a meeting with her uncle in order to tell him that he, not she, was going to be the one bequeathing Cedar Court to the National Trust.

If they would accept it.

If Francis were really dead.

The taxicab swerved to a halt outside the main entrance of the hospital.

With her black hair swept softly into a knot at the nape of her neck and wearing a dove-grey suit with a white silk shirt tied in a loose cravat at the neck, she looked stunningly elegant as she stepped from the cab and paid the driver. Fifteen minutes later she was seated facing Mr Zimmerman.

Like most Americans, he had an unpretentious, direct manner.

'The prognosis isn't good, Miss Grant,' he said after going through the formalities of greeting her. 'But then, I think you already know that, don't you?'

Geraldine ran the tip of her tongue over her bottom lip. 'Yes,' she said, as outwardly in control as if they were talking about nothing more important than the weather, only the whiteness of her knuckles betraying her inner turmoil. 'How many treatment options am I now left with?'

'With your type of aplastic anaemia, severe aplastic anaemia, there is, as we discussed on your last visit, a complete failure of production of all types of blood cells, resulting in fat cells in the bone marrow instead of the blood-producing cells which would normally be present.'

He paused, leaning forward and resting his elbows on his desk, steepling his fingers together. 'The only real, definitive cure is a bone marrow transplant.'

'And?' Geraldine could feel her heart slamming against her breastbone. What was he saying to her? That she could be cured if she underwent a transplant? And if that was the case why had he said that the prognosis wasn't good?

'And transplants are usually only carried out on patients under the age of forty who have a brother or sister as a suitable match.'

She opened her mouth to speak. No sound came. She had no siblings. And she was certainly no longer under the age of forty. Once again, she licked her bottom lip. 'And when those conditions aren't applicable?'

'In some cases where a sibling donor isn't available a matched donor transplant can be carried out using a donor from a volunteer donor registry. However, the risks are higher with a matched unrelated donor transplant than with a sibling one and suitable donors, especially for someone of your age, are not plentiful.'

His face was sombre.

'And supportive treatment?'

Geraldine had never been a panicker, and she didn't panic

now. She did, though, have a giddying sense of unreality. How could she be continuing with the conversation so coolly and calmly? Was there something unnatural about her? She thought of the way she'd long avoided close personal relationships and thought that perhaps there was.

'We can continue treating the symptoms as we have been treating them, with transfusions and antibiotics. Another course of action is an immunosuppressive therapy called ALG. This treatment suppresses the immune system allowing the bone marrow to recover. The dangers are that with your immune system 'damped down' in this way you are open to a high risk of infection – and left with no way of fighting it off. And it only allows improvement to a level which minimizes the need for transfusions. It isn't a cure.'

Vaguely she was aware that she was grateful he wasn't pussyfooting around and giving her hope where hope didn't exist. He hadn't, though, yet told her the real nitty-gritty. He hadn't told her how long she had left to live if no donor transplant was forthcoming.

Reading her mind, he said gently, 'Without a successful transplant you have a year, Miss Grant. Maybe a little more, maybe a little less.'

A year. Her head spun. She heard herself thanking him. As if from a distance, she saw herself rise to her feet.

Saw herself leave the room. Leave the hospital.

Outside, on the Boulevard Victor Hugo, the traffic was as heavy as ever. She stood, staring at it, reviewing her options, such as they were.

A transplant was possible – just. And she could have ALG therapy, which carried the risk of her dying from an infectious disease that her damped-down immune system could not fight off. Or she could continue with her monthly blood transfusions and antibiotics and put her affairs in order.

As pragmatic as any Frenchwoman, the last option was the one she knew she was going to embark on whether she decided to have ALG or not. As for a transplant – that was in the lap of the gods. Mr Zimmerman would do his best for her, but it was no use assuming that a suitable donor would be found.

Not attempting to flag down a taxi, she began walking

without aim or purpose, wondering how she felt about the obscene prospect of dying in her early fifties.

Not good, of course. And not frightened. This realization interested her and she knew that, later, she would try to analyse why. She couldn't do any such analysis now, though, because she was too angry. Too ragingly, scorchingly, *searingly* angry.

How *dare* her body betray her in such a subversive, sly, deceitful way? It was unforgivable. Insupportable. Vile beyond belief.

Still oblivious to her surroundings she crossed to the far side of the Boulevard Victor Hugo and into the smaller, though still busy, Avenue du Général Leclerc.

The indications that there was something wrong with her had, at first, been deceptively mundane. She'd begun feeling tired during the day. She'd lost colour. She'd become aware of bruises appearing for no good reason.

'You are anaemic, *chérie*,' Dominique had said to her over lunch at Beauvilliers, their favourite restaurant. 'You need a pick-me-up – a tonic.'

'If I'm anaemic, I need lots of red wine,' she had said, thinking that Dominique's diagnosis was perhaps right and not worrying about it. 'How about we share a bottle of Burgundy?'

Her doctor had taken blood from her to be tested and, until the results were received, had prescribed an iron supplement.

Then had come the blood test results.

They had shown an alarmingly low blood count.

It was then that her doctor had referred her to Mr Zimmerman at the American Hospital.

Mr Zimmerman had arranged for her to have a bone marrow sample taken. A needle had been inserted into her left hip bone and a sample of marrow – together with a sample of bone – had been taken.

It had only been then, whilst waiting for the results, that she had begun to wonder if she might be suffering from something a little more serious than general anaemia.

'Your platelet count is less than twenty,' he had said to her gravely, 'and your reticulocyte count is less than twenty-five.'

'Which means . . . ?'

'Which means that they are severely abnormal. The platelet count should have been in the range of a hundred and fifty to four hundred, the reticulocyte count between fifty and a hundred and fifty. I want you to come into hospital so that further blood samples can be taken and analysed and so that I can give you a transfusion of red blood cells immediately.'

There had been endless other blood tests, further bone marrow tests, further transfusions.

The end result had been the definite diagnosis of bone marrow failure and the pathology results that had led to the prognosis she had just been given.

As she walked into Boulevard du Bois le Prêtre, the words 'Without a successful transplant you have a year, Miss Grant. Maybe a little more, maybe a little less' hammered in her ears.

It was certainly a prognosis that concentrated the mind.

Once she had made sure she was on every possible donor list, she would put her affairs in order. If a year, give or take a little, was all that was left to her, then there were places she wanted to go and people she wanted to see. Dominique could take over the escort agency. She wasn't going to spend her last days putting consenting adults in touch with one another. Those days, though challenging and, for the most part, fun, were over.

Wryly, she reflected that they had also been profitable, for what she had created was a management consultant's dream – a business with a steady supply of highly motivated labour, extreme mobility, low overheads due to focused use of laptops and mobile phones, eager customers and outrageously high profits.

It hadn't been the way she'd thought, when she was young, that she would spend her life, but it had been surprisingly agreeable. She'd always been her own boss. She'd liked almost every girl she'd agreed to manage. And she'd enjoyed much more matching the right girl to the right client than she had having her own list of clients.

In retrospect it surprised her that, for a short time, she'd once done escort work herself, because sex was very low on her list of priorities. It had happened, though, during a period of time when she hadn't cared about anything. When, after she'd lost her one and only dream of founding a new dynasty at Cedar Court, nothing had mattered at all.

And now she had reached the one person her thoughts always returned to.

Francis.

Though his father had never been able to understand why he hadn't returned to England after he had ceased being Kiki's manager and live-in lover, she had always believed it was because he was ashamed – ashamed of the drug addict he had become and ashamed of his behaviour towards her. Unable to face either her or his father, he had simply slid away, losing himself in the vastness of America.

And so she had never been able to tell him that she was sorry.

'*Tiens!*' Dominique had erupted explosively when she had once voiced this regret. 'Why should you feel sorry for anything, *chérie*? You didn't walk out on him on your wedding day. You have nothing to reproach yourself for.'

'I was the one who wanted us to marry,' she had said. 'It wasn't Francis's idea. It was mine – and my mother's and his father's.'

With the clarity of maturity she could see now that when it had come to the question of their wedding Francis had simply done what he'd always done. He'd been pleasantly agreeable and let himself be swept along in the wake of people more forceful than himself. And then had come Kiki and his experience of managing her and being part of the pop world – and he'd loved every minute of it. Exciting, glamorous and fast, it had been his spiritual home. He hadn't wanted to abandon it. When he'd done so in order that they could hit the hippie trail to India, it had only been because she had insisted he do so.

And the minute they'd returned, even if Kiki hadn't been desperate that he become her manager again, he would have been itching to pitch himself once more into her racy, chaotic lifestyle.

He'd never been interested in Cedar Court. It's history – and their joint family history – had never meant anything to him. It was another of the reasons he'd been happy to go through his teens accepting that they'd marry when she was twenty-one. He knew she'd take the burden of Cedar Court from his shoulders and that his father would happily accept her doing so. And Cedar Court was another of the reasons he'd never returned to England. He hadn't wanted the bother of it – and so he'd simply walked away from it.

Someone bumped into her, jarring her from her thoughts, and with a startled shock she realized she was in the Place des Abbesses, in Montmartre. She wondered how long she had been walking and hadn't a clue. She didn't feel tired, though, and – miracle of miracles – she had none of the bone pain that was usually so persistent.

Ignoring the Art Nouveau decorated entrance to the Metro, she took the steps at the right of the church of St-Jean l'Evangéliste, wondering, now that she'd been forced to face the fact that she wasn't immortal, what her life had all been about. One thing she knew with certainty was that it had never had a spiritual dimension. Even now, coming to terms with the fact that it might soon be over, she had no impulse to enter St-Jean l'Evangéliste.

She continued to the end of the street and turned right into Rue Ravignon, reflecting on the sum of her existence.

There had been her youth. There had been Bickley High and Primmie, Artemis and Kiki. With difficulty, she mentally transported herself to the days before her violent rift with Kiki; to the days when she had been just as close to Kiki as she had been to Primmie and Artemis. They had been good days. They had been the best days of her life. Primmie's voice saying 'It will always be the four of us, won't it? We'll be friends for ever and ever, won't we?' rang in her ears as clearly as if Primmie were standing beside her.

She closed her eyes, fighting back a long-delayed wave of fatigue and an almost overwhelming yearning for the past. She should have kept in touch with Primmie and Artemis. Cutting Kiki from her life with surgical precision had been no reason to fight shy of remaining in touch with Primmie and Artemis. The few short months when she had been an escort girl would have shocked them both, but would have been the kind of shock they would have got over.

Uncaring that she was walking further away from her home, she continued up the hill towards a small public garden.

Her girlhood friendships had been some of the most precious things in her life – and the others had been her relationship with Francis and her passion for Cedar Court.

261

She crossed the green oasis of the garden, no longer walking aimlessly. On the crown of the hill was the Auberge de la Bonne Franquette and, with her fragile resources of energy fast deserting her, it was as far as she intended going. From there she would telephone for a taxi to take her home and, once home, she would telephone her uncle. She was his main beneficiary and he needed to be told that she was unlikely to outlive him.

As for the future left to her, she would leave Paris and return to England.

And she would stay at Cedar Court.

She would stay at Cedar Court for as long as her health permitted her to do so. She would also get in touch with Artemis – that is she would if Artemis was still at the same address or in the phone book.

She stepped into the cool interior of the restaurant feeling extremely purposeful for a woman who, an hour or so ago, had been poleaxed by shattering news. Unlikely as it seemed, she had discovered things to look forward to.

There was Cedar Court.

There was the possibility of a reunion with Artemis.

And, in Cornwall, there was Primmie.

She seated herself at a small corner table, a knot of anticipation beginning to coil deep in the pit of her stomach.

'A glass of Chablis, please,' she said to the waiter, reflecting on how delighted Primmie would be to see her.

Incredibly, she realized she was smiling.

Primmie would be more than delighted to see her.

Dearest darling Primmie would be over the moon.

Twenty-Three

September 2003

A s Primmie stepped inside her front door she put down her basket of freshly gathered mushrooms and turned her attention to the letter, addressed to Mrs Amelia Surtees, she'd picked up from her post box. When she'd first moved into Ruthven, there had been a steady stream of letters for Amelia. Most of them had been letters from organizations Amelia had supported, such as the RHS and RSPB. Each time she had written back, informing the sender that Amelia had died and, over the last month or so, the stream had reduced to a trickle.

She seated herself at the kitchen table and opened the envelope. The heading on the notepaper was that of the Claybourne Children's Home, Nottingham. Assuming it was yet another of the many charities her aunt had supported, Primmie smoothed it out and began reading.

Dear Mrs Surtees,

This is to confirm that five of our ten-year-olds, three boys and two girls, will be arriving with you on Saturday the 13th of September, as arranged after last year's most successful stay at Ruthven, to spend a fortnight with you. Miss Rose Hudson, a young care-worker at Claybourne, will accompany the children. As always, our many thanks for giving our children the opportunity to experience a week of country living, by the sea.

Yours sincerely,

Arthur Bottomly, Superintendent.

Primmie sucked in her breath, blinked and read the letter again. She hadn't been dreaming. The Claybourne Children's Home superintendent really was about to send five children to her for a fortnight's holiday. Her first instinct was to telephone the number on the letter heading to tell him that he couldn't possibly do so, to explain to him that Amelia had died five months ago and that, as she hadn't known about this long-standing arrangement, she'd been unable to cancel it earlier.

She pushed her chair away from the table and walked into the hall, where her telephone sat on a small black lacquered table. And hesitated. The 13th of September was only ten days away. Would the superintendent be able to arrange an alternative stay near the seaside for the children? She remembered how excited she had always been as a child before yearly

263

holidays to Whitstable or Broadstairs. If their holiday were cancelled, the children would be devastated.

She picked up the phone, and instead of dialling the super-intendent's number she dialled Matt's.

'Did you know about this?' she was saying moments later after reading the letter to him.

'I knew about the Claybourne Children's Home arrange-ment, but I understood Amelia's solicitors had cancelled it along with all the other holiday arrangements they'd cancelled.'

'What other holiday arrangements?' she asked, exaspera-tion rising. 'How many children was Amelia in the habit of providing holidays for? And why didn't you ever tell me about them? That two of the bedrooms were fitted out with bunk beds as well as a single bed has been puzzling me ever since I arrived. Why didn't you explain to me?'

'Because you never asked,' he said reasonably.

She gave a sigh of capitulation. 'OK. Pax. But what am I to do, Matt? The children are due here in ten days' time and I don't want to cancel what is most likely going to be their only holiday, but I don't know what will be expected of me. What did Amelia do for them? There's no entertainment nearby and . . .'

'You're flapping, Primmie.' It seemed to fascinate him. 'I've never known you to flap before. Not even when the hens went missing. If the children who are due to arrive are anything like the children that have been before, the only entertainment they'll need is that of the novelty of staying on a smallholding. They'll love the hens – and so it's a good job we retrieved them all. They'll love feeding them and collecting the eggs and generally running wild in the orchard and down at the cove, collecting shells and paddling in rock pools and that sort of thing.'

'Yes,' she said slowly, understanding all too well what bliss Ruthven would be for city children and coming to a decision. 'And I'm not panicking any longer, Matt. I'm going to honour the arrangement.'

'Good.'

Though she couldn't see him, she knew he was smiling.

The next morning he had taken her to the local cattle market in order that she could do something she'd been promising herself she would do for a long time. Buy a cow.

Looking and feeling like a true countrywoman in a waxed sleeveless jacket over an open-necked blouse, her trousers tucked into green Wellingtons, she had, with his help, bought a small, docile-looking Jersey.

When she'd christened her Maybelline, Matt had cracked with laughter, but she hadn't cared. Maybelline had long-lashed gold-flecked liquid brown eyes, and she'd told him that an animal so pretty deserved a pretty name.

If not quite as much a part of her day-to-day life as Matt, Hugo Arnott, too, had become a good friend.

'I moved here to escape the rat race, Primmie dearest,' he'd said to her in his attractive American drawl when, shortly after Matt had introduced him to her, she asked what had brought him from New York to a tiny fishing village in Cornwall. 'I was fifty-six, master of my own fate and bored with rustling and hustling. You might call this early retirement. It's certainly a novelty – and until the novelty wears off, here I shall stay.'

Peggy Wainwright, Calleloe's postmistress, had also become, if not a close friend, then a friendly acquaintance, as had Peggy's sister, who was married to a farmer over near Tregidden, Peggy's sister-in-law, who ran a tea shop in nearby Coverack, and John Cowles, the local vicar.

All in all, though Primmie had feared that she would feel isolated and lonely at Ruthven, she hadn't felt either. Which was perhaps just as well, for despite issuing invitations to Joanne, Millie and Josh that they come and stay with her for a few days, or even for a couple of weeks, none of them had taken up her invitation.

As she went upstairs to check on the state of readiness of her guest bedrooms, she philosophically shrugged the disappointment away. Her children would come down and visit her in their own good time and, until they did so, she had lots and lots to occupy her – her imminent guests, for one thing.

For a week she would be baking and cooking for five growing children, plus their carer. She was going to need to be organized where her grocery shopping was concerned, and she was going to have to think about entertaining them. Matt was no doubt right about the ways they would entertain themselves out of doors, but what if it rained? She would need to have plenty of jigsaw puzzles and games such as draughts, Monopoly, Cluedo, dominoes and Scrabble. Buying them wouldn't be an extravagant expense, for they would be useful to have in for her future bed and breakfast guests.

After reassuring herself that, where the rooms were concerned, all she had to do was air the beds, she went into her bedroom for her jacket and her handbag, intending to go into Calleloe to see what board games were on offer. Having children around her again, even if only for a fortnight, was going to be fun.

She heard the car coming down the rutted track towards Ruthven long before she saw it. Wondering who it could be, she stood by the window, waiting for the car to come into view.

When it did so, her eyes widened. Instead of being the kind of serviceable vehicle most people living in and around Calleloe drove – either a small car that was easy to park in Calleloe's steep, narrow streets or a Range Rover that took rough ground in its stride – the car was an open-topped, metallic-silver Ferrari. Despite the private road signpost, tourists seeking a secluded spot to picnic in occasionally ventured down the track to the cove. This obviously was one such and, by the look of the car, the tourist in question was extremely rich.

Five minutes later, as she drove the Corsa down towards the gates, it was to find the Ferrari parked smack on the other side of them. The driver – a woman – was still in the car, which was a relief. If she hadn't been, if she'd gone for a walk, then there was no telling how long she, Primmie, would have been trapped this side of the gates.

Musing on the oddity of the Ferrari driver's choice of parking space when there was the entire headland she could have parked on, she continued driving towards the gates, her mind half on what she was doing and half on the necessity of ordering foodstuff for Maybelline for the winter.

At her approach, instead of turning on the Ferrari's engine and driving away in order to give access to the lane, the driver opened her door and stepped out of the car.

She was tall, slim and spectacularly well groomed. Glossy black hair was coiled into a sleek chignon. Her jacket and its matching knee-skimming slit skirt were ice-white and French couture elegant. Primmie felt her mouth tugging into a smile of amusement. Whoever she was, she was hardly a typical tourist. Perhaps her interest was the church not the coastline. She was just about to roll her window down and ask if she could help in any way when the woman rounded the bonnet of the Ferrari and she saw her full on for the first time.

Though the Corsa was only crawling along, she slammed her foot on the brake with all the urgency of an emergency stop at speed. It was thirty years at least since she had last seen Geraldine, but there was no mistaking that beautiful, classically sculpted bone structure.

She scrabbled for the door handle, flinging the door open, half falling out of the car in her haste.

'Geraldine!' she shouted, regaining her balance, beginning to run. '*Geraldine!*'

Geraldine came to a halt, flashing her the same dazzling smile with which she had greeted her on their first day at Bickley High.

'Oh my God!' Primmie felt as if her heart was about to stop beating. 'It *is* you! What are you doing here? How did you find me?'

As she was tumbling the words out, she was pulling the gate wide.

'Primmie!' Geraldine's black-lashed, violet-dark eyes were bright with tears. 'Dearest darling Primmie!'

Seconds later, the gate no longer between them, they were hugging as if their lives depended on it.

'It's been so long!' Primmie's voice cracked and broke. 'Why didn't you keep in touch, Geraldine? You haven't changed. You haven't changed one little bit. I would have known you anywhere!'

Even as she gasped the words, still hugging and being hugged, she knew they weren't a hundred per cent true. Geraldine *had* changed. She'd always been as slender as a reed, but now there was a certain fragility to her slenderness and her wonderful cheekbones were a tad too pronounced and hollowed.

267

'It's been thirty-one years, three months,' Geraldine said, at last pulling away so that she could take a proper look at her. 'And *you* have changed, Primmie! You look every inch a countrywoman. Do you always wear Wellingtons when you go out in your car, and what are those clinging to your skirt? Feathers?'

Primmie grinned. 'Yes, they'll be from the hens. Oh, Geraldine, it's so good to see you! You can't know how often I've wished and wished you would just turn up out of the blue. I always imagined that if you did, though, it would be in Rotherhithe. How did you find me? You *did* find me, didn't you? This isn't just the most amazing piece of luck, is it?'

'No, of course it isn't just luck.' Geraldine tucked her arm in hers. 'Your message on the Friends Reunited website said you were living on the outskirts of Calleloe, on the Lizard. I didn't need to be Brain of Britain to find you. I simply made enquiries at the post office in Calleloe.'

Primmie hugged her arm tightly and, ignoring both cars, began walking her up the track towards the house. 'Now you're here, you're going to stay, Geraldine, aren't you? I've got masses of room. You *have* to stay. There's so much to catch up on. So much I want to know. Are you still living in Paris? I saw your photograph in a newspaper gossip column a few months ago and you were with a very handsome Frenchman. Are you married?'

With a smile of amusement, Geraldine held up a left hand bereft of rings.

Primmie giggled. 'Well, then. Have you *been* married? What have you been doing for this last thirty years?' The giggles died. She stopped walking, turning to face her. 'And why didn't you keep in touch, Geraldine?' she asked, a world of bewilderment in her voice. 'Neither Artemis nor I ever understood it.'

'Aah, that needs a little explaining, Primmie.' Geraldine's eyes darkened fractionally and for the first time Primmie noticed that there were shadows of tiredness beneath them. 'Perhaps later, over a bottle of wine or a couple of strong scotches?'

Primmie nodded, feeling a stab of concern. Was Geraldine not very well? And what had happened in Paris, all those years ago, that she was still reluctant to talk about to her?

Geraldine smiled across at her, the fleeting darkness in her eyes no longer discernible. 'What made you move from London to Cornwall, Primmie? And this isn't a smallholding. It's a farm!'

They were nearly at the house now and the meadow, where Maybelline was grazing and the hens were roaming around free, was on their left-hand side, the paddock on their right.

'Hardly.' Primmie couldn't keep a giggle of happiness out of her voice. 'It is wonderful, though, isn't it? I was left it by an aunt – not outright, but to live in and enjoy for my lifetime. It once supported quite a lot of animals, but I only have a cow and hens – and the hens were here when I came.'

'And the cow?' Geraldine asked, not knowing when she'd last felt such fun fizzing in her throat.

'I bought Maybelline a short time ago. She's very beautiful. Very tame and gentle. When I've milked her she loves me putting my arms round her neck and stroking her behind the ears.'

'*You* milk her?' Geraldine rolled her eyes to heaven and Primmie was immediately transported back in time, remembering how she'd had to stifle her giggles when, on that first day at Bickley High, Geraldine's mother had asked her to look after Geraldine and, behind her mother's back, Geraldine had rolled her eyes to show just what she thought of such a needless suggestion.

'I'll have you know that I'm getting very accomplished at milking,' she said with mock severity. 'A friend, Matt, taught me how. He isn't a farmer – he was a fisherman until he retired, a year or so ago – but he can turn his hand to anything.'

Geraldine quirked an eyebrow. 'And is he single and good looking?'

Primmie had the grace to blush. 'As a matter of fact, he is. But I don't think he's looking for a wife. He's never been married and so I don't imagine he'll start thinking about it now.' They'd reached the house and she came to a halt. 'Well, here we are. This is Ruthven.' Pride shone on her face and filled her voice. 'What do you think of it, Geraldine? Isn't it marvellous?'

Geraldine saw an unremarkable-looking, large, slate-roofed

stone house. It stood four-square and sturdy, its only redeeming feature its green French-looking window shutters.

'It's wonderful,' she said, well aware of just how wonderful it would seem to someone who had never lived in anything other than a London council house. Her mouth tightened fractionally as she remembered that Primmie had, once upon a time, lived somewhere very different. When they'd been at Bickley High, she had lived, Monday to Friday, at Kiki's.

Primmie hadn't yet asked if she'd renewed any contact with Kiki, but she would, and when she did she would have to tell her that, where Kiki was concerned, her feelings hadn't changed. Even at this distance of time, she had no intention of seeing or speaking to Kiki, ever again.

'This is the sitting room,' Primmie was saying, continuing with her guided tour of the downstairs rooms. 'It looked very dowdy when I arrived and so I painted the walls white and re-covered the sofa and chairs in yellow.'

It was a lovely large room with an open fireplace and bookshelves floor to ceiling in the recesses at either side of the chimney breast. In the nearby hearth a copper kettle was stuffed full of marigolds, their colour the exact shade of the many Penguin paperbacks on the shelves.

'I haven't had to decorate the guest bedrooms,' Primmie said as she led the way upstairs. 'My aunt provided holidays for children in residential care and all the bedrooms – except the one that was her own and is now mine – are all beautifully decorated. These two rooms,' she indicated the two rooms on the left-hand side of a spacious landing, 'both look out over the headland.'

'And are you going to provide holidays for under-privileged children as well?' Geraldine asked, as Primmie led the way into the first of the two bedrooms.

'Only unintentionally. There are five children arriving here in ten days' time, only I didn't know until a few hours ago.' She sat down on the neatly made-up single bed as Geraldine strolled across to the window to look at the magnificent view. 'What I will be doing is becoming a bed and breakfast landlady. I've already got myself a fire safety certificate and someone from the local council has been out and has approved the amenities I'm offering. It means I'll be included in the list of B&Bs in local tourist brochures. I've left it too late to really get under way this year, but by next spring I'll be up and running.'

Geraldine remained standing at the window, looking out over the headland to the church and the enormous vista of sea and sky. The house would make a wonderful B&B. And a wonderful holiday home for children. Thinking about children prompted thoughts of Artemis.

Still looking at the stunning view, she said, 'Are you still in touch with Artemis, Primmie? I'd love to see her again. I know about the child she lost. I saw the death notice in *The Times*. It must have been a terrible time for her. Absolutely ghastly.'

The expected response – the agreement that it had been an utter nightmare for Artemis – didn't come. There was no response at all. Only a ringing silence.

Wondering if perhaps Primmie hadn't heard her, she turned her head and looked towards her.

Primmie was still seated on the bed, but this time her face wasn't glowing with happiness at their reunion and her eyes weren't shining with the pride she felt in her home. She looked as if she were on the edge of some terrible abyss, as if Artemis's tragedy hadn't occurred twenty-five years ago, but was a tragedy that had occurred only recently; a tragedy she was still struggling to come to terms with.

'I'm sorry, Primmie,' she said, shocked at the depth of Primmie's reaction to what she had said. 'I didn't mean to distress you. I should have realized you would have known the child, that you wouldn't just feel bad about what happened on Artemis's behalf, but that you would have grief of your own. She would have been like a niece to you, wouldn't she? It was a little girl, wasn't it? And I seem to remember she had an unusual name. A name that didn't seem at all like the kind of name I would have imagined Artemis choosing.'

'Artemis didn't choose the name.' Primmie's hands were clasped tightly together in her lap. 'I chose the name.'

Geraldine frowned, not understanding, only the sensitive subject preventing her from asking if Artemis had been unable to think of a name for herself.

'And Destiny wasn't like a niece to me, Geraldine.'

271

Primmie's eyes held hers, harrowed. 'She was my daughter. She was my baby and, because I wasn't married when I had her, because I couldn't give her all the things I wanted her to have, Artemis and Rupert adopted her.'

For several seconds Geraldine couldn't move. The enormity of what Primmie was telling her was just too great. Her pulse beats roared in her ears.

'Simon Lane?' she said, reading the answer in Primmie's eyes. 'Oh, Primmie! Oh, darling, darling Primmie.'

Swiftly she crossed to the bed, sitting down at Primmie's side, taking hold of one of Primmie's hands. 'Why didn't you tell me?' she asked, more deeply moved than she'd thought herself capable of being. 'I had no idea. Did anyone else know?'

The realization that Primmie had had Kiki's father's baby was so staggering even her orderly mind boggled at the possible emotional fallout. The baby had been Kiki's half-sister. How on earth had Kiki felt about it? And how had she felt about Artemis adopting her? More incredible still, just why hadn't Simon Lane been more supportive to Primmie? He'd had money. Primmie needn't have faced financial difficulties as a single parent. Kiki's name wasn't one she'd wanted to bring up, but she did so now. 'Kiki,' she said. 'Did Kiki know?'

Primmie shook her head. 'No. No one knew. Not even Simon. And I couldn't tell you, Geraldine. You'd gone to Paris. I had no address for you, no telephone number.'

Geraldine winced, well aware of how selfishly she'd cut herself off from everyone in the aftermath of Francis's desertion and Kiki's betrayal. 'I'm sorry,' she said inadequately. 'Oh God, Primmie. I'm so sorry.'

Primmie squeezed her hand. 'You don't have to be sorry, Geraldine. You had heartache of your own, and though it was never easy for me, living on my own without Destiny, I always had the comfort of knowing that Artemis loved her with all her heart and I knew lots of other things that were a comfort. I knew what her bedroom looked like. I knew what the garden looked like and so I could easily imagine her playing in it. I'd patted and stroked the pony Rupert and Artemis had bought for her. In the first year or two I met Artemis regularly for lunch and she would bring me photographs of Destiny and

272

tell me what she was doing and how she was progressing. I wasn't completely cut off from her.'

'But you didn't see her?'

Primmie shook her head. 'No,' she said, her voice bleak. 'All the adoption advice given to Artemis and Rupert was against it. Artemis would have disregarded it. She wanted me to be a part of Destiny's life, for Destiny to regard me as a much-loved auntie, but Rupert couldn't cope with being constantly reminded that Destiny wasn't his. He put an end to the regular lunch meetings I had with Artemis. And then . . .'

She paused, taking a deep breath. 'And then Destiny drowned in the pool at Rupert and Artemis's villa in Spain. And neither I nor Artemis was at her funeral. Artemis was in hospital in England, recovering from a serious car accident, and Rupert didn't contact me about the funeral arrangements. Quite simply, he wouldn't have wanted me there. She was his little girl and I suppose at such a terrible time for him he didn't want reminding that she was adopted.'

They were silent. Through the window they could see a brassy blue sky and seagulls wheeling. After a little while, Geraldine said gently, 'And what about your other children, Primmie? It said on the website that you had four. Are any of them married? Do you have grandchildren?'

Primmie unclasped her hands and wiped the tears from her cheeks. 'Two of them are married, Joanne and Millie. I don't have any grandchildren, though. Not yet.'

'And the other two? What do they think of this adventure of yours into Cornish country living?'

Primmie managed a smile. 'Josh and Lucy? I'm not sure what Josh thinks. He's every inch a south-Londoner and I doubt he truly knows just whereabouts Cornwall is. Lucy is a world traveller. At the moment she's in Australia, but I'm hoping she'll be back in England soon. And when she is, she'll stay here and she'll love it, though I doubt she'll stay for long – staying in one place for any length of time isn't Lucy's style.'

She took hold of Geraldine's hand. 'And you'll stay here as well, won't you, Geraldine? And next year, when I'm really organized, will you stay for the whole of the summer?'

Geraldine slid an arm round Primmie's shoulders and pulled her close so that Primmie's head was against her shoulder and Primmie couldn't see into her eyes. 'I'm not in a position to make plans for next summer, Primmie,' she said. 'But I'd like to stay here now. I'd like to stay here for a couple of months, if it's all right with you.'

'Of course it's all right with me! It's more than I could have ever hoped for! There are the children arriving in ten days' time, though. It doesn't matter about rooms, because there are three guest rooms, but perhaps you won't want to be here when the place is full of children?'

She pulled away from Geraldine a fraction so that she could look into her face.

Geraldine grinned. 'Of course I'll want to be here. After some of my work experience of the last thirty years, children should be a doddle.'

Primmie grinned back at her, wondering just what kind of work Geraldine had done. She would ask later. For the moment, all that mattered was that Geraldine was back in her life – and was going to stay back in her life.

'I missed you, Geraldine,' she said thickly. 'You'll never know how much.'

Geraldine smiled and pulled her close again. 'If it's half as much as I missed you, Primmie, then I do,' she said, and kissed Primmie's hair, regretting to the very depths of her being all the years of friendship she had so foolishly wasted.

Twenty-Four

Wearing black leather trousers, a turquoise T-shirt emblazoned with a sequinned panorama of Las Vegas and a black leather jacket, Kiki stood at the door of her flat, saying goodbye to it. It was an absolute tip. For the last six weeks, ever since her catastrophic Grantley gig, she'd done very little but hole up in it, drinking heavily, mulling over the greatest decision of her life – whether or not she was going to end it.

In retrospect she knew she should have driven away from Grantley the minute suicide first entered her mind and committed the dreadful deed there and then. After all, what was the alternative? Now it had finally permeated her thick skull that, apart from a few brief glory days in the late seventies and early eighties, she had never ever been a major rock star – and that she was most definitely now never going to become one – what was there left to live for? Looking round her uncared-for flat, the answer was 'bloody little'.

With her head pounding from her mammoth vodka binge and her body feeling as if it had been run over by a truck, she slung her bag and laptop on the back seat of her clapped-out Fiat Uno, eyeing the car with loathing. Even just being seen behind its wheel robbed her of all self-respect and self-esteem. It was bad enough no longer being a star, but without some remnants of a star's lifestyle, she couldn't even enjoy living on reputation.

And she no longer had rock-star dosh. Though she still received royalties from the songs she had written with Geraldine, it wasn't enough to support her in the style people expected. There was no pleasure in having people recognize her – which they still did – if they then immediately became aware that she was virtually impoverished. Every time it happened, the humiliation was so great she didn't know how she survived it.

Nauseously she slid behind the wheel and turned the key in the ignition. Lots of other old rock stars that she knew had carved out new careers for themselves in other aspects of the music business: management or production. She'd never attempted either. Being behind the scenes hadn't been what she'd wanted. Being up front and having all eyes on her had been what she'd wanted.

As she surged away from the kerb, she realized that she was already thinking in the past tense. Well, so be it. She wasn't going to endure another two or three decades as a has-been as clapped out as her car. There was such a thing as having a rag of pride. It would have been different, of course,

275

if she'd had the sense to have married money – the kind of money that would have enabled her to still hold her head high – but the idea of marriage had never appealed to her. It was too tying. Too conventional. Too boring. She'd always had a masculine attitude to sex, liking a lot of variety with little commitment. She'd felt it went with her job description. Where it had left her, of course, was alone.

Grim faced she pulled out on to the North Circular. Despite all the rock paraphernalia of endless parties, when it came to the bottom line, she'd always been alone – or she had been ever since she'd moved out of the Kensington flat she'd shared with Primmie, Artemis and Geraldine – and that was so long ago it seemed to have been in another lifetime.

It suddenly occurred to her that she had no road map in the car and that the last time she'd been to Cornwall she'd been driven there. She shrugged her shoulders. Cornwall was west and was big.

It couldn't be that hard to find.

Primmie and Geraldine were seated on a garden bench looking out over Ruthven's overgrown flower garden towards the sea.

'You could make a patio here,' Geraldine said, a plate of buttered toast balanced on her knee, a mug of tea cupped in her hands.

'I could – when I have the time. Lack of time is why the flower garden is so overgrown. I'm aiming at self-sufficiency and so the vegetable garden has been my first priority.'

'And what are you growing?' Geraldine had abandoned her highly unsuitable white linen suit and was dressed a little more appropriately for her surroundings in a shirt, slacks and flat shoes. That the peach-coloured shirt was Chanel, the cream slacks Armani and the cinnamon leather shoes Gucci ensured she still looked a million dollars.

'Spinach, carrots, lettuce, celery, leeks, onions, cabbages, potatoes – and kale, for Maybelline.'

'And what do you do with it all? You surely can't eat it all. You'd be as big as the house!'

Primmie giggled. 'I'm getting on that way. This skirt is a size sixteen. The first size sixteen I've ever had to buy.

Geraldine regarded the shapeless pleated garment in

question. 'And where did it come from?' she asked quizzically, a throb of laughter in her voice. 'British Home Stores?'

'The local Oxfam in Calleloe. As for what I do with my surplus veg – do you remember Peggy asking you to ask me if I'd exchange some eggs for mulberries? That's because amongst local people produce is used as currency. Matt lives in a traditional fisherman's cottage and the garden is too tiny for him to raise many veg, so when he worked on the cowshed, making it habitable for Maybelline, I repaid him with whatever was cropping from what Amelia had sown last year. I'm also starting to bottle and pickle things and I'm thinking of putting a little stall and an honesty box at the end of the track, where it meets the road. That way I'll be able to make a profit from whatever excess I have.'

'And what about the milk? Are you going to carry a pole across your shoulders with milk pails hanging from either end and go door to door?'

Primmie's shoulders shook with laughter. 'No, I'm not. I don't know much about selling surplus milk, but I think it's a bit tricky if it hasn't been pasteurized. There's someone called a dairying officer who keeps an eye on things like that. He came round to inspect the cow shed and to make sure I was cleaning the dunging passage every day and not letting dung build up in it.'

'The dunging passage?' Geraldine could hardly keep her voice steady. 'I dread asking this, Primmie, but is that a part of the shed or a part of Maybelline?'

Primmie gurgled with laughter. 'It's a part of the shed. I'll show you this evening, when I next milk her.'

'And you've already milked her this morning?'

'I have. You were still asleep and so I didn't disturb you. Milking her is very restful. I love doing it. I sit beside her on a little stool and rest my forehead against her warm flank and she's all soft and velvety and delicious smelling.'

Geraldine's expression was so comic, Primmie, more supremely happy than she'd been since Ted died, giggled again. Having Geraldine with her made her feel young again. Everything, even the most mundane things, was fun. She drank the last of her tea and said, 'Shall we to try to get in touch with Artemis? I have an old telephone number for her.'

277

'Yes, and if you have a telephone number for her, why haven't the two of you kept in touch?' She hesitated and then said gently, 'Is it because of what happened to Destiny?'

Primmie's giggles died. 'I think Artemis felt guilty,' she said at last, slowly. 'Guilty that she hadn't ensured Destiny had a responsible, fully trained nanny with her when Rupert took her to Spain. And I felt . . .' she made a despairing movement with her hand. 'I felt too many things. I didn't want to share my grief with anyone. Not even Artemis.'

'And now?'

'And now it wouldn't be an issue. I still grieve for Destiny. I'll always grieve for her, but I'm no longer frightened of harbouring feelings of blame towards Artemis for her death. In loving Destiny, Artemis and I shared something wonderfully precious. I'd love to see her again. I'd love it if we could persuade her to come down here, whilst you're still here. It would be just like old times again.'

'Except that Kiki wouldn't be with us.' Geraldine's voice was suddenly abrupt. 'That's one reunion I don't want to have, Primmie. Telephone Artemis. I, too, would absolutely love to see her again. But Kiki is a no-go area. Sorry.'

Primmie remained silent. There was a lot she wanted to say to Geraldine about Kiki – and a lot of questions she wanted to ask about Francis – but now was not the time.

'I'm going to telephone Artemis now,' she said, rising to her feet. 'What do you bet she shrieks with disbelief when I tell her I'm living on a smallholding in Cornwall and that you're staying with me?'

Five minutes later, when she rang the number of Artemis's Gloucestershire home, there were no shrieks of any kind. 'Mrs Gower no longer lives at this address,' a young woman said indifferently.

'Oh dear. I'm sorry for having troubled you. Do you perhaps have Mr and Mrs Gower's present address and telephone number?'

'This *is* Mr Gower's present address and telephone number,' the young woman said again, and this time, if a voice could have a smirk in it, hers had. 'Mrs Gower no longer lives here, though. She moved out three weeks ago.'

'And you don't have a telephone number for her?'

'No. Why should I?' The connection was smartly severed.
Primmie stood, eyebrows raised, the telephone receiver still
in her hand.

'Trouble?' Geraldine asked.

'It would seem so.' She put the telephone receiver back on
its rest. 'Artemis has moved out and another woman, who
sounds to be very young, has moved in – and says she has
no number for Artemis.'

Geraldine gave a Gallic shrug. 'Rupert ditching Artemis
was bound to happen eventually. I'm only surprised it didn't
happen within months of their marriage.'

'It would have been easier for her if it had happened then.'
Primmie's eyes were troubled. 'Having your husband leave
you after thirty-two years must be horrendous. I can't see
Artemis coping well in such a situation, can you?'

'No. Under the circumstances, I think we're duty bound to
find her. A phone call this evening, to Rupert, is called for.
He might not want to admit to having a contact number for
her, but he must have and, if he doesn't, his solicitor will no
doubt have one. If he doesn't, we'll hire a private detective.'

Primmie's eyes widened. 'A private detective will cost a
lot of money, Geraldine.'

'So?' Geraldine gave a wicked wink. 'I have stacks of
money, Primmie. Oodles and oodles of it. Which is why I
mentioned the patio, because if you'd like one, you shall have
one – and any other repairs or renovations that Ruthven needs.'

'But you can't do that, Geraldine! We're all getting older,
and whatever money you have you'll need for yourself, for
your future.'

Geraldine was just about to take a deep breath and tell her
that she didn't have a future – or not a very long one, when
the noise of a vehicle, approaching down the track towards
Ruthven's gates, halted her.

Primmie raised a hand to her eyes, squinting into the hot
morning sunlight. 'It's Matt,' she said with pleasure.

Geraldine watched with interest as a small, extremely
battered truck pulled up behind her Ferrari. Ever since she'd
arrived, Primmie's conversation had been peppered with
Matt's name and it was obvious that he had become a very
important part of her life. Was he worthy of being so important

279

to Primmie, though? That was what she, Geraldine, wanted to know and, with her wealth of experience where men were concerned, it was something she was totally confident of assessing.

Blissfully unaware of the kind of scrutiny he was under, Matt, unable to gain access to the track leading to Ruthven because of the Ferrari blocking the gates, jumped out from behind the wheel of the truck and, after circling the Ferrari in stunned admiration, began walking towards the house.

Even from a distance, Geraldine was approving of what she saw. A strong-looking man, he didn't move as if he was in his early sixties, he moved like a man who had always been active and still was. Though not very tall, he was well built, with thick hair shot through with silver. He wasn't wearing elderly clothes, either, which was, as far as she was concerned, another point in his favour. His navy fisherman's jersey was ageless, as were the jeans he was wearing with it.

There was no direct access to the front of Ruthven from the track and as he followed it round into the cobbled yard at the rear, he waved across to them and then disappeared out of sight.

'Do you need to let him in?' she asked, as Primmie made no sign of moving.

Primmie shook her head. 'No. The side door is off the latch – and even if it weren't it wouldn't matter. Matt has a key.'

'*Has* he?' Geraldine raised beautifully shaped sleek eyebrows high.

Primmie blushed rosily. 'It's easiest,' she said demurely. 'And he spends a lot of time here.'

Geraldine would have liked to explore the subject further but, with Matt about to join them at any moment, put her curiosity on hold.

There came the sound of his walking through the house and then he stepped out of the front door, a few yards away from them, and she saw that her first impressions had been correct. Matt Trevose was a very handsome man. His eyes were a warm amber-brown, his skin hard-tanned by constant exposure to the elements.

'I'm sorry, Primmie,' he said, walking towards them. 'I

didn't realize you had company. I thought the Ferrari had been parked by a tourist.'

Before Geraldine could apologize for blocking the gates, Primmie jumped to her feet and, slipping her hand into Matt's, said eagerly, 'Matt, I want you to meet one of my dearest, *dearest* old friends, Geraldine Grant. Geraldine, Matt Trevose.'

Aware that, if the way Primmie had slipped her hand into Matt's was anything to go by, Primmie and Matt were more than dearest friends, Geraldine rose to her feet.

'I'm very pleased to meet you, Matt,' she said truthfully, shaking his proffered hand.

'It's nice to meet you, too.' Matt gave her his easy smile. 'Primmie's mentioned your name lots of times when talking about her school days.'

'Geraldine is going to be staying with me for a little while, Matt. Hopefully for several weeks – and, if I'm lucky, even longer. We're just about to go down to the cove. Would you like to come with us?'

'I'm sorry, Primmie. I can't. I'm taking some tourists out for a day's sailing. I called in here on the way to let you know that Dave Clegg, over at St Keverne, has a goat he'd like to offload. It's a nanny and I wondered if you were interested.'

Primmie didn't hesitate. 'I'm interested. So interested I'll drive over there this morning with Geraldine.'

Vastly amused, Geraldine fought her fatigue. She was about to go and inspect a goat. It was an activity as far removed from her sophisticated lifestyle in Paris as anything she could imagine. Summoning all the reserves of her energy, she said, 'We are only going to look at this animal, aren't we?'

'Yes, that's all we can do until I sort out where I'm going to house it.' Primmie beamed sunnily across at her, hardly able to believe that the two of them were doing things together just as they had done when they were girls. 'And can we go in your car, Geraldine? When we pull up at Dave Clegg's in a Ferrari his eyes are going to pop out of his head!'

Kiki headed out on the M4 towards Bristol, staying firmly in the outside lane, pushing the Fiat to its top speed and keeping it there, no matter how the engine protested. All she had with her was one bag and her laptop and she was uncaring of the rest of her worldly goods. Her prized record collection had been sold off for drug money, in the years before she'd cleaned up her act where drugs were concerned. As for everything else – when her landlord finally got round to entering her flat to find out where the hell she was and why the rent wasn't being paid, he was welcome to whatever he found.

She rode hard on the tail of a family saloon, forcing it over into the middle lane. Little Richard's 'Lucille' was now belting out from her souped-up speakers. It had been recorded in 1957, when she was six years old. She'd loved it then, and she loved it now.

As junction 17 came and went, she reflected darkly that the whole thing wrong with her life had been her having been born just too late to be a performer of the kind of music that held her heart. Brenda Lee, whose songs she never tired of, had recorded her biggest hit, 'Sweet Nothin's', in 1960. Jerry Lee Lewis's heyday had been almost entirely pre-1963. She hadn't first strutted her stuff on stage until 1966, when she'd sung Saturday nights at the Two Zeds. After that, by the time she'd been professional and Francis had been managing her, it had been the early '70s and original rock and roll had already become nostalgia rock.

As signs came up for the M5 and the West Country, she finally began changing lanes. From the '70s on she'd ridden every new wave there had been, enjoying some high spots and a whole long litany of staying-in-the-business-only-by-the-skin-of-her-teeth lows. The trouble was, success as a rock star wasn't simply down to how good a performer you were. There were lots of sensational performers. What mattered was who heard you, when – and what they were in a position to do about it.

For mega-fame, luck was needed as well. Barrow loads of it. And luck – the right person handling her career at the right time and with the right backing group and the right songs – was something she'd never had.

Now on the M5, she pressed her foot on the accelerator as far down as it would go. As far as her career was concerned, she'd been humiliated for the last time. The sound of The

Stones had long since replaced Little Richard. With 'Little Red Rooster' blasting her eardrums, she left junction 18 behind her and bowled along towards junction 19.

Ten miles short of it, the Fiat's protesting engine gave a high-pitched wail and the car began losing speed. Within another half a mile it was crawling and within three quarters of an hour, as she pulled over on to the hard shoulder, it ground to a stop.

With the bonnet up and indicator lights flashing, she stared, clueless, into the engine. There could be no question of phoning the AA on her mobile, because she never did sensible things like belonging to the AA, and using the emergency phone to summon a tow truck seemed pointless. She'd be charged for doing so and would then have to pay for garage repairs, which might take days.

She slammed the bonnet shut, aware that it had started to rain. In high dudgeon, she yanked the nearside rear door open and dragged the laptop and her zip-up bag from the seat. Then she stood by the car and began thumbing a lift.

Within seconds, a truck driver pulled off the motorway on to the hard shoulder in front of her Fiat. With rain now plastering her hair to her head, Kiki ran towards it. The driver leaned across a large, unkempt-looking dog and threw the passenger seat door open for her. She tossed her bag up to him and, the laptop under her arm, hoisted herself nimbly up to squeeze into the seat beside the dog.

'Where d'you want to get to?'

'Cornwall.'

He rolled a cigarette from one corner of his mouth to the other. 'You're in luck. I'm going to Penzance. What part of Cornwall d'you want?'

'The Lizard.'

'I'll let you off at Helston. Don't mind the dog. Just shove him out of the way.'

Kiki was tempted to ask where on earth she could shove the dog to, but, as it was obvious there wasn't anywhere, shifted herself over so that there was more room for her and it.

The dog licked her face appreciatively.

'What kind of a dog is he?' she asked as the driver settled

on a steady eighty miles per hour and they thundered on through heavy rain towards Exeter. 'Is he a sheepdog?'

'Dunno. My missus bought him as a guard dog, but he's soddin' useless, neither use nor ornament.'

Kiki looked at the dog. The dog looked at her. Or she thought it was looking at her. It's hair was such a matted, bedraggled tangle it was hard to be sure.

The fug of engine fumes, damp dog and cigarette smoke was so unpleasant she closed her eyes, deciding that the best way of surviving the journey was to sleep through it.

When she woke, the dog's head was on her shoulder.

'We're crossing Bodmin Moor,' the driver said glumly. 'I hate Cornwall. It never does anythin' here but soddin' piss it down.'

Helston was presumably either on the Lizard or very near to it. From there she'd have to hitch a lift to Calleloe and then, in Calleloe, make enquiries as to where, exactly, Ruthven was.

The dog farted. It wasn't pleasant in the confines of the cab.

'Phaugh!' its owner said, winding down his window and letting rain in. 'Bleedin' animal! I'd sell him if I could get anything for him.'

The dog, unaware of the offence he was causing, continued to loll against Kiki as if they were bosom pals.

Before a huge roundabout just outside Helston the truck driver pulled over to the side of the road, coming to a halt with his engine still running. 'That's the road you need for the Lizard,' he said, nodding in the direction of the roundabout's first exit. 'From here to Lizard Point is only about eight miles, so you can't be far from where you want to be.'

'Ta.' She eased herself away from the dog, yanked open the door, threw her bag to the ground and jumped after it.

The dog followed her.

The truck driver smartly slammed the door shut so there could be no question of the dog leaping back in again. As he put the truck into gear again, he was grinning, showing yellowed teeth.

'You can have him,' he yelled to her as he began pulling away. 'I don't soddin' want him.'

The dog sat by her side, looking up at her. 'I don't suppose you want him, either,' she said, hoisting the strap of her bag up and over her shoulder. 'Come on. Nothing's going to stop for us on a roundabout. Let's drag ourselves a few yards down the first exit – and when we do get a lift, don't fart. Got it?'

The dog wagged its tail. Feeling curiously energized, Kiki began walking. It was still raining, but she wasn't particularly bothered. England was a country of dog lovers. Someone would stop and give the two of them a lift – and Primmie would take the dog in. Even though it was over thirty years since she'd seen Primmie, she didn't have a second's doubt on that score.

Primmie regarded the tethered nanny goat doubtfully.

The nanny goat stared stonily back at her with yellow eyes.

'Does she give milk, Mr Clegg?' she asked uncertainly.

'Oh aye. And she'll be grand at rearing orphans.'

From behind her Geraldine made a stifled, snorting sound.

Wildly Primmie wondered if Dave Clegg knew of the children who were due to arrive in just over a week's time, and then he said, 'Calves do real well on goat's milk, better'n they do on their mother's milk. Lambs, too. Fact is, you can rear near anything on goat's milk. Piglets. Foals. Alice here will rear anything you put nearby her.'

Deciding that if what Dave Clegg said was true Alice must have a nice nature, Primmie tried to overlook Alice's yellow eyes. 'Then I'll take her, Mr Clegg. I'll come back for her with Mr Trevose. He has a truck and I haven't.'

'Ah, no.' Dave Clegg dragged his eyes away from Geraldine's Ferrari and regarded her regretfully. 'I'm going in to Helston Cottage Hospital this afternoon and I want Alice settled afore I go.'

'But I haven't got anything to take her home in! Even if you go into hospital this afternoon, she'll be all right here. I'll come tomorrow with Matt and untether her and pop her in the back of Matt's truck.'

'Ah, no,' Dave Clegg said again, rubbing a stubbly chin with a grubby hand. 'I have someone else who's interested in giving her a home, see? It's either you takes her now, or you don't takes her at all.'

Ever hopeful, Primmie turned towards Geraldine.

'No.'

'But . . .'

'It's a *Ferrari*, Primmie. Not a cattle truck. Don't even think it, let alone ask it. No. Never. Not in a million years.'

Primmie's shoulders sagged. 'I'm sorry, Mr Clegg,' she said, turning back towards him. 'But it just isn't possible . . .'

Geraldine heaved a huge sigh. 'Oh, all *right*. But he has to provide us with something to cover the rear seat. And that something has to be clean, Primmie. And waterproof!'

'We're nearly there, young lady,' the Reverend John Cowles said to Kiki as he turned off the narrow main road on to a track marked 'Private'. 'This track isn't actually private, of course,' he continued, not at all disconcerted by the huge damp dog on the back seat poking its head out of the window. 'It has to be used to gain access to the church – which is one of the five churches I serve – but Mrs Surtees put the notice up when she got tired of hordes of trippers scattering litter all over the headland on their way to the cove. And the cove itself is private, and so the notice does make some sense. Leastways, no one living locally objects to it – and of course locals use it when they attend church. Which isn't,' he added cheerfully as they bumped down a track high with brambles and bright with wild orange montbretia, 'that often, as I only conduct a service here once every three months.'

He came to a halt beside a pair of rusty iron gates. 'This is Ruthven.' He indicated an even narrower track. It led up gently rising ground, between fields, to an immensely solid-looking grey-stone house. 'Give Mrs Dove my best wishes. If she should want to see me for anything – surplus eggs or milk – I'll be in the church for half an hour or so checking a genealogy request in the register. 'Bye, God bless.'

Kiki hauled her ass – and her bag and the dog – out of the car. No one, as far as she could remember, had ever said 'God bless' to her before. And as the blessing had come from a vicar, she supposed it carried a bit of clout. She shrugged her shoulders. Even if it did, it wasn't going to interfere with her plans for finding a cliff – and as the sea was so near she could hear it and smell it as well as see it, finding a cliff wasn't going to be hard to do.

With her bag hoisted over one shoulder, the laptop under her arm and the dog keeping close to her side, she walked towards the house. It had stopped raining now, though there was still a light drizzle. Though she'd thought herself beyond having an interest in anything, the beauty of Ruthven's location impinged even on her consciousness. Though not on the headland itself, there was a panoramic view of sea and sky and, apart from the vicar's car still beetling its way to the tip of the headland and the church, there wasn't a person in sight.

She wondered how Primmie stood it.

Ever since she'd kicked the dust of her childhood home from her heels, she'd lived in cities, surrounded by restaurants, clubs, shops, noise and people. Where did people who lived in places like the Lizard go on an evening, for God's sake? What did they do?

With the question still mystifying her, she neared the house and discovered that the track didn't lead, as she'd expected it to, to Ruthven's front garden and front door, but curved round to the side the house, leading into a large cobbled yard surrounded by outbuildings.

One of the buildings, its doors wide open, housed a shabby-looking Vauxhall Corsa. With rising anticipation, she crossed the yard to a side door of the house. Hens squawked and flapped in dismay at her approach and at the sight of the dog.

The dog barked at them, but didn't give chase. Instead, as she dumped her bag on the ground and knocked at the door, he sat expectantly by her side, tongue out, ears up.

There was no reply. Impatiently, Kiki tried the door and, when it opened, didn't give a second thought to entering the house. 'Primmie!' she shouted as she stepped into a stone-floored porch. There was a scarred wooden bench, under which was a pair of new-looking Wellingtons. An ancient-looking waterproof hung from a hook.

'Primmie!' she shouted again, for all the world as if she were entering the old flat in Kensington and Primmie were expecting her. 'It's me! Kiki!'

The only reply was a ringing silence. Undeterred, she walked through the porch and into a large, roomy kitchen. It smelled of fresh paint. There were colourful rag rugs scattered on a slate floor, two tables, an enormous one with a jug of fresh flowers in its centre, a smaller one laden with jars of what looked to be home-made jam. A cream-coloured Aga nestled beneath an old mantelpiece, a red gingham tea towel hanging on its rail.

The dog stretched himself out on one of the rag rugs and, with a contented sigh, closed his eyes.

A door at the far side of the kitchen led into a white-painted hallway, the walls full of paintings and framed photographs. The door of what was obviously a sitting room stood wide open.

She went in. It was a large, sunny room, its windows giving out on to views of the headland and the sea. There was no wasted wall space. Where there weren't bookshelves, full of neatly arranged books, there were yet more paintings, mainly watercolours.

There was a silver-framed photograph on the mantel over the open fireplace. It showed a middle-aged woman surrounded by four teenage children, three girls and a boy. One of the girls looked as if it could be Primmie, but the woman wasn't Primmie's mother. Though she hadn't visited Primmie's Rotherhithe home as often as Geraldine and Artemis, she still remembered Primmie's mother and would have recognized her.

Beside the fireplace a broad shelf housed a music system and several stacks of CDs. She stepped nearer, curious as to just what Primmie's musical taste now was. There were several opera compilations. A lot of Mozart. A lot of Chopin. And then, on CD after CD, she saw her own name.

Everything she had ever recorded was there, from 'White Dress, Silver Slippers' to the last album, which had been released only in America. Which meant that Primmie had gone to a great deal of effort to obtain a copy.

She never cried. Lovers had come and gone. Managers had come and gone. Success had come and gone. And she had never cried. She took one of the rock and roll compilation CDs she never travelled without from her bag and switched on the stereo, tears stinging the backs of her eyes. Primmie had never forgotten her. All through the long years of non-

288

contact, Primmie had been loyally buying everything she had ever recorded.

With her eyes overly bright, she slid the CD into the player and turned the volume up high. Then, hugging her arms, she stood looking out over the headland to the sea, waiting for the friend who had never forgotten her to come home.

'We could have sold tickets for this,' Geraldine said grimly as she swung the Ferrari off the main road and on to the track leading to the headland.

Primmie didn't answer her. She was too busy struggling to keep Alice firmly anchored in the rear of the car. Dave Clegg had put a collar round Alice's neck with a long length of rope attached to it and, from the front passenger seat, Primmie was doing her best to hang on to the rope so that Alice could neither leap from the car nor scramble up on to the cream leather upholstered rear seats.

As they'd driven past Calleloe, tourists had taken snapshots of them. On the hill leading up the turn-off for the headland, a group of schoolchildren had laughed themselves silly. As they approached the turning, a couple of startled hikers cheered them on their way.

Only when they began bumping down the track did Alice stop tugging on the rope. Primmie's aching arm muscles gave heartfelt thanks.

'I think she likes the sea air,' she said, seeing with surprise that the gates to Ruthven were wide open. In the distance, parked outside the small churchyard, was the distinctive shape of the Reverend John Cowles's Volkswagen.

Assuming he had called at Ruthven en route to the church and had neglected to close the gates after him, she didn't give them another thought. And then Geraldine said, 'I can hear music coming from the house. You didn't leave the radio or the stereo on, did you, Primmie?'

'No. I didn't have the radio on this morning – and I don't have the Everley Brothers on any of my CDs.'

As they veered into the yard, the volume of the music was ear-splitting.

'Does anyone else have a key, apart from Matt?' Geraldine asked, bringing the Ferrari to a halt, finding it impossible to imagine that it was Matt playing the Everly Brothers' 'Wake Up Little Susie' so offensively loudly.

'No.' There was deep concern in Primmie's voice. 'And it isn't Matt in the house. Matt doesn't like rock and roll.'

As she said the last three words, the same incredible thought occurred to both of them simultaneously.

Primmie's reaction was one of incredulity and hope.

Geraldine's was one of white-hot rage.

Heedless of Alice, they scrambled from the Ferrari and began racing across the cobbles.

Geraldine reached the side door first. It stood wide open and she sprinted into the house, her eyes blazing. Hard on her heels, Primmie ran through the porch and into the kitchen, only to be brought up short by the sight of a huge, tangled mass of fur reclining on one of Amelia's rugs.

Geraldine, heedless of the dog, catapulted into the hallway beyond and then hurled herself into the sitting room.

'What the *fuck*,' she demanded, as Kiki spun away from the window to face her, 'are *you* doing here?'

Kiki, totally unprepared for the sight of Geraldine, gasped, falling backwards a step. 'I could say the same to you,' she managed, doing her best to sound aggressive and not defensive. 'I came here to see Primmie. If I'd known you were here, I would have put my visit on hold till you'd gone.'

'*I'm* not going anywhere. *I'm* staying here. *Living* here. You're the one that's going!'

'Kiki! Oh, Kiki, darling! How wonderful to see you!' With the dog gambolling at her heels Primmie ran into the room, raced past Geraldine and threw her arms round Kiki.

Kiki blinked. The woman hugging her was the middle-aged woman in the photograph – the woman that she hadn't recognized.

'Primmie?' She gathered her wits with difficulty. 'It is OK for me to stay here, with you, isn't it? It will probably only be for a few days, and . . .'

'He never came home.' The skin was taut across Geraldine's cheekbones. 'After you dumped him, Francis never returned to England. He never came back to Cedar Court. Neither I, nor his father, have ever seen him again. You destroyed him, Kiki. You took him away from me and then, when you'd no further

290

use for him, you ditched him as if he was dirt under your shoe! You destroyed his life, my life, his father's life . . .'

'Hey! Steady on.' Kiki was over her shock now, her fighting spirit kicking in. 'The only person who destroyed Francis's life was Francis. He was a drug addict – and it wasn't me who turned him into one. He came back from his hippie-trail expedition with you an addict. *I'm* not to blame for that, Geraldine. If anyone is to blame, it's you.'

'Kiki, sit down.' Primmie valiantly tried to defuse the situation. 'You, too, Geraldine. I'll make some tea. Or would whisky be better?'

Neither Kiki nor Geraldine took any notice of her.

'And if it hadn't been for my running off with him,' Kiki continued, getting into her stride, 'you wouldn't have spent the last thirty years living a privileged existence in Paris. And I know you *have* been living a privileged existence, because I've seen your picture in the gossip columns.'

'And did the caption beneath the pictures say I was a madam, running high-class call-girls?' Geraldine asked acidly. 'Because that's what I was. That's how my "privileged" existence was funded.'

Primmie sucked in her breath, her eyes widening.

Kiki opened her mouth to continue her verbal attack, registered what it was Geraldine had just said, and gaped at her.

'Truly?' Primmie forgot all about making tea to calm the situation down. 'Is that why you didn't keep in touch with Artemis and me?'

'Yes. How could I? And before you ask, no, I'm not remotely ashamed of the way I've lived my life. I simply paired pretty, intelligent girls up with rich men. End of story.'

The atmosphere in the room had suddenly changed. Geraldine's furious outburst had utterly exhausted her. She'd had a blood transfusion immediately before setting off for Cornwall, but wasn't feeling the full benefit of it yet and, the last reserves of her energy spent, simply couldn't continue venting bitterness and anger on such a gargantuan scale.

Kiki, who had no reason for anger, except as a defence mechanism, was too interested in Geraldine's lifestyle in Paris to want to continue their furious slanging match.

Primmie, aware that the crisis had passed, put the million

and one questions she was dying to ask Geraldine on hold and let out a deep, heartfelt sigh of relief.

Her moment of thankfulness lasted a second, maybe less.

'Oh, no!' she suddenly shouted, looking out of the window. 'Alice is in the garden and is eating everything in sight!'

Whirling round, she darted from the room, making for the front door.

'Who's Alice?' Kiki asked Geraldine, perplexed. 'A child?'

'A goat – and don't just stand there, Kiki. Goats are strong. We need to be out there with Primmie, helping her.'

It was as much of a flag of truce as Geraldine was ever likely to offer her, and Kiki knew it. On the stereo, Jerry Lee Lewis was singing 'Whole Lotta Shaking Going On'. It was yet another of her favourite tracks. She didn't hang about to listen to it. Instead, she ran out into the garden to give chase to the goat.

Twenty-Five

'Wine or whisky?'

It was four hours later and they were in the sitting room, Primmie and Kiki grubby and exhausted after chasing Alice the length and breadth of Ruthven and the headland.

'Wine, please.' Geraldine was sprawled full length on the deep-cushioned sofa, her face so pale it looked carved from alabaster.

'Whisky.' Kiki, the dog beside her, was seated cross-legged on the rag rug in front of the fireplace. The grate was empty of coals but made glorious by a jug of marigolds. She ran a hand through her fox-red hair, making her youthful, spiky hairstyle spikier than ever. 'And what do we do with that black-hearted goat now we've finally tethered her? Where does she sleep tonight? With the cow?'

Sitting back on her heels next to the coffee table, Primmie poured Geraldine a glass of red wine. 'I don't know. I haven't a clue what sleeping arrangements goats need. I'm not sure Maybelline would like sharing with her, though.'

'Sensible Maybelline,' Geraldine said dryly, taking the proffered glass from Primmie. 'And what about other sleeping arrangements? The dog's, for instance?'

All three of them looked at the dog. The dog, happy at being the centre of attention, looked back at them from beneath its matted fringe of hair.

'What about the kitchen?' Primmie poured Kiki a slug of Bell's. 'He seems to like being on the rag rugs.'

The dog lolled a little more closely against Kiki.

'By all means give the kitchen a try, Primmie.' Still holding her wine glass, Geraldine closed her eyes in exhaustion. 'But every dog I've ever met prefers sleeping on its owner's bed. Which brings us to the subject of Kiki and whether there's going to be room for her here once the children arrive.'

'Or room for you!' Kiki shot back instantly. 'Why this assumption that if anyone is going to leave here it's going to be me?'

'Because I'm working on the old trade union principle of last in, first out.' Geraldine opened her eyes again. 'And because for you to stay here when the children are here would mean your sharing a room with me and I'm not prepared to do that, Kiki. I'm being civil towards you for Primmie's sake, but I'm not going to be *that* civil.'

Primmie, who had made a pot of tea for herself, poured a cup and said, 'In the old days, Kiki and I always shared a room. If you move out of the guest room into my room, Geraldine, Kiki and I can move into the guest room. Problem solved.'

Kiki flashed Primmie a face-splitting grin. 'Wicked,' she said, momentarily forgetting her reason for being in Cornwall.

Primmie grinned back at her, glad that another potential crisis had been avoided. 'You speak like my daughter Lucy. Everything is 'wicked' or 'cool'.

Kiki took another deep swallow of whisky. 'So tell me about your kids, Primmie. How old are they? Where are they? What are their names?'

Primmie paused for a moment, struggling not to make eye contact with Geraldine, well aware that Geraldine would know how heart-stoppingly difficult it was going to be for her not to speak Destiny's name.

She took a steadying breath. 'Joanne is twenty-three. She's office manager at D. P. International, a London advertising agency, and is married to one of the agency's account directors. Millie is thirteen months younger and married as well – though doesn't always remember it – and lives in London. Josh is twenty and single and a bit of a Romeo. Lucy is nineteen and is travelling in Australia.'

'No grandchildren?'

Primmie shook her head.

Kiki shrugged. 'I don't suppose it matters, does it? They've all still got acres of time. Do they visit you a lot? Are they the "children" you and Geraldine keep mentioning?'

'No.' Primmie sat a little more comfortably on the floor and hugged her knees. 'My aunt – who left Ruthven to me – gave holidays to groups of children who are in care. In an arrangement left over from last year, five of them are due to arrive in nine days' time.'

'Cool.' There was no real enthusiasm in Kiki's voice. Children had never been of any great interest to her – unless they bought her records.

'And you still haven't told us what brought you to Cornwall, Kiki,' Primmie continued, full of curiosity. 'Have you been appearing at a rock festival? And how did you get here? Where's your car?'

'And why is your dog in such a disgraceful, uncared-for condition?' Geraldine said from the sofa, her eyes again closed. 'He doesn't look as if he's ever been brushed in his life, let alone bathed.'

The lines of Kiki's jaw tensed. It would be easy to make up a reason for being in Cornwall that would enable Primmie to keep her illusions about her. For a second she was tempted to say that she'd arrived by helicopter and that in a couple of day's time she would be whirling off again, back to London and then on to New York, to a flash, rock-star-style apartment in the Dakota. Primmie would believe every word, but she doubted Geraldine would.

Geraldine had always been far too sharp for comfort. When people had money – real money – they could smell it on someone a mile away. And it was obvious that Geraldine had real money by looking at her Ferrari. Geraldine would know that she was flat broke and her lying about it would only make her look pathetic. Besides, she'd finished with all the humiliating business of pretending to be something she wasn't – and of enduring the knowing, contemptuous looks when she hadn't quite pulled off the deception. Her determination to be done with all that was why she was en route to the highest cliff she could find.

'The dog isn't mine,' she said, taking the easiest question first. 'My car broke down on the motorway and I hitched a lift to Helston. The dog belonged to the truck-driver who stopped for me. He and the dog didn't get on.'

'But what about your car?' Primmie asked, perplexed. 'Is someone bringing it down here for you, when it's fixed? Your agent, or manager, or minder . . . ?'

'Agents and managers don't act as gofers, Primmie, and minders are for rock stars who need them to keep the fans at bay.' Still sitting cross-legged, her hands resting on her knees, she paused, gazing at Primmie and Geraldine defiantly. 'And I no longer need to keep fans at bay,' she said at last, bitterly. 'I'm a has-been. My career is over. Finished.'

It was the first time she had ever put the fact into words.

Primmie stared at her. 'But how can it be? In April, in St Austell, I saw posters of a rock festival you were appearing at.'

'Ah, the great Easter Rock Revival Concert!' Kiki breathed in hard. The St Austell gig had been good – mainly because two old buddies, Marty Wilde and Eric Burden, had flown over from the States to be onboard for it. It had been her swan song, though. For a long, ghastly period before the St Austell gig she'd had no work to speak of, and after it there had only been the death she had died at Grantley. 'Yeah, well. That was a one-off, Primmie,' she said, her voice weary. 'Despite anything you may have read to the contrary, I've been on the skids for at least a decade.'

There was a long silence.

Geraldine, well aware of how much the admission must have cost Kiki, was conscious of a flicker of respect for her. In the overall scheme of things, it wasn't much, but it made a decided change from the loathing and contempt she'd been nursing for the last thirty-one years.

'I'm sorry,' Primmie said at last, inadequately. 'I hadn't realized . . .'

'Why should you?' Kiki managed to sound almost philosophical. 'I don't suppose anyone's life is all it seems to be, is it?'

'No, indeed.' It was said with a wealth of feeling as, with great effort, Geraldine summoned the strength to push herself up against the cushions on the sofa.

Primmie looked towards her – and saw that bruises were beginning to show on Geraldine's arms. 'What on earth have you done to yourself?' she asked, concerned. 'Those bruises weren't there this morning!'

Geraldine tugged the sleeves of her cinnamon-silk shirt down as far as they would go. 'No, they weren't. Don't worry about them, Primmie. They'll soon fade.'

'I have some arnica tablets somewhere. I'll find them for you. You shouldn't bruise so quickly and so easily, Geraldine. You must be anaemic.'

Geraldine shot her a strained smile. 'Very probably.'

Kiki, uninterested in Geraldine's bruises and not wanting the conversation to return to the subject of her dead career, said, 'Neither of you has said a word about Artemis. Has she stayed here yet? That snobbish prick she married couldn't father children, could he? What was his name? Richard? Robert? What did they do? Did they adopt?'

'His name is Rupert,' Geraldine said smoothly, saving Primmie from having to answer. 'And yes, they did adopt. Primmie thinks they have two boys – though they won't be boys now. They'll be in their late-teens or early twenties.'

Kiki shifted her position to give the dog a little more room on the rug. 'What do you mean, Primmie "thinks"? You didn't both lose touch with her, did you?'

'I didn't stay in touch with her for the same reason I didn't stay in touch with Primmie. And Primmie . . .' Geraldine gave Primmie a swift glance, saw that she was still struggling to control her feelings, and said, 'Primmie's life with Ted and the children was very different from Artemis's way of life. They drifted apart. It happens.'

'Geraldine and I tried to make contact with her yesterday.' Primmie, her thoughts full of Destiny, kept her voice steady with difficulty. 'She and Rupert have separated. According to him, they're getting divorced. Last night, when Geraldine spoke to him, he said Artemis had gone on a cruise, that he didn't know when she would be returning to England and that he didn't have a mobile number for her.'

'I bet he was lying.' Kiki slid her arm round the dog's neck. 'He *must* have a mobile number for her. He just doesn't want her old friends telling her how much she should be squeezing out of him in a divorce settlement. Wasn't the house a huge old rectory in the Cotswolds and didn't he have a string of polo ponies? If he was loaded thirty-odd years ago, when she married him, he must be really rolling in it now. If Artemis plays her cards right, she should come out of the divorce a wealthy woman.'

'You're telling me I can't have the house?' Artemis's voice rose in hysterical disbelief. 'But why not? *I'm* not the one breaking our marriage up! *You're* the one who is being unfaithful! *You're* the one who wants to leave!'

She was facing Rupert in the drawing room of their home, still wearing the floral silk print dress and jacket she'd travelled from Southampton in. Her handbag and travelling make-up box were at her feet and the rest of her luggage, which the taxi-driver had brought indoors for her, was standing in the large square entrance hall.

'If you'd stayed in England, instead of haring off in a fit of pique on a cruise to the West Indies, you would have known from the beginning that this was the arrangement that was going to be made.' Rupert's eyes flicked beyond her to the open door leading into the hall.

Wildly, Artemis wondered if he thought the taxi driver was still waiting to be paid and was about to walk in on them.

'And in the eyes of the law,' he continued, standing completely at ease with his hands in the pockets of his chinos, '*you're* the one who has left the marital home.'

'Me?' Her voice rose to a disbelieving squeak. '*Me?* How? When?'

'When you walked out of here with your bags and baggage six weeks ago.' There was dry satisfaction in his voice. 'I informed both my solicitor and yours of your action.'

'I didn't walk out!' Artemis felt as if she were struggling in treacle. 'I went on a *cruise* because I was so distressed I was *ill*. I hoped that by the time I got back you'd have become bored with the Serena creature just like you did with all the others. I hoped that we could sort things out and . . .'

'And that you could continue being a middle-aged, fifteen-stone dead weight around Ju's neck for a little longer?' an unmistakable Chelsea-set voice said from behind her.

Artemis spun round.

With pert, bra-less breasts pushing against a crimson silk shirt and wearing nothing else, apart from black silk panties, the Serena creature stood at the foot of the stairs, leaning against the mahogany newel-post, her waist-length hair mussed and tumbled as if she had just got out of bed.

Artemis sucked in her breath, her eyes bulging in disbelief.

Serena smiled. 'You moved out, and I moved in,' she said with a fait accompli shrug.

Artemis whirled back to face Rupert. 'You've had her living in my house?' she gasped. 'Sleeping in my bed?'

His high-boned face looked weary beyond belief. 'We are in the throes of a divorce, Artemis. You left the marital home, and as I shall be marrying Serena at the earliest opportunity, yes, she has been . . . *is* . . . living here and sleeping in the bed you mistakenly refer to as still being yours.'

Artemis had never been violent in her life, but she didn't hesitate. She clenched her fist and, putting all the weight of her fifteen stone into the punch, went for gold, making thumping contact with his jaw.

Taken totally by surprise, he went ricocheting backwards, flying off his feet – and, when he landed, he didn't move.

Artemis didn't care.

Hoping she'd killed him, she scooped up her handbag and make-up box and, without even deigning to look at Serena, stormed past her, out of her defiled home.

Her car was in the double garage and the keys were in her handbag. Uncaring about her luggage, uncaring that she was leaving without any personal items – items Orlando or Sholto would have to collect for her – she unlocked the car door and yanked it open. Then, hunched behind the wheel, finally accepting that her marriage was over beyond all possible doubt, not knowing where she was going to go, or what she was going to do, she sobbed and sobbed until she could sob no more.

The next morning, when Primmie returned to the house after milking Maybelline and failing to milk Black-Hearted Alice, only Geraldine was up and dressed. Unlike the cinnamon shirt she'd been wearing yesterday, the white shirt she was wearing with grey flannel slacks and a soft grey Shetland sweater was fastened tightly at the wrists.

'I don't suppose we'll see Kiki for hours yet,' she said as Primmie put the pail of frothing milk down. 'This is probably the time of day she usually rolls home after partying or clubbing. How did you get on with Alice? Was she cooperative?'

'No. She *glared* at me. Those yellow eyes are like something out of a horror film. And she's too close to the ground to milk. I just couldn't figure out how to do it.' She lifted the chrome lid on one of the Aga's hotplates and set a frying pan on it. 'I think maybe she was cross at sleeping tethered and out in the open. With luck Matt will be round this morning to tell me how I should house her and feed her.'

'And milk her?' Geraldine asked, amused.

'And milk her. Do you like mushrooms, Geraldine? I picked these myself.'

'As long as they're safe to eat, I love them.' Geraldine seated herself at one of the large deal tables. 'I've been thinking about your kitchen garden, Primmie, and have a couple of suggestions to make.'

'What kind of suggestions?' Primmie drizzled oil into the frying pan.

'I've been thinking that you could grow just as much veg in a far prettier way if you made a classical French potager.'

'A potager?' Primmie began peeling the mushrooms. 'Do you mean vegetables in small beds edged with box?'

'It does. The beds are called *carrés*. Instead of growing vegetables in boring long lines, they're planted out in chequerboard patterns and by colour. Jade-green carrot leaves next to the red of beetroot leaves, for instance. And golden-green celery next to the blue of Solaise leeks.'

'And the icy green of lettuce next to orange pumpkins, and purple cabbage with tomatoes?'

'That's it. You've got the idea. And we can bring flowers into the equation, too, by edging the beds with contrasting colour. Scarlet begonias with the green of salad crops, for instance.'

Primmie dropped the mushrooms into the frying pan and swirled them round to coat them with oil. 'And beds of pumpkin with orange rudbeckia.'

They grinned across at each other, full of enthusiasm for a shared project that would be truly creative.

'We'll need to make sure that we plant vegetables together that crop at the same time. With really careful planning we should be able to get two different crops from each bed every year.'

She cracked two eggs into the sizzling pan. 'And can we grow fruit, too?'

There was no reply.

With more energy and zest than she'd felt for months, Geraldine had left the kitchen in search of pen and paper so that she could start planning out an ornamental kitchen garden as aesthetically pleasing as her flower garden in Paris; a garden worthy of a Renaissance château or a medieval monastery.

When Kiki eventually emerged from her comfortable cocoon in the pin-neat bedroom she was sharing with Primmie, it was lunchtime. The sound of Eva Cassidy filled the house with mellow music. The table with the vase of wild flowers on it was set for four. Primmie was standing at the Aga, stirring soup in a saucepan, and Geraldine was standing with her back against the sink, one foot crossing the other at the ankle, a mug of coffee cupped in her hands. By her side was a rugged-looking man wearing a bulky jersey and jeans.

'You're just in time for lunch,' Primmie said with a beaming smile, for all the world as if Kiki had just come in after a hard morning's work. 'Matt is dying to meet you. Matt, Kiki Lane. Kiki, Matt Trevose.'

Unused to such polite introductions so early in her day, Kiki summoned up the manners to shake his proffered hand.

It was a strong handshake and to her vast relief he didn't gush about how thrilled he was to meet a seventies/eighties rock star and to lyingly say, as most people did, that he had every record she'd ever recorded. All he did was look a little bemused and say that he was pleased to meet her.

'Matt is a neighbour and a good friend,' Primmie said, still stirring the soup. 'Ever since I arrived at Ruthven he's helped me with absolutely everything. Would you like a coffee? You look as if you're gasping for one. There is lashings in the pot.'

'And so it didn't matter about Black-Hearted Alice being left out of doors last night?' Geraldine said to Matt, ignoring Kiki completely. 'Primmie thought she might have been unhappy about it.'

'Not in the warm weather we're having at the moment. In the winter she'll need housing, though. Goats don't like cold and they hate rain.'

Kiki poured herself a coffee, not adding milk or sugar to it. She'd spent most of her life waking up in strange beds and strange places, having to fight off hangovers and get to grips with where the hell she was – and whom she was with. This morning, with no hangover and no unwelcome bed mate, was, though, the most disorientating morning she could remember.

For one thing, she was in a lovingly cherished home, not a hotel room or her littered London flat. For another, both Primmie and Geraldine were with her. It was almost like the days decades ago, when, with Artemis, they'd all lived together in Kensington. And last, but not least, there was the conversation. Goats? *Goats?* Who cared whether they didn't like cold and rain? And where was the dog? It had gone to sleep on the rug beside her bed, but was now nowhere to be seen.

'Rags is enjoying the September sun,' Primmie said, opening a door of the Aga to check on the fish she was baking. 'The hens aren't too keen on him, but he's leaving them well alone.'

'Rags?' Kiki took a deep drink of coffee. 'Who named him Rags?'

'I did, because of his liking for the rugs.' Primmie closed the Aga's door again and, from another of the its generous compartments, took out a soup tureen that had been warming. 'I'm quite happy for you to re-christen him, if you want to. He is your dog, after all.'

'No. Rags is fine.'

'There's homemade soup for lunch – and fish that Matt caught early this morning. Geraldine's made the vinaigrette dressing for the salad.'

'I can't cope with lunch just yet; I need a bit of fresh air. Does the headland end in cliffs? Are there walks there?'

'There are no cliffs – which is a good thing because I won't have to worry about the children who are coming to stay falling over the edge of them. You can walk for miles, though. The coastal footpath runs right across the headland. And if you want really dramatic cliffs, Kynance Cove is only ten minutes away by car. Turn left at the main road and just keep driving. You'll soon come to signposts for Lizard Point and Kynance Cove.'

Kiki made no response and, looking across at her as she poured soup from the pan into the tureen, Primmie said perceptively, 'If you want to borrow my car, you can.'

'Thanks.' Kiki drained her coffee mug and put it down on the table. 'I'll do that, then. See you all later.'

Minutes later she was bumping down the track in Primmie's Vauxhall Corsa, Rags's untidy bulk in the passenger seat beside her. He hadn't been a companion she'd intended having, but the minute she'd stepped from the house he'd careered across to her, and when she'd opened the Vauxhall's door he'd been inside the car even before she was.

The expedition she was making was only a recce, but as she turned left into the narrow main road it occurred to her that, when she made her final expedition, she was going to have to go to great lengths to make sure Rags wasn't with her. She didn't want him scrambling down the cliff face trying to reach her after she'd jumped, or, even worse, simply leaping off the top of the cliff with her.

She chewed the corner of her lip. When she'd left London, she hadn't had a shadow's doubt about what it was she was going to do – or why she would be doing it. Now, though, things no longer seemed quite so clear-cut. Somehow, almost without her being aware of it, her mood had shifted.

Primmie, of course, was partially responsible. Primmie had always been sunshine and light, and still was. It rubbed off.

302

She'd actually found herself wishing she'd got up a bit earlier so that she would have had the appetite for the lunch Primmie had prepared. There'd been the smell of bread to go with the soup and she hadn't had homemade bread since . . . when? She couldn't remember. Never, probably.

She also hadn't woken up with a hangover, which was a rare change. Though she'd seen the red light years ago where all drugs but weed were concerned, alcohol had always been a prop she'd never even tried to do without – and alcohol was something she obviously needed to get back into suicide mode. One thing she was sure of, there wouldn't be enough of it at Ruthven. Primmie might have had a bottle of Bell's and some red wine in the house, but it was a certainty that where the whisky was concerned Primmie bought it a bottle at a time – and not all that often.

Instead of the countryside being as bleak as it had been on Bodmin Moor, the road out to Lizard Point ran between fields that had once been full of corn and that now, the corn cut, were a stubble-fired, faded yellow. Other fields had cattle in them and every now and again there were strings of small, squat, whitewashed cottages, their gardens bright with white marguerites and brilliant blue agapanthus.

She pressed the button for the passenger-seat window, opening it low so that Rags could stick his head out. It was a beautiful day, with hardly a hint that it was no longer high summer. Occasionally there were clusters of trees at either side of the road, their branches interweaving so that she would find herself driving through dappled groves of light.

It certainly wasn't a day for committing suicide – or even for contemplating it.

High above Kynance Cove she parked in the National Trust car park and, having no interest in the cove itself, didn't bother walking down to it. Instead, Rags at her heels, she set off along the top of the cliffs, the tough grass springy beneath her feet.

The cliffs weren't as she had imagined they would be. They were high, certainly, and the drop was steep, but the cliff face shelved outwards from its lip, not inwards. In throwing herself off it, she would be at great risk not of instant death, but of agonizing injuries as she bounced off first one rocky protuberance and then another.

303

Standing as near to the cliff edge as, with Rags, she felt it was safe to go, it occurred to her that the only way she could have drummed up the nerve to throw herself over the edge was if she'd driven down to Kynance the night the idea had first entered her head. Then, anaesthetized by alcohol and in pitch blackness, she would simply have taken a running jump and that would have been that. Now, though . . . ? Now, as she stood, staring down at the ribbon of sand at the cliff's foot, it no longer seemed such an easy, obvious option.

For the first time it occurred to her to wonder who would find her body. The beaches and coves of Cornwall were popular destinations for families with children and, though not unduly caring about children, she certainly didn't want one to live with nightmares because of her. And then there was the question of who would identify her. When she didn't return to Ruthven, Primmie would report her missing to the police. And it would be Primmie who would be asked to identify her.

She'd gone through life not giving a damn about anyone but herself, but she couldn't do that to Primmie.

As if reading her thoughts, Rags tugged at the sleeve of her leather jacket, trying to get her to move backwards, away from the cliff edge.

Suddenly, his doing so struck her as being eminently sensible. She had, after all, things to do. If she was going to stay with Primmie in Cornwall – and it went without saying that she was – then she needed to get herself other clothes apart from the ones she was standing up in. With luck, Calleloe would have a charity shop.

And Rags needed a trim and a bath.

Putting all thoughts of suicide on hold, she stepped away from the cliff, beginning to walk back over the grass towards the car park. Before she found a charity shop, she needed to find a dog-grooming parlour. Geraldine could be as rude as she liked to her, but she wasn't going to have her being rude about Rags. When Rags returned to Ruthven, he was going to look like an entrant for Crufts.

Artemis drove nervously into Calleloe. The streets were so narrow and steep she didn't know how cars were managing to pass each other and she was so tired that driving had long ago ceased to be either effortless or automatic. When she'd disembarked from the MS *Caronia*, ten hours earlier, she'd had faint hopes that the nightmare of the last few weeks would be at an end; that Rupert would have ended his affair with the Serena creature and that she and Rupert could continue with their marriage as if the word divorce had never been mentioned.

Finding Serena installed in her home, in her bed, had put an end to her pipe dream. She still couldn't quite grasp that Rupert could have been so uncaring of her feelings as to desecrate the one place that had always meant more to her than anything else: her home.

Only the beautiful Georgian rectory wasn't her home any longer. How could it be, with every room reeking of Serena's presence? And, worst of all, when everyone knew about it. And people did know, a distressed telephone call from the car to Olwyn had left her in no doubt of it.

'Rupert told everyone that you'd walked out on him, tired of his philandering, and that Serena had moved in. The general attitude was that he was acting a bit precipitately, but as his affair with Serena has been common knowledge for yonks, no one was overly surprised,' Olwyn had said, full of concern for her. 'What are you going to do now? Hole up in a hotel until your solicitor thrashes things out on your behalf? Or would you prefer to come and stay with me?'

It had been a kind offer, but if she'd gone to stay with Olwyn, everyone she and Rupert knew would be aware of it. It was a humiliation she couldn't even contemplate enduring.

Even worse had been the next two telephone calls she had made.

'I know it's grim, Mother, but it isn't the end of the world,' Sholto had said, unfazed at the news. 'Dad may have dug his heels in over the house, but he isn't going to be mean with the divorce settlement. Everything will work out OK in the end. You're better off being able to look around for something that will really suit you. Perhaps a swish flat in London or a house on the coast.'

That he'd thought her concerns were primarily financial had incensed her. Her father was a millionaire. If she'd wanted a swish flat in London, or a house on the coast, she could have had one – or both – any time she'd wanted.

'And Serena's a brick,' he had added. 'She won't make waves. Not now she's got her own way over the house.'

That Sholto had met her – that he was quite obviously approving of her – was a betrayal so great she'd thought her heart was going to give out.

Not wanting to hear another word from him, she'd severed the connection and had only then taken on board the fact that Rupert was insistent on keeping their home not because *he* felt fiercely about doing so, but because Serena wanted him to.

Almost apoplectic with distress, she'd speed-dialled Orlando's number.

'Have you met her, too?' she'd demanded hysterically, seconds later. 'Aren't *either* of you appalled at your father's behaviour? We've been married for thirty-two years and he leaves me for a . . . for a . . .' she'd been sobbing so hard she could hardly get the words out, ' . . . for an oversexed *tart* and neither of you are up in arms about it!'

'Lady Serena Campbell-Thynne can hardly be described as a "tart", Mother,' Orlando had said, sounding vaguely amused. 'And of course I'm pretty appalled at what has happened – as is Sholto. But it's been on the cards for years and Dad stuck by you all the time we were children . . .'

He'd made it sound as if Rupert deserved a medal for having done so.

Distraught at not getting the response she'd needed, she'd severed her connection to him, too, and then, still crying, she'd put her car into gear and driven away, having absolutely no idea where she was driving to.

It was only when, on the outskirts of Bath, she'd seen the signs for the M5 that she'd known where it was she was going. She was going to Cornwall. She was going to find Primmie – Primmie, whom she should never have lost. Primmie, who had always been the very best friend in the world to her.

At the bottom of the hill she was driving down were a harbour, a small car park and, wedged between a general store and a greengrocer's, a post office. She breathed a sigh of relief. In a place as small as Calleloe, she would

306

probably have to go no further to find out where Ruthven was.

'You can have my ticket,' a young girl said to her as she squeezed her way into the tiny car park. 'I'm just leaving and there's still half an hour on it.'

It was a kindness that, in her overwrought condition, had her on the verge of tears again.

Appalled at how near to a complete breakdown she was, determined that she was not going to ever cry again, she parked her car. It was four thirty, she'd just driven all the way from Gloucestershire and she hadn't eaten since breakfast aboard the MS *Caronia*. Telling herself that it was no wonder she was in a fragile, jittery condition, she changed out of her driving shoes into her high heels and began walking back to the foot of Calleloe's precipitous main street, intent on going first to the post office and then into the nearest tea shop.

Outside a sophisticated-looking art gallery she paused before crossing the road, disorientated at the number of tourists thronging the area round the harbour. It was almost as if it were August, not September. There was a small ice-cream stall and another stall selling picture postcards and holiday souvenirs, both of them doing a roaring trade.

With seagulls screaming above her head, she moved forwards to cross the road – and left her right shoe behind. Tottering in an ungainly fashion, she tried to retrieve the shoe, but its stiletto heel was wedged in a crack in the pavement. A couple of mothers, pushing prams, awkwardly circumnavigated her.

'You'll find it easier if you step out of the other shoe as well, dear,' an elderly woman said helpfully. 'If you don't, you're going to fall over.'

With senseless panic bubbling up in her throat, Artemis did as the woman suggested. The pavement struck cold through her stockinged feet. As she bent almost double to tug at her shoe she felt unutterably undignified and, aware of the figure she must be cutting from behind, scorchingly embarrassed.

At last, with a suddenness that unbalanced her, the shoe came away in her hand, minus its heel.

It was the last straw.

307

Unable to think further than that her marriage was over; that her sons were unsympathetic; that she'd never felt more lonely or lost in her life and that she was going to have to either limp back to her car with one shoe on and the other off or wearing no shoes at all, she did what she had just vowed she would never do again.

She leaned her back against the plate-glass window, covered her face with her hands and burst into tears.

Hugo Arnott dropped the Sotheby's catalogue he had been studying, his concern immediate. He had registered Artemis's presence when, outside his art gallery, she had paused in order to cross the street. Blonde, statuesque, beautifully dressed ladies of a certain age were not the norm on the streets of Calleloe.

Always immaculately suited himself, to see someone as impeccably groomed and beautifully dressed as the woman in floral silk who had emerged from the car park had been, for him, a treat of the highest order. For a brief second he had felt himself to be in Rome or Milan; to be in a city where women still gave thought and care to their clothes and where formality in dress wasn't an anachronism, but something to be aspired to.

Then had come the heel incident.

His temptation had been immediately to go out and offer assistance and only the prospect of her taking offence had deterred him. He still hadn't quite recovered from a recent experience in London when, on a crowded tube train, he had risen to his feet to offer his seat to a young woman. 'No, thank you, Grandad,' she had said rudely, rejecting his offer. 'My legs aren't so old that I can't still stand on them.'

There had been sniggers from everyone within hearing and, though he didn't for one moment think a mature lady, dressed as the one outside his gallery was dressed, would react to his offer of assistance in a similar manner, once bitten was twice shy.

Then she'd tugged her shoe free, wrenching it from its heel as she did so. As she reeled back against the window of his gallery, her hands to her face, he hesitated no longer. He sprang to his feet and, as fast as his rather corpulent bulk would allow him to, made for the door.

'Can I be of assistance, ma'am?'

The American voice was a rich, deep baritone and through her tears Artemis saw a bear of a man, dressed in an expensively tailored pale grey suit and with a pink carnation in his button-hole.

She tried to speak, failed, and vainly shook her head, the tears continuing to stream heedlessly down her face.

Taking no notice of what was obviously meant to be a 'no' and not a 'yes', Hugo withdrew a spotlessly white Irish linen handkerchief from his breast pocket and pressed it into her hands.

Artemis took it gratefully. 'I'm sorry . . .' she said incoherently, quite unable to regain control now that she had so completely lost it. 'It's just that . . . that my shoe heel is wedged . . .'

As a reason for such a torrent of tears it wasn't remotely adequate, and knowing it only made her more unable than ever to stop crying.

With deepening concern, Hugo gently took hold of her arm. 'Would you care to step inside and sit down for a few minutes while I try to get your shoe heel free? There's a cobblers thirty yards or so away. It may be possible to have your shoe mended.'

Artemis nodded, wanting nothing more than to be no longer in full view of so many curious passers-by.

With his free hand Hugo scooped up her shoes and, with his other hand still beneath her arm, ushered her into the gallery.

To Artemis, it was like stepping into an oasis of calm. The carpet beneath her stockinged feet was deep-piled and rose pink. Oil paintings and watercolours in gold frames hung against walls that were covered in pearl-grey watered silk. Bach played softly. The chair he led her to was a nineteenth-century replica – or perhaps even an original– French gilt-wood arm chair.

She sank down on it gratefully, regaining control of her breathing, fighting for control of her tears.

309

'A cup of tea is called for, I think.' Hugo hadn't lived in England for the past three years without becoming aware that tea was the acceptable palliative in every kind of crisis.

'Thank you.' He was being so kind she couldn't bear the thought he might think she was in a state of collapse over something and nothing. 'It isn't the shoe,' she said, mopping her tears with his handkerchief. 'It's . . . my husband's just asked for a divorce and I've come to Calleloe to stay with a friend . . . though I'm not sure exactly where Primmie lives . . . and . . .'

As he looked down at the top of her head, he saw that her hair was naturally blond, as pale as barley in September, and then she lifted her tear-ravaged face to his. Looking into eyes that were a true china-blue, he registered the lift to his heart the word 'divorce' had occasioned, decided he would mull over all it might mean a little later, at his leisure, and said, 'Primmie? There can only be one Primmie and she lives a mere ten-minutes' car ride away.'

As she gasped in relief, he beamed down at her. 'And she's obviously having quite a reunion party. My buddy Matt tells me there are already two other old friends staying with her. Kiki Lane, who used to be quite a popular singer in America some years ago, and an extremely glamorous, Ferrari-driving lady by the name of Geraldine.'

'Kiki and Geraldine are here? In Calleloe? With Primmie?'

Artemis forgot all about her intention, three decades ago, never to speak to Kiki again. Too much water had passed beneath the bridge for that to matter now, when she was so in need of the friends of her youth.

Seeing the expression of incredulity and joy on her face, he said, 'I take it that they are friends of yours, too,' happier at being the bearer of good news to her than he could remember having been for a long, long time.

'Oh yes!' Rupert's betrayal no longer seemed like the end of the world. She might not have a husband any more, but she did have friends. Friends she couldn't wait to be reunited with. The realization that Primmie, Kiki and Geraldine were only minutes away was too much for her. Tears came again in a great, unstoppable flood.

Hugo wasn't in the least disconcerted.

He had other handkerchiefs. He had all the handkerchiefs this lovely lady was ever going to need.

Twenty-Six

'It's so good to have you back in my life, Geraldine,' Primmie said, as, arm in arm, she and Geraldine walked along the silver sliver of sand in the cove.

'It's good to be back in it.' Geraldine's voice was heartfelt. 'And now I am back, I'd like to make a difference, Primmie. I've got a sinful amount of money – quite literally – and I'd like to spend some of it on Ruthven.'

'But in what way? I've got everything I need, Geraldine.'

It was coming up to six o'clock and there was a hint of approaching dusk in the light on the sea. Far out in the steely grey waters a freighter was making its way towards Southampton or Dover. A seagull, hoping for a tidbit of food, stalked them from a few feet away.

'What about the children your aunt regularly invited here? This is such a perfect place for children to holiday. I know the ones coming in nine days' time are a one-off for you, but what if they weren't? Wouldn't you like to do what your aunt did, and have children at Ruthven regularly? The barn could be converted into a dormitory for them, and that way you would still have room in the house for bed and breakfast guests.'

'Or for you and Kiki?'

'Or for me and Kiki.' Geraldine looked away from her, out to sea, not wanting to say that it was unlikely she would be around for too much longer, and not wanting to talk about Kiki.

The freighter was fast disappearing out of sight, beyond one of the low-lying arms of the cove. Watching it, as it slid from view, she said, 'You'd make me very happy, Primmie, if you'd let me arrange for the barn to be made into living accommodation and for the other outbuildings to be refurbished.'

As they began walking away from the beach, back towards the house, Primmie looked across at her with concern. 'Well . . . if it means so much to you . . .' she said uncertainly, wishing that Geraldine would tell her what it was that was so clearly troubling her.

Geraldine turned her head, all dark thoughts suppressed. 'Good. I'll speak to Matt tomorrow. He'll be able to put me in touch with a reliable local builder. And the first task we can give someone is to have suitable sleeping quarters made for Black-Hearted Alice. What was it Matt said she needed? An airy but draught-proof shed to sleep in at nights, with a sleeping place with low sides?'

'And he said I'd find it easier to milk her if she had a little platform to stand on and that if it had a feeding trough at one end it would coax her into the right position.'

'Particular little wench, isn't she? Is Maybelline so fussy?'

'No. Maybelline is a sweetheart.'

'And Black-Hearted Alice is a witch.'

Giggling like schoolgirls, they walked in deep mutual contentment past the church.

'Hugo is here,' Primmie said ten minutes later as they approached the house and saw a parked Mercedes.

'Good. I can't wait to meet him. An art dealer who prefers Cornwall to New York is either madly eccentric or else has his priorities right.'

'Hugo is and has,' Primmie said as they walked past the field where Maybelline was happily grazing and Black-Hearted Alice was crossly tethered. 'He's a lifelong bachelor who looks gay – he dresses totally inappropriately for Cornwall. Very Oscar Wilde.'

'And is he gay?'

'Not according to Matt. Hugo's problem is that he hasn't moved with the times. Women's lib is anathema to him. He likes his ladies to look like ladies – and to be helpless and dependent, like lilies of the field. There aren't many women like that these days, are there?'

'No, thank God.'

They giggled yet again and then, a minute or two later,

Geraldine said, 'I take it the Pavarotti-built gentleman unhappily knee-deep in hens is Hugo, but who is his companion? Do you know her?'

Primmie squinted into the light of a sun that was beginning to go down, seeing, for the first time, that Hugo had someone with him. 'Not a clue. They're both dressed as if they're about to go to a wedding. Perhaps it's someone visiting him from New York. A sister or a sister-in-law.'

As they stepped from the track into the cobbled yard, the woman in the floral dress and jacket turned and, from a distance of thirty feet or so, looked towards them uncertainly.

Primmie and Geraldine looked back at her, aware that she looked familiar, but unable to place her.

Slowly Geraldine said, 'It isn't, is it? It can't be, can it?'

'It is. It *is*!'

As Artemis's face changed from momentary doubt and confusion to blessed relief, Primmie hurtled towards her, arms outstretched. 'Artemis! *Artemis!*' she gasped. 'How wonderful! How absolutely, fantastically, gi-normously *wonderful*!'

Her arms went round her and, as Artemis felt herself being hugged by someone whose love she had never in her life had to doubt, she filled with tears yet again.

Watching her fondly, Hugo reached for the spare clean handkerchief he'd had the forethought to bring with him. All his life he'd been attracted to women who brought out his sense of chivalry and gallantry. He'd always been drawn to damsels in distress who needed to be looked after. And Primmie's friend quite obviously fell into the needing to be looked after category with bells on.

As the striking-looking woman who had walked into the yard arm in arm with Primmie, and whom he presumed was Geraldine, now began hugging Artemis tightly, he decided that he was definitely de trop and that a discreet exit was in order.

'For Artemis,' he said, pressing the handkerchief into Primmie's hand, and then walked out of the yard and across to his parked car. He would come back in the morning. As he drove away, he could see in his wing mirror that the three of them were still hugging and kissing and squealing with joy. He wondered where the missing member of their four-some was, and narrowly avoided her as he turned out of the track into the lane.

'Apologies,' he shouted as he swung the wheel quickly in order to give her more room to drive in. He wound his window down. 'You're Kiki, I assume.'

Kiki, her window already down so that Rags could hang happily half out of it, nodded, riveted by the sight of his pink carnation.

'There's quite an emotional scene taking place up at the house,' he said, almost equally riveted by the sight of what looked to be a snowy-white polar bear in the seat beside her. 'Your friend Artemis has just arrived.'

Kiki didn't hesitate. She swung the wheel and pressed her foot down hard on the accelerator, zooming off up the track towards the house in a blaze of dust and scattered pebbles with Rags, excited by his beauty treatment and the sudden urgency, leaning even further out of the passenger-seat window, barking frenziedly.

When she reached the house, she skidded into the cobbled yard as if into a pit stop at Le Mans.

'Temmy! *Temmy!*' she shouted, hurling herself from the car and, with Rags hard at her heels, sprinting across to where Artemis was the centre of a tight-knit threesome. 'My God, but you've changed! How much do you weigh? Sixteen stone?' She was hugging her, laughing and crying at the same time.

If it had been anyone else, Artemis would have been mortally offended. As it was, she was so glad to see Kiki again she only said, hiccuping from tears to laughter as she hugged Kiki and kissed her and hugged her again, 'Fifteen stone and *you've* changed as well. Why is your hair all gelled and spiky? You look like a hedgehog.'

'I look hip,' Kiki said, gurgling with laughter. 'My good-ness, isn't this wonderful?' She beamed round at Geraldine and Primmie, her green cat eyes dancing. 'We're all together again. After how many years? Thirty? Thirty-one? Have you any champagne in the house, Primmie? I think we should crack open a bottle. Moments like this don't happen very often.'

Primmie hadn't any champagne and so, tearing herself away from Artemis and with money Geraldine gave her, she zoomed off in the Corsa with Rags to buy some.

'I want to make this evening's meal special,' Primmie said as she, Geraldine and Artemis went into the house. 'Will you lay the dining-room table, Geraldine? My best tablecloth and napkins are in the bottom drawer of the sideboard. You sit in the chair near the Aga, Artemis, and just *be*. We'll catch up with what has brought you here when Kiki gets back and we're all seated together around the table.'

As she was talking, she was taking things from shelves and cupboards: a flameproof lidded casserole dish, olive oil, tomato purée, white wine vinegar, salt, black pepper, a tub of bay leaves.

'I don't want to just sit here,' Artemis said, slipping her foot from her good shoe and easing her other foot gingerly out of her hastily repaired and extremely fragile other shoe. 'I want to help. What can I be doing?'

'You could heat some oil in the casserole dish.' Primmie took a chicken from the fridge and began jointing it. 'And there are some tomatoes in a bowl on the window-sill. If you skinned them, it would be a great help.'

As Geraldine came back into the kitchen, Primmie was peeling and slicing onions and the oil in the casserole dish was sizzling.

'Have you a candlestick and candles?' she asked. 'And a small flower vase?'

'There's a cut-glass candlestick on the sitting-room mantelpiece and a small flower vase in the bathroom.'

With the onions peeled, Primmie began placing the chicken joints in the shimmering oil.

Artemis, busily dipping tomatoes in boiling water and slipping the skins from them, said, 'Your friend Hugo is a very kind man, isn't he? My shoe heel broke in the street and he went to a cobbler's repair bar to get it mended for me. Rupert would never have done that, not in a hundred years.'

She paused in what she was doing. 'And this is so nice, Primmie. Making a meal together. It reminds me of when we lived in the flat. I knew I was happy, way back then, but at

315

the time I never appreciated just how precious those days were.'

Later, as they sat round the candlelit table, replete after the chicken cacciatore, Primmie, serving raspberries into small glass bowls, said, 'You don't actually have to explain what brought you here, Artemis. Geraldine and I did try to contact you. The young woman who answered the phone told us you were no longer living with Rupert and then Rupert, when we phoned again, told us that you and he were getting divorced.'

'And so we are.' Artemis took one of the small glass bowls from her. 'After thirty-two years. Can you believe that, Primmie? I can't.' There was a wobble in her voice. 'He's always had affairs, but nothing's ever come of them and then this . . . this Serena creature appeared on the scene and he's become a *monster*.'

Picking up her dessert fork, she stabbed a raspberry with unnecessary violence.

'And when I went away on a cruise, Serena moved into the house – and she's still there and no one seems to mind! Orlando and Sholto have both met her and Sholto says it isn't the end of the world and Orlando says I should be grateful his father stuck by me all the time they were children and it's all so bloody, bloody *unfair*!'

There was a silence and then Kiki said, 'Well, not completely unfair, Tem. Look on the bright side. You don't have to go through life trying to please someone it's impossible to please any longer, do you? And if your grown-up kids are being so unsupportive, you don't have to consider them when making future plans. You're your own woman again. You can do what the hell you want. And the first thing you can do is to move in here with Primmie. Geraldine and I have already moved in, so I'm sure you doing the same thing isn't a problem.'

'Of course it isn't,' Primmie said, knowing that someone would have to move out temporarily when the children arrived, but determining to cross that bridge when she came to it. 'It's the four of us again, only this time, instead of our all living together in a Kensington flat, we'll be living together in Cornwall, in a house by the sea.'

Artemis brushed the tears from her cheeks and managed a

smile. 'Can I stay here, Primmie? Truly? For as long as I want?

'Dearest Artemis, you can stay here for ever.'

Artemis's smile deepened. 'That's the nicest thing anyone has said to me for years and years.' She looked across at Geraldine. 'I can't tell you how wonderful it was when Hugo told me you and Kiki were here as well. Did you drive down together?'

'God, no.' The thought made Geraldine flinch. 'There are still too many issues between Kiki and me. I don't want to shatter too many of your illusions all at once, Artemis, but I'm barely speaking to her.'

'Oh, goodness. I'm sorry. When I saw the two of you together I thought that you'd made things up . . . though of course I know that what happened was so awful that . . .' She broke off, deeply flustered, aware she was floundering and quite possibly making matters between Geraldine and Kiki worse. In a desperate attempt to steer the conversation into safer waters, she said hastily, 'So what is it that brought you here, Geraldine?'

'Retirement from running an escort agency.' Geraldine passed her a jug of cream. 'And before you ask, Artemis, the word "escort" is a euphemism for call-girl, which in turn is a euphemism for prostitute.'

Artemis stared at her goggle eyed and, as she seemed to have lost all power of movement, Geraldine obligingly poured cream on her raspberries for her.

'And I can probably top that,' Kiki said, determined not to let Geraldine steal the show, 'because I came here to commit suicide.'

This time everyone was goggle eyed.

Kiki shrugged. 'Well, I told you that my career was washed up, didn't I?' she said, looking from Geraldine to Primmie. 'And suicide seems a better option than going through life as a has-been.'

'But you aren't a has-been!' Primmie stared across the table at her, appalled. 'You're a woman who was a top-of-the-charts rock star in the '70s and who, because she's moved out of the age range for being a rock star, has said goodbye to it, just as successful footballers and Olympic athletes say goodbye to their careers.'

'Well, that's one way of looking at it, Primmie, but it isn't mine.'

'And are you still intending to commit suicide?' Geraldine asked, as if asking about the weather.

'Yes. But it's on hold at the moment.'

'Because of Rags?'

'For one thing.' Kiki looked across to where Rags, resplendently trimmed, bathed and blow-dried, was lying on the rug in front of the fireplace. 'And for another, because I have Artemis to get into shape.'

'Excuse me?' Artemis pushed her plate of raspberries and cream to one side, unable to concentrate on them.

'You need to lose weight, Artemis. I know you've nearly always been pleasingly plump, but now you're simply heavy and matronly. It's ageing. When was the last time you wore a bikini or a pair of jeans?'

'I don't like jeans.'

'And bikinis?'

There was no answer.

'I've always had to stay slim and supple because of what I do.' Kiki paused and corrected herself. 'Because of what I did. You can't bound around a stage in a huge arena carrying even a centimetre of excess flesh on your hips and bottom, especially not wearing the outfits I wore. Is there a gym in Calleloe, Primmie? Because if there is, I'm going to join it and Artemis is going to join it as well – and if there isn't, there'll be one in Helston and we'll join that.'

Without waiting for Primmie to answer her query, she looked across at Geraldine and said, deliberately provocatively, 'When I was living with Francis in Los Angeles, I part owned a gym, but way back then fitness regimes were more for athletes than for everyone.'

Primmie sucked in her breath.

Artemis froze.

Geraldine said icily, 'You always were an insensitive little bitch, Kiki. This is supposed to be a wonderful reunion dinner party and, though it goes without saying that the wonderful reunion bit doesn't apply to you and me, there's no need for you to bring things to a head between us by mentioning Francis.'

318

'Why not? I think it's time we stopped pussyfooting around the subject of you and Francis and me and Francis, because, to tell the truth, Geraldine, I never thought that what I did was so very terrible.'

As Artemis gasped and Geraldine's face drained of blood, she continued relentlessly, 'If you're totally honest with yourself, you were only marrying Francis because you wanted Cedar Court—'

'I was marrying Francis because he was the only person I ever wanted to marry!' Geraldine pushed her chair away from the table with such force water spilled from the vase of marigolds that she'd placed in the centre of it. She stood up, trembling violently. 'Thanks to you, Kiki, I've never married, never had children . . .'

'No.' Kiki's voice was still perfectly level and conversational. 'If you've never married and had children, Geraldine, it's because you've never really wanted to marry and have children. You've liked the way you've lived. You've liked being answerable to no one but yourself. You've enjoyed doing what you liked, when you liked. You could hardly have run an upmarket Parisian call-girl ring if you'd been married with children, could you? And I doubt that anyone involved in providing sex for money actually enjoys sex or yearns for a long-term monogamous relationship. I know that you loved Francis, Geraldine, but I don't think you ever analysed in quite what way.'

'And you did, I suppose?' Geraldine's knuckles, as she gripped the back of her chair, shone white.

'Analyse Francis and your relationship? Yes, I did. You were cousins who were more like brother and sister. Only your mutual family home – which you loved passionately and which he saw as a liability – was destined to be his only. The only way it could ever be yours – and be passed on to a child of yours – was if the two of you married. And so you used sex to get what you wanted and Francis, who knew with what passion you'd care for Cedar Court, enabling him not to have to, happily went along with it. When I ran off with Francis, I behaved badly – as did he – but I didn't ruin one of the world's great love stories, and perhaps if you could face that truth honestly, the two of us could be friends again.'

There was a silence.

Primmie and Artemis exchanged glances, mutually terrified that the shit was now truly going to hit the fan.

Geraldine's hands squeezed the back of the chair even more tightly. At last she said, her voice raw, 'I'd like to know what you think, Primmie. Are you in general agreement with Kiki?'

Compassionately, Primmie's eyes held hers. 'Yes, Geraldine. I am. I think that when you were a child you fantasized about Cedar Court being your actual home, not just the family home that your mother had been born in. We all have childhood fantasies of one kind or another and, because they're usually impossible to bring to fruition, we outgrow them. You saw a way of making yours come true – and as you and Francis were so close, it was easy for you to slip from being cousins who were best friends into being lovers who would marry. If it hadn't been for Cedar Court, I don't think either of you would ever have thought of marrying each other.'

'And you, Artemis?' Geraldine's voice was as brittle as glass. 'What do you think?'

Artemis looked towards Primmie for help, realized that, as Geraldine had asked her specifically, any such help would be inappropriate and said reluctantly, 'I'm not a very good person to ask, Geraldine, because I don't know much about men. If I'd known more, years ago, I would have known that Rupert wasn't marrying the real me – the me who's pretty crap at just about everything but running a home – and that when he found out I wasn't the successful, soignée model he had me down as being our marriage was bound to keep running into trouble.'

'I'm not asking about Rupert and you, Artemis. I'm asking about Francis and me.'

'And that's what I'm coming to, Geraldine. Just as we were never perfectly matched and able to give to each other what the other lacked, so I never thought that you and Francis were perfectly matched. You were strong and he . . . wasn't. I liked him, though,' she added hurriedly. 'I always liked him. It's just that I always thought it must be a bit tedious for you, always getting him out of scrapes.'

For one terrible, tense moment, Geraldine simply stared at her and it was then that Primmie realized that Geraldine was ill – probably desperately ill. Instead of her face looking merely finely chiselled, it looked gaunt, and she was more than race-horse thin. Looking at her, Primmie doubted if she weighed much more than eight stone.

Slowly Geraldine's grip on the back of her chair eased. Unsteadily she sat back down. 'OK,' she said in a tight voice. 'Now I know what you all think. And you're probably right. Francis was weak. That's no revelation to me at all. And maybe I would have been marrying him for Cedar Court – which, ironically, I'm no longer obsessed by. But running off with your friend's husband-to-be on their wedding morning is still the lowest, shittiest, most despicable act possible. Especially when you then don't even marry him, but simply stay with him while you have a use for him and drop him like a hot brick when his usefulness comes to an end.'

Kiki opened her mouth to make an indignant reply.

Beneath the table, Primmie kicked her hard. Given what had happened to Francis after his break-up from Kiki – or what was believed to have happened to him – she knew it would be fatal for them to start talking about it. It was subject matter for another day. For now, all that mattered was that some kind of rapprochement between Geraldine and Kiki was at last in sight.

Anxious for it to continue, and judging that the best way of helping it to do so was to shelve the subject by giving everyone something to do, she said, 'We'll have coffee in the sitting room. Kiki, would you take in the tray I've set? Geraldine, could you reach the box of cubed brown sugar on the top shelf of the cupboard next to the Aga? I always have to stand on a chair to get to it.'

As they moved their chairs backwards, away from the table, the subject of Francis was temporarily dropped. Breathing a sigh of relief, Primmie followed Artemis into the sitting room.

'Nice work,' Artemis said to her. 'Will Kiki have a bruise on her leg in the morning?'

'Very probably.'

They looked at each other, Destiny's unspoken name lying heavily between them.

Artemis stepped towards the television and picked up the silver-framed photograph that sat on top of it.

321

'It was taken about ten years ago,' Primmie said, watching her as she looked at it, 'when the children were still at school.'

Artemis put the photograph back down without saying anything.

'Destiny's photograph is in the bedroom.' Primmie's throat was so tight, it hurt. 'By my bed.'

'Rupert would never let me do that.' Artemis's eyes were again bright with tears. 'He said it wasn't healthy having a photograph always present that would constantly remind us of what we had lost. I used to speak of Destiny to Orlando and Sholto, but Rupert used to get so angry at my doing so that I stopped. And when I longed to share my grief with you, he said that doing so would only prolong it.'

'He was wrong.' Primmie's voice was quiet and steady and full of infinite pain.

'I know.'

Simultaneously they stepped towards each other, holding each other close, sharing their long-carried grief at last.

From the doorway Kiki, the coffee tray in her hands, said, 'What on earth is going on here?' She stepped into the room, Geraldine behind her. 'Who was Destiny? A friend?'

No one spoke.

Geraldine cleared her throat. 'I think,' she said, 'that we need the bottle of Bell's.'

Kiki put the tray down on Primmie's glass-topped coffee table. 'I'm always happy to see a bottle of whisky,' she said pragmatically. 'But I'd like to know why you three suddenly need one. Who was this Destiny person? Someone's granny?'

Geraldine took the bottle of Bell's and four glasses out of the sideboard cupboard and put them on the table, next to the tray.

'No,' she said, as Primmie and Artemis still didn't speak. 'Destiny was Artemis's adopted daughter. She died in a drowning accident when she was five years old.'

Kiki blanched at her crassness. 'Oh, gosh, Artemis. Forgive me. Primmie told me you'd lost a child and I just didn't put two and two together. I'm so sorry, Tem.' She looked from Artemis to Primmie. 'And were you Destiny's god mother, Primmie?'

322

Geraldine shot Primmie a swift glance and began pouring generous amounts of whisky into each glass.

'No.' Primmie took tight hold of Artemis's hand. 'No, Kiki. It wasn't quite like that.'

Geraldine handed Kiki one of the glasses.

'Artemis was Destiny's adoptive mother and I was her natural mother.'

Kiki's jaw dropped. Gobsmacked, she looked from Artemis to Primmie and back again. 'I don't understand . . . are you saying that you had a baby, Primmie, and Artemis adopted it?'

Primmie nodded.

'But why? I still don't understand.'

'It was before I was married. I couldn't provide Destiny with all the things Artemis could provide her with and, as Artemis and Rupert couldn't have children of their own, and as I couldn't have borne to have had her adopted by strangers, it seemed the obvious solution to both our problems.'

Kiki took a drink of her whisky to help her assimilate the unbelievable information that Primmie had had an illegitimate baby. If it had been anyone else, she wouldn't have batted an eyelid, but Primmie?

'When was all this going on, Prim? After I'd moved off to America, obviously.'

Primmie moved towards the table, took a glass of whisky from it and took a deep swallow. 'No,' she said, still nursing the glass. 'No. I was pregnant with Destiny when we were all three being fitted for our bridesmaid's dresses for Geraldine's wedding.'

Kiki stared at her, totally perplexed. 'But you couldn't have been, Primmie. That was just after I got back from my tour of Australia, and you were dating Simon. I remember that clearly because . . .' She was about to say 'because we had lunch together and he said he was going to marry you and I bullied him out of it,' but thought better of it.

Primmie didn't say anything, and neither did anyone else.

'So I don't see how . . .' she began, and then stopped.

The silence was profound.

In dawning horror, Kiki looked from Primmie to Artemis to Geraldine, and back to Primmie again. 'No,' she said, her voice strangled. 'No. It isn't possible. You would have told me if you were having Simon's baby, Primmie. You would have told me. Wouldn't you?'

'Yes,' Primmie said again, her voice full of remembered hurt. 'But only after I'd told Simon. And I never got the opportunity to tell him. We were going to make our secret engagement public when you came back from Australia and when he'd been able to tell you of our plans face to face. Then he fell ill and went away to recuperate – though I'm not sure now that he really was ill at all. I think he wanted to be on his own in order to come to a decision to end our relationship. It was while he was away that I discovered I was carrying Destiny and we didn't see each other again until the morning of what should have been Geraldine's wedding day.' She lifted her shoulders in an eloquent shrug. 'And when he said he no longer wanted to marry me, I decided not to tell him about the baby. If I had, he would have changed his mind, and I didn't want him marrying me out of a sense of honour or duty.'

'Oh God!' Kiki looked as if she was about to pass out. 'Oh Christ! Oh hell!' She drained her glass in a swallow. 'You're telling me you had Simon's baby *and he never knew*?'

Primmie nodded.

Kiki looked round her, as if for support. As she did so, Rags trotted into the room and sat by her side.

Dazedly Kiki looked back towards Primmie. 'I can't believe this. I can't believe any of it. I had a half-sister – a half-sister who was your daughter – and you never told me?'

'How could I? If I'd told you, then Simon would have had to know as well – and Simon knowing, when he didn't want to marry me, was a complication I simply couldn't face.'

'But Simon *did* want to marry you!' the words were blurted out before she could stop them.

Still standing near the door, Geraldine folded her arms.

Primmie bit her lip.

Artemis, who had never shared Geraldine's suspicions as to just why Simon Lane had broken off his relationship with Primmie, merely looked bewildered.

Kiki looked like a woman on the brink of an abyss.

'Come on, Kiki,' Geraldine said, pitilessly. 'How do you

324

know that at the time your father ended his engagement to Primmie, he was still in love with her and still wanted to marry her?'

'Because . . . because . . .' She put her hand down to Rags and knotted her fingers in his fur. 'Because we had lunch together when I came back from Australia and he told me then. I was . . . appalled. I couldn't even begin to imagine having Primmie as my stepmother. The thought seemed . . . indecent and I . . . and I . . .'

She couldn't go on.

'And you begged him not to do it?' Geraldine finished for her.

'I . . . Yes. Oh God, Primmie. I'm so sorry. So very, very sorry. If I'd known about the baby . . . If I'd been a bit older . . . If I'd had more sense . . .'

Her words tailed off into a silence no one attempted to break.

At last, in a haze of misery, she said, 'It could all have been so different, couldn't it? And it's all down to me that it wasn't, isn't it?' Her face was ashen, her flame-red hair only emphasizing its pallor.

Primmie dragged in a deep breath, feeling like a vertigo sufferer who, seeing the world tilt crazily, can only wait for the dizziness to pass. She'd suspected that Kiki might have had a hand in Simon's decision to end their love affair, but she'd never been certain of it; had never wanted to be certain of it. Now it confronted her in a way there was no avoiding.

She closed her eyes, the past of thirty years ago as close and as real as yesterday. If Kiki hadn't so cruelly sunk all her dreams for her then there would never have been any question of her giving Destiny up for adoption. She and Simon would have married and, with Destiny, would have lived at Petts Wood. Destiny would never have been taken to Spain by Rupert; would never have drowned. Destiny would be with her here, now.

She opened her eyes. And she would never have had the life she had lived with Ted. There would have been no love-filled little house in Rotherhithe. No Millie, Joanne, Josh and Lucy. What had happened had happened. Kiki wasn't to blame. If Simon had truly loved her – as Ted had truly loved her – then no amount of Kiki's pleadings would have made him change his mind about marrying her.

325

She looked across at Kiki, Kiki who no longer seemed at least fifteen years younger than her actual age, but who, perhaps for the first time in her life, was visibly sick with anguished regret and guilt.

'Nothing is all down to you, Kiki,' she said quietly. 'What you did caused me a lot of pain, but the aftermath of that pain wasn't your fault – Simon didn't have to take notice of what you said and I had a choice as to whether to keep Destiny or have Artemis and Rupert adopt her. There are no hard feelings, Kiki. Truly. What matters now is the present, not the past. And the present is the four of us being together again, just like we used to be.'

Kiki bit her lip and then, without a word, spun round, heading out of the room.

'Kiki!' Primmie slammed her glass of whisky down on to the coffee table. 'Kiki, come back!' She ran across the room after her. 'Don't leave, Kiki! There's absolutely no need for you to leave!'

Out in the hallway, at the foot of the stairs, Kiki paused. 'I'm not leaving, Primmie,' she said, turning to look at her, one hand on the newel post. 'I'm going to your bedroom. I want to see Destiny's photograph. I want to see if my little half-sister looked anything at all like me.'

Twenty-Seven

The next morning Kiki did something she had never, by choice, done before. She got up early. With Rags at her heels, she let herself quietly out of the house and set off down the track. In the meadow Black-Hearted Alice was tearing grass and thistles out of the ground, and the air was so still she could hear the sound of her jaws chewing relentlessly. There was no sign of Maybelline, who presumably didn't come out to graze until after she had been milked. Marvelling at the way Primmie had turned herself from a Londoner into a woman who could quite equably milk cows and goats she opened Ruthven's double gates.

It was a glorious morning, full of the promise of Indian-summer heat, and she paused, taking off her trainers, tying the laces together in order to hang them round her neck. Then, closing the gates behind her, she set off across the dew-wet grass, towards the headland and the sea.

There wasn't another soul in sight. With Rags repeatedly streaking off in front of her and then pounding back to circle her and race off again, it was as if she had the whole of Cornwall to herself. The two low-lying arms of the cove were a muted, misty green, the sea a shimmering, glittering silver.

With Rags's white plume of a tail leading the way she slipped and slithered down the shallow incline to the ribbon of sand, grateful for the emptiness and the tranquillity, aware she had a lot to think about.

That her father had died having had a child he had known nothing about seemed, to her, surreal. How on earth had Primmie managed to keep such a secret? She picked up some small flat stones from the shoreline and began spinning them out to sea. Rags, thinking it a game, plunged into the waves after them. She watched him frolicking in the shallows, reliving the moment in Primmie's bedroom when she had looked down at the face of her little half-sister. Nothing in her life had prepared her for such a mind-blowing, absolutely indescribable experience.

The photograph had been taken at a birthday party, for Destiny had been holding a balloon in one hand, printed with the words 'YOU ARE 4', and her dress was a ruffled and flounced pink party dress. Her eyes were shining and she was laughing with glee. Somehow, she had expected that Destiny's hair would be red, like hers. It wasn't. It was fair, like her father's; like Primmie's. And, like Primmie's, it was curly. Destiny had her short, kitten-shaped face, though. And her stubborn chin.

She sat down on the sand, hugging her knees, grieving for the half-sister she had never known, overcome by all she had missed out on.

She had hardly cried since childhood – and very rarely then – but tears rolled mercilessly down her cheeks and on to her clasped hands.

327

Rags, seaweed in his mouth, padded up to her, shaking water from his fur. For once she ignored him. Dropping seaweed from his mouth he flopped down beside her, and not for a long time – not until his coat had dried in the early morning sunshine – did either of them move.

When she returned to Ruthven, it was to find both Matt and Hugo in the kitchen, drinking mugs of coffee.

Primmie was grilling bacon.

Geraldine, wearing a narrow turquoise dress, her silk-black hair hanging long and heavy down her back, was seated at the kitchen table, chatting to Matt and making notes in a small notebook as they talked.

Artemis, still wearing her floral dress and jacket, was recalling a number on her mobile.

Hugo, flamboyant in a pink sweater and grey slacks, was scrutinizing a drawing that seemed to consist of nothing but brilliantly coloured, geometric shapes.

'Brett Kenwyn is your best bet if you want an all-round, dependable workman,' Matt was saying to Geraldine. 'He's a carpenter by trade, but he turns his hand to practically anything. He'll certainly be able to convert the barn into sleeping accommodation and he'll knock up a stand for Primmie to milk Alice on in no time at all.'

'And his phone number?'

As Matt gave it to her, Artemis said despairingly, 'Orlando isn't replying and Sholto's mobile is switched off.'

'Why are you ringing them?' As she asked the question, Kiki crossed the kitchen to where Primmie was now carving thick slices of bread.

'I need them to collect luggage I took with me on the cruise. Plus I want personal possessions I treasure taking out of the house before that bitch Serena rifles through them.'

'Wouldn't it be better to do that personally?' Hugo put the diagram for the proposed potager down on the kitchen table, giving her his full attention. 'I could take you. I'd quite like a long drive to . . . where would we be going?'

'Gloucestershire . . . but I couldn't ask it of you, Hugo. It's too far and besides . . .' Her cheeks flushed pink. 'Besides, collecting my things personally will be a little awkward.'

Kiki, busy forking slices of crispy bacon on to the hunks of bread, said impatiently, 'For crying out loud, Temmy, how can it be awkward? It's your *home*, for God's sake. And you are going to fight for it, aren't you? You're not just going to accept this statement of Rupert's that it's his and he's keeping it?'

'No, of course I'm not.' Artemis looked affronted. 'Though I'll only be doing so on principle. I don't want to live in it again – not after Serena's polluted it.'

'Well, then,' Kiki began passing around a plate stacked high with bacon butties, 'what's the problem?'

Artemis flushed even pinker. 'Before I walked out of the house I was a little violent.'

'Well, if you threw everything you could lay your hands on at him, no one could blame you.' Geraldine closed her notebook. 'Just as long as they were things he treasured and you didn't give a damn for.'

'They weren't things at all.'

Everyone looked at her with interest.

Looking deeply uncomfortable, Artemis said, 'I hit him. With my fist. On his jaw.'

Hugo choked on his coffee. Kiki gave a whoop of delight. Geraldine cracked with laughter. Primmie said incredulously, 'You mean you *decked* him?'

Artemis nodded.

'And hurt him?'

'Well, he was flat on his back and not moving.'

Kiki and Geraldine collapsed in gales of laughter. Primmie tried to keep a straight face, and couldn't. Matt looked horrified. Hugo looked dazed.

'And so you see Hugo taking me to the house to collect things might be a little awkward,' Artemis finished with masterly understatement.

All eyes turned to Hugo. Manfully he came to terms with the realization that his Rubenesque goddess wasn't quite as helpless as he had imagined. He reminded himself of how shamefully she had been provoked and indignation, on her behalf, flooded through him. 'Let's set off now,' he said decisively. 'We can be there and back by early evening.'

'But what will Rupert think?' It was a reflex question born

of thirty-two years of married life. 'He doesn't know you and . . .'

Kiki groaned. Geraldine rolled her eyes in despair. Primmie said patiently, 'If Rupert was to say that his affair with Serena had all been a ghastly mistake and he wanted a reconciliation, would you agree to one?'

Artemis paused for an infinitesimal moment and then shook her head. 'No.'

'And so you want a divorce as much as he does?'

'Yes.' There was surprise at the realization in Artemis's voice. 'Yes, Primmie. I do.'

'Then it doesn't matter *what* Rupert thinks about you being in the company of a man he knows nothing about. Far better to have Hugo take you and for you to collect everything you want yourself than to ask one of your sons to do it for you, which is what Rupert – and Orlando and Sholto – will be expecting you to do.'

'And if you don't leave now, this very minute, I shall never speak to you again,' Geraldine said in mock severity as Artemis still hesitated.

Artemis hesitated no longer.

'I'll get my handbag from the bedroom,' she said to Hugo. 'And be right with you.'

She was back downstairs a minute later, her clutch bag in her hand. Automatically, without thinking about it, everyone followed Hugo and her out to Hugo's parked Mercedes.

'They make a nice couple, don't they?' Primmie said as Hugo opened the passenger-seat door for Artemis.

Geraldine chuckled. 'Give them time, Primmie. Artemis only left the marital home yesterday.'

'Maybe, but her marriage has been over for ages, probably for years – though I don't think she's aware, yet, of just how long it's been dead.'

'It sometimes takes a long time to realize things.' Kiki's eyes were on the Mercedes as Hugo drove it out of the yard and on to the track leading down between the fields to the gates. 'I realized something only this morning.'

'And that was?' Geraldine, too, was still watching the car.

'That yesterday, when you said that my running off with Francis on your wedding morning was the lowest, shittiest, most despicable act possible – you were right. It was. And I want to tell you that I'm sorry, Geraldine. I shouldn't have done it.'

Primmie, standing only a foot or so away from them, waited for Geraldine's response with bated breath.

It was a long time in coming.

At last, as the Mercedes turned out of the gates inland, beginning to pick up speed, she said, without turning her head towards Kiki, 'Apology accepted – and there's something I want to say to you, too.'

Kiki looked towards her, her eyes apprehensive.

Aware that Kiki was expecting her to say something heavy, the corner of Geraldine's beautifully sculpted mouth twitched slightly. 'Congratulations on taking Rags to the beauty parlour. He looks the bee's knees.'

Later, as Geraldine walked with her across the meadow, towards the hen arks, Primmie was tempted to say how glad she was that the estrangement with Kiki had finally been laid to rest. She decided against it. Just because an apology had been given, and accepted, didn't mean the subject matter was no longer hurtful.

'Do you always keep the hens in their runs until midday?' Geraldine asked, breaking in on her thoughts. 'I thought they were happiest running free.'

'They are.' Primmie put the basket she'd brought with her on the grass and knelt beside the first of the arks. 'And this is when I let them out – at midday, when they've finished laying. If I let them out earlier they lay their eggs under hedges and all over the place and I never find half of them.'

She slid the door back that gave access to the nesting boxes.

Watching her as she began lifting the eggs and placing them in the basket, Geraldine said, 'There's something I need to tell you, Primmie.'

Primmie stopped what she was doing and leaned back on her heels, her tummy muscles tightening. This was the moment she'd been waiting for – and dreading – ever since she had realized that Geraldine was ill.

Geraldine sat down, her long legs coiled elegantly beneath her, her back against the wire mesh of the hen run. 'I'm suffering from something called severe aplastic anaemia,' she said starkly. 'Unless I have a bone marrow transplant – and the chances of having one aren't high – it's terminal.'

The blood drained from Primmie's face. She felt her head swim and for one dizzying moment thought she was going to faint.

Aware of the effect her news had had, Geraldine said, 'I'm sorry, Primmie. It isn't the kind of news that can be broken gently.'

It was the understatement of all understatements.

Primmie pressed the back of her hand hard against her mouth, knowing that for Geraldine's sake she had to remain calm. If she were to give way to the howls of protest and anguish clutching at her throat, then Geraldine's self-control – control she must have battled hard and long for – would also break down.

Licking dry lips, her voice raw, she said, 'What is aplastic anaemia, Geraldine? I've never heard of it.'

'It's a blood disease.' Her voice was perfectly steady. 'Instead of blood-producing cells in my bone marrow, all I have are fat-producing cells.'

'And a bone marrow transplant will rectify that?'

Geraldine nodded, her violet-dark eyes grave. 'Yes. If I have one.'

Primmie stared at her, confused. 'I'm sorry, Geraldine. I don't understand. If a transplant will cure you, why haven't you already had one? You have money. You're not dependent on NHS treatment.' Despite all her fierce determination to remain calm, there was the unsteadiness of fear in her voice. 'So what's the problem? What is it you haven't yet told me?'

Geraldine shifted her position in order to avoid the attentions of a Rhode Island Red that was trying to peck her hair through the wire mesh. 'Transplants are only usually carried out on patients under the age of forty who have a brother or a sister as a suitable match – and I'm fifty-two and an only child.'

Primmie struggled to remain calm. It wasn't easy – not when she wanted to sob in anguish at the unfairness of it all. How could Geraldine be facing a death sentence when they had only just found each other again? When, together

332

with Kiki and Artemis, they had so much to look forward to? It was too utterly monstrous. Too vile. Too bloody, bloody cruel.

'But the over-forty thing won't be impossible to get around, will it? Not when you can afford to go anywhere in the world for treatment?'

'And the sibling issue?'

Violet eyes held grey.

'There are donor registries, of course, and my consultant in Paris will be in touch instantly if a suitable match is found.' Geraldine gave her a lopsided smile. 'Until then I'll be travelling between here and Paris pretty regularly for treatment.'

'Which is?'

'Blood transfusions and antibiotics.'

She saw the sudden hope that lit Primmie's eyes.

'The prognosis is a year, Primmie,' she said gently. 'Maybe less.'

Primmie didn't speak. She couldn't. She took hold of Geraldine's hand, their fingers intertwining.

'I'm not going to tell Kiki and Artemis.' Geraldine looked across the sunlit field to where Maybelline was placidly grazing. 'Not yet. Artemis would go to pieces – and I'd find that hard to cope with.' Black humour entered her voice. 'And Kiki would begin treating me differently. She might even start being sensitive and caring – and that would unnerve me completely.'

Incredibly, Primmie felt the corners of her mouth twitch in response. The grimmer things were, the more important laughter was going to be. And, fortunately for Geraldine and her, laughter had never been a problem.

'The name is Brett Kenwyn. Are you Miss Grant?'

Primmie regarded the leather-jacketed and jean-clad Brad Pitt lookalike in bemusement.

'No. Are you the builder she's expecting?'

'That's me.' White teeth flashed in a dazzling smile. 'She said she had quite a bit of work for me. A barn to convert, a custom-made goat shed to build, a patio to lay.' He swung a heavy tool bag easily from his shoulder on to the ground. 'Which has priority, d'you know?'

Primmie registered that, as if all his other handsome attributes weren't enough, he also had a slight cleft in his chin, and said, 'The goat shed. Geraldine is having a rest at the moment, but I'll show you around and you can decide where it would be best placed. I'm Primmie Dove. Would you like me to show you the barn? Then you can tell me how much work will be involved.'

As she was talking, Primmie was leading the way across the cobbled yard towards the farm buildings. 'I have another two friends, as well as Geraldine, living with me, and as I'm going to be giving holidays to groups of children I desperately need more sleeping accommodation.'

As they came to a halt in front of the dilapidated barn, Brett Kenwyn tucked his thumbs into the front pockets of his jeans and assessed it.

'Is it going to be an impossible job?' Primmie asked anxiously.

'Nah.' Brett eyed the exterior with a knowing eye. 'It'll be a piece of cake. Miss Grant said dormitory accommodation was wanted.'

'Yes. We thought young children would find a dormitory more fun. And we'll need very safe access for them – ladders with handrails.'

'Your wish is my command,' he said, shooting her another dazzling smile. 'And what about the goat shed? Do you want it squeezing in around the yard, next to the cow shed, perhaps? Or d'you want it tucked out in the field where she grazes?'

'Next to the cow shed, if you can manage it. It will be less of a trek when I milk her.'

'I charge seventy pounds a day,' he said, 'and if you want me to start work right away, I can.'

Primmie smiled sunnily. 'Then please do, Mr Kenwyn.'

'The name is Brett. Do you want the goat-shed roof thatching?'

'Yes, please, Brett. And call me Primmie.'

'OK, Primmie.' She was treated to yet another dazzling smile. 'Then I'll start digging the foundations out now.'

'If he were on the books of the agency I've just divested myself of, he'd be earning himself a fortune,' Geraldine said an hour or so later as, standing at the side door, a mug of tea in her hands, she looked across to where Brett Kenwyn, naked to the waist and muscles rippling, was hacking out foundations for the goat shed with a pickaxe.

Primmie's eyes widened. 'Did you have *men* escorts on your books, as well as young women?'

'Goodness, but you're naive, Primmie! Of course I did. They had to be intelligent, though, as well as good-looking. When women are paying for a man to escort them to public functions they don't want it to be obvious, the minute he speaks, that he's hired out by the hour. My agency was top-of-the-market and all the escorts who worked for it were deluxe in every sense of the word.'

'And you now have nothing at all to do with it?'

Geraldine's mouth tugged into a smile. 'That's right. My pimping days are well and truly over – though looking at our builder, I can't help seeing dollar and pound signs. There must be well-heeled women in Cornwall who would be happy to pay for a handsome young escort – especially one with such a torso.'

Primmie didn't know if Geraldine was teasing her or not, but was taking no chances. 'Well, if they are, you're not going to be the one providing them with someone,' she said spiritedly. 'I could explain a lot to Matt, but not that!'

Geraldine eyed her curiously. 'Forgive me if I'm being a little too nosy, Prim, but is having Kiki, Artemis and me here cramping Matt's and your style?'

Primmie didn't pretend to misunderstand. 'Well, it is a little bit,' she said truthfully. 'But Matt has a very cosy little cottage in Calleloe – and I shall probably begin spending the odd evening or so there.'

'Or the odd night or so?'

'Or the odd night or so.' She smiled. 'Good men are hard to find. Matt reminds me of Ted – and I loved Ted with all my heart and still miss him.' Her eyes were overly bright. 'I'll always miss him, because what we had together was so very perfect.'

'And is it perfect with Matt?'

Primmie's smile deepened. 'Not yet, but I think it will be some day. And that's worth working towards, isn't it?'

*   *   *

335

When Kiki came back after an Oxfam trawl with Rags, it was late afternoon.

'There's a bloke digging to Australia next to the cow shed and he's playing one of my Rock 'n' Roll Greats CDs,' she said indignantly. 'Who lent it to him? I don't want him sneaking off with it.'

'No one.' As the sound of Gene Vincent singing 'Blue Jean Bop' drifted from the far side of the farmyard, Primmie continued laying the kitchen table for three, certain that Artemis wouldn't be back from Gloucestershire till late. 'The bloke in question is the builder who's going to convert the barn and make a shed for Alice. His name is Brett and if he's playing a rock and roll CD it's his own. That sequinned beret is nice. Did you find it in Calleloe?'

'Helston, in a boot sale.'

In skin-tight jeans, leather jacket and gaudily sequinned beret, Kiki strode back out of the kitchen and into the porch, opening the side door so that she could hear the music more clearly. 'Blue Jean Bop' was followed by Little Richard's 'Long Tall Sally.'

'Are you *sure* it isn't my CD?' she shouted back to her, over her shoulder.

'Positive.'

'Forgive me if I'm not convinced. I'm going over to check.'

Geraldine, who had been sitting in the rocking chair near to the Aga, put down the gardening magazine she had been leafing through. 'How old would you say Brett Kenwyn is, Primmie?'

'Early thirties.' Primmie put a bottle of Merlot on the table. 'Why?'

'No real reason.' It wasn't the truth, but there was no point in putting her thoughts into words. Kiki had always done exactly as she wanted to – and Brett Kenwyn looked like a young man who could take care of himself.

After dinner, Geraldine, looking desperately fatigued, went straight to bed and Kiki announced she was going into Calleloe, to meet Brett Kenwyn for a drink.

Primmie, assuming Kiki's interest was entirely musical, was quite glad of her plans. It meant she would have time to herself until Artemis returned, and time to herself was something she had wanted ever since her talk with Geraldine out by the hen arks.

Going into the small room that looked out over the front garden, she sat at Amelia's big old desk and switched on her laptop. Five minutes later she was online. She didn't check in on the Friends Reunited website. Instead she entered 'Missing Persons, USA' in her search box. Geraldine might not have a brother or a sister who could give her a bone marrow transplant, but she did have a cousin. Minutes later, knowing that her search would be long and involved, she typed in 'Francis Sheringham'.

Twenty-Eight

When Artemis returned late that night with a mountain of luggage, she was in reasonably good spirits. 'The Serena bitch wasn't there,' she said, as she and Primmie curled up on either end of the sofa, drinking milky cocoa, 'but Orlando was. I explained that Hugo was a friend who was kindly going to ferry some personal items to Cornwall for me. I don't know why, but both he and Rupert looked quite dazed.'

'Good.' Primmie, comfy in a shabby woollen dressing-gown, took a sip of her cocoa and grinned at her over the rim of her mug. 'I don't know about Orlando, but Rupert was always difficult. The last thing he would have expected was for you to be in the company of a highly eligible man.'

Artemis, resplendent in a Rigby & Peller lace-trimmed peignoir, shot her a sheepish grin. 'It was very good for my self-esteem that he couldn't quite work out my relationship to Hugo. Now I know why escort agencies have male escorts for hire, as well as girls. Somehow, having Hugo with me helped me to keep my dignity.'

'And was his retaining the house mentioned again?'

'No. I didn't want to get into that kind of a discussion in

front of Hugo – and if he suggests that part of the settlement will be our home in Corfu, I shall sell it. I've done a lot of thinking this last forty-eight hours and one decision I've come to is that I don't want to live with reminders of a marriage that is over. I was a very loyal wife to Rupert and he was never loyal to me in return.'

She slipped off the fluffy mules she was wearing and wriggled pearly-pink-painted toes against a cushion. 'The most terrible thing I'm having to come to terms with, Primmie, is that I don't think he ever really loved me at all. Not in the way Ted loved you. Not in the way I always wanted to be loved. I thought being married to a man with everything would be a fairy tale, and it wasn't. Nearly all Rupert's friends have the attitude that extramarital affairs are perfectly OK – it's all some of them seem interested in, apart from hunting – and that it's middle-class to behave differently.' She gave a despairing shrug. 'And I *did* behave differently. I was never unfaithful to Rupert – not once.'

'Don't get weepy,' Primmie said gently as Artemis looked as if she was about to fill with tears again. 'Start thinking about what you're going to do with your future.'

Artemis blinked the pending tears away.

'I'm going to buy a house on the Lizard – near to you,' she said purposefully. 'And instead of simply being a glorified party-caterer for Rupert, I'm going to help you look after the children who come here for holidays and I'm going to act as a part-time receptionist at Hugo's art gallery.'

Primmie's eyebrows rose quizzically. 'Does Hugo know this yet, or is it going to be a happy surprise for him?'

'He suggested it to me over dinner this evening.' She saw Primmie's eyes light with prurient interest and added quickly, 'We wouldn't have got back to Calleloe in time for dinner and so we stopped off at a restaurant in Launceston.'

She looked at the clock on the mantelpiece. It was after midnight and she said gratefully, 'It was nice of you wait up for me, Primmie. Did Kiki and Geraldine go to bed ages ago?'

'Geraldine did. Kiki isn't in yet.'

This time it was Artemis's eyebrows that rose high. 'In from where?' she asked, as if Kiki were fifteen, not fifty-two.

'In from an evening out in Calleloe with the builder who started work here this afternoon.'

Artemis's jaw dropped. 'How come she's in the mood to be dating workmen? I thought she was supposed to be feeling suicidal?'

'She's obviously feeling suicidal no longer. And she hasn't gone out with a gang of work*men*, Artemis. She's gone for a drink with a work*man*. The carpenter-cum-builder Matt recommended.'

Artemis put her empty cocoa mug on the coffee table, rose to her feet and stretched, myriad lace ruffles rippling down her arms. 'No disrespect, Primmie, but I can't quite see Kiki hitting it off with a retired friend of Matt's.'

Primmie was about to correct Artemis's assumption that Brett was of pensionable age and then decided against it. It would do for another day. For the moment, it was too late and she was too tired.

She did wonder, though, as she went to bed, if she'd been a little naive in assuming that Kiki and Brett had met up for a drink for no other reason than to chat about a mutual love of rock and roll – and when, much later, the sound of the front door being opened woke her and she saw by the clock that stood next to her photograph of Destiny, that it was ten past three, she was almost a hundred per cent sure she had been naive.

The next morning, at breakfast, no one brought up the subject of Kiki's evening out with Brett Kenwyn. Kiki, much to everyone's surprise, was with them for breakfast, looking incredibly sparky in a mint-green T-shirt, faded jeans and Cuban-heeled boots.

'Nice to see you've got your luggage back, Tem,' she said as Artemis appeared wearing a matronly cream silk dress and jacket ensemble. 'But there's no garden party in Calleloe today. If all your clothes are as unsuitable as that Queen Elizabeth-style outfit then I suggest you hit the shops in Truro. And if you don't want to go as far as Truro, there's always the Oxfam shop in Helston.'

Artemis gave a ladylike shudder. '*You* may be able to get away with shopping at Oxfam. You're only a size ten. I

339

couldn't. Not even if I wanted to, which I don't. I didn't look good in jeans when I was sixteen and I certainly wouldn't look good in them now. I shall find out where the nearest Jaeger stockist is and buy myself a whole new wardrobe of classic country clothes.'

'Well, don't go by yourself or the chances are you'll still end up looking like an aged member of the Royal family.' Kiki helped herself to a slice of toast from the toaster and began slathering it with honey. 'Take Geraldine or me with you.'

'I notice you don't suggest I go with her,' Primmie said in pretended umbrage as she spooned scrambled eggs on to plates. 'Is that because you don't think much of my dress sense either?'

Kiki eyed Primmie's aged Marks & Spencer pleated skirt, well-worn sweater and flat shoes, and grinned. 'You're not exactly cutting edge, Prim.'

'No, but I'm comfy. Does anyone want more scrambled egg? There's still lots left.'

'Not for me.' Geraldine poured herself a black coffee. 'Is it Brett Kenwyn I can hear in the yard? He's nice and early.'

'He is considering he had such a late night,' Primmie said with an impish look towards Kiki

Kiki didn't rise to the bait. Still eating toast, she walked across the kitchen to the door leading into the porch, Rags at her heels. 'I'm going to walk Rags,' she said laconically, 'and then I may try my hand at a bit of building work.'

The instant the porch door closed behind her, they all three left the table and crossed to the window.

Straight as an arrow, Kiki walked over to where Brett was unloading bags of cement from the back of a van.

'I know what you're both thinking,' Artemis said in shocked tones, 'but you can't be right. He's young enough to be her son.'

'So he is, at a pinch,' Geraldine said dryly. 'It won't weigh with Kiki, though. I never thought the day would come when I would say this, but I do have a sneaking admiration for her.'

'Mine isn't sneaking,' Primmie said as Brett's handsome face lit up at the sight of Kiki's approach. 'It's boundless.'

*   *   *

340

As the days passed and it became accepted that Kiki and Brett were a romantic item, Primmie's bemused admiration grew. It was the fact that Kiki and Brett managed to look like a regular couple, not a bizarre oddity, that most impressed her. She wasn't sure, but she thought it was because Kiki's emotional and mental development had, in many respects, been set in stone when she was a teenager. Whatever it was, it was keeping tongues in Calleloe happily wagging.

'Kiki's twenty feet high on a rafter, nails between her teeth, a workman's tool belt slung around her hips and a hammer in her hand,' Artemis said, as, the goat shed completed, Brett began work on the barn. 'Do you think she's a help to him, or a hindrance?'

'God knows.' Geraldine gave a Gallic shrug of her shoulders. 'But at least she'll be out of our hair tomorrow, when the children arrive. And at least we don't have to worry about where she's going to sleep whilst they're here.'

'You do know that the whole of Calleloe knows who she is and that she's moving into Brett's caravan with him, don't you?' This time Artemis spoke directly to Primmie. It was late afternoon and the three of them were sitting in the garden, enjoying a bottle of Chardonnay. 'It'll be in the local papers soon and I can't help wondering how she'll feel about that.'

'It will depend on whether they use the word "has-been" about her, or not,' Primmie said sagely.

'Well, if they do and she copes with it, a great corner will have been turned.' Geraldine stretched out to put her wine glass back on the garden table, fresh bruises showing on skin that was deathly pale. 'Shall we get on with adding to the list of what we're going to do for the children's entertainment? Artemis's idea of a sandcastle competition is a good idea, but we'll have to make sure we have plenty of buckets and spades.'

Later in the afternoon Geraldine zoomed off in her Ferrari into Calleloe to buy buckets and spades, taking Artemis with her. Artemis, who had initially intended moving into a hotel when the children arrived and who, instead, had accepted Hugo's suggestion that she move into the spacious, unoccupied flat above

341

his art gallery, wanted to shop for bits and pieces of household items she felt the handsomely equipped kitchen lacked.

Primmie baked. Tomorrow her home would be full of children and she was looking forward to their arrival with great expectancy. It would be just like twenty years ago, when Ted's and her little house in Rotherhithe was full of their children's chatter and laughter.

'The kids are on their way!' Kiki shouted just after four o'clock the next day, from her vantage point with Brett high on the barn's roof. 'There's a minibus heading down the lane towards the gates!'

Primmie left the house and began walking down the track towards the double gates, full of happy anticipation. Buoyantly she opened the gates as the minibus creaked into view, a radiant smile on her face. 'Welcome to Cornwall!' she called out to the children. 'Welcome to Ruthven!'

Minutes later the children were scrambling from the minibus into the yard and the plump, rosy-cheeked young woman who had been driving was trying to marshal them into some sort of order, saying to Primmie as she did so, 'I'm Rose Hudson. It's very kind of you to give children from Claybourne a holiday, Mrs Dove. I did think they'd be tired by now, but I obviously underestimated them!'

'Please call me Primmie,' Primmie said, as a little boy with glasses and a very bad squint said indignantly, 'Where's the sea, then? I thought we were staying by the sea.'

'It's over there, where you can't see any more land, silly,' a freckled-faced girl said and then, smiling winningly up at Primmie, 'I'm Daisy and he's Jimmy. That's Jimmy's friend, Frankie.' She pointed towards a skinny boy, tall for his age. 'And that's Marlon.'

Marlon was black and was looking around him a trifle apprehensively.

'And I'm Ellie,' another little girl said forthcomingly, a battered teddy bear in her arms.

'Thank you, Daisy and Ellie,' Rose Hudson said as Primmie led the way into the house and then, to Primmie, 'Goodness, but you've made some changes here! I came last year with a group of ten-year-olds and the decor is much nicer now.'

'I'm glad you like the changes I've made.' Primmie took hold of a little hand that had slid into hers. 'I have some introductions to make, too,' she said, glancing down and seeing that her newfound friend was Daisy. 'Artemis is going to be here every day helping me with the cooking and the housework, and Geraldine is living here with me.'

As Artemis moved forward away from the Aga, a vision in cream silk and pearls, Rose Hudson's jaw dropped. Primmie, well aware that Artemis looked nothing like anyone's idea of household help, suppressed a giggle. 'And this is Geraldine,' she said, as Geraldine strolled through the maelstrom of children towards them. 'Geraldine is living here with me, and so you'll be seeing a lot of her.'

Rose Hudson's jaw dropped even further. If Artemis was bizarrely overdressed, Geraldine, wearing a scarlet linen dress by Chanel, her hair twisted into a loose knot held in place by a tortoiseshell comb, was mind-bogglingly elegant.

'Where's our rooms?' Jimmy demanded, as Geraldine shook Rose's hand. 'Where are we sleeping? Me, Frankie and Marlon ain't sleeping wiv the girls, are we?'

'I'll show you where you are sleeping.' Primmie began leading the way out of the kitchen into the hallway just as Kiki and Brett tramped into the kitchen from the porch.

'We thought we'd bring the luggage in from the bus,' Brett said, a suitcase in either hand and one tucked under his arm.

Primmie paused, aware that further introductions were necessary. 'Brett is converting a barn into sleeping accommodation and Kiki, who lives here with me and has moved out temporarily while the children are here, is helping him,' she said as Brett flashed Rose a smile that must have left her weak kneed.

With a brief 'Hi' to Rose, Kiki ploughed past them towards the foot of the stairs, as laden as Brett.

Ellie scurried after her.

'One of those bags is mine,' she could be heard saying as she followed Kiki upstairs, Primmie, Brett, Rose and the other children in her wake 'You look like someone I've seen on the telly. Are you famous?'

In the kitchen, Artemis's eyes met Geraldine's.

'No,' they heard Kiki say. 'I used to be, but I'm not now.

Which room do you and your friend want to have? A pink one, a blue one or a lilac one?'

Artemis reached for a pair of oven gloves. 'Whatever Kiki's state of mind when she drove down here, I think she's beginning to come to terms with her situation, don't you?' she said, taking the scones from the Aga. 'Perhaps having a new young lover has helped.'

'A new lover of any age is always a help.'

Artemis looked startled, not knowing whether Geraldine was teasing her or not.

To show that she wasn't, Geraldine said, 'And you should take a leaf out of Kiki's book, Artemis. Hugo is obviously besotted with you. Why don't you go for it? He has all the right qualifications. He's a giant of a man and so you'll always look femininely fragile in comparison. He's a bachelor. He's intelligent and cultured. He's kind and caring. He dresses with wonderful aplomb. Nothing seems to faze him. If I were in your shoes, I'd be leading him into the nearest bedroom as fast as light.'

Artemis flushed scarlet. 'That's because you've a whole lot more expertise in the bed department, Geraldine. I wouldn't know how to start going about having an affair. I can't begin to imagine taking my clothes off in front of anyone other than Rupert.'

'Well, it's about time you did.' There came the sound of several pairs of feet clattering back down the stairs. 'Time to butter the scones,' she said, pleased that Artemis hadn't indignantly said that she didn't fancy Hugo, for it meant that she did – which, if she'd judged Hugo correctly, meant that the chances of Artemis's life being turned round in the near future were very, very high.

The next day Rose Hudson, accompanied by Primmie, took the children down to the cove. Artemis spent the day learning the ropes of reception work at the art gallery. Kiki spent the day with Brett.

The day afterwards, on Monday, Matt took Rose and the children out on his boat.

On Tuesday Rose and Primmie took them for a picnic to Lizard Point and, when they came back, Brett told them stories

344

about the nineteenth-century smugglers who used to live in Calleloe.

On Wednesday they spent the day at Ruthven, helping Primmie feed the hens, collect eggs and play in the grazing pasture, giving Black-Hearted Alice a wide berth as they did so.

'Why ain't there no swings round here?' Jimmy, always the spokesman, asked Kiki.

Kiki, who hadn't gone out of her way to spend time with him, or any of the other children, ignored him. Half an hour later, though, Geraldine saw her wrestling old car tyres out of the back of Brett's van and towards a far corner of the pasture where a couple of oak trees gave shade to Maybelline on hot days. Five minutes later she was back at the van, hauling a heavy coil of rope and a tool bag from it.

Bemused, she strolled out to the pasture to see what was going on.

'I'm hanging the tyres from the trees,' Kiki said, sweat beading her forehead as she swung a weighted rope up and over the branch of a tree, 'so that the children can swing on them.'

It was an effort that met with great success. Marlon, who had been apprehensive about the countryside, especially his introduction to the hens and to Maybelline, lost the last of his reserve, whooping and yelling like a banshee as he, Jimmy and Frankie had bets as to who could swing the highest and the furthest and Rags barked dementedly, egging them on.

'And tomorrow I want you to take me to buy a donkey.'

It was mid-afternoon and Primmie was lying in post-coital comfiness with Matt, in his brass-headed bed in Calleloe.

'Excuse me?' He rolled over, lying on one elbow, looking down at her with comic disbelief.

She giggled, her fingers playing slowly across his well-muscled chest and down towards his stomach. 'I want you to take me to buy a donkey. Jimmy said this morning at break-fast, "Ain't you got nuffink to ride here, missus?" and I had to admit that I hadn't. I also agree with him that I should have.'

'But he and the other children go home on Saturday!'

'True.' She moved her hand lower and saw, with gratification, that his eyes began to darken with desire again. 'But a donkey is obviously an essential for next year, when children will be staying regularly, and so I thought I'd buy one now, and make Jimmy happy. Do you know where I can get one from?'

'There's a donkey sanctuary on the outskirts of Penzance.' With that information out of the way, he bent his head and kissed her long and tenderly.

Primmie closed her eyes in happiness. She was fifty-two and the impossible had happened. She was in love again – and just as deeply in love as she had been with Ted.

'We can go tomorrow,' he said when he finally raised his head from hers. 'And we can take Jimmy and one of his cohorts with us, if you think they'd like to come.'

'I'm sure they'd love to.'

Their eyes held. Gently he cupped a full breast in a strong, capable hand. 'I love you, Primmie,' he said simply.

'Yes.' She smiled. 'I know.' She curled her legs round his, determined not to tell him yet that she was in love with him. It was a long time since she had embarked on a love affair and she wanted to take every step slowly in order to savour it. The relationship she and Matt were building between them was very special and she was determined that its foundations would be deep and solid. There was no need to rush things. In another week, then perhaps she would tell him that she loved him – and she would tell him that he was her peace and her future, for she was certain that he was.

For now, she merely drew his head down to hers again, whispering softly against his ear, 'Love me again, Matt. Please love me again.'

'And so I'll be in Paris for three days, maybe four, to see my consultant, Mr Zimmerman, and to have my monthly blood transfusion,' Geraldine said to Primmie the day before the children were to leave. 'There's no need to go into explanations with Kiki and Artemis. They both have so much going on in their lives at the moment that I doubt they'll even know I'm gone.'

It wasn't quite true, but certainly neither Kiki nor Artemis asked any awkward questions. For several days, as Kiki remained with Brett in his caravan at nearby Coverack and Artemis spent a great deal of her time at the art gallery with Hugo, Primmie almost had Ruthven to herself again. She used the time productively, able to appreciate, for the first time, just how much produce she was going to be able to garner from the orchard. As well as apple trees there was also a pear tree and a plum tree, its branches bending earthwards under the sheer weight of its fruit.

With Rags her companion whenever he got bored with watching Kiki and Brett working on the barn, she gathered the ripe plums into large plastic buckets and then later, listening to *Woman's Hour* on the radio, began the mammoth job of stoning them.

As she worked, her thoughts were full of Geraldine. When Geraldine had first told her what it was she was suffering from, and that two of the main drawbacks to a successful bone marrow transplant operation were the difficulty of getting a match, unless the donor was a sibling, and that transplants were generally only carried out on patients under forty, she had thought that the age difficulty was simply a case of priority being given to younger people, not that there were medical difficulties in a successful transplant in older patients. Now, thanks to the Aplastic Anaemia Trust website, she knew differently. Which meant that even if she succeeded in tracing Francis, and even if his bone marrow tissue was a suitable match, a transplant was still not a foregone conclusion.

She was still mulling the difficulty over as she sprinkled cinnamon on the stoned plums, doused them in clear honey and then began cooking them in relays in the oven.

When the telephone rang, and Geraldine's voice, taut with tension, said, 'Mr Zimmerman has found a bone marrow match for me and he's going to carry out the transplant,' she thought at first that she'd dozed off and was dreaming.

'But that's wonderful news! Mega news!' she gasped, as reality sank in.

'Isn't it just?' There was indescribable emotion in Geraldine's voice. 'I'll ring you again, Primmie, when I have further news. For the moment, just keep fingers crossed.'

As Geraldine rang off, Primmie sat down abruptly in the

rocking-chair, certain that her legs were going to give way. Geraldine was being given the chance of a full return to health – and it could very well be the only chance she would ever have.

'What are we going to do for Christmas?' Artemis asked a little prematurely at dinner that evening. 'Are we going to have Christmas dinner here, at Ruthven, with Hugo and Matt as guests?'

'Excuse *me*,' Kiki said heavily, before Primmie had the chance of replying, 'but aren't you forgetting someone? What about Brett?'

'And Brett, too, if he hasn't parents who will expect to see him for Christmas Day dinner.'

'He hasn't. But what about Primmie's kids, and yours? Won't they be expecting to spend Christmas with you?'

'Mine probably will be,' Primmie said, not sounding very sure. 'And I shall be inviting them, though Joanne and her husband nearly always spend Christmas Day with his parents and Millie usually goes abroad with whomever it is she's with at the time. With luck, Josh might come and stay for a few days and Lucy intends being home from Australia for Christmas.'

She looked across at Artemis. 'What about Orlando and Sholto, Artemis? Would you like to ask them to come and stay over Christmas? The more guests we have, the merrier it will be.'

'I'd love to ask them.' The familiar wobble was back in Artemis's voice. 'I know they've been a bit insensitive about things, but I do love them and I do miss them. They may even like to do a bit of house hunting with me. Did I tell you that I've spoken to all the local estate agents, detailing the kind of property I'm looking for?'

The conversation drifted on to other things and Primmie's thoughts went back to Geraldine. If Geraldine's transplant were a success, would Geraldine also be spending Christmas with them at Ruthven? And would Geraldine, too, like to invite someone to spend Christmas with her in Cornwall? Perhaps her French friend, Dominique?

* * *

If it hadn't been for her anxiety over what was happening in Paris, Primmie would have enjoyed the next couple of weeks. With the plums batched up in plastic containers and stacked in the deep freeze, she had turned her attention to poaching pears in red wine, spiced with cinnamon and cloves and sweetened with sugar. Artemis, too, had caught the autumn freezer and bottling bug.

'I've found a recipe for tomato chutney I'd like to try,' she said, 'It will put your glut of tomatoes to good use.'

Companionably, they had begun skinning the tomatoes, putting them in a large conserving pan with sugar, spiced white vinegar and a pinch each of salt, paprika and cayenne pepper. As the brew simmered and reduced, Artemis said, 'I think I'm happier now than I've ever been. It's incredible, isn't it, when only a short time ago I thought my world had come to an end?'

'It's not too incredible, Artemis. My world has changed pretty drastically, just as quickly, more than once in my life.'

Artemis stirred the tomato mixture, a frown puckering her forehead. 'But mine has only changed because of you, Primmie. If it hadn't been for you, I would still be in Gloucestershire with everyone I met knowing Rupert had dumped me for an upper-class bimbo – and I'd be mortified and unable to envisage any other kind of life but the one I'd led for the last thirty-two years. I certainly wouldn't be working as a receptionist in an art gallery. I wouldn't be surrounded by friends.' She paused, her cheeks flushed. 'And I wouldn't have met Hugo.'

'And Hugo is exceptionally special, isn't he,' Primmie said, more as a statement than a question needing an answer.

Artemis answered her, though. 'Hugo is *wonderful*.' Her eyes glowed. 'He's the kindest man I've ever met – not just to me, but to everyone he comes into contact with. I can't imagine why he's never been married.'

Primmie began putting bottling jars into the oven to heat. 'Perhaps it's because he's an incurable romantic who never found his dream package – though I think he's found it now.'

'Me, do you mean?' Artemis scooped a spoonful of the tomato mixture from the pan and put it on a cold plate to test its consistency. 'I do hope you're right, Primmie,' she said fervently. 'Oh God, I do hope you're right!'

A few days later, when shopping in Calleloe, Primmie went into the art gallery to see for herself just how much Artemis was enjoying her new lifestyle. Seated behind an elegant nineteenth-century French writing desk, surrounded by opulently framed works of art, Artemis looked utterly at home in her surroundings in a way Primmie had never seen her do before. Her pink and mauve floral silk dress was softly draped at the neck and three long strands of pearls lay at just the right depth on her magnificent bosom.

Set against the background of the Arnott Gallery's sumptuously over-the-top decor, all grey silk wallpaper and glittering chandeliers, Artemis looked almost understated. Primmie had heard Hugo tell Matt that American tourists were absolutely bowled over by Artemis, and now she could quite clearly see why.

'Primmie!' Artemis rose instantly from behind her desk, smelling fragrantly of Patou's Joy. 'I didn't know you were coming into Calleloe today. Have you time for a coffee or a white wine?'

Primmie put her basket of groceries down and flexed her aching arm muscles. 'It's only eleven o'clock, Artemis. Isn't it a bit early for wine?'

'Hugo says wine should always be offered to clients who look as though they're going to spend a lot of money – which usually means American clients.'

'Well, that rules me out. I'll have a coffee though, and a biscuit if you have any.'

While Artemis walked with poise born of her modelling days towards the rear of the gallery and the kitchen, Primmie, fearful she would find that her favourite picture had been sold, went in search of it.

It was still there.

Somehow, now that she, Artemis, Geraldine and Kiki had all been reunited, the large oil painting of the four girls in an Edwardian summer garden moved her even more than it had the first time she had set eyes on it. As she looked at two of the girls on the wide swing, the two who, one golden haired

350

and one titian haired, reminded her of Artemis and Kiki, she wondered what their lives had been like when they had reached Artemis and Kiki's age. Had they, like Artemis and Kiki, reached a moment in time when all seemed to be disappointment and unfulfilled dreams? And had they, as Artemis and Kiki were doing, discovered a whole new lease of life just when all seemed most hopeless?

'It's gorgeous, isn't it?' Artemis handed her a bone china cup of freshly percolated coffee, a bourbon biscuit resting in its accompanying saucer.

'It's us,' Primmie said simply, filling with emotion. 'It's us, when we were schoolgirls, sunbathing in Kiki's garden at Petts Wood. The two girls with their arms round each other are you and Kiki, and the dark-haired girl looking so coolly and clearly out of the picture, her head resting against the rope of the swing, is Geraldine.'

Artemis drew in a deep, unsteady breath. 'And that's you, looking towards the three of us, with a pale blue sash round your waist and a beribboned sun hat in your hand.'

'Except that our garden idyll wasn't in Edwardian times, but in the sixties, and we weren't wearing white broderie anglaise dresses, but either hideous Bickley High uniforms or skinny-rib jumpers and mini-skirts!'

Artemis gave a chuckle of reminiscence and then, still looking at the painting, said, 'I wonder who the girls were? I wonder what happened to them?'

It was an echo of her own thoughts. 'I don't know, Artemis,' she said, 'but I do know that this is my favourite painting in all the world.'

She was still thinking about the painting as she turned down the high-hedged track towards Ruthven, wondering if perhaps Hugo, who would know the provenance of the painting, could find out for her the identity of the four girls in their garden idyll.

As she rounded the last curve of the track, before reaching Ruthven's gates, she sucked in her breath, almost rigid with shock. Parked this side of the closed gates was Geraldine's Ferrari.

Her heart began to race. Geraldine wouldn't have returned

without telephoning first to say that she was doing so and that her transplant had been successful. Only if she had bad news would she not have been instantly on the telephone.

With hands clammy on the wheel, she came to a halt behind the empty Ferrari. There was no sign of Geraldine and, after glancing up the track leading to the house and seeing it empty, she trusted instinct, slammed her car door behind her and set off across the headland to the cove.

The instant she saw Geraldine's tall, ethereally slender figure, a silver-grey metallic raincoat tie-belted round her waist, the collar turned up in protection against the sea breeze, she knew that the transplant had failed. Despair was in every line of Geraldine's body and when, her hands thrust deep into the pockets of her raincoat, she raised her head at her approach, Primmie read everything she needed to know in the dark, hopeless depths of her eyes.

'It never happened, Primmie,' she said starkly as Primmie ran towards her. 'It seemed like a perfect match, but it wasn't.' And then, as Primmie's arms went round her, she lost all her tightly reined control, tears spilling down her cheeks at the knowledge that, for her, the sands of time were fast running out.

Life settled into a routine for the four of them. Geraldine remained at Ruthven for most of the time, conserving her strength. Kiki divided her time between Ruthven and Brett's caravan, seldom mentioning her three decades as a rock singer and, instead, talking with increasing knowledge about foundation excavations and different brick courseworks as she accompanied Brett as a glorified labourer on whatever building job he was working on. Artemis remained living in the flat above the gallery, spending part of every day acting as the gallery's receptionist and most of the rest of every day with Hugo, looking for a suitable house to buy.

'Though she's wasting her time, of course,' Hugo said to Matt, 'because when we marry she won't need a separate property of her own.'

'And when do you intend popping the question?' Matt asked, fascinated by his friend's decision to venture down the aisle after fifty-six years of bachelorhood.

'When her divorce comes through,' had been Hugo's confident reply. 'And uncontested divorces don't take long these days, so you'd better start thinking top hat and tails, buddy.'

At Christmas, Orlando and Sholto made Artemis radiantly happy by driving down to Ruthven on Christmas Eve for a three-night stay. It was a visit enlivened by Josh, who brought a great deal of south-east London Jack-the-Lad chutzpah with him.

'Your son and my two are never going to get on,' Artemis had said frantically before they had arrived. 'Orlando and Sholto are too much like Rupert – they're very snobbish.'

'It won't worry Josh,' Primmie had said serenely. 'He isn't easily put down. Just you wait and see.'

To Artemis's relief, Orlando and Sholto hadn't been stand-offish with Josh and were more than perfectly civil towards Hugo. They'd even been kind about Cornwall, saying that they intended coming back in early summer to check out the surfing.

There had been no Lucy or Dominique. Dominique had telephoned Geraldine from Rome, where she was spending Christmas with an Italian count who was, she assured Geraldine, on the verge of popping the kind of question that would make her a countess.

Lucy had telephoned on Christmas Eve, just as Primmie came into the house weighed down with armfuls of holly and ivy. 'I'm in Hawaii, Mum. I'm coming home the pretty way and it's taking longer than I thought,' Geraldine heard her say and then, a little while later, 'My goodness, Mum! You sound as if you're having an enormous house party. Who are Orlando and Sholto? They sound very top drawer. And who is Hugo and this Matt person you seem so fond of? I'm not going to come home to find you married again, am I?'

Primmie had laughed and told her not to be so silly, but Matt, who had taken the holly and ivy from her arms and was decorating the room with it, had also overheard the remark and Geraldine thought he looked more as if a secret were out, rather than embarrassed at Lucy having come to the wrong conclusion.

Later that evening, as Kiki went off with Brett to deliver presents to his married sister, who lived in Penzance,

Geraldine, Primmie, Matt, Artemis and Hugo went into Calleloe to a Christmas carol concert, whilst Orlando, Sholto and Josh checked out the local pubs.

On Christmas Day morning, while the younger members of the house party were still in bed, there was more than one surprise where presents were concerned.

'A Harley? A *purple* Harley?' Kiki said dazedly when Brett roared up to Ruthven at the crack of dawn astride her present. 'But how can you afford it? You *couldn't* have afforded it! It must have cost thousands!'

'Well, it's second-hand, but even so, it did rather stretch the budget,' Brett said with masterly understatement. 'I figured we'd be riding it together most of the time, though, and that we'd have a lot of fun with it.'

'A lot of fun?' Kiki threw her arms round him, ecstatic with joy. 'I'm going to have far more fun than that! I'm going to have the most fun I've had since I was fifteen!'

'A ring? Oh, Hugo. It's beautiful, absolutely beautiful.'

The square-cut antique sapphire, surrounded by diamonds, glittered on a bed of black velvet. Knowing that she was going to cry, grateful that they were alone in the Christmas-tree-decorated sitting room, Artemis lifted it from its box and slid it on to the fourth finger of her right hand.

Very gently, Hugo removed it and slid it on the fourth finger of her left hand.

As she sucked in her breath he lowered his powerful frame down on one knee, saying emotionally, 'I was going to wait till you were free before I did this, my darling, but I simply can't wait any longer to know what your answer is going to be. Will you marry me, Artemis? Will you light up my life as no one else could possibly do? Will you be my wife, as well as my friend?'

'Oh, yes!' Artemis didn't even try to restrain her tears of joy. She was loved again – and this time loved for the person she really was, not for the person she seemed to be. 'Oh yes, Hugo!' she said, taking hold of the large white Irish linen handkerchief he was, not for the first time, so dependably offering her. 'I want to marry you more than anything else in the world!'

* * *

Even before Primmie was faced with the stunning surprise of her own Christmas present, her morning had been joyously memorable. Whilst it was still dark she had milked Maybelline in the warm, electrically lit cow shed, and Black-Hearted Alice in her spanking new, equally modern convenience-equipped shed, hardly able to believe that her life had changed so drastically since Christmas last year, when she'd been a Londoner hardly knowing the front end of a cow from the back.

She'd walked out of Alice's cosy sleeping quarters just as Brett had roared up on the Harley.

From then on, after he and Kiki had sped euphorically off for a Christmas-morning ride, she had had her holly-and-ivy-decorated kitchen to herself for an hour or so. Listening to carols on Classic FM she had stuffed the turkey with the chestnut stuffing Artemis had made before going to the Christmas Eve carol service, rubbed it all over with butter, layered its breast with bacon rashers, covered it loosely in foil and put it in the oven.

By the time Hugo arrived, a small gold-wrapped present in one hand, she was peeling potatoes.

She didn't find herself peeling them for very long. When Artemis rushed into the kitchen to tell her that she and Hugo were engaged, all Christmas-dinner preparations were put on hold.

Orlando and Sholto were woken by their mother announcing her news. Geraldine was woken by Primmie with the same news.

As a bleary-eyed Orlando and Sholto manfully made it downstairs in order to toast their mother and her fiancé in champagne, Matt had arrived and even a hungover Josh had put in an appearance.

It was after all the congratulations had been given that Matt said, 'And now it's time for me to give you your present, Primmie.'

'Now? In front of everyone?' she had said, bemused. 'Can't it wait until after I've made the bread sauce?'

'Absolutely not. But I can't bring it into the sitting room unless I blindfold you first.'

Giggling, aware that everyone seemed to be in on the secret

but herself, Primmie allowed herself to be blindfolded with the turquoise silk scarf Geraldine had been wearing.

'Right,' Matt said authoritatively. 'Now you must sit down on the sofa, Primmie.'

Primmie did as she was told, aware that something heavy was being brought into the room and that a lot of activity was going on.

Geraldine sat down on one side of her and took hold of her hand, and Artemis sat down on the other side of her and took hold of her other hand.

'Right,' Matt said again. 'Now this present is a bit of a concerted effort, Primmie. I wouldn't have known how much you wanted this if Artemis hadn't told me. And I wouldn't have been able to buy it unless Hugo had lowered its price to one I could afford. It does, though, come with all my love, dearest Primmie – and all my thanks, for having changed my life far more than I could ever have imagined.'

From behind her, with one hand lovingly on her shoulder, he took off her blindfold.

In front of her, hanging in luminous, jewel-coloured glory, was *Summer Memory.*

Disbelief, gratitude and radiant joy flooded through her in so many successive waves that for a moment she thought she was going to do an Artemis and burst into tears.

Covering Matt's hand with hers, she turned her head, looking up into his ruggedly handsome face. 'Thank you so much, Matt,' she said sincerely. 'It's the most beautiful, *wonderful* Christmas present anyone has ever given me.'

After Christmas was over, life settled into a domestic routine that Primmie would have found blissful if it hadn't been for her escalating anxiety where Geraldine was concerned. At the end of January, Geraldine made another trip back to Paris, to see Mr Zimmerman, but this time there was no telephone call from her saying that there was news of a bone marrow match.

'Just what *is* the matter with Geraldine?' Artemis said to her as they tramped together across frost-rimed grass towards the hen arks. 'She's constantly tired, bruises as soon as you look at her, has nosebleeds more often than anyone I've ever known. When I ask her, she just says that she's anaemic, but it must be something else, surely?'

Wishing desperately that she could share her burden of knowledge and knowing she couldn't possibly break her word to Geraldine, Primme slid the door of the nesting boxes back and said; 'Geraldine does have anaemia, Artemis. Truly.'

'Then her doctor should prescribe iron tablets for her. There's a herbalist in Calleloe. I'm going to go in there tomorrow and see what he advises.'

The next morning, just as she was about to leave the gallery's flat, the telephone rang.

She put down her handbag and lifted the receiver, expecting it to be Hugo.

'Artemis?' The voice was young, female, cut-glass and so distressed as to sound on the verge of hysteria. 'It's Serena Campbell-Thynne. There's been an accident. Rupert was thrown from his horse and it rolled on top of him. He's . . .' She broke off, sobbing, and someone else, a man, took the telephone from her and said, 'Mrs Gower? Rupert is badly hurt and he's asking for you. He's in Bristol Royal Infirmary, in intensive care.'

Artemis could feel herself swaying as if she were about to faint. 'The boys . . . Orlando and Sholto . . . do they know? Are they with him?'

'Orlando is on a ski-ing trip in America. He's been contacted and is on his way back to Britain. Your younger son is at the hospital.'

In a daze Artemis tried to grasp what was being said to her. 'Is Rupert's life in danger? I'm sorry, but you're not being very clear.'

'He's in a critical condition,' the man said again, not answering her question, 'and he has asked to see you.'

'Then I'll be there. It will take me about three hours.'

When she severed the connection, she immediately telephoned Hugo. 'It's Rupert,' she said unsteadily, aware that she was shaking with shock. 'He's been badly hurt. Perhaps fatally hurt – whomever it was who spoke to me said that Orlando was flying home from America. He wouldn't do that, would he, unless Rupert were in danger of dying?'

357

It was a question Hugo couldn't possibly answer. Aware that his beloved angel was in no state to be driving to wherever her estranged husband had been hospitalized, he said merely, 'I'll be right with you,' and put the phone down.

Seated beside him as he drove at ninety miles an hour in the outside lane of the motorway, tears rolled down Artemis's cheeks.

'I'm not distressed because I'm still in love with him,' she said, clutching a familiar white linen handkerchief in her hands. 'But I do still have some feelings for him. How could I not when we were married for thirty-two years? And he wants to see me. I won't be able to bear it if it's because he wants to say sorry. Rupert *never* says sorry. The word just isn't in his vocabulary.'

At the hospital, clutching hold of Hugo's arm, Artemis allowed herself to be led, with rising apprehension, into the intensive care unit. In the waiting room attached to it were Sholto and Serena.

'Dad's been badly crushed,' Sholto said, white faced. 'He's had surgery but it's going to be a miracle if he pulls through.'

Artemis looked across at Serena and barely recognized her. There were deep circles carved under her eyes and her breath was coming in great shuddering gasps.

Leaving Hugo with Sholto she was escorted by a nurse into the room where Rupert lay.

He was attached to a plethora of monitoring screens, tubes and drips, an oxygen mask over his nose and mouth, his eyes closed.

Weak kneed she sat down on the chair beside the bed. Not for one minute did she think he was going to ask her, if he recovered from his injuries, to give their marriage another go. Instead, she was certain that he was going to apologize to her for his years of unfaithfulness and the way he had so insensitively and abruptly ended their rocky marriage.

'Rupert?' Her voice was a hoarse whisper. 'I'm here, Rupert. It's Artemis.'

His eyes flickered open.

Very lightly, she covered his hand with hers.

He made a gutteral noise in his throat and the nurse stepped forward, lifting his oxygen mask away from his mouth.

'A . . . bugger,' he said with enormous effort. 'Bloody horse . . .' He closed his eyes again, rallying strength. When he opened them again, he said, 'There's something I have to tell you, Artemis.'

His words were rasping and slurred.

Tears blurred her eyes. 'It doesn't matter, Rupert. I don't want an apology. I just want you to recover.'

He made a slight movement of his head. 'It isn't to do with you and me, Artemis.' He shut his eyes again and then, his eyes still shut, he said, 'It's to do with Destiny.'

Artemis felt as if the world had stopped revolving. It was so unexpected, so moving. He'd never granted himself the comfort of talking about Destiny and now, when he thought he might be dying, he wanted to do so. And he wanted to do so with her.

He opened his eyes again, the expression in them one of quite dreadful reluctance.

'She isn't dead,' he said after an interminable pause. 'I'm sorry, Artemis. I acted for the best. She didn't drown. She didn't die. Destiny is alive.'

Twenty-Nine

For a second she just sat, poleaxed, hardly able to grasp that after all these years of resolutely not uttering Destiny's name he so desperately wanted her still to be alive that his partially anaesthetized brain had made the wanting a reality to him.

Leaning towards him, she said gently, 'You're hallucinating, Rupert. Please stop trying to talk. The effort is too much for you. If you want me to stay here at the hospital, I will. Sholto is here and Orlando is—'

He interrupted her by making another hideous guttural sound in his throat. 'Sweet Christ, Artemis,' he said on a gasp, when he at last managed to speak. 'Just for once, listen to me, will you? Really listen.'

The little jagged green lines running continually across the screen of the nearest monitor increased in unevenness. Artemis glanced at it fearfully, wondering if she should ask the nurse if she should leave.

'I was never going to tell you . . . I couldn't see the point.' He sucked in another deep breath, making a whistling sound as he did so. 'It was your fault, Artemis. Destiny should have been in a home for children with special needs and you wouldn't even consider it. You wanted to saddle our home with a child who needed far more attention than our way of life could tolerate. It was unfair to you. Unfair to me. Unfair to her. And so I resolved an untenable situation the only way I knew how. When you were in hospital, unable to leave it, I put Destiny into a long-term care home – and told you that she'd drowned in Spain.'

He broke off, his eyes closed, the lines on the monitor dancing wildly.

'Right. That's enough,' the nurse said abruptly. 'Please leave the room, Mrs Gower. Please leave immediately.'

Artemis did no such thing.

She gripped Rupert's hand tight, desperate for him to open his eyes, to remain conscious. 'Where did you leave her?' she demanded frantically. 'If you're telling me the truth, where did you leave her?'

In her anxiety to be near enough to hear even a whisper in reply, she half slid and half fell off the chair on to one knee beside him. 'Rupert! Please God! What home did you put her in? Where is she now? *Where is our daughter?*'

There wasn't a reply, or even the merest hope of her remaining to hear any reply he might make.

An entire team of doctors and nurses surged into the room, most of them concerned only with Rupert, two others heaving her to her feet and frogmarching her back into the waiting-room.

'What on earth . . .' Hugo began, hurrying forwards to extricate her from their grasp.

'What's happened?' Serena shrieked. 'Is Rupert dead?'

'She's alive,' Artemis said incoherently to Sholto as Hugo

put a steadying arm round her. 'Destiny is alive. Your father's just told me. She's alive and he's always known she was alive.'

It was the moment she should have collapsed into tears, but for the first time in her life she was beyond tears, she was beyond anything but the most profound, mind-numbing shock.

'And Dad?' Sholto hadn't the least interest in whether an adopted sister he had never known was alive or not. 'Why has everyone gone rushing in to him? Has he taken a turn for the worse? He hasn't died, has he?'

Numbly Artemis shook her head. 'She's alive,' she said again, this time to Hugo. 'My little girl is *alive!*'

Hugo, who hadn't a clue what she was talking about, but was aware from the fevered activity going on in the intensive care room that cataclysmic bad news was probably imminent, said, 'Let's go out into the corridor, darling. You can talk to me there. Explain to me there.'

As she leaned against him so heavily he was almost totally supporting her, he led her out of the waiting room and into the relative privacy of the corridor. 'What daughter, darling?' he asked as she started to tremble violently. 'The little girl you told me about who drowned when she was only five years old? How can she still be alive?'

Artemis's trembling increased. She was juddering now, shaking from head to toe. 'He did it. Rupert did it,' she said through chattering teeth. 'She was a slow learner . . . and he hated it. He was ashamed of it. He wanted us to put her in a home. But she didn't *need* to be in a home, Hugo. She was loving and happy and quite clever at some things . . . things like drawing and painting. And he . . . Rupert . . . he took her to Spain . . . to our villa in Spain . . . and he telephoned me with the news that she'd died . . . drowned . . . and she hadn't. She hadn't!'

The horror of what she was telling him almost took his breath away. 'You mean he *lied* to you? But how could he lie about a thing like that and get away with it? You have her death certificate, don't you? And you know where she is buried?'

At the blank incomprehension he met with, he knew just how easy it would have been for Rupert to have pulled the wool completely over Artemis's eyes. Without her having to say anything, he knew that Artemis had never given a thought to a death certificate; that she'd believed Destiny had been cremated.

'He put her in a home. He put our five-year-old little girl into a home *and left her there*!' As Artemis thought of how bewildered, how frightened Destiny must have been, how she must have cried and cried for her, she thought she was going to faint. 'How could he do such a thing, Hugo? How could anyone be so cruel, so wicked . . . ?'

'Dad's dead.' A door whisked shut behind Sholto as he stood staring at his mother in Hugo's protective arms. 'I think I should stay with Serena, don't you?' he said tightly, his face drawn and white. 'She probably needs me to be with her far more than you do.'

As he turned abruptly away from her, Artemis made no attempt to run after him, or to call him back. She could only think of one thing, and it wasn't Sholto's grief.

'He didn't tell me where he left her!' Her eyes met Hugo's, appalled. 'How can I find her, Hugo, if I don't know where he left her?'

He tightened his arm round her and began walking her down the corridor towards the stairs and the exit.

'We'll find her,' he said confidently. 'The first thing to do is to contact whatever organization you have in Britain that is the equivalent of America's Missing Persons Bureau.'

Artemis stopped walking, swinging round to face him. 'No,' she said, as a new realization hit her with all the force of a tidal wave. 'The first thing I have to do is to tell Primmie!'

It was seven o'clock when they turned in through Ruthven's opened gates. Behind cosily drawn curtains all the downstairs lights were on, so that in the otherwise bleak emptiness of the headland the house looked as glowingly welcome as a house on a Christmas card.

'How am I going to tell her? How can I possibly prepare her for such earth-shattering news?' she said as Hugo drove into the yard and Rags came bounding out of the house to greet them.

Hugo, who was still rallying from the shock of learning that Destiny had been Primmie's love child, said gravely,

'You can't prepare her, Artemis, darling. You couldn't prepare anyone for news such as this. Just tell her straight out, as simply and directly as possible.'

They entered the house by the side door, walking through the porch and into the kitchen. Primmie, Kiki, Geraldine, Brett and Matt were all seated at the gingham-clothed table. Primmie was ladling soup into bowls from a large, steaming soup tureen, Matt was cutting thick slices from a loaf still warm from the oven and Brett was pouring generous amounts of red wine into glasses.

'You're just in time,' Primmie said, rising to greet them and still smiling at something Brett had just said. 'The soup is carrot and parsnip, but I've some pâté in the fridge, if you'd prefer it.'

'No. The soup is fine, Primmie.' Artemis stood in the welcoming warmth of the kitchen, aware that Rags was again settling himself down by the Aga. Through lips that were dry, she said, 'I think you should sit down, Primmie darling. I have some news. Monumental news.'

It certainly wasn't the way she would have prepared her for the news that Rupert had died, and Primmie stared at her in bewilderment.

'Good news? Bad news?' she asked, nervously aware that though Artemis's eyes were shining with fevered excitement, her face was a shell-shocked white.

'I want you to listen to me very carefully, Primmie, because when Rupert told me this, I didn't at first believe it. I couldn't. It's both too terrible and too wonderful.'

Brett put the wine bottle down and, pushing his chair away from the table a little, placed his ankle on his knee. Kiki lit a cigarette. Geraldine took a drink of her wine, a slight frown puckering her forehead. Matt merely looked towards Primmie, concerned.

Slowly Primmie sat down. 'OK,' she said, her nervousness growing. 'Go on.'

Artemis licked her lips and then said, very quietly and steadily, 'Destiny didn't drown twenty-five years ago, Primmie. When I said to you that as a toddler she was a little slow, it wasn't the whole truth. Destiny had learning difficulties. They

363

weren't severe, but Rupert was embarrassed by them. He didn't want people assuming he'd fathered a child who wasn't academically bright. When I was in hospital after my car accident in 1978, he took advantage of the situation by putting Destiny in a long-term care home, phoning me, from Spain, and telling me that she had drowned.' She licked her lips again. 'He told me all this just minutes before he died. It must be the truth. It *has* to be the truth.'

For a long, long moment time stood still.

No one moved.

It seemed to Artemis that no one even breathed.

Then Primmie said devoutly, 'Oh God.' Slowly and unsteadily she rose to her feet. With tears blinding her eyes, she stepped towards Artemis. 'I can't believe this is happening. I can't believe I'm living through this.' Tears rolled down her cheeks. 'If Destiny is alive, then we can find her, Artemis. We can find her and have her in our lives again.'

With sudden burning overwhelming hope, they fell into each other's arms.

Brett, aware something momentous had happened, but not certain what, said in an undertone to Kiki, 'Who is this Destiny person? Is she Artemis's daughter? Her sister?'

Kiki ran a hand through her spiky red hair. 'No,' she said, for once looking her age. 'She was Primmie's illegitimate child. Artemis adopted her. When she was five years old, on holiday in Spain with her father, she drowned. Or he said that she had drowned.'

'Jeez.' As Primmie and Artemis continued to cling to each other, sharing the most profoundly emotional moment of their lives, he said, 'Pretty traumatic, discovering your dead child isn't dead at all. No wonder they've both gone to pieces.'

'And me,' Kiki said, looking dazed. 'Inside, I'm all in pieces, too.' She reached out for his hand. 'I never knew her, but Destiny was my half-sister. The only sister, of any sort, I've ever had.'

As Brett took on board what this meant where Primmie and Kiki's father's relationship had been concerned and stared at her, round eyed, Matt said to Hugo, 'The first thing we're going to have to ascertain is whether Artemis's husband put Destiny in a care home *before* going to Spain, or afterwards.'

'If it was before, finding her should be relatively simple.' Hugo opened a cupboard where he knew he would find a bottle of Bell's. 'How old will she be now? Twenty-nine? Thirty?'

'Thirty,' Geraldine said, as Hugo put the bottle of whisky on the table, adding quietly, so that Artemis and Primmie shouldn't hear, 'And if Rupert put her in a care home in Spain, then finding her won't be simple at all, Hugo.'

She kept quiet about her worst fear, which was that Rupert Gower had offloaded his adopted daughter in Spain under a different name to her birth name. It wouldn't have been hard for him to do so. Rupert had always had money – money that had quite obviously paid for Destiny's care for years and years. And money would have enabled him to do anything he'd felt was necessary to prevent his action ever being discovered.

As to whether Rupert had continued paying for residential care once Destiny had reached adulthood, that depended on just how severe her learning difficulties were. Artemis had always insisted that they were slight. Rupert had judged them to be severe enough to be an embarrassing social handicap. Where the truth lay was impossible to know. If, however, Rupert had still been paying residential fees, then details of the payments would, presumably, be amongst his personal effects – and as Artemis was his widow, there would be no problem about her having access to them.

The same thoughts were obviously going through Hugo's mind, for as Artemis and Primmie finally drew apart, he said, 'As your husband's next of kin, you're going to have to go back to Gloucestershire in the morning, Artemis. However much you don't want to, there are arrangements it's down to you to make. And you need to go through all Rupert's personal papers before anyone else does so, just in case there should be information about Destiny in them, payments to an adult care home, that kind of thing.'

Artemis gazed at him blankly. 'But Destiny wouldn't need to be in a home now, Hugo. She's thirty. She's a woman. And she never needed special care. Truly she didn't.'

Matt and Geraldine exchanged glances, both of them aware that it was a catch-22 situation, for if Artemis was right, Destiny would be far harder to find.

Primmie said quietly, 'I'm going to take Rags for a walk. I need to be on my own for a little while.'

'But it's pitch black out there, Primmie.' The concern in Matt's amber-brown eyes deepened. ' If you need to be on your own, be on your own in the house. We can all go home. Geraldine can stay with Artemis.'

'No.' She shook her head. 'No, I don't want you to all go home. I just want to walk, and think, and to have Rags with me.'

She walked out of the kitchen into the porch and at the sound of her shrugging herself into Amelia's old Barbour, Rags roused himself and trotted after her.

Seconds later the outside door closed after them both.

'OK,' Hugo said, pulling a chair out for Artemis at the table. 'Let's get moving. With luck, there will be information amongst Rupert's papers that will lead us to Destiny pretty quickly. If there isn't, we're going to have to explore other search avenues. Ideas please.'

Once out in the cold darkness of the headland, Primmie raised her face to the starlit sky and took a deep, steadying breath. Her child was alive. The daughter she'd grieved for, for so long, was alive. And she was going to find her. Of that she hadn't a second's doubt.

With Rags at her heels, she set off down the track towards the gates. It was icily cold, and though the Barbour kept the wind out it wasn't particularly warm. She didn't care. She didn't care about anything but the breathtaking realization that a miracle had taken place. A miracle that should never, ever, have been necessary.

Rupert Gower had injured Artemis and her in a way that was so vast and terrible she wasn't sure if she would ever come to terms with it. He'd robbed both of them of a daughter. He'd cheated them of her childhood, her teenage years and the years of her young womanhood. And what he had done to Destiny was far, far worse.

Turning left at the gates, she headed across the moonlit headland towards the cove. When she thought of the crime Rupert Gower had committed against Destiny, depriving her of Artemis's unconditional love and supportive care, depriving her of her home, she was swamped by all-consuming rage.

Drawing great gasps of air into her lungs, she slid and slithered down the dunes to the soft crescent of luminous pale sand. Rupert was dead. What was done was done. What mattered now was not the past. What mattered was the present – and the future.

Facing the dark glitter of the sea, the night breeze tugging at her hair, she raised her face to the stars, praying that Destiny would re-enter her life – certain that when she did so she would never again leave it.

Next morning the whole atmosphere at Ruthven had changed. Instead of comforting routine, there was urgent activity. Artemis phoned to say that she and Hugo were driving back to Gloucestershire.

'Naturally I'm not going to be so insensitive as to parade Hugo in front of Orlando and Sholto at the funeral. He'll book into a nearby hotel and I'll have the comfort of knowing he's nearby and there if I need him. And I'm sure I shall need him. Orlando will help me with the funeral arrangements, of course, but my real priority is going to be gaining access to Rupert's personal papers, because there must be something amongst them that will give us a clue as to the home he left Destiny in, or where she is now. There *must* be.'

Kiki looked completely transformed as she ate toast and drank coffee on the hoof. 'Artemis told us last night, when you went for your walk, that Rupert's and her holiday villa was in Marbella,' she said to Primmie, pacing the kitchen, fired with a sense of purpose. 'Both Brett and I think it's more likely that Rupert took Destiny to Spain and put her in a care home there, rather than doing so in England. Regulations would most likely have been laxer, for one thing. '

'And so the records of residential care homes in the Marbella area need checking out,' Geraldine interposed from where, in a white-piped navy silk dressing-gown, she was putting slices of bread into the toaster.

'And they need checking out in person, not by phone.' Kiki patted the small leather travelling bag she'd brought down into the kitchen with her. 'Which is why Brett and I are setting off this morning for Spain.'

Primmie didn't even go through the motions of telling her that she couldn't possibly do such a thing. Childcare organizations in Spain were already on top of her investigative list.

'But will you be able to get a flight at such short notice?' she asked.

Despite the tension they were all feeling, Kiki grinned. 'We're not flying, Primmie. We're going on the Harley. And the way I ride it, we'll be there just as soon as going by plane!'

With Artemis and Hugo en route to Gloucestershire and Kiki and Brett en route to Spain, Primmie sat at the kitchen table with the telephone and pen and paper and Geraldine sat opposite her, her mobile in one hand, her black notebook open in front of her.

'I'll check out Destiny's medical card number with every possible government office,' Geraldine said. 'It's a long shot, but it might come off.'

'I'll start with the Salvation Army. They are the most experienced people I know when it comes to searching for missing family members.'

'You're going to need lots of copies of Destiny's birth certificate, Primmie,' Geraldine punched in a number on her mobile, 'so make a phone call to the Public Records Office as well.'

Primmie did so and then, after a long, exhaustive telephone call to the Salvation Army Missing Persons Programme, phoned Joanne, knowing that she, of all her children, would be best able to give calm, concrete help.

She wasn't let down.

'It is,' Joanne said flatly from her office in London, high above Hanover Square, 'the most terrible story I've ever heard. If it hadn't been that Rupert Gower obviously knew he was dying, he would never have told Artemis, would he?'

Primmie's silence was her reply.

Joanne didn't pull any punches. 'Then I'm glad he's dead. What he did was monstrous. Totally and utterly unforgivable. As for the copies of Destiny's birth certificate, don't wait to receive them in the post. I'll collect them and drive down to Cornwall with them. I want to see you, Mummy. I want to give you what support I can.' She paused and then said, 'As far as the Public Records Office is concerned, there may be another certificate there, apart from Destiny's birth certificate. If she is now thirty, she could have married. A recent marriage certificate would have her address on marriage on it. I'll do a search covering the last fourteen years – and I'll phone Millie with the news.'

'Thank you, darling. I'll phone Josh. I doubt he'll register just how cataclysmic Destiny still being alive is for me, but he'll be as supportive as he can be. And thank you for the idea of there possibly being a marriage certificate. If there is, it would be the best possible short cut to finding her.'

When she and Geraldine had rung every phone number they could think of that could possibly be useful, Geraldine took a break by taking Rags for a walk and Primmie switched on her computer.

The list of helpful websites was huge. Taking a deep breath, she logged on to the first of the sites her search engine had pulled up for her – Comprehensive People Search – and registered Destiny's details.

By early evening she was still ploughing through every website she could find, making notes of whatever advice they gave where searching for a missing person was concerned, registering Destiny's details time and time again.

It was so like what she had been doing for weeks past in trying to trace Francis that before logging off she switched to the American Missing Persons sites. There was no ticked box against Francis's name on any of those sites on which his name was posted; no messages waiting to be read.

Closing down all the sites, she opened her email. There was nothing there, either, apart from a cheery message from Lucy, this time from California, where she had stopped off after finally leaving Hawaii. Lucy always used internet cafés to send and receive messages. She pondered Lucy's hotmail address, wondering whether to tell her by email about Destiny or to wait until she next telephoned her, and decided that the news would be more appropriately given over the phone.

With that decision made, she continued to sit in front of

369

her computer, suddenly aware of the simplicity of hotmail addresses.

What would happen if she typed in Destiny's name as a hotmail address? It was an unusual enough name to perhaps not need other letters or figures after it. Lucy's email address was simply LucyDove@hotmail.com.

In the address line she typed in destinygower@hotmail.com, and the simple message *Please respond to sender*. And then, after a moment's thought, destinysurtees@hotmail.com, with the same message. Surtees was, after all, the name Destiny had been born under. Perhaps Rupert had put her in the care home under that name, not her adoptive surname.

Weary beyond belief, her neck and shoulder muscles aching after the long hours she had spent hunched over the telephone and the computer screen, she typed another address into a new message as an afterthought: francissheringham@hotmail.com. This time her message was a little longer.

> The Francis Sheringham I am seeking is the Francis Sheringham of Cedar Court, Sussex, England. Dearest Francis, if this reaches you, please, please contact me. I'm living at Ruthven, Calleloe, Cornwall, and this is very possibly a matter of life and death. Primmie.

Then, having done all she could possibly do for one day, she went back downstairs to make herself a restorative cup of tea.

Any hopes she'd had that Artemis would find documentation amongst Rupert's personal papers relating to Destiny were quickly dashed.

'There isn't a thing,' Primmie. My solicitor has been with me, making sure I have access to everything I should have access to, and it's a complete blank. The will is straightforward. Nothing left to Serena, because Rupert must have thought it unnecessary to alter his present will when it would have been null and void on our divorce. She isn't left high and dry, being a spoilt little rich girl, but Sholto still seems to think it unfair.'

Two weeks later, the funeral over and the house she had lived in for thirty-two years with Rupert locked up until it could be put on the market and sold as part of Rupert's estate, Artemis returned to Calleloe with Hugo to find that Kiki and Brett had drawn just as complete a blank in Spain and that Primmie's efforts with hotmail addresses had also come to nothing.

It was all very dispiriting.

'We may be in for a long haul, but we'll get there in the end, Primmie dearest,' Matt said, his heart hurting at the depth of her dejection. 'For the next few weeks let's cheer ourselves up at the thought of Hugo and Artemis's wedding. What date have they finally decided on? Is it Easter or May?'

It was May, and though there was no let-up where phone calls, emails, hours on the Net and telephone calls to government departments in their search for Destiny were concerned, there was at least the joy of a wedding to look forward to.

'Has Artemis told you that when she moves out of the flat and in with Hugo – which she's ridiculously refusing to do until they're married – Hugo is going to let Brett have the flat?' Kiki said to Primmie as Primmie came in from a rain-lashed yard after ensuring that her animals – including the donkey she'd acquired in September, when the children were with them – were snug and warm.

'That's smashing news, Kiki.' Primmie shook rain from her hair. 'The caravan can't be much fun in weather like this.'

'The caravan has been a haven almost as magnificent as Ruthven.'

Kiki rarely expressed depth of feeling and Primmie took advantage of her mood, 'You never talk about how you're now feeling, Kiki, but I'm assuming life isn't as bleak for you as it was when you arrived here.'

Kiki, seated cross-legged on one of the rag rugs Rags favoured, hugged her knees. 'It isn't. When I arrived I couldn't see the point in carrying on living – there simply didn't seem to be anything to carry on living for. The only thing was, when I actually stood on top of the cliffs I'd decided I'd throw myself from, I knew I could never do it. I didn't have the bottle. Because I was here, with you and Geraldine and Artemis, my failure to follow through mattered less and less. Ruthven has been a lifeline. I'd forgotten what regular living was like. And so things are OK now. I'm writing. I'd started

371

a novel of sorts months and months ago, which was getting nowhere. It is now. And Brett is ace. It helps.' Her solemnity vanished, 'Whether he'll still be around when I'm seventy-two and he's the age I am now, remains to be seen.' There was laughter in her voice. 'It wouldn't surprise me, though. I've every intention of being a very hip old lady!'

The next morning the rain had vanished and the January sky was a bright, hard blue. 'I'm going into Calleloe,' Primmie called out to Geraldine, who was, as was her habit nowadays until at least half past nine, still in bed. 'I'm out of soap powder and we need bacon and oil and a long list of other groceries. Is there anything you particularly need bringing in?'

'A newspaper, Primmie, please. Not a tabloid. And if Peggy Wainwright has some more coconut chocolate bars in stock, a chocolate bar.'

Primmie eased her faithful old Corsa down the rutted track to Ruthven's gates and then turned right, towards the main road, reflecting on how nice Joanne's visit to Ruthven had been. Everyone had taken to her immediately and the only cloud had been that Joanne had failed to find any trace of a marriage certificate for Destiny at the Public Records Office. It had been wonderful showing Ruthven off. Joanne had thought the barn conversion was absolutely brilliant – which it was. She'd been tickled pink at watching Maybelline and Black-Hearted Alice being milked, and had said about Matt, 'If he asks you to marry him, Mummy, for goodness sake say "yes".'

As she headed down into Calleloe, the Reverend Cowle's little Fiesta chugged past her, going in the opposite direction. She gave him a cheery wave, making a mental note to speak to him about Destiny. As a vicar, he might well have ideas as to what other methods they could use in searching for her. It occurred to her that, if Matt did ask her to marry him, John Cowles would be the person performing the service, just as he was going to perform the service for Artemis and Hugo in three months' time.

In Calleloe, she parked in the little car park near to the harbour and then crossed the road towards the post office. She was only going in there to buy Geraldine her bar of coconut chocolate – a delicacy no other shop in Calleloe sold – and was slightly annoyed to find a long queue ahead of her. When the unkempt, elderly man in front of her at last reached the counter, she breathed a sigh of relief. Hopefully he was only collecting his pension and in another couple of minutes she would have paid for Geraldine's bar of chocolate and be on her way to the grocers.

'I wonder if you can help me?' a voice no older than her own, and with a transatlantic twang in it, said to Peggy Wainwright.

Primmie sighed and tried to control her impatience. She should have realized he was a tourist by his overcoat, which, though shabby and none too clean, definitely had a look of American tailoring to it. His hair, too, was worn longer than any local man would have worn it. It had obviously once been fair, but was now so streaked with grey as to be almost white. Even though his shoulders were stooped, now that she'd heard his voice she mentally revised her assessment of him as being ancient. He was probably no older than Matt.

Deeply grateful that Matt was so physically fit and still so attractive, she'd stopped listening to the conversation taking place in front of her, and it was only when Peggy Wainwright said, 'Ruthven? Did you say it was Ruthven you needed directions to?' that she snapped out of her reverie.

'Yes. I'm trying to trace an old friend. Her name is Primmie. Her married name is, I think, Primmie Dove. Dove was part of her email address. When I knew her, though, her surname was Surtees.'

Blood began beating thunderously against Primmie's eardrums. It couldn't be. This almost frail, unkempt figure in front of her could not possibly be the Francis Sheringham who, when last she'd seen him, had looked like a courtier of Charles II. Common sense told her he wouldn't still look as he had all those years ago, but he couldn't possibly have changed so much. No one could.

'Well, aren't you in luck!' Peggy said to him gleefully. 'Because Primmie Dove is standing right behind you in the queue!'

In a moment that seemed to Primmie to take for ever, the figure in front of her turned round.

She was wrong in thinking that no one could possibly change so much. His hair at the front was even thinner and more lack-lustre than the hair on the back of his head. His eyes were bloodshot, his skin dull and heavily lined. But it was Francis. Without a shadow of doubt, it was Francis.

'Primmie? Dearest, dearest Primmie! I'd forgotten how wonderfully efficient British post offices could be. Ask for a name and they produce the person instantly.'

She began to laugh, weak with relief that beneath the phys-ical wreck he had become, the old charm and sense of fun were still there; dizzy with relief that she had found him.

'Oh, Francis, thank God you're here!' Uncaring of the number of people queuing behind her, she threw her arms round him, hugging him tight. 'Geraldine needs you so much, Francis. She needs you more than anything else in the world.'

His drew away from her, his face suddenly drawn, the skin tight over his cheekbones. 'Geraldine's here? In Calleloe, with you?'

'Yes. And don't run away, not until I tell you why she needs you.'

He waited – as did the rest of the queue and Peggy Wainwright.

'She needs the bone marrow of a close blood relation, Francis – and you're the closest blood relation she has. It doesn't necessarily mean that your bone marrow will be the match she needs, but there's a chance it will do. And it's the only chance Geraldine has got, Francis. Without a bone marrow transplant, she will die within the next few months. So you do see why I had to find you, don't you? You do see why it was so important that you came?'

Thirty

Once out in the street, he said tautly, 'What is Geraldine suffering from? Is it leukaemia?'

'Not exactly, though it's similar. It's something called aplastic anaemia. Her bone marrow is failing to produce blood cells and platelets.'

'What the devil are platelets?'

'They're something in the blood that helps form clots to stop bleeding.'

As he mulled this over in sombre silence, Primmie ignored the grocers and walked him across the road to the car park.

'Did you drive here?' she asked.

'Not a hope. Money isn't exactly coming out of my ears, Primmie. I got the cheapest flight I could get – Air India – and then a train to Helston and a bus from Helston to Calleloe.'

They'd reached the Corsa now and, as she unlocked the driver's door, he paused by the other side of the car. 'And to make the flight even cheaper, I bought a single. It was all I could afford.'

Their eyes held over the car's roof. 'You went to such lengths in response to an email from someone who, over thirty years ago, was only a casual friend, without even emailing back to find out why you were so needed?' she said, deeply moved.

He shot her a rueful smile. 'I did it because you said it was a matter of life and death, Primmie. And in the days when I knew you, I never knew you to exaggerate – and anyway, you were never just a casual friend. During the last thirty years I've had a whole barrowful of casual friends and you have nothing in common with any of them. You were always a real friend. I don't think you'd know how to be anything else.'

They got in the car, and not until he'd fastened his seat belt and the engine was engaged did she say, 'There's something you have to prepare yourself for, Francis. Kiki is living in Calleloe. She's at Ruthven now.'

He sucked in his breath, slamming his hand down hard on the dashboard like a driving instructor giving a learner emergency-stop practice. 'What the hell, Primmie! I'm not prepared for a confrontation with Kiki!'

'Neither was Geraldine when Kiki first showed up here.' Primmie continued driving uphill, out of Calleloe. 'It took a little time for their relationship to shake down into their old friendship, but it's done so. Things may be awkward between you and Kiki to begin with, but she's indifferent to the past and, under the circumstances, I think you'll find that you can tolerate her presence. '

She turned left on to the main road that was signposted Lizard Point.

'She's given up the rock-star scene, is heavily into writing a book and is living with someone I like very much. He's a local builder, much younger than her and one hundred per cent genuine. I think it's safe to say that she's changed since living in Calleloe. The old self-obsessed Kiki isn't half as much in evidence as she used to be.'

Francis didn't respond, but she could sense his tension.

As they drove the heavily wooded road towards the turn-off for Ruthven, she said, 'Where were you last living in America, Francis? What have you been doing? Why did you never return to England?'

'Thirty years in three minutes, Primmie? It's a bit of a tall order.'

He fell silent and she didn't push him. At last he said, 'For the last three years I've been living in Wisconsin, making a living by being a gardener. As to why I never came back . . .' He looked away from her and out of the window to where the coastline was visible through the now thinning trees. 'At first, after my break-up from Kiki, it simply wasn't an issue. I was into hard drugs and no way could I ever have put in an appearance at Cedar Court. The whole thing was out of control. It was out of control for years. The late 1970s to the early 1990s were a wasteland of addiction: first cocaine, and then heroin. It was self-destruction on a massive scale. Someone I met who knew me from London said they'd heard my father thought I was dead. It seemed the kindest way to leave it.'

'And now?' Primmie slowed down and turned off on to the single-track road that led across the headland.

'I don't know. I never wanted saddling with the responsibility and the debts of Cedar Court when I was young and fit, so I sure as hell don't want saddling with them now. If that issue could be resolved, I'd quite like to see the old man again. I know he's still alive. I used to anonymously check every year.'

'And family? Did you ever marry and have children?'

'God, no. My only experience of ever living with anyone for any length of time was with Kiki and that put me off the idea of long-term relationships for life. I was never marriage material, Primmie, though I was too young to realize that way back in the days when I intended marrying Geraldine. In 1992 I met someone who took me out of the gutter and helped me turn my life around. It was a sexual relationship I was totally committed to.' There was the merest pause and then he said, 'He died five years ago.'

She turned her head briefly from the track ahead of them, and as their eyes met he knew that she wasn't shocked – or surprised.

'Since then I've simply managed as best I can. No drugs, not even anything soft. No close friends either, more's the pity.'

'Did it never occur to you to contact Geraldine?'

'After what I did to her? Destroying her life's dream of having children who would be born and raised at Cedar Court – and of one of them inheriting it? I wouldn't have insulted her by even trying to contact her. I used to read the *International Herald Tribune* in order to keep up with the news in Europe and every so often I would see her photograph in the gossip column. She was always attending some embassy banquet or other on the arm of an ambassador or millionaire steel tycoon. So I'd bin the paper and get on with self-destructing – apart from this last few years when I'd bin the paper and get on with manuring a rose-bed or mulching clematis.'

Primmie drew to a halt at Ruthven's gates. 'Let's walk up to the house, not drive, and then I can introduce you to Maybelline, Black-Hearted Alice and Ned, en route.'

'Who are they?' he asked, vastly relieved at having a little more breathing space before the cataclysmic experience of being reunited with Geraldine. 'The local Mafia?'

Primmie giggled. 'Maybelline is a very gentle, very docile Jersey cow. Even if it has never occurred to you to fall in love with a cow, you will fall in love with Maybelline. Everybody does. Black-Hearted Alice is a nanny goat. The idea was that she'd be an extra attraction to the children-in-care I intend giving holidays to, but I came a cropper. One look from Alice's malevolent yellow eyes and no child in their right mind goes near her. Ned is a donkey. Matt and I bought him from a donkey sanctuary last September.'

'And who,' he asked, as they walked up a track flanked by a paddock on one side and grazing pasture on the other, 'is Matt?'

Primmie came to a halt at the paddock gate. 'Matt is my very special friend,' she said, her dancing eyes leaving him in no doubt as to the nature of the friendship. 'And now I think it would be a good idea if I left you here, whilst I break the news of your arrival to Geraldine. Ned is over there, in the far corner, but he'll be ambling over here any minute now to see if you have anything for him.'

Francis registered that the small donkey that had been head down, foraging in the long grass at the foot of the fencing, was now looking alertly across at him.

'What do you mean "break" the news to Geraldine that I'm here?' he asked, alarmed. 'Surely she knows you were trying to contact me?'

'No. Incredibly, it never seems to have occurred to Geraldine that, being her cousin, you are possibly the best chance of a bone marrow transplant that she has. And truth to tell,' she added, alarming him even more, 'I suspect Geraldine is of the same opinion as your father. I think she thinks that you are dead.'

When she entered the house by the side door, walking through the porch and directly into the big live-in kitchen, she was relieved to find Geraldine on her own.

'Kiki's Harley is in the yard, so I'm assuming she's still here,' she said, as Geraldine automatically pushed the book she had been reading to one side and rose to her feet to make Primmie a cup of tea.

'She's in the sitting room, sulking because Brett is doing mega high roof work in Truro and says it's too dangerous for her to be working alongside him.'

To prove her point, as she finished speaking the sound of Jerry Lee Lewis's 'Whole Lotta Shaking Going On' suddenly blasted into life in the sitting room.

'Where's the shopping?' Having filled the kettle, Geraldine registered that Primmie was unladen.

'I got diverted. I've got your chocolate bar, though.' She fished it out of her coat pocket and put it on the kitchen table. 'I have some news for you, Geraldine. It's pretty momentous so take a few deep breaths will you? I don't want you collapsing on me.'

Geraldine put the kettle down on the Aga with a clatter. 'Destiny? There's news? You've found her?'

'No.' With great difficulty Primmie steadied her voice. 'No, Geraldine, but I've found someone else. Francis is down by the paddock, talking to Ned. I think he'd like you to join him.'

For a terrible second she thought she'd misjudged the blunt way she'd broken the news. Geraldine gave a small, animal-like moan, her face – always pale – draining almost to translucence.

'If you'd like me to go with you . . .' Primmie began uncertainly.

She needn't have bothered.

'Oh . . . my . . . God! Oh, my *dear* God!' Geraldine pushed herself away from the Aga and shot past Primmie at the speed of light.

'Francis!' Primmie heard her calling as she ran across the yard and on to the track leading down towards the paddock. *'Francis! FRANCIS!'*

Primmie stood for a moment or two, waiting for her heart-beats to approach something like normality, and then walked out of the kitchen, down the corridor and into the sitting room.

Kiki was slouched in the wing-chair, a trousered leg slung over one of its arms, looking as mutinous as a teenager.

Primmie turned the volume down so that Jerry Lee Lewis, instead of blasting their eardrums, could hardly be heard.

'What is it, Prim? You've got your "I've Got News For You" expression on.'

'That's because I have.' She hesitated for a moment, praying that she was right in her assumption of how Kiki was going to take the news. 'As well as trying to find Destiny, I've privately been trying to find someone else, Kiki.'

Kiki shifted her position in the chair, her cedar-red hair catching the February sun streaming through the window.

Primmie hesitated again. Until now she'd respected Geraldine's wish that Artemis and Kiki not be told just how

379

ill she was. Now, though, in order for Kiki to appreciate how necessary Francis's presence was, Kiki was going to have to be told.

'Geraldine's illness is far more critical than she's made out to you and Artemis,' she said, seeing with relief that Kiki no longer looked as if her attention was on Jerry Lee Lewis. 'If she doesn't have a bone marrow transplant her life expectancy can be measured in months – and for any chance of success, especially at her age, the transplant needs to come from a sibling. As the nearest thing to a sibling that Geraldine has is Francis, I've been trying to contact him. And succeeded. He's here now. Being reunited with Geraldine down by the paddock.'

There were times when Primmie felt that Kiki really came into her own, and this was one of them. There was no need to ask her not to make a problem or a drama out of Francis's presence. All Kiki was interested in was Geraldine.

'Why didn't she say how ill she is?' she demanded, springing to her feet. 'Why didn't she say she needed a transplant? I could have samples of my bone marrow taken to see if it would match. I can still do that. Where do I have to go to have it done?'

'Francis's bone marrow is a far likelier bet, Kiki. Unrelated bone marrow tissue rarely, rarely matches. Volunteer donor registries worldwide have Geraldine on file as needing a match and so far there's only been even one near miss.'

Kiki strode across to the window to see if she could catch a glimpse of Geraldine down by the paddock. What she saw was Geraldine with a frail-looking, shabbily dressed man who looked to be at last fifteen years her senior. 'Wow!' she said expressively. 'If that's Francis, then I wouldn't have recognized him on the street in a hundred years.'

'It isn't going to be difficult for you, meeting him again?'

'In what way?' Kiki looked at her blankly. 'It's *decades* since we were an item. All I want from Francis Sheringham now is help for Geraldine.'

'And so Geraldine and Francis are, as we speak, on their way to see Geraldine's consultant, Mr Zimmerman, in Paris,' Kiki said to Brett as, naked in the cosy warmth of their caravan, she straddled him, moving in slow, languorous rhythm.

'And this bone marrow tissue that her cousin is going to have taken? What are the chances of it being a successful match?'

'According to Primmie, heaps and heaps higher than a random match, but not as much of a dead cert as a brother or a sister match.'

Propped by a couple of pillows and with his hands folded behind his head, Brett kept tight rein on the almost unbearable sexual excitement she was arousing in him and regarded her with deep fascination.

It was a fascination she had exerted on him from the moment they had met and which, in the five months since then, hadn't waned. When she'd told him about Primmie having contacted Geraldine's long-lost first cousin – a cousin she had, some thirty years ago, been on the point of marrying – and when he had idly queried as to why their marriage had never taken place, she had said simply, 'Because I ran off with him on the wedding morning. We were together for quite a few years – I can't remember how many – but the experience was no very big deal. His being my manager and agent and my being his ticket to glitz and glamour was really what our relationship was about. I thought our being a couple would mean he'd work his arse off for me, but my judgement, as always, was way off beam. All Francis wanted was to be out of his head on cocaine.'

She'd been just as prosaic when she'd explained the Primmie/Artemis/Destiny situation to him. 'Primmie fell in love with my father – who was divorced – and he with her. It would have been all wedding bells and confetti, but I took exception to the prospect of having Primmie as my stepmother and told my father so in no uncertain terms. I didn't know, though, that Primmie was having his baby – and neither did he.

'He called the wedding off. Primmie never told him she was pregnant. Artemis and Rupert couldn't have children and when Destiny was born they adopted her. Everything in the garden was lovely until Destiny showed signs of having a learning disability. Rupert was mortified at the thought of people knowing his daughter wasn't very bright – especially

381

as he seems to have taken the line that she wasn't really his daughter, being adopted – and he solved his problem by offloading her into a residential care home, covering his action with his "she's drowned in Spain" story. None of which,' she had finished bluntly, 'would have happened if I hadn't emotionally blackmailed my father into not marrying Primmie.'

'Jeez,' he'd said expressively. 'So you fucked up both Geraldine's *and* Primmie's life. What about Artemis? How did you trash things for her?'

'I didn't,' she'd said, affronted. 'Just the opposite. When we were teenagers I probably saved Artemis's life.'

The story of the Vietnam anti-war battle in Grosvenor Square had been light relief after some of the other glimpses into her past.

What intrigued him about her was that, though carelessly amoral and endlessly thoughtless, there was no real meanness in her. The other thing that constantly intrigued him was her attitude to their own, where their ages were concerned, bizarre relationship. She was twenty years his senior and yet not once had he been aware of her being self-conscious about it. She never needed her confidence boosting where her looks or figure were concerned. In the past, he'd had girlfriends who'd constantly needed to be told that their bums weren't big, or that they truly were the most glam babe in the room. Kiki just took it for granted that she was head turning. Which she was. And she also took it for granted that he should consider himself bloody lucky to be her boyfriend. Which he did.

There was unfettered pleasure in his eyes as, having imparted all her information re Geraldine and Francis, Kiki tilted her head back, her eyes half-closed, and began to move her hips with increasing speed.

Her breasts were small and firm, her nipples a dark wine red. He removed his hands from behind his head to cup them and then, as she gave a soft, vibrant moan, abandoned all thought of anything but lovemaking.

With Geraldine and Francis en route for Paris, Primmie took a solitary walk across the headland, not to the cove, but to the church. When she'd first arrived at Ruthven the church doors had been firmly locked on all but a few, rare occasions. Since asking the Reverend John Cowles if she could periodically polish the pews and the brasswork, she had been entrusted with a key, and regular quiet time within it was now something she treasured.

After arranging a posy of snowdrops in the small vase that stood near the foot of the altar, she seated herself in one of the lavender-waxed pews, her thoughts on Geraldine. 'Please, Lord,' she prayed silently, 'please let Francis's bone marrow tissue be a perfect match for Geraldine. Please let her be able to have a successful transplant. Please. *Please.*'

In the days that followed, she kept herself busy by making marmalade with the Seville oranges that were still glutting the greengrocers in Calleloe.

'Are you going into full-time production, sweetheart?' Matt asked, stepping into the kitchen to be met by the sight of preserving pans, muslin sieves, a huge stoneware bowl, piles of fruit, stacks of sugar and a vast array of glass jars. 'Because unless you are, we're going to be eating marmalade from now until doomsday.'

'No we're not. Peggy's been too busy to make marmalade this year, and so she's going to be taking at least a dozen jars from me.' With her back towards him, she continued stirring the contents of her preserving pan. 'John Cowles is unmarried and so he'll be grateful of a gift of half a dozen jars – and I'm sure he'll have lots of parishioners who'd be happy to be given a gift of home-made marmalade. Artemis is too busy making wedding plans to be knee-deep in oranges, so she'll be grateful for some as well. All of which means that far from being snowed under with it, we're going to be lucky if we have enough to see us through the year. That's nice,' she added, as he kissed her on the back of her neck.

As the pungent aromatic scent of oranges filled the kitchen, Matt said, 'Hugo has asked me to be best man. Did you know?'

'No, but I'm very pleased. Will you have to hire yourself a morning suit?'

'I expect so. I can't imagine either Hugo or Artemis settling for anything less.'

Primmie turned away from the Aga and gave him a kiss.

'You'll look splendid. Almost as splendid as Kiki is going to look as her maid of honour.'

Matt's eyes creased at the corners. 'Speaking of which, I didn't see the Harley when I arrived. If she isn't in, could we perhaps take advantage of the fact?'

Primmie gave the preserving pan an assessing look, judged that its contents would be quite safe left to their own devices for a half hour or so and, sliding her hand into his, said equably, 'What a jolly good idea, Matt.'

The next few weeks, as February gave way to March, were taut with tension. First came Geraldine's telephone call to say that Francis's bone marrow tissue was a match. Then came a moment so dreadful she never knew how she survived it.

'They're not going to use it.' Francis's voice over the telephone had been raw. 'It's deemed unsuitable because of my long history of drug abuse. But there's another donor, Primmie. They've found a match. A transplant *is* going to take place.'

Even after the transplant had taken place, the tension was excruciating. Not until Francis finally telephoned to say that there was no longer any fear of the graft being rejected did Primmie give way to boundless relief and joy.

There was no quick return to Cornwall for Geraldine. 'Mr Zimmerman wants me where he can keep a close eye on me for a few weeks,' she said over the telephone to Primmie, 'and so I'm back in my house in the Opera quarter and Francis is staying with me. Since being here, he's been in contact with his father and when I do get the final all-clear we'll be paying a visit to Cedar Court before continuing on down to Ruthven for Artemis and Hugo's wedding.'

'But is she coming back to Cornwall just for the wedding, or for good?' Artemis said to Primmie, when Primmie relayed Geraldine's news to her. 'And do you think she and Francis might get back together?'

Primmie, remembering the depth of feeling there had been in Francis's voice when he had told her of his lover who had died, said, 'I hope she's coming back to Cornwall for good, but you can forget about a wedding where Geraldine and Francis are concerned, Artemis. They both know now that marriage isn't what their relationship is about. If they live together, it will be as cousins and friends.'

'Then though it's selfish of me I hope they do so in Calleloe and not Cedar Court. Isn't it wonderful news that Lucy will most definitely be home from her travels by the end of April and that she'll be at my wedding, and that Sholto and Orlando are both coming down to Cornwall for it? There have been times when I thought Sholto might cry off, but he seems quite happy now about my marrying Hugo. Perhaps it's because he has a steady girlfriend – or so Orlando has hinted. Oh God, Primmie. I can't believe that in five weeks time I'm going to be married to Hugo. I'm so happy, I could burst!'

Primmie well understood that Artemis's thoughts were now centred almost entirely on her approaching wedding day. Her own thoughts, though, were still centred almost entirely on the ongoing search for Destiny.

Every morning, after her animals were tended and fed and the breakfast things were cleared away, she sat at the kitchen table with the telephone, a county directory and her laptop.

With no responses coming from any of the organizations that she, Geraldine, Artemis, Kiki, Matt, Hugo and Brett had contacted, she had begun devoting herself to the task of telephoning every residential child-care home in the country, asking the bursar if he, or she, would search their records for 1978 to see if a five-year-old child named either Destiny Surtees or Destiny Gower had been handed into their care by her father.

Where Northumberland and Cumbria were concerned, she had now contacted not only every care home for children with special needs, but every other type of care home, orphanages included. It had been a long, laborious task, for no one was ever able to check records immediately. She had to trust that people would telephone her back. And when they didn't, which was often, she had to telephone them again. There was also the constant brick wall refrain of 'We're not at liberty to divulge that information' to be met with and, whenever possible, overcome. For all the numberless times it couldn't be overcome, the name and address of the care home was marked with an asterisk on the mammoth list in her laptop file, so that, at a future date, they could be approached again, with legal back-up.

Now she was trawling through Yorkshire, a huge task that was likely to take her many weeks. 'Good morning, I wonder if you could help me,' she said for the fiftieth time one glorious morning, as palest pink drifts of clematis montana nodded against her kitchen window. 'I'm trying to trace whether my daughter, Destiny Surtees, was in your care some time from 1978 onwards. It's possible that she may have been known as Destiny Gower. She was born on the sixth of January, 1973, in London. My name is Primmie. Primmie Dove, formerly Surtees.'

'Destiny?' a woman's voice said musingly. 'We've ever only had one Destiny at Rydal Hall. It isn't a name to forget, is it?'

Primmie was so locked into expecting a negative response that at first she didn't register that she hadn't met with one. She was, in fact, beginning to write a shopping list as she waited for the voice on the other end of the telephone to say either that she would telephone back when she'd had the time to check the home's records, or that such information wasn't disclosable.

'I don't remember her surname offhand, but she was a pretty little thing. When she left here she went to York to train as a nursery care assistant. Just hold the line, Mrs Dove, and I'll have a quick zip through our files.'

Primmie dropped the pen she had been writing with, her heart beginning to slam like a piston. Could the woman be referring to Destiny? *Her* Destiny? But how could her Destiny have gone on to train as a nursery care assistant if she had learning difficulties? She remembered Artemis's adamant assertion that Destiny had only been a slow learner, nothing more. A nursery care assistant wouldn't need to be a high achiever. She would need a love of children and a caring nature more than scholastic ability. With the telephone pressed hard against her ear, she closed her eyes. 'Please!' she whispered, with all the fervour with which she had prayed in church for Geraldine. 'Please. Please. *Please!*'

She could hear drawers being opened and closed and folders being rustled. She tried to steady her breathing, and couldn't.

386

For the first time ever, she was meeting with a hopeful reaction – and an incurious one. If Rydal Hall had information on anyone with the name Destiny, she was going to be told it.

'Yes, here it is,' the woman said cheerily, oblivious to the cataclysmic importance of her response. 'Destiny was with us until 1989, when she went to Chalgrove, a residential children's home in York, as a trainee nursery care assistant.'

'Her surname?' Primmie said, her throat so tight it was a miracle she was able to speak at all.

'I remember thinking at the time that she'd be very good with small children. Certainly the younger children here loved her and we were all very sorry to see her leave.'

'Her surname?'

'It was nice to think, too, that she'd been so happy at Rydal she wanted to work somewhere similar. That was very gratifying, we all thought.'

Primmie sucked in her breath, about to scream, '*For the love of God! What was her surname?*' but was saved at the last second as the woman continued fondly, 'Destiny Gower was a little ray of sunshine. Everyone at Rydal thought so. Unfortunately, we've lost contact with her. When you next see her, Mrs Dove, please give her our best wishes.'

It was totally beyond Primmie to be able to correct the bursar's misunderstanding, to ask further questions or to finish the conversation in any adequate way.

She simply dropped the telephone, covered her face with her hands and wept tears of relief and joy. For eleven years Destiny had been in care at Rydal Hall in Yorkshire – and had been happy there. And from there she'd gone on to train as a nursery care assistant at Chalgrove, a residential home in York. Which is where she might still be. The enormity of what she had discovered in one, not very long, telephone conversation overwhelmed her. She knew she should get straight on the telephone to Artemis, but she couldn't do it. She was shaking too much.

Eleven years of her daughter's life were now no longer a mystery to her – and even if Destiny were no longer at Chalgrove, Chalgrove would surely know her next place of employment, for they would have had to supply references.

387

Though she hadn't yet found Destiny, she was well on the way to doing so. Perhaps only hours from doing so. With tears of joy still streaming down her face, she finally managed to steady her hands enough to be able to punch in the gallery's phone number.

When Artemis answered the phone she said without preamble, 'Artemis! Oh, Artemis! I've found the home Rupert left Destiny in! It's called Rydal Hall and it's in Yorkshire. And Artemis, darling Artemis, Destiny was *happy* there and you were quite right. She wasn't severely handicapped. She couldn't be, for when she was sixteen she went to a residential home in York to train as a nursery care assistant.'

There was a gasp from the other end of the line.

'The home in York is called Chalgrove. I don't think she's still there, because the bursar at Rydal Hall said they'd lost contact with her. But if she did her nursery care assistant training there, they would have supplied references for wherever she moved on to. We're only a smidgeon away from finding her, Artemis. And, according to the bursar at Rydal, she was happy despite all the awfulness of what happened to her. Isn't that just the most wonderful relief? And she's working, just like any normal young woman. It's such fantastic news I don't think I've truly taken it all in yet. I've never been so happy. Never. Never. Never.'

There came the sound of Artemis stumbling to her feet. 'I must tell Hugo,' she said, her voice no longer competent and assured but almost incoherent. 'I must tell Hugo and then I'm coming straight over to Ruthven.'

Seconds later Primmie phoned Matt, then Geraldine, and then Kiki on her mobile. Then, armed with Chalgrove's number from directory enquiries, she rang Chalgrove, her heart in her mouth.

'Don't get despondent just because she's no longer there and they were unable to help,' Matt said gently to her that evening. He rose from the sofa they were sitting on and put another log on the fire. 'It was, after all, pretty unlikely that she'd still be at Chalgrove fourteen years after beginning to train and work there.'

'Yes, I know, but I expected them to be able to tell me where her next place of employment was.'

'It's fourteen years ago, Primmie.' Matt sat beside her again, slipping his arm comfortingly round her shoulders. 'Chalgrove is a children's home, not M15. Though they would have given Destiny references when she left, they would have no reason to keep a record of them, nor of whom they were given to.'

'Yes. You're right.' She took hold of his hand, giving it a squeeze. 'I'm wrong to feel disappointed when everything is so wonderful. We know now where she spent the years from five to sixteen. We know where she was living and training until she was eighteen. We know what surname she is known by. We know the kind of work she does. We know the area of England she thinks of as home. It's just a question of more telephone calls, isn't it? My beautiful eldest daughter is out there, living a normal life but thinking she has no family, and soon she's going to have more family than she could ever imagine.'

'That's true.' Matt's well-shaped mouth tugged into a smile. 'A natural mother, an adoptive mother, two half-brothers, three half-sisters and two adoptive half-brothers.'

'And another half-sister. You're forgetting Kiki. Until a few months ago, Kiki lived her life believing herself to be an only child – and an only child without children of her own. When we find Destiny, it's going to have a huge impact on her life.'

Matt gave a chuckle. 'You've had a huge impact on mine,' he said wryly. 'A year ago, almost my only social contact was a weekly drink with Hugo. Now I'm surrounded by the most extraordinary collection of friends. Geraldine – who even when ill looked as if she'd just stepped out of *Vogue* and is certainly the only woman in this part of Cornwall to go shopping in a silver Ferrari. Kiki, who I can safely state is like no one else I've ever met before. Artemis, who, next to you, is possibly the sweetest, kindest woman in the whole world and is a perfect soulmate for Hugo. The only thing is, they do rather cramp our style, don't they, dear love? Finding private time together is becoming a nightmare. It would be much easier if we were married.'

389

'Is this a proposal?'

He put a finger beneath her chin, turning her head so that he could look into her eyes. 'It most certainly is,' he said solemnly. 'Will you marry me, Primmie Dove? Will you continue to make my life interesting and full of fun?'

She giggled. 'There's nothing I would like better, Matt Trevose. But can we keep our intentions to ourselves until we find Destiny? When we make our announcement, I want all my children to be happy for me – and that includes Destiny.'

He nodded assent, drawing her closer. 'We'll find her soon, Primmie, I promise.' And then, a very happy man, he lowered his head to hers.

Matt wasn't a man who would ever break a promise and, as preparations for Artemis and Hugo's wedding grew ever more fevered, Primmie, Artemis and Kiki spent every spare second telephoning children's homes in Yorkshire, certain that the promise was about to be fulfilled.

Day after day, they drew a blank.

'I've engaged a private detective,' Geraldine said from Paris in one of her daily telephone calls. 'He says with all the information we already have, it will be a piece of cake.'

It wasn't. By the fourth week of April, there was still no new lead.

Conscious of the children she hadn't lost, but whom she saw far too little of, she rang Joanne, Millie and Josh. 'There's to be a wedding at Ruthven on the first of May, and though it's not my wedding I want you all be to be here. It's an opportunity for a family get together and Cornwall is magic in May. Husbands and partners are invited as well, and this time I'm not taking no for an answer!'

To her great satisfaction, they'd all turned up trumps and said yes.

Adding to the frenetic activity of the wedding preparations were the telephone calls now being made to Ruthven from the many children's homes and organizations that Primmie had contacted months and months earlier, when she'd made her decision to offer disadvantaged children holidays by the sea.

With only a week to go until the 1st of May, Primmie over-heard Kiki saying to one such caller, 'Next weekend? *Next weekend?* That's far too little time and, besides, we couldn't do those dates even if we'd had proper advance warning. I'm sorry. Later in the year, perhaps.'

When she'd put the phone down, Primmie said curiously, 'Who was that?'

'The Claybourne Children's Home. They've been let down by another holiday home and want to bring six five-year-olds down on Saturday, Artemis's wedding day. I told them it wasn't on.'

'Would it be so disruptive?' Primmie paused in her task of setting the table for lunch. 'We're all organized for the wedding now and the children will be sleeping in the new dormitory in the barn, not the house, so it won't encroach on the guest-room situation.'

'And that isn't acute,' Artemis chipped in, busy drizzling a vinaigrette on the green salad that was to accompany cheese omelettes. 'Orlando and Sholto have arranged to stay at the Tregenna Castle Hotel in St Ives, and Josh is staying at Matt's.'

'As are Joanne and her husband,' Primmie added, thrilled to bits at the close relationship that was growing between some of her children and the man she knew she would soon be marrying.

'Which leaves a guest room here for Lucy, when she arrives – which she should be doing any moment,' Artemis continued. 'And if Geraldine shares a room with Primmie, as she did for ages when it was the four of us here, it means there's room at Ruthven for Francis, as well.'

'And when are Geraldine and Francis getting here?' Kiki asked, pouring herself a healthy slug of red wine.

'Later today. Perhaps tomorrow.'

'And so we could have the Claybourne children here next week,' Primmie said, bringing the three-way conversation back to its beginning. 'And it would be rather nice starting off the holiday year with children from a home we already know. Rose was lovely and she'll have news of the children who came in September.'

'Shall I ring the Claybourne back, then?' Kiki asked, the phone still in her hand.

'Yes.' Primmie turned her attention to the omelettes. 'And tell whoever it is you speak to about the wedding. Tell them that it would be wonderful if the children arrived on Saturday in time for it.'

Thirty-One

The last few days before the wedding were days of arrivals. At ten in the morning Primmie answered the telephone and found herself speaking to her dearly beloved youngest daughter.

'Hi, Mum!' Lucy said, fizzing with high spirits. 'I'm at Helston station and I have someone with me. I hope you don't mind. If there isn't enough room at the house, he can bunk up at a nearby hotel.'

'I don't mind at all, and he can stay here until Saturday, when I have half a dozen children coming to stay. Is your friend someone you met in California?

'He is, and Jon isn't just a friend, he's my boyfriend.' She gave a happy giggle. 'You can think of him as my fiancé, Mum, because though he doesn't know it yet, he's going to marry me. Can you come and pick us up, or is there a bus we can catch from here to Ruthven?'

'There's a bus from Helston to Calleloe, but there's no need for you to catch it. I'll be down to pick you up in twenty minutes.'

'Great stuff. What are you driving these days? Do you still have your old banger?'

'I do, but I won't be driving it.' Giggles that were an exact replica of her daughter's rose in her throat. 'I'll be driving a silver Ferrari.'

'Of course you can take the Ferrari,' Geraldine said minutes later when, rather belatedly, she asked if this were possible. 'I changed the insurance so that you could use it while I was in Paris. You did take advantage of the arrangement, didn't you, Primmie?'

392

'I did the shopping in it a couple of times, but felt that my headscarf and Barbour let it down.'

Geraldine made a sound of exasperation and Primmie, overcome with love for her, hugged her. 'God, I'm so glad you're back here, fit and well,' she said, thickly.

'Me too,' Geraldine said with profound sincerity. 'Now off you go to be reunited with your world-travelling daughter. If the Ferrari doesn't impress her, nothing will.'

When she swooped to a halt outside Helston Station, attracting attention from passing motorists and pedestrians alike, Lucy whooped with disbelief and delight.

'What a *wicked* car!' she said, abandoning rucksacks and a tall young man and rushing towards her. 'Oh gosh, Mum! I've missed you so much! It's *great* to be home – even if the location has changed! Which of your friends does this car belong to? Is it Kiki's?'

'No. Kiki rides a Harley Davidson and I rather baulked at borrowing that.'

'I'm not surprised!' Ecstatically, Lucy dragged her across the pavement to where her companion, looking amused, was waiting to be introduced.

'Jon, my Mum. She'll want you to call her Primmie, not Mrs Dove. Mum, Jon. Jon's a medical student. We met on the steps of the public library in San Diego when the bag I was carrying collapsed and my books toppled everywhere.'

'I've very pleased to meet you, Jon,' Primmie said, shaking his hand and liking the steadiness, as well as the good humour, that she saw in his eyes.

'It's great to be meeting you, Mrs . . . Primmie. On the flight over, Lucy talked non-stop about your adventure in leaving London for Cornwall. I've got confused between people and animals, though. Is Maybelline your friend who lived in Paris for years? And is Kiki a person, or a cow?'

Knowing very well that Geraldine would have replied that Kiki was a person and, quite often, a cow as well, Primmie kept a straight face with difficulty. 'She's a person,' she said to him as he loaded Lucy's and his rucksacks into the Ferrari. 'And Maybelline is a cow. My friend who lived in Paris for many years is Geraldine – she's at Ruthven now, waiting to meet you. The friend who is getting married on Saturday is Artemis.'

'Great. Got it,' he said affably, piling into the rear of the Ferrari with Lucy. 'What a fantastic car. I didn't expect to be met by a Ferrari. I thought all Brits drove Minis.'

The next couple of hours were sheer bliss for Primmie, because Lucy was over the moon at everything she saw.

'Ruthven's a wonderful house, Mum. Fantastic. When I think of Millie trying to persuade you to sell it, sight unseen, I could weep.'

'Well, fortunately, selling was never an option I had. It didn't look quite as wonderful when I first moved in, though. Its present splendour is all down to Geraldine. She had the patio laid, so that we could eat in comfort outside in the summer, and she paid for the barn to be made into living accommodation.'

'And is this where Jon will be sleeping, until the children arrive?' Lucy asked, viewing the sky-blue painted walls and the shining oak floor of the barn's dormitory with approval.

'Yes. When he and Geraldine have finished chatting about San Diego – and I have to say that until ten minutes ago I'd no idea Geraldine was so familiar with San Diego – he can bring his rucksack over here and make himself at home.'

'Gosh, Mum. I feel at home already. The Lizard reminds me of New Zealand. Everything is so green and open and clean. I love the way it's nearly separate from the rest of Cornwall and the way it's entirely different to the rest of England.'

'I love the sea best,' Primmie said, aware, not for the first time, that her youngest daughter was a kindred spirit, '. . . being able to hear it at night, in winter, when there are gales, being able to see the sun glinting on it in summer, from the garden. Matt says that the coastline for miles on either side of Ruthven's cove is very much as it was a century ago.'

'All thatched cottages nestling around tiny harbours?'

Primmie nodded. 'And fishermen still bringing in hauls of pilchards – which is what Matt still does occasionally.'

'And you're happy, Mum? Really in love with him? Just like you were with Dad?'

Primmie took hold of her hand. 'Yes,' she said gently. 'It's real love, to last down all the days, just as it was with your dad. And please don't think that my being in love again – which is an absolute miracle to me at my age – is taking away anything from the love I had, and will always have, for your Dad. Matt knows that Ted is locked away in the safekeeping part of my heart, and he wouldn't want it any other way.'

In perfect harmony they walked out of the barn. 'I'd like to see the church next,' Lucy said as Jon showed no signs of tearing himself away from Geraldine and joining them. 'Did Artemis have to get some kind of special dispensation to be able to be married in it?'

'No. It's still a working church – if that's the right terminology. There are five churches in our local vicar's benefice. Regular services are held on a rota basis in the other four churches, but because our church is so isolated from the rest of the parish, services are only held once every three months or so.'

'And is it where you and Matt will one day get married?'

They had begun walking down the track, towards Ruthven's gates. 'Yes,' Primmie said, 'When we've found Destiny.'

And she began telling Lucy of how close she believed that day was.

The next arrivals, on Thursday morning, were Joanna, Josh and, much to Primmie's amazement and delight, Millie.

'Neville couldn't come,' Joanne said, referring to her husband, 'and so Millie said she'd come in his place. She and Alan are at sixes and sevens again and I think she wanted to do a mysterious disappearing act for a few days, in order to make him think she might have someone else in her life. Which, for once, she hasn't.'

Primmie didn't care about Millie's motives in being at Ruthven. As far as she was concerned, Millie was there, and that was all that mattered.

'But the house is huge, Mum. And is all this land yours? The orchard and the field with the donkey in it and the other field, with the cow and the hens?'

Looking round her, dressed in teetering high heels, an above-the-knee black skirt with a side split and a silky, T-strap purple top, Millie's bewilderment was pitiable. 'And your friends . . . You never told me you had rich and famous friends, Mum. Alan would have come if he'd known he'd meet Kiki Lane here. He loves all those old disco numbers from the seventies. And how you could have the use of a Ferrari, and not tell me, is just unbelievable. Do you know how much those cars cost? Your friend Geraldine must be a millionairess.'

'Close,' Primmie said, resolving not to let Millie know just how Geraldine had come by her wealth. 'Let's go down to the paddock and give Ned some carrots and, after that, I'll introduce you to Maybelline.'

As Lucy had no intention of allowing Millie to share the barn dormitory with Jon, Francis obligingly agreed to do so, moving out of the front guest bedroom, so that Millie could move into it.

'And when the Claybourne children arrive, I'll book into the Tregenna Castle Hotel,' he said to Primmie, looking extremely dapper in the chinos and coffee-coloured cotton shirt that were part of the wardrobe he'd returned from Paris with.

'Good. It means you'll be able to keep an eye on Josh, Orlando and Sholto. They arrive tomorrow, and when they were last here it took Calleloe's young single female population weeks to settle down to normality.'

'But if Sholto now has a steady girlfriend, why hasn't he brought her with him?' Artemis asked Orlando minutes after Sholto's and his arrival. 'He must know that I'd love to meet her.'

Her eldest son, who had driven straight from a board meeting and was immaculate in a grey Savile Row suit, Turnbull & Asser shirt, silk tie and handmade shoes from Lobbs, looked desperately uncomfortable.

'You have met her,' he said, as Sholto, who had hared off to the Tregenna Castle Hotel bar on a quest for coffee for Artemis, showed no signs of making an early return. 'Sholto's nervous of telling you her identity, though. He thinks you might go through the roof when you're told.'

Artemis looked at him blankly. 'Go through the roof? Why

on earth should I do that? I'd love you both to have steady girlfriends.'

Orlando fiddled with one of his cufflinks.

'He's dating Serena,' he said baldly. 'Sorry, Ma. But there it is. They've been inseparable for months now.'

Artemis stared at him.

'Serena,' he said again, just in case she hadn't cottoned on to whom he was speaking about. 'Serena Campbell-Thynne.'

'Yes. I heard you the first time.' Her voice was absolutely calm, her face expressionless.

In rising panic, Orlando waited for hysterical waterworks. They didn't come.

With every atom of her energy Artemis was forcing herself to assimilate the appalling news sensibly and rationally. The first point she was struggling to bear in mind was that if her youngest son wanted to shack up with his late father's mistress it was, after all, up to him. At this stage of the game, nothing she could say or do would make any difference. He was over twenty-one, of sound mind – though she now had a private opinion on that score – and financially independent. The second point, the most important point, was that she was marrying her beloved Hugo in the morning and she was going to allow nothing to spoil their wedding day, *nothing*. And that included Serena Campbell-Thynne. And the third, and last, point, was that at least Sholto had had the sense not to bring the family tart with him.

She wondered if she might, one day, have to accommodate herself to having Serena as a daughter-in-law and decided that, if such a dark day ever dawned, she would simply ride with it and make the best of it. Serena had, after all, been unknowingly responsible for turning her life around. Without Serena, Rupert would never have wanted a divorce – and if he had never wanted a divorce, she would never have driven in need of refuge to Primmie and to Ruthven. And if she hadn't done that, she would never have met Hugo and Hugo was, undoubtedly, the love of her life.

'I don't want a discussion of this when Sholto comes back with coffee,' she said, rather as if her thoughts were already on other things – which they were. 'Later on, when I'm no longer with you both, you can tell him that you've told me.

I think he could have looked further afield for a girlfriend, but there you are. It's his choice. Now, about tomorrow, you are au fait with everything that will be expected of you, darling, aren't you? It's not every son who gives his mother away in marriage.'

Orlando resisted the temptation to check his forehead for beads of perspiration, said he was completely au fait with his duties and wondered if Sholto was going to have the sense to bring a couple of large brandies back with him.

'You obviously behaved with wonderful cool, Temmy,' Kiki said that evening, when, with Primmie and Geraldine, they had a pre-wedding supper at Ruthven.

All the men were in Calleloe, enjoying a stag night that Matt had faithfully promised would not be too wild – or at least not where he and the groom were concerned. Joanne, sensitively aware that Artemis would probably like to spend her pre-wedding evening with only Kiki, Geraldine and Primmie, had taken Lucy and Millie into Penzance for an Italian meal.

'I did rather surprise myself,' Artemis confessed. 'But then, a second before I threw the greatest wobbly in the world, I suddenly thought: does it matter? Sholto's quite able to take care of himself. If what he wants in life is Serena, then that's his affair. And she did actually do me a very good turn. If it weren't for her, I wouldn't be marrying Hugo.'

Primmie collapsed into giggles, Kiki cracked with laughter and Geraldine chuckled, saying, 'That's pragmatism on an almost French scale, Artemis. I couldn't do better myself.'

'Everything is all absolutely, perfectly, wonderfully organized for tomorrow, isn't it?' Artemis said, turning her attention to a subject that really mattered. 'I know the church is looking magnificent, because I went there on the way here. The flowers are breathtaking, Primmie. It's a veritable bower of lemon and white.'

'And as Hugo has made all the arrangements for the reception, down to the last detail, you don't have a thing to worry about,' Primmie said, lifting a bottle of champagne from an ice bucket. 'Especially as the Tregenna Castle Hotel is well known for the immaculate smooth-running of its functions.'

'And Brett booked the bus that is to take everyone who hasn't a car from the church to St Ives,' Kiki said. 'And if you're thinking of opening that champagne yourself, Primmie, don't. Give it to someone who has the experience. Geraldine or me.'

'And the cake?' Artemis said, too anxious about the arrangements for her big day to take offence at being judged as inexpert as Primmie where the opening of champagne bottles was concerned. 'It has *six* tiers. Do you think the caterers are going to be able to transport it safely?'

'Relax, Artemis,' Geraldine chided. 'Tomorrow is going to be flawless. Now, have you all got your champagne flutes at the ready?'

As the three most important people in the world to her nodded their heads, she released the cork with a wonderfully festive bang and poured the fizzing contents of the well-chilled bottle into their proffered glasses.

'A toast,' Primmie said, raising her glass high. 'To Artemis and Hugo.'

'No.' Artemis's free hand flew high to forestall them. 'There will be lots of toasts to Hugo and me tomorrow. Tonight needs a different toast.'

Not about to argue with her, Primmie, Kiki and Geraldine waited, glasses raised.

'To the four of us,' Artemis said, her eyes aglow, her face radiant.

'To the four of us,' they all said in heartfelt unison.

It was, Primmie thought, as they clinked glasses and drank, a moment never to be forgotten. A moment when they were all deeply aware that, though they had lost each other once, nothing in the world would make them lose each other again.

Thirty-Two

The next morning Primmie was awake by six o'clock as usual. Before she did anything else she pulled back the

399

curtains to see what kind of a day it was going to be. There had been plenty of April showers over the last few weeks but now, the 1st of May, the early morning sky was crystal clear, promising a cloudlessly warm day.

Her relief was vast. Artemis may have coped with almost unnatural calm over the news of Sholto's relationship with Serena, but she would never have taken rain in her stride on her wedding day.

Quietly, so as not to disturb Geraldine, she dressed in a comfy corduroy skirt and, to combat the dawn chill, a polo-neck sweater. Artemis's wedding day or not, there were daily tasks that couldn't be skipped. Her animals had to be fed and Maybelline and Black-Hearted Alice milked.

She always milked Maybelline first, because it was such a pleasant task. 'This is a very wonderful, special day,' she said to her, pouring barley meal into her manger. 'Ruthven is going to be *en fête* and you are going to wear a big blue bow.'

Maybelline mooed agreeably and then mooed again as Primmie pulled her milking stool close to her side.

Milking Black-Hearted Alice was always a very different kettle of fish. First, she had to be coaxed into position with feed, for as far as Alice was concerned, no feed, no milk. This meant that milking her was always difficult, for only when Alice was well into her stride eating would she remain still.

'Come along, Alice. No tantrums this morning,' Primmie said in her best businesslike voice. 'I've got one of Maybelline's cow cakes for you and a new salt lick, and in return for these treats, I'd like you to allow me to put a bow on you.'

From the milking stand that Brett had made, Alice glared at her. Without too much hope of her entering into the spirit of the thing, Primmie began milking her. The rhythm that was so relaxing with Maybelline was a time of great tension with Alice, for the second she'd finished eating she would begin kicking and skittering to be off the stand.

Today was no exception and by the time she left Alice and went to let Ned out of his stable and into the paddock, she felt as if she'd done three rounds with Lennox Lewis.

With Ned happily ambling free, she set off for the cove. It

400

was after seven o'clock now and as she began slithering down the shallow dunes, the sea flashed and glittered in the sunlight, shifting in colour from serpentine green to a silvery steel-grey.

Reaching the sliver of sand that was Ruthven's beach, she breathed in deep, blissful breaths of crisp, salt-laden air. The day was still untouched and hers alone, the silence profound.

Wishing Rags hadn't so easily accommodated himself to sleeping on Brett and Kiki's bed in the caravan and was, instead, with her, she walked along the shingle, her face lifted to the sea breeze, counting her many blessings one by one.

The instant she returned to the house with the milk, there was no further time for quiet contemplation. Artemis had been adamant that she was going to leave for the church from Ruthven and was already there, eating a scrambled egg break-fast, her cheeks flushed with excitement.

'Kiki's blowing up balloons and is going to tie great clus-ters of them on Ruthven's gates,' she said, her eyes glowing. 'And Geraldine is finding me something old, something borrowed and something blue.'

The something old that Geraldine found was a length of white satin ribbon it was decided could be used to deco-rate Artemis's posy of lemon roses and gypsophila. The something borrowed was a lace-edged handkerchief and the something blue was a garter Geraldine had bought espe-cially for the occasion in Paris.

'The Claybourne rang this morning whilst you were out,' Kiki said, entering the kitchen holding a dozen balloons in either hand, rather like a hip Mary Poppins. 'Just as they don't send the same children year after year, they don't send the same carers, and as this year's care-worker doesn't drive, the driver accompanying her is going to need accommodation. They said not to panic. If we don't have room for him, he'll put up at a bed and breakfast in Calleloe.'

'Well, we don't have room for him,' Primmie said, refusing to be rattled, 'but as the summer season hasn't started yet, he'll have no trouble finding somewhere to lay his head.'

Later, as countdown time to the two o'clock wedding began in earnest, Geraldine came into the bedroom where Primmie

401

and Kiki were dressing and said, 'For the first time in her life, I think I can truthfully say that Artemis has chosen a dress perfect for the occasion.'

Kiki grinned. 'You mean it's not white organdie with a train and a veil?'

'No, thank God. It's a mid calf-length dress and floaty jacket in cream silk and antique cream lace. She's wearing her favourite three-stranded pearl necklace with it and diamond and pearl drop-earrings and she looks, I might add, absolutely stunning.'

So did Geraldine. Striking and understated as always, her night-black hair was looped into a glossy knot on top of her head and her narrow emerald crêpe de chine sheath dress and bolero jacket were a masterpiece of French designer fashion.

'You are not,' Geraldine now said in horror, seeing Kiki's nails for the first time, 'going to wear blue nail varnish?'

'I am, as it goes,' Kiki said, steelishly mulish. 'I'm keeping Artemis happy by wearing a dress that pleases her, not me. And, as the dress is pale lemon, the blue varnish will look stunning, not tarty. Also, it will match my mascara.'

Geraldine's eyes flew to Primmie's for help.

'It could be worse,' Primmie said philosophically. 'At least the dress covers up the butterfly tattoo on her shoulder.'

Her own wedding-day outfit was far more modest than Geraldine's or Kiki's. She was wearing a long floral skirt in shades of soft pinks and soft greens, a white lace-edged blouse and a grey velvet jacket that she had found in one of Helston's excellent charity shops. Her wide-brimmed hat, in the exact same pink as the roses on her skirt, was a present from Geraldine.

'Is Orlando here yet?' came a frantic cry from the bedroom Artemis was using. 'It's one thirty. He should be here by now. Try his mobile again for me, Kiki.'

'No need,' Kiki said, as they heard the sound of Orlando's BMW speeding up the track to the house.

'Is Artemis going to let us have a look at her dress before we leave for the church?' Lucy called up to them from the bottom of the stairs, where she had been helping Joanne put the final touches to Millie's complicated hairdo.

'Tell her no,' Artemis shouted from the bedroom. 'No one

sees the bride's dress till she enters the church. That's traditional and I'm sticking to it.'

Prudently keeping quiet about the fact that Geraldine had already seen the bride in her wedding glory, Primmie relayed the message downstairs. 'And it's time the three of you were on your way,' she added, as Orlando, looking as handsome as a film star in his cutaway coat, grey striped trousers and grey waistcoat, squeezed past them to run up the stairs, grey gloves and top hat in one hand.

Five minutes later, she and Geraldine were driving down the track and across the headland to the church, in the Ferrari.

'Let's hope Hugo and Matt are in situ,' Geraldine said wryly as they bumped to a halt on the rough grass outside the lych-gate. 'I don't think Artemis's nerves will take it if she arrives here before them.'

'They are. That's Hugo's car parked the other side of the vicar's car and Matt's truck is squeezed between Joanne's car and Peggy Wainwright's Mini.'

They stepped out of the Ferrari, put on their hats, smoothed their skirts and walked into the tiny church.

Organ music was already being played. Through the stained-glass windows, shafts of jewelled sunlight illuminated a packed congregation of family and friends. Sholto, in a morning suit, was seated in the front left-hand pew. Brett and Francis, jaw dropping in their formal dress, were acting as groomsmen.

Josh, wearing a light-coloured suit she had never seen before, looked incredibly handsome, seated between two of his sisters. Lucy was resplendent in a simple white dress, her long fair hair held away from her face by an Alice band.

Joanne was wearing a pale blue suit with a knee-skimming straight skirt and a breathtakingly dramatic wide-brimmed black hat.

For one panic-stricken moment, as she walked down the aisle with Geraldine to take her place in the pew behind Sholto, she thought Millie wasn't in the church.

'She's over there,' Geraldine said in a whisper, reading her mind. 'On the right-hand side of the church, seated next to one of Hugo's nephews.'

Primmie turned her head, saw that the nephew in question

403

was somewhere in his late-twenties and good looking in a rather flashy way. She heaved a deep sigh. If Millie had been unencumbered by an extramarital relationship when she arrived in Cornwall, she had a shrewd suspicion the situation would have changed by the time Millie returned to London.

Jon, too, had elected to sit on the groom's side of the church, presumably because Lucy was hemmed in by the wall on one side of her, and Josh on the other.

Having checked that all her family was safely present, Primmie turned her attention to Hugo and Matt, who were standing only yards in front of her, talking to John Cowles.

Hugo, of course, looked as if he had been born to wear nothing but formal day wear. His morning coat fitted in a way that no hired morning coat could ever do. Rather touchingly, he looked nervous. It was Matt who made her suck in her breath, though.

In his hired morning suit, Matt looked magnificent.

The organist fell silent. There was a sense of charged antici-pation.

Then the stirring, magnificent opening chords of Handel's 'Arrival of the Queen of Sheba' thundered through the church.

Primmie turned to see Artemis's entrance, the hairs on the back of her neck standing up, her throat tightening with emotion.

Artemis looked breathtaking. The delicacy of her cream silk and lace dress set off her classic English rose beauty to perfection. Her china-blue eyes shone. Her barley-gold hair was swept upwards in undulating waves beneath a glorious hat drowning in pink rosebuds and swirls of veiling.

Kiki, in a floaty lemon silk dress, a gardenia tucked behind her ear, a posy of them in her hands, looked almost conven-tional until she moved the posy, revealing midnight-blue nails.

The first hymn was 'Praise My Soul the King of Heaven'.

After it, as Artemis stood at Hugo's side, looking, despite her above average height and weight, almost diminutive in comparison to him, the Reverend John Cowles said with clear pleasure, 'Dearly beloved, we are gathered together here, in the sight of God, and in the face of this congregation, to join together this Man and this Woman in holy Matrimony.'

Primmie listened to the familiar words with a full heart,

remembering her own wedding day so long ago, remembering Ted and how she had loved him, and he her.

'I require and charge you both, as ye will answer at the dreadful day of judgement, when the secrets of all hearts shall be disclosed, that if either of you know any impediment, why ye may not be lawfully joined together in Matrimony, ye do now confess it.'

Artemis had insisted that her wedding service be conducted from the 1662 Book of Common Prayer and John Cowles had been happy to oblige her. Primmie was glad he had done so. She liked thinking of the long history of the words, and of the countless couples who, down the ages, had heard and responded to them,

John Cowles was now saying to Hugo: 'Wilt thou have this Woman to thy wedded Wife, to live together after God's ordinance in the holy estate of Matrimony? Wilt thou love her, comfort her, honour, and keep her in sickness and in health; and, forsaking all others, keep thee only unto her, so long as ye both shall live?'

Hugo's booming 'I will' could have been heard in Calleloe.

Primmie's eyes moved from the back of Hugo's head to the back of Matt's. For a man of sixty-two he had a wonderful head of hair, grizzled with silver, but as thick and curly as a ram's fleece. Overcome at her good fortune in having had a long and lasting marriage and, as a widow, finding the same rock-solid quality of love a second time round, Primmie listened to Artemis's responses, wondering how long it would be before she was standing beside Matt, saying the same responses, in front of the same minister, in the same church.

'For as much as Hugo and Artemis have consented together in holy wedlock,' John Cowles was now saying, 'and have witnessed the same before God and this company, and thereto have given and pledged their troth either to other, and have declared the same by giving and receiving of a Ring, and by joining of hands, I pronounce that they be Man and Wife together, in the name of the Father and of the Son, and of the Holy Ghost. Amen.'

While the register was being signed, the organist played 'Jesu, Joy of Man's Desiring'.

Then, after another hymn, a psalm reading and a benediction,

Artemis and Hugo turned away from the altar, walking back down the aisle, beaming like Cheshire cats.

'Have you seen the number of video cameras Hugo's side of the church have with them?' Geraldine said as they squeezed out of their pew to follow the happy couple. 'They're making our cameras look very tame.'

The crush on the doorstep of the church was enormous. As the professional photographer Hugo had engaged began taking charge, assembling Matt and Kiki at either side of Hugo and Artemis, Primmie manoeuvred her way to the lych-gate, where there was more breathing space.

As she reached it, she heard the sound of a vehicle making its way down the track towards Ruthven. The minute the vehicle came into view, she knew what it was. It was the Claybourne children's minibus.

She looked to where Artemis and Hugo were still being rearranged by the photographer for photographs with their best man and maid of honour and decided that she had plenty of time in which to bring the children across to the church so that they could join in all the fun of the eventual confetti-throwing.

As she began taking a short cut to Ruthven's gates, striding over the grass of the headland, a not very tall, stockily built, fair-haired young woman jumped down from the minibus's passenger seat.

'Never mind the balloons, Destiny!' the driver bawled in a south-London accent. 'Get the bloomin' gates open, gel!'

Primmie came to such a sudden halt that she nearly fell. Had she heard correctly or had she been imagining things?

'Destiny! Destiny!' the children hanging half out of the minibus windows began chanting. 'Can we have a balloon, please, Destiny!'

The girl at the gates began laughing and untying the balloons, running back to the minibus with them.

'The *gates* Destiny!' the driver shouted exasperatedly. 'Open the blooming things, for Pete's sake!'

Primmie didn't wait to hear any more. Her Destiny had trained as a nursery care assistant and here was a care worker, working with young children, looking as if she were in her late twenties or early thirties, as fair-haired as herself and with Destiny's distinctive name.

She began running over the rough grass. Running as if her life depended on it, running as if she had wings on her heels.

As the young woman registered that she was racing towards her, a look of confusion and apprehension crossed her face.

'I'm s-sorry,' she stammered as the children, still aboard the minibus, waved the balloons from the open windows in glee. 'I didn't mean to do anything wrong. It's just that the balloons looked so pretty and the children did so want them . . .'

Primmie, hatless now and gasping for breath, floundered to a halt.

'It's . . . OK,' she gasped, struggling for breath. 'The children . . . can have . . . the balloons.'

The look of anxiety on the young woman's face cleared. She smiled sunnily. It was a smile Primmie would have known anywhere. It was her own smile. Joanne's smile. Millie's smile. Lucy's smile.

'I wonder,' she said, knowing that she mustn't cry tears of happiness; that she mustn't act in any way out of the ordinary. 'If you would tell me your surname, Destiny?'

'Gower,' Destiny said, her smile even broader as the impatient children surged out of the bus and began gathering round them.

Primmie made a sound in her throat that Destiny and her driver thought was a belated gulp of air after her run, but which was a sob.

'And are you Mrs Dove?' the driver asked, still doggedly behind the wheel. 'Because if you are, would you mind opening these flippin' gates so I can drive up to the house?'

'Yes.' Primmie didn't turn her head towards him. She couldn't. She couldn't look at anything but her daughter's face. It wasn't beautiful in a classical way, but it was a pretty face, full of character and good humour. Her wide-spaced eyes were grey and thick lashed. There was a look of Kiki about her nose and cheekbones, and her mouth was the full, generous mouth she saw every day when she looked in her mirror.

'There's a wedding taking place at the church,' she said, her heart feeling as if it would burst. 'Shall we walk the

407

children over to it, so that they can see the bride and throw confetti?'

Destiny gave a gasp of pleasure. 'That would be lovely, Mrs Dove. Can the children take their balloons with them?'

'Of course they can, and my name is Primmie.'

As, with the children still running in circles round them, they began walking across the headland, Primmie had no fears about Artemis's and Kiki's, or anyone else's, reaction. They would all instinctively know that nothing could be said to Destiny here and now. She would need to be properly prepared for what she would be told, by someone she trusted. Perhaps Arthur Bottomly, Claybourne's superintendent, or Claybourne's bursar.

She didn't think, when the news was broken to her, that Destiny would be disorientated by it. From the little she'd seen of her daughter, she thought that her reaction would be one of joyous wonderment.

With the children's balloons dancing round them, the sea breeze tugging at their hair, she said with joy so deep there were no words for it, 'There are people at the church who have waited a long time to meet you, Destiny.'

Destiny turned to her with shining eyes. 'Then let's run,' she said, her voice full of laughter and delight.

She slipped her hand into Primmie's and gave it a squeeze. 'Let's run towards them as fast as we can!'